I0617621

"Maxim," she rasped, "you scared me half to death."

He gave a sheepish smile and looked down. "I'm sorry. I was just looking for the bathroom."

She gave a slightly forced-sounding giggle. "Well, Javan's room is a hog wallow, but it's not the bathroom. Although, it does kinda smell like one."

Maxim gave a small, breathy chuckle and looked up at her. Her body was rigid, and he realized that he was still holding onto her. His cheeks flamed and he immediately removed his hands.

Alyx smiled at his obvious awkwardness and she pointed to the door on the right. "There's the bathroom."

He nodded, still keeping his eyes away from hers. "Thanks." He escaped into the room and let out a relieved breath. Alone, at last. He closed his eyes and tried to calm his nerves. When he got over the feeling that he was going to hyperventilate, he left the bathroom and went back outside, where Javan was leaning up against the car, waiting.

Javan frowned. "You're looking kinda nasty, Maxim," he remarked.

Maxim took a deep breath and glanced up at him. "Can I just"—he pointed to the back seat—"you know, ralphing and all that."

Javan raised an eyebrow. "Yeah, man. Go ahead and get in. It's unlocked."

Maxim hurried into the car, clutching his backpack to his chest as if it was the only thing keeping him alive. He could still feel the warmth of Alyx's skin on his hands. That was weird. Her skin had been so soft...

"Hey," Javan said through the open window, "you need a bucket or something?"

Maxim smiled tremulously and shook his head.

"You sure?" he prodded. "'Cause I don't want chunkage decorating my car."

Maxim's smile grew slightly against his will, and Javan grinned.

"We ready?" Alyx's voice came.

"Sure are," Javan replied. "We are gone!"

"I'm driving," she declared. Javan tossed her the keys and hopped into the passenger seat. She started the car and turned in her seat to look at Maxim. "You okay?"

Maxim's heart made a small lurch, and he swallowed hard. Geez...she was so beautiful. He nodded slowly. "Look," he said, "I'm not really into this kinda thing. I'm uh—"

"I know," Alyx interrupted. "Alex told me." She pushed her glasses up so that Maxim could see her eyes. She smiled. "You don't need to worry about anything. Javan and I will do our best to make you as comfortable as possible."

He sighed. "I haven't been around a whole lot of people...a lot." He frowned, feeling like an idiot. What kind of stupid sentence had he just rattled out? Writer? Yeah, right. He couldn't even formulate a coherent thought.

Alyx retained her warm smile. "That's all right. Being shy isn't a crime."

He raised an eyebrow. "Shy? I'm socially inept."

"I'm sure you'll be just fine." Her cheek dimpled as she smiled wider and turned back in her seat.

Maxim sighed and sat back against his seat, releasing the death grip on his bag just slightly.

Alyx steered the car out of the driveway, and Javan let out a monstrous cackle that made Maxim jump.

"This rocks!" he shouted. "Man, I am so in need of a vacation!"

"Um...where exactly are we going?" Maxim murmured.

"Wherever the road takes us!" Alyx laughed. "Anywhere away from here." Javan patted her on the shoulder and they pulled out on the open road.

Maxim swallowed and concentrated on looking out the window. If he just looked out the window, maybe everything would not seem quite so terrifying... Maybe.

Praise for *The Road Less Traveled*

The Road Less Traveled was brilliantly touching and funny! I could relate having taken so many road trips myself. The people you meet along the way will always stay with you. I know I will never forget these Characters. Brieanna Robertson is a shining star that truly stands out. Her flare to write about people in their everyday lives and make you feel apart of it is truly something remarkable. I enjoyed this book immensely and will be reading it again. I would love to read a story on Jeff, Alex and Javan.

-Sensual Reads and Reviews

To find out which path each of these characters takes is one that as a reader you cannot deny yourself. The Road Less Traveled is a story from the heart, delivered with eloquence, thought, understanding and passion. Each character is written with such quality and detail, that you can't help but find yourself immersed in their journey. This was a very absorbing read and has me reaching for another of this author's works, even as we speak.

-Blue City Romance

From the first page this morning, to the last page this evening, I have been absorbed in your words. I could relate to everyone of the characters in some way. I laughed when they laughed and cried when they hurt. What a gift you have. If this book is any indication of what your future holds... the skies the limit my dear. My hat is off to you!! Fabulous, from beginning to end!

-Adelle Laudan
Author of Juliana

You know how they have those warnings for movies... PG-ratings, and those warnings on books... Explicit sexual or Violent content. Well, I think you need to put a warning on your book. You know, like a MW-rating, as in Medical Warning.

Examples:

AAA - Asthma Attack Alert - for people like myself with asthma who can't catch their breath from laughing so hard when the humor is beyond funny.

IIW - Incontinent Issue Warning - for people who laugh so hard they can't make it to the bathroom in time.

PLAW - People Living Alone Warning - for people who live alone and laugh so hard they can't breathe and have no one to resuscitate them.

Keep making good reading happen...

-Bouzwha
Emily Wade-Reid
Author of Bittersweet Chocolate

The Road Less Traveled

Traveled

Book One in the Serendipity Series

Brieanna Robertson

Whimsical Publications, LLC

Florida

First Edition Copyright © 2008 by Brieanna Robertson
Revised Edition Copyright © 2013 by Brieanna Robertson

www.breiannarobertson.com

Published in the United States by
Whimsical Publications, LLC
Florida

www.whimsicalpublications.com

Cover art by Traci Markou, with help from Brieanna Robertson

ISBN-10: 0-9787738-5-3
ISBN-13: 978-0-9787738-5-4

Printed in the United States of America

ACKNOWLEDGEMENTS

First and foremost, I would like to say thank you to the most important person in my writing career as well as my life. My mother. Without you, I would be nothing. You are the wind beneath my wings and the best editor, promoter, and fan I could ever have. You truly are my hero.

Thank you also from the bottom of my heart to J.R Ward and all of the people who took a chance on me and helped me realize my greatest dream of being a published author. A huge thank you goes to Janet Durbin, my publisher, editor, and friend. Thank you for helping me make *The Road Less Traveled* the best it could be.

Thank you to all of my fans and those who have loved *Road* even from its first rough ebook printing. Your loyalty is amazing and so appreciated.

A special thanks to William Robertson for writing the lyrics to "Consuming." And to my dear friend Jimmy Bigley, who has been such a huge inspiration and wonderful writing partner. Also to the people I harassed into reading this book in its original notebook form way back in high school: Jessica Poulin and Rebecca Donato-Hardie.

And finally, thank you to my wonderful husband. Your steadfast support means more to me than I can express in words. Thank you for choosing to walk down "the road less traveled" with me and for giving me my very own storybook romance.

To the trips we make with our dearest friends, and the resulting adventures that build lifelong memories.
And to anyone who's ever had their life touched by a beautiful stranger

Chapter One

Ashland, Oregon

The rain was worse than it had been all year, pouring down in driving sheets that soaked and stung. The heavy drops mingled with the hot tears that coursed down Alyx's cheeks as she ran from the small house on the outskirts of town. The house that she had at one time thought was peaceful, a place of solace. His house. She could hear him shouting from the front porch, demanding that she return, but she ignored him. She continued to her car, knowing that he would not step outside and risk ruining his perfect hair to chase after her.

She got in her car and turned on the ignition with a shaky hand. Headlights split the darkness and she backed out, leaving the screams and the pain behind her. She glanced in her rearview mirror and could see the beginnings of an ugly, purple bruise marring her left eye. The coppery taste in her mouth let her know that her lip was still bleeding. She heard his voice still echoing in her ears. *Why do you like to piss me off, Alyx? You know I don't like to have to hurt you!*

She cringed and tried to shake the words away, but they wouldn't leave her. *You think you're going to leave me? You'll never leave because you could never find anyone better than me! No one else would put up with you!* The words were horrible, but she remembered the names the most...the awful things he had called her... She didn't even want to think about it.

Fighting more tears, she returned her gaze to the road and sped through town, coming to a screeching halt in front of a tan two-bedroom house she knew very well. She turned off the ignition and stumbled out of the car, making her way to the front door. She knocked loudly, casting a glance behind her for good measure. She was met a moment later by a pair of light green eyes that gave her instant comfort.

"Alyx?" his soft voice questioned.

"I left," she sobbed, her raven locks dripping and hanging in her face. "I really left this time, Javan."

Javan's eyes filled with worry, and he opened the door wide. He held his arms out and caught her, pulling her close and inside.

"I just couldn't take it anymore," she cried. "I thought he was going to kill me. I've never seen him look so evil. He hit me like he always does, but this time when he went to hold me and tell me how sorry he was, I screamed at him to stay away and I got out of there."

He stroked her hair softly. "You did the right thing," he assured. "No one should have to take that. Especially you. I'm glad you finally left him for good."

"I really thought he loved me." She buried her face in Javan's shirt, feeling foolish, hopeless, and lost.

"Alyx, anyone who could hurt you on purpose doesn't love you."

She let out another sob. "I'm so stupid!"

"Shhh," he soothed, sitting her down on the nearby sofa. "It'll be all right now."

"Is my brother home?" she asked, wiping at her nose.

He shook his head. "Alexi had to work late tonight. He should be home soon, though." Alyx trembled silently, and Javan reached out to touch her cheek. "Babe, you did the right thing."

She looked up at him. Javan. Her best friend in the whole entire world. He had been with her through the best and worst times of her life. She gave him a meager smile. "I know."

He pressed a kiss to her forehead. "I'll get some ice for your eye and something to clean your lip up with. I'll be right back."

She leaned back against the couch, remembering how Rick had kissed her one minute and lashed out at her the next. She could still feel the mind-numbing pain of that first blow. And she couldn't get past the things he had called her... For no reason at all. He never had a valid reason, for any of the crap he pulled. But he never had a problem always blaming it on her.

She shivered. She would never go back there, and in the morning, she would get the lock to her apartment changed. The last thing she needed was him appearing on her doorstep and cornering her when she least expected it.

"Here's one of Alex's sweatshirts," Javan said, coming back into the room. "Change into that before you catch a cold."

Alyx smiled at Javan's concern and unfolded the sweatshirt as he disappeared into the kitchen. It was her brother's Southern Oregon University sweatshirt and it smelled like Alexi. Like cologne and coffee. It was a smell she always associated with safety, for her big brother had always been her protector. She replaced her soaking top with the warmth and comfort of the sweatshirt and seemed to tremble less.

"Here's some ice," Javan's voice came again. He sat down next to her and made her place the ice pack against her eye as he cleaned the dried blood from her lip.

"Thank you, Javan," she murmured.

He met her eyes and sighed. He pulled her close and she nestled against him. "I'd do anything for you, kid. You know that."

It was true. Her junior year in high school, she had been stood up for the prom. Javan had managed to land himself a date with one of the prettiest cheerleaders in the school, but he had left when he realized what had happened to Alyx. They spent the night sitting on the couch in their formalwear, watching old movies and eating ice cream until they thought they would explode. That was only one instance. He'd walloped a neighbor kid when he'd been bullying her; he'd helped her sneak out of her bedroom to go to a party full of underaged drinking at age seventeen then had tackled a dude who was trying to grope her and helped her sneak back in again after the entire thing had ended up a disaster. For better or worse, good decisions and bad, Javan had always been right there.

"Alyx?"

"Yeah?"

"If you don't mind me asking, what set him off this time?"

She sighed. "You know when Alex, Jeff, you and I went to Lassen two weeks ago when Rick was in New York?"

He nodded.

"Well, I got my pictures back the other day and I had

them sitting in my purse. Rick found them and started raging when he saw this one of you and me in your sleeping bag together. I tried to explain to him that I had been freezing and that a skunk had sprayed mine, but he wouldn't listen. I actually think he was always intimidated by you."

"Who in their right mind would be intimidated by me?" Javan grumbled. "I'm an actor and my best friend is a chick. Half the people who meet me think I'm gay."

She shrugged, but couldn't help a tiny giggle. "I don't know, but I guess he thought I was sleeping with you or something."

"That's pathetic."

"Right? Like I would actually have someone take a picture while we were sleeping together." She sighed. "I'm glad it happened, though. It gave me the courage to leave. It was just one time too many..."

He gave her a comforting squeeze. "Rick was pond scum masquerading as a guy worthy of you. You're so much better than him."

She frowned, and tears leaked out of her eyes again. "Whatever," she muttered. "I'm nothing but a weak, pathetic girl."

Javan turned her so he could look into her eyes. "I've known you all my life, Alyxandra Oncidezzerro," he breathed. "You are not a weak person. You just thought he loved you. You wanted to believe the best of him. That's not a crime." He wiped her tears gently. "Hey, come on, you're one of the best people I know at taking a tough situation and making something good come out of it. In high school, when the less than serious actors in the plays threatened to ruin show after show after show, who pulled it together?"

"You did," she stated, wiping at her nose. "That's why everyone thinks you're gay. It has nothing to do with the fact that your best friend is a girl. It has everything to do with the fact that you were always super actor and wearing some kind of flamboyant pink shirt or something."

He laughed. "Ouch. Shoot. There's the Alyx I know and love."

She laughed through her sniffle.

"Now enough comments about my wardrobe in the nineties. Come on, Alyx. You *always* saved the day when it came to improv and the kids who were only in drama for an easy credit. You somehow always got them to get it together. You have made it through heartbreaks, car crashes, and disasters on stage. You made it into the Oregon Shakespeare Company, and you've survived having me as a friend all your life!" He gave her a little shake, making her giggle further.He smiled. "You'll make it through this too, kid, and you'll be stronger and wiser in the end."

Alyx stared up into the eyes of her long time friend. "Why didn't I ever go out with you?"

He arched an eyebrow. "Are you insane? I've had to kiss you enough in plays! Besides, the first wrong move I made, you'd kick me! And then your brother would beat me into the ground! I don't know about you, but I have no driving need to get the crap kicked out of me by the ever desirable Alexi Oncidezzerro. There's a reason he's so desirable."

Alyx smiled. "Yeah, he's a stud. But you calling him desirable does nothing for your claim to be straight status."

Javan snorted. "Dude, the guy could probably bench press a small truck. I'm not hitting on him. I'm just stating the obvious. That's so gross…"

She giggled again, feeling momentarily better by the playful banter, and the front door burst open just as a whip of lightning illuminated the dark sky outside. Two soggy men ran in the room laughing.

"Holy cow!" the brown-haired one exclaimed. "Those drops could take your head off!" A clap of thunder punctuated the sentence. The other man, who was taller with slightly darker hair, laughed. The first man shook his head and turned toward the sofa. He stopped when he saw Javan and Alyx and his eyes widened. "Alyxandra?" He strode over to her and knelt in front of her, searching her face and assessing the damage. "What happened to you?" he whispered, brushing her hair back.

"I left Rick," she murmured. "I left him for good this time."

His face darkened. "Rick did this to you?" he growled. "I'll kill him."

He started to rise, but Alyx grabbed his hands. "No, Alexi, don't," she protested. "It's not worth it. Just come here and be a good brother."

Alexi met her eyes and let out a deep sigh. He let his gaze drift over her. Several different emotions flashed through his eyes. In the end, he sat down next to her and pulled her up against him. "Whatever you want, sweetheart," he whispered, apparently deciding that throwing his primal, barbaric instincts to the wind was the best course of action. Alyx had never had to worry about having bodyguards. Alexi was fiercely protective and had a bit of a temper and Javan, despite his overall gentle nature and eccentric personality, could pack a mean punch when necessary. She was surprised they hadn't put Rick in the hospital by now.

Alyx sighed and closed her eyes as she listened to the strong rhythm of Alexi's heartbeat. No one in the whole world was like her brother. He had always been her hero. "Hi, Jeff," she murmured, peeking at the other man in the room.

He smiled, still standing by the door, not wanting to intrude. "Hey, Alyx," he said softly.

"Jeff's gonna crash here tonight," Alexi explained. "He's too tired and had a few too many beers after work to go all the way back to his place."

Jeff shrugged. "I wasn't paying attention."

Alyx opened her eyes all the way. "There was a girl somewhere, wasn't there?" Jeff chuckled and she smiled. "Would you mind if I stayed here tonight also?" she yawned. "I really don't want to be alone tonight."

"Stay as long as you like," Alexi said, hugging her close. "You know we all love you here."

"Yeah...I know."

Jeff flopped down in a chair as another roll of thunder shook the house. Alyx jumped and felt stupid for the reaction, especially when she noticed that Jeff had caught it. She hunched her shoulders self-consciously.

"Did you get those pics back from Lassen yet?" Jeff asked, flashing her an encouraging smile.

She sighed and filled with affection for the man. He was obviously trying to take her mind off her troubled thoughts and terrible night. She had awesome friends. "Yeah, there's this really stupid one of you." She sat up and reached for her purse.

The stereo suddenly let out a sound resembling a strangled goose, which sent everyone jumping.

Jeff frowned. "What the crap?"

Music began to blare.

"Finally!" Javan exclaimed. "The station blew off the air about a half hour ago." He got up and went to turn the volume down.

"Just turn it off," Alexi said.

"Wait, I like this song," Javan protested, noticing it was *Follow* by Bleeding Passion. He started to play the air guitar.

Alexi rolled his eyes. "Whatever," he muttered. "Let's see your pictures, Alyx."

She opened her package of pictures and tried to ignore the aching pain in her head. She flipped through them until she came to one of Jeff. "Look," she said, handing it to him. "You look like a donkey."

"...That was *Follow* by Bleeding Passion, the second most requested song of the week..." the radio announcer's gravelly voice came. "I tell you, those guys are awesome. Every song they put out is a hit. Y'know, they're going to be playing in San Francisco on July eighteenth. That's gonna be a great show..."

Javan's eyes widened and he riveted his attention to the radio.

"...I have five tickets here that are just itching to be given away... Tell ya what; I have five Bleeding Passion trivia questions also. We don't usually do it this way, but these are the last tickets available for the show. Let me say that again. These are *the last* tickets. The show is completely sold out. Whoever calls in and can answer all five questions first wins the tickets. All of them. I'm handing 'em right out in a block. Good luck finding another radio station that'll give you such a sweet deal..."

Javan gasped and looked around the room frantically. "Phone!" he shouted. "Phone! Phone! Phone! Phone!"

Alexi frowned as Javan all but ran in circles. He picked up the white cordless from the end table. "Here," he called, tossing it to him. Javan grabbed it like someone dying of hunger might grab at a steak. "Spaz," Alexi muttered.

Alyx smirked.

"So, did you tell him it was over?" Alexi asked, looking back down at her with concern mirrored in his eyes.

Alyx swallowed and nodded. "He hit me in the mouth after seeing that picture of Javan and me. He didn't go for my eye until I told him I was leaving and we were through."

"Do you think you should go back to your apartment?"

She shrugged. "I'm going to get the lock changed tomorrow, but I think it'll be all right. Rick's violent, but I don't think he's psychotic."

"I won!" Javan bellowed, jumping up and down. He flung the phone like it was a football and he had just made a touchdown. Part of the back popped off and flew into a dark corner.

"Hey!" Alexi shouted. "That's my phone, you jerk!"

Javan ignored him. "I just won five tickets to see Bleeding Passion in Frisco!"

Alyx's eyes widened. "You are so taking me with you."

"Who's Bleeding Passion?" Alexi questioned.

"One of the best bands on the planet!" Javan answered.

"They are pretty good," Jeff put in.

"I can't believe I won!" Javan screamed, jumping again. He pointed to Alyx and grinned. "You and me, baby. We are so there."

Alyx smiled and part of her heart suddenly didn't feel so heavy.

"Hey, you guys want to come?" Javan asked Jeff and Alexi.

"Yeah, come with us!" Alyx urged, grasping her brother's hand.

Jeff's eyes lit up, but Alexi stomped on the idea that he saw blossoming. "We can't," he said. He noticed Jeff's disgruntled look and sighed. "We have that big meeting on the eighteenth, remember? You know, with that Roscoe guy from New York?"

Jeff groaned and let his head flop back against the chair. "Man," he whined, "sometimes being your business partner sucks."

"We won't have a problem at the theatre, will we?" Alyx asked Javan.

"Nah. Neither one of us has taken vacation yet. Or...hardly ever. Besides, that's what understudies are for."

"Who else can we get to go?" she asked.

"You should take my brother Maxim," Jeff yawned. "That dude could use a vacation."

Javan shrugged. "That's fine. Tell him we'll leave next week. We can go on a road trip. Sound good, Alyx?"

She noticed Jeff and Alexi exchange a look of surprise, but she didn't give it much thought. "Sounds heavenly, I need to get out of here."

"We can just scalp the extra tickets when we get there.

They should fetch a good price."

"It'll be good for you to get away, Alyx," Alexi said, pressing a kiss to her temple. "Get a new perspective on things. Clear your head."

Alyx smiled up into her brother's slightly violet eyes. "You're the best, Alex. Are you sure you can't come?" She did her best to imitate the pout that used to get her everything when she was a little girl.

He chuckled and shook his head. "I wish I could, but this guy's a major client."

"You really want to take Maxim?" Jeff asked.

"Sure," Javan replied with an indifferent shrug.

"Uh… Is that such a good idea?" Alexi asked, frowning.

Jeff grinned. "It's perfect," he snarled. He followed the statement with a very loud, evil overlord laugh that would have found its home in a Disney movie. "Maxim won't even know what hit him."

Chapter Two

The quiet little town seemed quieter than usual as the cool night air wound its way through the open window and brushed across Maxim's cheek like a caress. He frowned and stirred, slowly opening one eye. His frown deepened when he raised his head with a wince. He brought his hand to the back of his neck and tried to rub the painful stiffness away. The lyrics of "The Sound of Silence" played softly and he reached over to turn off his radio. Since when did he listen to Simon and Garfunkle? He squinted at the station, noticing for the first time that his glasses were askew. He positioned them correctly and glanced at the radio again. It hadn't been on that station before. He shook his head and looked to the glowing monitor of his computer.

The letter H repeated itself enough to cover the entire screen. He scrolled down and saw that it went on for about fifty pages. He sighed and touched his cheek, feeling the imprints of the keys on his skin. When had he fallen asleep? And how had he managed to sleep on his keyboard and not know it? He tried to erase the colony of H's and his screen went entirely black. He blinked, watching as the screen flashed blue while the computer restarted itself. He heaved another sigh. Well, there went that story beginning.

Not that it really mattered. They were never any good and never got anywhere anyway. He hadn't written anything good since high school. Considering he was twenty-five years old, he found that rather pathetic.

Maxim pushed his chair away from his desk and stood, stretching his back muscles. He went to the window and looked down at the glistening black pavement. Rain. He closed the window and glanced at the clock. 5:05 A.M. He walked over to the door and took his gray coat from the rack. Knowing he wouldn't be getting back to sleep, he decided the crisp morning air might be refreshing.

He opened the door and closed it quietly behind him. The staircase creaked and groaned as he made his way down, and as he went to open the main door of the apartment building, the handle broke off. Maxim stared at it for a second, then put it back on and managed to shove his way outside. He took a deep breath of the cleansed air and stuffed his hands into his pockets before continuing his way down the street. He had been walking this street all alone for years.

Loneliness was not something that was new to Maxim. He had been feeling alone practically all his life, but it had never really bothered him until now. In fact, it had never really been loneliness until now. He had just thought of it as solitude...life.

He had always lived in his older brother's shadow. Jeff was the charismatic deBoer brother. There was no limit to his contacts and friends. Maxim didn't care. He was quite happy to have Jeff do the entertaining at social functions. Jeff's shadow was a nice place to be as he was a rather nice older brother. Out of all of his siblings, he and Jeff were the closest.

Maxim let his mind wander back to his childhood. He had always been a shy person, but he had gone completely inside of himself when his father left and his mother died of breast cancer. He had been sixteen. He had gone through high school sitting in the far corner in the back of the room, speaking only when he had to. He'd had Jeff until his junior year, and then no one. It had never really bothered him. He had the story characters he created. They were companions enough.

He had stayed at home for awhile after graduation, helping Jeff take care of their younger brother Barrett and little sister Meg. He had stayed until Jeff's wild college parties had gotten to be too much. While Jeff had always been careful to not allow their younger siblings access to such things, Maxim had been caught in between. And he'd never been much of a social butterfly. He'd found his little apartment on the top floor of a building and that was where he remained.

It had been five years since then. Jeff was now a major attorney with his law school buddy, Alexi. They had a private practice called Oncidezzerro and deBoer, or something ridiculous like that. Maxim had always thought that it would sound better if it was just Jeff and Alexi, but he supposed that wasn't professional enough for them.

Barrett managed a bookstore, and Meg was going to Southern Oregon University to study physics. Maxim was the only one in his family who had yet to make something of himself. He tried every day, but it seemed that his ideas had dried up like a grape left in the sun to raisin. He could no longer find anything good to write about, and perhaps that was why he now felt the loneliness heavy upon him, making his heart ache in his chest.

He worked at Barrett's bookstore, which he enjoyed, but he never spoke to anyone unless it was absolutely necessary. He barely spoke to Barrett. People freaked him out beyond measure. They were conniving, manipulative creatures that stabbed you in the back or abandoned you as soon as you trusted them. It had happened with his father. He had led them to believe that he loved them, and then deserted them all without warning or reason. Maxim had listened to his mother cry by herself in her bedroom night after night because of him. Then, not even two years later, she had left them as well. Of course, it hadn't been by choice. She had been very sick, but that hadn't made the pain any more bearable.

And then, of course, there was Jeff. He was one of the best people Maxim had ever known. He was a good friend who would give the shirt off his back to help anyone. Maxim couldn't understand how anyone would want to hurt Jeff, but he was continuously walked on and betrayed by people he thought he could trust. Maxim saw how much it hurt his brother, and he had no desire to experience the same pain.

A horn blared suddenly and Maxim jumped as a car sped by, nearly drowning him with the water it splashed everywhere. He turned away so that only his back got wet and he shivered as a few icy droplets found their way down his collar. He ran a hand through his thick brown hair, which tended to stick up in every direction all at once, and continued on, the ache in his heart worse than usual.

* * * *

Alyx jumped and felt her brother tense also as Alexi's

alarm, which sounded like a stuck foghorn, shattered everyone's peaceful slumber.

"Dude!" Javan shouted from the other room. "Shut that thing off!"

Alexi swatted at his nightstand until he managed to turn the alarm off. He heaved a sigh and nudged at Alyx, who was lying across his chest. She'd fallen asleep there by accident after talking to her brother for hours into the night about what had happened between her and Rick. "You need to move, kiddo," he said.

She groaned. "Now I know why I never stay over," she mumbled. "You and Jeff get up way too early."

"I get the same complaint from Javan. Come on, sweetie." He pushed her off gently. "I need to get in the shower."

Alyx yawned and rolled over. "Maybe I'll go and bug Javan," she said, blinking the sleep out of her eyes. She sat up and her hand went to her eye, which was swollen. She winced. "Man, my head hurts."

Alexi turned, the muscles in his back rippling as he did so. He studied her. "Look at me," he commanded.

She did so, frowning. She saw a muscle twitch angrily in his jaw and she gave him a gentle smile. "It'll look better later," she assured. "Don't go killing anyone, all right?"

He made a growling noise and turned back toward the door.

Alyx stood and stumbled her way into Javan's room, where she fell across the bed with a sigh.

"Go away!" Javan groaned, flipping over and pulling the pillow over his head.

Alyx giggled. "Come on, Javan," she teased. "You know you thrive on adventure. What better time to start one than five A.M.?"

"Adventure?" Javan questioned. "You know what I thrive on? Sleep. That's what."

She grinned.

"Every morning I have to wake up to that obnoxious alarm! One day I'm gonna stuff it right up Alexi's butt! It takes me, like, two hours to get back to sleep every morning. Then, when I do finally wake up, I have one of those sleep headache things that you get when you're forced awake and then fall back to sleep. You know, one of those ones right behind your eyes?"

The front door banged open with a crash, making Alyx jump.

"Rise and shine!" Jeff's voice sang. "The morning is *FINE!*" The last word was bellowed in a baritone that seemed to shake the entire house.

Javan half-groaned, half-growled and flipped back over. He sat up and his pillow fell to the floor. "Shut *up!*" he shouted, his voice cracking.

Alyx laughed. Javan's sandy hair stuck straight up and he looked ridiculous.

"I brought donuts!" Jeff called.

Javan's eyes widened. "Donuts!" He leapt out of bed, almost knocking Alyx right off, and he ran into the kitchen. He lunged at Jeff, who staggered backward to keep the pink box from flying right to the floor.

"Hey, Jeff," Alyx greeted as she trudged in after Javan, rubbing her good eye.

He grinned and went to Alyx, taking her gently by the shoulders and pressing a kiss to her cheek. "Good morning, beautiful."

Alyx snorted. "Right! I look so good in black and blue!"

He smiled and tucked a piece of hair behind her ear. "I brought donuts."

"He sure did!" Javan exclaimed, diving into the box and pulling out a glazed one.

"How come you're already dressed and ready to go?" Alyx asked, noticing that Jeff was showered, shaved, and in his favorite blue pinstripe suit.

He shrugged. "I woke up around four and couldn't go back to sleep, so I just got up. Thought I'd surprise you guys." He pointed to her hair. "When did you put the red streaks in your hair anyway?"

Alyx touched her crimson-streaked black hair. "Oh, last week. Do you like them?"

"Yeah, it really makes your eyes stand out. The red contrasts with the green."

"These are so good!" Javan gushed as he started to help himself to a second donut, this one cream filled.

"Hey man, you ready to go?" Alexi asked, coming out of the bathroom with his tie hanging untied around his neck.

"I've been ready for hours," Jeff said. "You're the one

who's half dressed."

Alexi smiled and tucked in his shirt.

"Wannawonut?" Javan mumbled, his mouth full of cream and cake.

Alexi frowned. "No thanks, Javan." He looked at Alyx. "How do I look?"

She smiled and looked over her handsome brother. His dark hair was still wet but combed back, and his face was stubble free, revealing the square Oncidezzerro jaw that their father also possessed. He wore a gray suit, and Alyx tied his maroon tie for him. "You look splendid as always, Alex," she said, "but I do believe Jeff has more fun." She pointed to Jeff's tie, which was blazing silver.

Alexi smiled. "Yes, well, Jeff may have a stunning tie, but I have violet eyes." He batted them at her playfully.

Jeff frowned. "Dude, that looked really gay."

Alexi frowned at him. "Well excuse me for teasing my sister. Geez."

Jeff shrugged. "Just saying, is all. I mean, what good alpha male says 'violet' anyway?"

Alexi rolled his eyes and shook his head. "One that doesn't want to say 'purple.' I mean, do my eyes look 'purple' to you? That implies that they're the color of eggplant, or Barney the Dinosaur."

Javan paused in his voracious eating to shoot a glance from Alexi to Jeff with a curious frown. "You do realize that you two 'good alpha males' are standing in the kitchen arguing over the color of Alexi's eyes? I no longer feel like the one who should be confused as homosexual."

Jeff scowled playfully at him. "Who asked you?" He went over and peered into the donut box. He selected a third one and stuffed it into Javan's mouth.

Alyx smiled as her brother pressed a kiss to her forehead. "Be good," he said. "I'll see you tonight. Don't forget to get your lock changed."

"I won't," she assured.

Jeff winked at Alyx and waved. He snatched a jelly donut from the box and made his way out the door after Alexi.

"Man, that dude loves you," Javan remarked. He set the donut box down on the counter.

Alyx frowned. "Huh?"

He pointed toward the door. "Your brother. Even as kids,

that guy would have moved heaven and earth to keep you happy."

She smiled and sat down on a barstool at the kitchen counter. She took out a donut with sprinkles and started to pick them off one by one. "Yeah, I know."

He took a seat next to her. "We all love you, you know."

She sighed and frowned as a memory of Rick socking her one flashed through her mind. She pushed it away. "I know, Javan, but don't get all sappy and psychologistlike on me now, okay? I'd rather just forget last night ever happened."

He smiled and nodded.

* * * *

"Did you drive my car this morning?" Alexi asked as he and Jeff got in his black Subaru WRX.

"Yeah," Jeff said. "I left mine at the office last night, if you recall, and I needed to get to the donut store somehow."

Alexi glanced at him. "You know, other people have been killed for that."

Jeff grinned and slipped on his sunglasses. "Yeah, but if you kill me, you'll go bankrupt." He bit into his jelly donut and a great glob of raspberry jam oozed out the back and fell on his pants. "Crap!" he shouted.

Alexi raised an eyebrow. "That's gonna look good."

"Dang it," he moaned. "Hey, drop me off at Maxim's. I'll wash them there and just be a little late."

"Fine, fine," Alexi sighed. "Leave me all alone to do your paperwork."

Jeff stared at him. "It's better than having red crap on my crotch! What do you think my clients will think of that?"

Alexi chuckled and switched on the radio as Jeff continued to mutter.

Chapter Three

Maxim climbed the steps of the building up to his apartment and sighed when he reached his floor. He brushed off the arms of his coat, which were still dripping water, and placed his hand on the doorknob. Same steps. Same apartment. Same door. He frowned as he heard Rob Zombie music blaring from the inside and he put his ear to the door. He blinked. A voice sang along with it. He opened the door and watched as a tall, brown-haired man danced through his apartment in a white button-down dress shirt, a silver tie, and a pair of bright yellow happy face boxers. Maxim took off his coat and made his way to the stereo, which he promptly turned off.

The yellow-clad underwear man stopped abruptly and scowled at Maxim. "Hey! I was listening to that!"

"So was the rest of the building," Maxim muttered. He frowned. "Nice shorts, Jeff."

Jeff grinned and admired his boxers. "Thanks!"

Maxim yawned. "Why did I ever give you a key?"

"Because you love me."

Maxim rolled his eyes. "What are you doing here?"

"I was on my way to work and my donut detonated all over my pants. I needed to wash them and you were closest. Since I didn't get to really eat either, I'm cooking breakfast too!" He flashed Maxim a wide, warm grin.

Maxim smiled and sat down on his sofa.

"Where were you anyway?" Jeff asked, going to the stove.

"I took a walk."

Jeff pulled open a drawer and the handle busted off. He stared at it, frowned, and set it on the counter. After retrieving the fork he was after, he closed the drawer. He started to hum to himself and opened up the refrigerator. "Geez, Maxim," he commented. "You have less food than me. What do you live off of? Ramen noodles?"

Maxim smiled and picked up a book he had recently bought. He flipped through the pages absently then set to reading it, stealing another glance at his brother.

Jeff closed the refrigerator with somewhat of a slam and some debris fell from the ceiling. He stared for a second then went back toward the stove. He stepped on a floorboard that bowed in the middle and frowned. "Dang," he muttered, "what's up with your floor?"

"Water damage," Maxim replied.

He shook his head and returned to his breakfast, but jumped back. "Holy crap!"

Maxim closed his book with an annoyed scowl and looked back at Jeff. "What is it?"

"You've got a granddaddy cockroach on your counter! Gimme a shoe! Where's a shoe?"

Maxim rolled his eyes and stood. "You don't need to kill it. He's not hurting anything."

Jeff stared at him in complete bafflement. "That's sick, dude!" He glanced around, then seized a pot and slammed it down onto the kitchen counter. The clanging rang through the apartment and sent the roach running for its life.

Maxim winced as he rushed over to his brother. "What are you doing? Not only am I pretty sure that you woke up everybody on the floor, but now I'll never catch the roach."

Jeff ignored him and continued to blindly bang at the counter.

"Stop it!" Maxim shoved him out of the way and grabbed a cup. The roach scurried frantically in search of a dark place to hide. Maxim tried to put the cup over it, but it dodged him.

"Don't you have any spray or anything?" Jeff asked. He opened up the cupboard under Maxim's sink and let out a triumphant shout as he spotted a half-used can of roach spray. He pulled it out and took aim.

"Jeff!" Maxim cried. "Are you out of your mind?" He yanked the can out of Jeff's hand and threw it aside right as he managed to corner and trap the roach. He looked up at his brother, who was giving him a very perplexed look, and

scowled. "Sure, just spray pesticide all over my kitchen counter. Poisoning me is a new torture you haven't tried yet." He
scooped the roach into the cup, opened the window, and flung
it out. "I have to get along with my roommates," he said,
turning back to Jeff. "Otherwise, they might turn on me."

Jeff screwed up his face. "Gross, Maxim! How can you
live here? This place oughta be condemned!"

"It's fine. I like it here."

Jeff's eyes bulged. "You *like* things spontaneously breaking off? You *like* asbestos falling from your ceiling? Maybe
one day you'll fall through the floor and *then* get a clue!"

Maxim glanced at his brother but said nothing.

"You bring girls here?"

Maxim cocked his head to one side and looked slightly
puzzled. "What's a girl?"

Jeff put his hand to his face. "Holy cow," he muttered.
"You embarrass me sometimes."

"Love you too."

"You need a life, Maxim!" Jeff cried. "This thing you've
got going isn't working out so well!"

"Your eggs are burning," Maxim stated with a sniff.

Jeff let out a strangled cry and ran to save his breakfast.
Maxim took the opportunity and went back to the couch and
his book. He did have a life... A boring, terribly lonely life, but
a life nonetheless. The last thing he needed was a lecture
from Jeff. He blocked out his brother and lost himself in the
words of Henry David Thoreau.

"Maxim," Jeff said with a sigh, bracing his hands against
the counter, "I have taken it upon myself to give you a bit of
a push."

Maxim frowned. "Do you mind? I'm trying to read about
Walden Pond."

Jeff ignored him. "You know my business partner Alex?"

Maxim turned a page, making a noncommittal noise.

"His sister Alyx got really hurt last night."

"Alex has a sister named Alyx?" He looked up at Jeff in
confusion.

"She's Alyxandra and he's Alexi. Their mother really liked
the prefix Alex."

"I guess," he muttered, turning another page.

"Anyway," Jeff continued, "she was beat up real bad by
her now ex-boyfriend."

Maxim raised his eyebrows. "That's terrible."

"Yeah. She's gonna get out of Oregon for a week or so. Her best friend Javan just won five tickets to go see Bleeding Passion in San Francisco on the eighteenth, so they're gonna go."

Maxim nodded. "That'll be good for her." He noticed Jeff steal a sidelong glance at him and then wince as if expecting a blow. An uneasy tingle worked along his spine.

"Yeah." Jeff cleared his throat. "It'll be good for you too, considering...Itoldthemthatyou'dgotoo." He sped through the last part and turned to Maxim with a cheesy grin plastered on his face.

Maxim's eyes bulged. He threw his book aside and jumped up. "You *what*?"

"They're happy you're going!" he threw in, grabbing a skillet and holding it out in front of him. "You leave next week!" He inched away as Maxim advanced, holding the skillet out as if to deflect bullets.

"Jeff, are you totally insane?" Maxim cried. "I don't even know who Bleeding Passion is! I don't really want to go traipsing all over California with a bunch of strangers either!"

"But Max—"

"I have a job!" he shouted.

Jeff waved the protest away. "Barrett will give you the time off. Come on, Maxim. Give it up. I know you can't say no. You lack the willpower." He put the skillet down and folded his arms, confident he had won the argument.

Maxim could only stare. Words completely failed him. His eyes narrowed and he peered directly at Jeff. "No," he finally stated. Jeff's eyes widened in surprise and Maxim gave him a triumphant smirk. "Take that, you traitorous jerk." He opened up his refrigerator and pulled out a bottle of root beer.

Jeff let out a dramatic sigh. "Come on, Maxim," he urged. "You need to do something. You're living terribly—"

"It's my life!" Maxim slammed the refrigerator door. More debris fell from the ceiling. "You have no right to interfere!"

"I do have a right!" Jeff insisted. "I have no desire to watch you turn into a disgruntled bachelor who turns into a mean old man. I love you too much for that."

Maxim set his root beer down on the counter and sighed. "Jeff, I don't even know these people!"

"Alyx is the sweetest girl I've ever known, and Javan is

really cool also. He lives with Alexi. They're not going to kill you or anything."

Maxim knew he looked unconvinced because he felt unconvinced.

"It's just a concert, Maxim," Jeff said with a whine. "Go and have some fun for once in your life... Just give it a chance, all right? Trust me."

His eyes were pleading, and Maxim had rarely seen his brother look pleading. He ran a hand through his hair. "You're a terrible brother," he muttered.

Jeff grinned and grabbed him, catching him in a headlock. He noogied him. "I'm a great brother!" He laughed. "I'm just a terrible friend."

Maxim pulled away and rubbed his head with a frown. "When are you gonna stop running my life?"

"When you decide to start running it yourself," Jeff stated, returning to his breakfast.

Maxim heaved a sigh. He felt very tired all of a sudden. "I can't believe I'm doing this. Jeff, what am I supposed to do? I barely say ten words to anyone. If a customer at work asks me one question too many I start to feel like I'm going to pass out!"

Jeff put his hand on Maxim's shoulder. "I have faith in you. Take a Xanax. You have no butter. I'm going to go next door and ask for some. You have a cute blonde over there."

Maxim frowned. "You going in your boxers?"

He nodded.

"Those boxers?" He raised an eyebrow.

"Why not?"

Maxim held up his hands. "Hey, whatever."

Jeff disappeared through the door and Maxim went back to his sofa where he promptly collapsed with a groan. He glanced at the framed picture of Jeff and him he had sitting on the end table. He picked it up and studied it. It had been taken a year ago at an office party. Jeff was laughing; his warm blue eyes sparkled, and he had his arm slung around Maxim's shoulders. Maxim had a small smile on his lips, but he looked awkward and uncomfortable.

His eyes were the same color as Jeff's, but they were hidden behind his black-framed glasses. Maxim's hair was a shade lighter and had blond highlights in it. He reached up and touched his hair. Most of the blond had grown out ages ago, but the tips of his hair still remained slightly lighter. Jeff kept telling him to reapply them. He claimed it would give him a "hipper" look.

His hair was always in disarray while Jeff's fell nicely around his face. He didn't know if that made them look like the sleek lawyer and his bum brother, or the skater lawyer and his snowboarder brother... He shook his head. It truly didn't matter all that much. It was easy to tell that they were brothers. They both had the same narrow faces with rather sharp features, and they both had the same lines around their mouths. Jeff's were a bit more prominent because he smiled more. Maxim's were very subtle.

That party had been a nightmare. It had been Jeff's last attempt to get him into a social circle. Some person Maxim couldn't remember had managed to get him to drink a few beers. Liquor had never been something he could handle well and he'd wound up spewing all over a girl who had been trying in vain to flirt with him all night. It had been so bad that Jeff had pretty much left him alone when it came to associating with people... Until now.

He set the picture back on his table then picked up his book again and flipped through it mindlessly. It had suddenly lost his interest. He flopped it down and snatched the picture again. "Why did I agree to do this?" he asked aloud. "Because I can't say no to you?" He rolled his eyes. "I really need to get a spine. You have been bullying me my whole life. It must be nice that you have so much charisma and find it so easy to associate with strangers. I've never been a people person. I never will be a people person. Why do I let you talk me in to crap like this? Why do I listen to you at all?" He frowned suddenly and shook his head. "Why am I talking to a stupid picture?" He put it down and leaned his head back against the couch with a frustrated growl.

Jeff burst back into the room with a stick of butter. "Man, that chick was cute," he remarked. He went to Maxim's dryer and pulled his pants out, whistling to himself. He doused them in wrinkle remover and pulled them on then leaned against Maxim's counter to eat the scrambled eggs and toast he had made. "You might want to call Alyx later. She'll want to know for sure if you're going. Just call Alex's number. If she's not there, someone will give you the number to her apartment."

Maxim blinked. Alyx and Alex and... He shook his head. There were too many people with the same name here.

Jeff finished his breakfast then shoved his shoes on and slipped back into his jacket. He tousled Maxim's hair as he went by and winked at him. "See ya, bro," he said. "Thanks for letting me use your stuff." He blew out the door, and Maxim heard a feminine voice on the other side say, "Well, you clean up real nice." Maxim sighed. Jeff had managed to charm his neighbor. That was not a great surprise. Jeff was one great big handsome gene pool of charm. He picked up his book again and, with an enormous sigh, began to read.

* * * *

There was a loneliness that always came after a break-up. Even after a break-up that was long overdue. The memories remained and swarmed a person when they didn't want to think about them. There were pictures everywhere in Alyx's apartment of her and Rick. A one-year relationship didn't just vanish. Her mind kept replaying moments over and over again...

"Hey, do you guys know what you want to order?"

Alyx looked up from her menu and her heart faltered for a moment at the handsome waiter's gorgeous grin. She smiled shyly and tucked her hair behind her ear. "Um... what would you suggest?"

"A date with me," he stated.

She ignored the sharp jab in her side from Javan's elbow and the snickers of her friends at the table. She stared at the waiter and glanced briefly at his nametag. Rick. She cleared her throat. "Excuse me?" she asked, her voice going up in surprise.

He grinned again and knelt down next to her chair, rest-ing his elbow nonchalantly on the table and letting his amber eyes slide over her face in appreciation. "Sorry, I don't tend to blurt stuff out like that." He gave a nervous chuckle. "You're just so beautiful. I couldn't help it."

There were more snickers and she felt her cheeks flush a bright shade of red. "How about you just give me some pasta and we'll see how the night progresses?"

Javan let out a loud peal of laughter and Rick gave Alyx a beguiling smile. "Sounds like a good start." He stood and pulled his order pad out of his pocket. "But don't hold it against me if the food sucks. That's not my job." He winked at her.

"And it is your job to flirt with the customers?" she teased.

He shrugged and gave her a boyish look. "Only the really cute ones..."

She shook her head. That had been the moment that started it all. She'd thought he was so charming. His boyish mannerisms had been what had drawn her to him. Too bad it had all been a ploy...

Her eyes widened in surprise as she came out the back-stage door after her show, laughing with Javan and a few other cast members. Rick was there! He was leaning suavely against the building, a black jacket clinging to his slender frame. She grinned in elation. He had never come to see her before! She ran to him and he caught her in a warm embrace. "What are you doing here?" she cried.

"I realized I'd never seen you at work before," he answered. "I wanted to watch my beautiful girl in the spotlight."

She gazed up at him in adoration. "Why didn't you tell me you were coming?"

He smiled and touched her cheek softly. "I wanted to surprise you."

"Hey, Alyx, we're all going out to get some ice cream. You guys want to come?" Javan asked. He stuffed his hands in his pockets and gave them both a warm smile.

Rick's arm went possessively around Alyx's waist and he pulled her up against him. "I was going to take Alyx somewhere," he said. "So she'll just have to go with you some other time."

Javan frowned and he met Alyx's eyes. She grinned and snuggled next to her boyfriend...

Alyx rolled her eyes. Javan had picked up on the signals before she had. That had been several months into their relationship and she had been hopelessly naïve. She'd thought he was so handsome and such a gentleman. And she really had believed that he'd loved her. He'd been very convincing. She snorted. Yeah, loved her like a possession, maybe. Ja-

Javan had seen it. Why hadn't she?

"What were you doing with him, Alyx?"
His voice was furious with an edge she had never heard before. She blinked in bewilderment, not understanding his anger. "We just went out, baby. That's all. We went shoe shopping." *She laughed a little, thinking the entire conversation was kind of silly. Why was he jealous of Javan, of all people? He was her best friend!*
His lip curled into a snarl, and he approached her with menace. "You were gone all day!"
She retreated a step and realized that he had backed her against the wall. "Well...we went to a movie and then got something to eat..."
"I don't want you seeing him again," he declared.
She laughed because she couldn't believe those words had just come out of his mouth. "Excuse me, Javan has been a part of my life a lot longer than you have! He's my best friend and I'm not going to ditch him because you're jealous!" *Her head jerked to the side as the flat of his hand met her cheek with a force that made her ears ring. She stared ahead for a moment, completely stunned. Slowly, she brought her hand up to her cheek to ease the stinging and met his eyes, shocked and hurt.*
Almost instantly, his facial expression morphed from one of anger and malice to one of grief and concern. "Oh baby, I'm sorry." *He reached out and touched her hair.* "I didn't mean it, baby." *He pulled her into his arms and held her, murmuring his apology over and over again...*

And so it began. There had been many more times after that, and she'd always just taken it. He'd made it sound like it was her fault, like he was justified in some way. *"I'm sorry, baby, but you just made me so mad. Why do you like to provoke me? Do you like making me this angry? I don't like hurting you, baby, but you need to learn to not make me so mad..."* She shuddered as she remembered those words. She'd left him once, but he had tracked her down and practically begged her to take him back. He swore that he would never hit her again, that he loved her with all of his heart and would never want to hurt her... Yeah, right. It had just gotten worse after that. He'd tried to seduce her, which hadn't gone over well, and he'd beat her up for not wanting to sleep with him. And for several months after that, she had just sat by and endured it while he smacked her around whenever he wanted to and called her abhorrent names.

Alyx sighed and put her head in her hand, entangling her fingers in her hair. He was a demon in disguise; she knew that, and it was sick that she missed him, sick that she'd actually been depraved enough to think about calling him earlier that day... But the person she had known was not the person who kept hurting her. He was not the man she had loved. She missed that person. The boyish, flirtatious man she had met at the restaurant. Where had he gone? When had he been replaced by someone so horrible? She wiped at an unwelcome tear and jumped as the phone rang suddenly. She frowned. It was probably Javan. He had been calling her all day.

She picked up the phone and rolled her eyes. "Pizza Hut."

"Oh...um, I'm sorry," a soft voice murmured. "I think I called the wrong number."

Alyx's eyes widened. "Wait!" she exclaimed. "I'm sorry, I thought you were someone else."

"I'm looking for someone named Alyx."

She drew her breath in involuntarily. The voice on the other end was gentle, like a quiet breeze. It captivated her, soothed her, and she found herself wanting to listen to it forever. All of the tension and pain she had just been feeling dissolved at the sound of the whispering voice on the other end. "This is Alyx Oncidezzerro."

"Miss Oncidezzerro... This is Maxim deBoer. I'm Jeff's brother."

She smiled. "Oh, hello. You're coming to see the concert with us?"

"Yes... What do I need to bring with me?"

"Luggage is preferable," she joked. Silence. She sighed. "Bring whatever you like. We'll be gone for about a week and a half. We're going on a road trip."

"When are we leaving?"

"Next Friday."

"Where should I meet you?"

She thought for a moment. "Let's say at Alex's house. We're taking Javan's car and he lives there."

"Alex is your brother?" he questioned.

"Yes," she said with a giggle. "I don't usually take to talking about myself in the third person."

"What time?"

"Noonish sound all right?"

"Yes. Thank you."

"I'll see you then."

"Thank you, Miss Oncidezzerro. Have a pleasant day."

Alyx raised her eyebrows in surprise as she heard the phone hang up. His manners were amazing. No one had wished her a pleasant day in...well, never. She sat back in her chair and glanced at the picture she had of her and Rick sitting on her table. They had gone snowboarding and were all dressed up in their gear. He had his arm around her and they were both grinning like a storybook couple. She stared at it for a minute, then went and turned it face down with a scowl.

What she really wanted to do was hurl it against the wall and watch it shatter, but she decided that probably wouldn't be the best course of action to take. Violence never got any-one anywhere. She knew that firsthand. She went around to every other picture she had of him and either took them off the wall or turned them face down as well. She could always take the pictures out and burn them. That might be thera-peutic...

She decided to make herself some tea instead and take a hot bath. That would probably be the best choice. She put on the tea kettle and smiled as she thought of Maxim again. She liked his voice.

* * * *

Maxim let out a deep breath. That hadn't been too bad. He hadn't died or anything. Although, if he kept all these people straight it would be a miracle. Go to Alex's house to meet Alyx and...Javan, right?

He shook his head, yawned, and left the front desk to go stock books. Barrett had been harping on him all day. He would worry about this trip later... Like, the day before should suffice. If he worried about it now, he would only give him-self ulcers.

Chapter Four

Maxim really didn't know how long he'd spent staring into the mirror. It had been awhile. He wasn't even sure why he kept staring into the mirror. What did he care what he looked like? These people had never met him, never seen him before in his life. He wasn't trying to impress anyone. He *never* tried to impress anyone. All he ever really wanted to do was blend into the background and disappear. Yet, for some reason, he'd put some gel in his brown locks, which succeeded in making his otherwise completely disheveled mass of hair look like a stylish disheveled mass of hair. And he'd changed his clothes three times. Which was completely stupid.

He'd packed one suitcase and a backpack. The suitcase contained clothing and other traveling necessities. The backpack contained enough reading material to last him his entire life.

He finally managed to tear himself away from the mirror and stand up. He heard a knock and instantly felt nauseous. He went to the door and opened it to his brother who stood there in his leather jacket and black shades.

"Hey bro, ready to go?" Jeff asked.

"No," Maxim replied miserably.

Jeff bent and picked up Maxim's bag. "Good. Let's go then." He started down the hallway.

Maxim sighed and slung his backpack over his shoulder. He would never forgive Jeff for this.

* * * *

Alyx threw her bag into Javan's trunk and grinned at him as she leaned against the back door. "Soon we'll be free!"

Javan smiled and touched her now healed eye. "Just us and the open road," he said. His slightly sad, concerned gaze turned to excitement, which she was grateful for. "And five Bleeding Passion tickets!"

She giggled and tried to ignore the tormenting memories lurking beneath the surface. This trip was to forget all of that. A new start. "This is going to be great! Where are we going to go first?"

"Who cares? Just so long as we have a good time!" He turned back to make sure everything was arranged in the trunk.

Alyx turned away from her friend and let out a large sigh, allowing her smile to fade for the moment. She didn't want Javan to know that she was feeling anything but excitement and happiness. She didn't want him to know that she still felt kind of broken inside. *A new start, Alyx,* she told herself. *Get a grip.*

"Alyx!"

She immediately plastered the smile back onto her lips and turned to face the front door of Alexi's house. She saw her brother emerge, dressed in his regular suit and tie, and she waved.

Alexi swaggered over to Alyx and caught her in an embrace. "I have to get to the office," he said. "Have fun, sweetie. Be good, okay?"

She grinned and kissed her brother on the cheek. "Always. I'll see you in a week or so. Don't work too hard."

"Call me when you get to your first stop. I love you." He turned. "Oh, and Alyx?" She frowned and he grinned. "Slay the beast."

She returned his smile. "And shine like the coming dawn."

He nodded and winked at her.

She could never hide anything from her brother. He always knew what she was feeling. He knew she was still hurting, despite her false bravado. "Slay the beast and shine like the coming dawn" had been a phrase they had used since childhood. Alexi had been Alyx's favorite playmate, and together they had made up grand stories and adventures. Alexi had made up that line while Alyx was facing a terrible, fire-breathing dragon that was going to eat Javan if she didn't stop it. At the time, the dragon had been the dryer and Javan had been placidly minding his own business playing video games, but the saying had stuck. It was something they still said to one another to encourage, to let the other know that they believed each other invincible.

"Take good care of Maxim," Alexi called back to Javan, rolling his eyes. "I still can't believe he agreed to go."

Jeff's car suddenly came to a screeching halt in front of Alexi's house and Jeff jumped out, waving at everyone. He grinned and pulled a suitcase out of the back seat. "Hey, guys! You all ready to go?"

Alyx grinned and gave an enthusiastic nod.

"Dude!" Javan shouted. "Do you know who's touring with Bleeding Passion?"

Jeff shook his head.

"Fat Stinky!" he exclaimed in glee.

Alexi frowned. "That is the most bizarre name I have ever heard," he muttered, getting into his car. "Come on, Jeff. We gotta go."

"Have fun, everyone!" He got back in the driver's seat and frowned when he saw Maxim still sitting in the passenger seat. He sighed. "Get out, Maxim!" he demanded. "Come on, man. Even a turtle doesn't get ahead until he sticks his neck out."

Maxim frowned. "I'm going to get out just to escape that comment," he muttered, forcing himself out of the car.

Jeff grinned. "Have a good time!" With that, he shifted gears and sped off, leaving Maxim standing in the dust his back tires kicked up.

"Hey, Maxim!" Alexi called as he drove past also.

Maxim did his best to smile and wave as Alexi disappeared down the road, leaving him there with his backpack as his only friend and ally. He swallowed and turned, glancing up at the two people loading the car. His heart was up in his throat and beating like a tom-tom. This may just kill him. Jeff had sentenced him to death. He shifted uncomfortably.

"Hi there."

He almost jumped completely out of his skin. His eyes went to the owner of the voice and his breath sucked in sharply. Tall, slender...creamy white skin, black hair streaked with crimson... shining, beautiful, silky black hair. The crimson only made it more attractive.

She glanced at her friend and walked over to Maxim. "I'm sorry, I didn't mean to startle you."

The goddess spoke! Maxim blinked and managed to close his mouth before he started to drool. She pushed her sunglasses up onto her head, revealing stunning green eyes, and she flashed him a grin that outdazzled the sun. He swore he stopped breathing altogether.

Alyx frowned a bit. Was he mute? Was he alive? Did she need to prod him with a stick? She thrust her hand forward. "I'm Alyx," she announced. "Alyx Oncidezzerro."

He blinked a few times as sense slowly seemed to return to him. "Oh, I spoke to you on the phone. Right." He cleared his throat and shook her hand slowly. "M-Maxim," he stammered. "I'm Maxim deBoer." He tried his best to give her what she expected was a charming smile, but it came off rather weak.

Alyx smiled. He was very handsome, but in a different way than his flashy brother. He reminded her of the college professor you secretly lusted after. "You can go ahead and load your things into the car," she said. "We'll leave as soon as I make sure everything's locked and unplugged in Alexi's house." She didn't miss the petrified look in his eyes, and she gave his shoulder a reassuring squeeze. Alexi had told her that Maxim was very shy and had a great deal of social anxiety. It must be difficult for him to go on a trip with complete strangers. She was kinda surprised he agreed to it.

"Hey, Javan!" she called. Javan, who had been checking out his tires, looked up. Alyx chuckled to herself at his expression. Sometimes, he managed to look completely like a confused cow. "Come here!" she demanded. "You're being rude!" Javan was there in a few long-legged strides. "This is Maxim," she introduced. "Be nice and load his bags."

He looked at Maxim and grinned. "Sure!" he exclaimed, flopping an arm around Maxim's shoulders.

Maxim jumped a little then closed his eyes as if to compose himself.

"I'm Javan!" he announced. "How're you doing, Maxim?"

Alyx saw Maxim pale and she glanced up at her friend. "Don't...frighten him, Javan," she warned.

He looked appalled. "I would never..."

She laughed and squeezed Maxim's shoulder again. "Don't worry," she assured, "sometimes he frightens *me*. I'll be right back." She sauntered back into the house, giving him a wink as she did so.

"Maxim, you're not looking so good," Javan observed.

Maxim looked up at him, hoping to convey a "help and get me out of here" expression. He asked himself for the millionth time *why* he was doing this.

Javan laughed like he knew what Maxim was thinking. "Come on. Let's get you in the car before you ralph or something."

Maxim nodded mechanically and was ushered over to the car by Javan, who took his bag and loaded it into the trunk. He winked as he shut it. "We don't need you trying to make a break for it," he teased.

Maxim swallowed as he watched his suitcase get eaten up by the trunk and disappear from sight. He was feeling sicker by the minute. "C-Can I have a glass of water or something?" he asked feebly. His throat felt like Death Valley.

"Yeah, go on in and get one before Alyx locks up."

He made a slow turn and headed inside. He managed to find a glass in the kitchen, root around in his pocket, pull out a Xanax, which he only took when necessary—and right now was definitely necessary—and swallowed it with a long drink of water, leaning back against the counter as he did so. His eyes involuntarily wandered around the layout of the house. It was something he couldn't help. He took in everywhere he went, logging pieces of description away in his memory to use as ammo for later story ideas.

The house was actually pretty barren. White stucco walls and beige carpet. There was a large fireplace in the living room with a brown leather couch and a chair that matched. There was also an entertainment center and a glass coffee table. The dining room had a large, round, wooden table that was strewn with a laptop, empty coffee mugs, and potato chip bags, as well as numerous papers. He smiled a little. It was apparent that was where Alexi did most of his work.

With a sigh, Maxim finished his water and decided to make use of the bathroom while he was in there. Who knew when a rest stop would be, and his nerves were wreaking havoc on his bladder. He left the kitchen and went to locate it.

* * * *

Alyx sat on the bed in Javan's room. Just sat there. She'd gone in to make sure that he'd unplugged the shaver in his bathroom and had sat down on the bed. She felt so tired, but she didn't know what she was tired from. She had a small idea that it had something to do with the fact that she kept smiling at everyone and insisting she was fine when she was anything but. She kept having nightmares about Rick, and memories of him plagued her throughout her day. The bad memories made her sick, and the good ones made her sick at heart. She just couldn't figure out what her problem was. Why couldn't she just get over it? The guy was a monster. Why did she dwell on memories of him at all?

Because you really thought he loved you, you sick freak.

She gave a dry chuckle as her own thoughts answered her. Yeah, well, there was always that. He had been so charming in the beginning, like a romance novel hero. Dashing and charismatic. She had written off his possessiveness as a fierce need to protect her, but she realized now that she had just been delusional. She'd always had some sick Prince Charming complex, probably because she'd grown up with the two men who mattered most in her life protecting her and guarding her from all evil. She had wanted Rick to be that for her so badly that she'd just glossed over all the warning signs. She was such a pathetic fool.

She sighed and shook her head. She looked around as if remembering where she was. What was she doing in there? Having a therapy session with herself? Javan probably thought she was never coming out, and Maxim had probably died of a heart attack by now. What was she thinking, leaving him out there for an extended period of time with Javan? Alone, no less. That was a sure way to get him to never go out in public again.

She stood, gave one more quick look around the room, and started out the door, ramming right into someone who had just come in. She screamed and jumped back, making the other person jump as well.

Maxim's nerves spasmed at her shrill shriek of surprise. He instinctively reached out to place his hands on her shoulders. His heart hammered so loud that he could actually hear it in his ears, and he drew in a deep, calming breath.

Alyx looked up at him and let her breath out slowly. "Maxim," she rasped, "you scared me half to death."

He gave a sheepish smile and looked down. "I'm sorry. I was just looking for the bathroom."

She gave a slightly forced-sounding giggle. "Well, Javan's room is a hog wallow, but it's not the bathroom. Although, it does kinda smell like one."

Maxim gave a small, breathy chuckle and looked up at her. Her body was rigid, and he realized that he was still holding onto her. His cheeks flamed and he immediately removed his hands.

Alyx smiled at his obvious awkwardness and she pointed to the door on the right. "There's the bathroom."

He nodded, still keeping his eyes away from hers. "Thanks." He escaped into the room and let out a relieved breath. Alone, at last. He closed his eyes and tried to calm his nerves. When he got over the feeling that he was going to hyperventilate, he left the bathroom and went back outside, where Javan was leaning up against the car, waiting.

Javan frowned. "You're looking kinda nasty, Maxim," he remarked.

Maxim took a deep breath and glanced up at him. "Can I just"—he pointed to the back seat—"you know, ralphing and all that."

Javan raised an eyebrow. "Yeah, man. Go ahead and get in. It's unlocked."

Maxim hurried into the car, clutching his backpack to his chest as if it was the only thing keeping him alive. He could still feel the warmth of Alyx's skin on his hands. That was weird. Her skin had been so soft...

"Hey," Javan said through the open window, "you need a bucket or something?"

Maxim smiled tremulously and shook his head.

"You sure?" he prodded. "'Cause I don't want chunkage decorating my car."

Maxim's smile grew slightly against his will, and Javan grinned.

"We ready?" Alyx's voice came.

"Sure are," Javan replied. "We are gone!"

"I'm driving," she declared. Javan tossed her the keys and hopped into the passenger seat. She started the car and turned in her seat to look at Maxim. "You okay?"

Maxim's heart made a small lurch, and he swallowed hard. Geez...she was so beautiful. He nodded slowly. "Look," he said, "I'm not really into this kinda thing. I'm uh—"

"I know," Alyx interrupted. "Alex told me." She pushed

her glasses up so that Maxim could see her eyes. She smiled. "You don't need to worry about anything. Javan and I will do our best to make you as comfortable as possible."

He sighed. "I haven't been around a whole lot of people...a lot." He frowned, feeling like an idiot. What kind of stupid sentence had he just rattled out? Writer? Yeah, right. He couldn't even formulate a coherent thought.

Alyx retained her warm smile. "That's all right. Being shy isn't a crime."

He raised an eyebrow. "Shy? I'm socially inept."

"I'm sure you'll be just fine." Her cheek dimpled as she smiled wider and turned back in her seat.

Maxim sighed and sat back against his seat, releasing the death grip on his bag just slightly.

Alyx steered the car out of the driveway, and Javan let out a monstrous cackle that made Maxim jump.

"This rocks!" he shouted. "Man, I am so in need of a vacation!"

"Um...where exactly are we going?" Maxim murmured.

"Wherever the road takes us!" Alyx laughed. "Anywhere away from here." Javan patted her on the shoulder and they pulled out on the open road.

Maxim swallowed and concentrated on looking out the window. If he just looked out the window, maybe everything would not seem quite so terrifying... Maybe.

Chapter Five

Maxim had managed to scrunch himself up against the door and use his bag as a barrier between him and the rest of the human race. He'd put his headphones on and started listening to some calming rock music, thus blocking out the people and the road that was separating him from everything safe he had ever known. Because of this, he had actually managed to get through about five pages of Thoreau. Reading about the tranquility of Walden Pond relaxed him somewhat, and he no longer felt like a spring coiled so tight it was about to snap. He leaned his head against the window and sighed.

Smiling, he watched the trees whiz past. Oregon had so many trees. It was like a thick, soft blanket... He blinked. That was all right. That was the first shred of decent description he had come up with in...geez, who knew how long. He concentrated on the denseness of the foliage, trying to find the right words to convey the way they interweaved with one another. They almost resembled a barrier, like he could step into those trees and emerge in a different world, a different time. His smile grew. They were—

Maxim's thoughts completely fled as metal music suddenly invaded his ears at a decibel not preferable. He grasped for his CD player and stabbed at the buttons until he succeeded in changing the song. What was Metallica doing on his Sting album? His frown deepened at the start up of the next song. Now he had George Straight twangin' away at him? He switched the song again and all but screamed aloud. He yanked his headphones off with a frustrated snarl. The Backstreet Boys? He flipped open his CD player and sighed when he saw that the CD had been burned by Jeff. He had forgotten about that. He supposed his brother thought he was funny. That was the last time he ever asked Jeff for a favor. Not that he had anything against Metallica or George Straight, but not on his Sting CD! The Backstreet Boys were all fine and good also, if he was fifteen.

The tennis ball Javan had been bouncing off the windshield for the past half hour suddenly rebounded and bounced off of Maxim's forehead. He blinked.

"Dude!" Javan exclaimed, swiveling in his seat to look at Maxim. "I'm sorry!"

Maxim smiled weakly.

Alyx screamed and slammed on her brakes, sending Maxim crashing into the back of Javan's seat. His face squished up against the upholstery as his neck twisted at an unnatural angle. "Ow," he muttered, straightening. "I guess a seatbelt would be beneficial."

"What the crap?" Javan questioned.

Maxim peered over the seat and frowned when he saw a tall, very hairy, bearded man standing inches away from Alyx's car, staring straight at her with beady eyes that looked as if they would burst from his skull at any moment.

"What's he doing?" Javan asked.

"Don't ask me! He just popped out of nowhere!" she exclaimed. "He's just staring at me!"

There were a few more moments of complete silence where the man only stared unblinking at Alyx. He then turned, still not speaking, and disappeared into the forest.

"That was...bizarre," Javan remarked.

Alyx continued down the road. "I think it was the missing link, or the Yetti."

"I think it was one of ZZ Top," Javan said.

Maxim grinned.

"Whoa!" Javan exclaimed.

Maxim jumped and looked at him. He spotted Javan watching him in the side view mirror.

"That's the first genuine smile I've seen out of you yet!"

Maxim felt his face redden. He smirked a bit and looked away. He scooted back into his seat and secured his seatbelt. He had no desire to break his neck anytime in the near future. Something suddenly started to ring in the vicinity of his backpack and he frowned in confusion.

Javan turned and looked at Maxim. He frowned. "Your bag is ringing," he announced.

"But I don't have anything that rings," he replied, befuddled.

"Well, *something* is ringing."

Maxim opened up his backpack and rifled through it, pushing books and snacks and CDs aside. The ringing grew louder as he reached the bottom, and he pulled out a black cell phone. He stared at it as if it was an alien life form. It continued to blare.

"Answer it!" Javan cried.

Maxim flipped it open and put it to his ear. "Hello?" he answered cautiously.

"Hey, brother!"

Maxim jolted at the sudden exclamation and scowled. "You!" he snarled.

"How do you like the surprise?" Jeff asked.

"What surprise?"

"The phone! It's one of mine! I gave it to you so I could keep track of you."

Maxim frowned. "*One* of yours?"

Jeff ignored him. "How's the trip so far?"

"Oh just peachy," Maxim said, his voice all sarcasm. "After you *left* me at Alexi's house, I was stuffed into the backseat of a car with two strangers and no possible way to escape. I have recently been hit in the head with a tennis ball and almost broke my neck because ZZ the Yetti was standing in the road!" He saw Alyx and Javan exchange glances and stifle laughter. "Not to mention," he continued, "that you completely *ruined* my Sting CD!"

Jeff laughed. "Glad you're having a good time, Maxim."

"I hate you," Maxim snarled. He snapped the phone shut.

"Harsh," Javan remarked.

"He's just my brother."

Alyx smiled. "So, where should we go first?" she asked. "We have a whole week and a half off and three days before the concert."

Javan leaned back against the seat and let out a contented sigh. "I love the randomness of this trip. Anyone feel likecamping in the redwoods?"

"I haven't been to the redwoods in years!" Alyx exclaimed. "Not since you came with my family that time when I was ten."

Javan grinned. "That was a trip I'll always remember." He turned and looked at Maxim. "Alexi convinced me that a bear was prowling through our camp. I ran myself right up a tree and stayed there all night, even after Alexi told me it had been a joke all along. Alyx's dad finally had to come and get me out." He shook his head and turned back around. "That was embarrassing."

Maxim raised an eyebrow. "Don't you know that bears can climb trees?"

Javan stared at him for a second, and Maxim swore he saw the color drain from his face. "Thanks, dude," he said sarcastically. "Thanks a lot."

Alyx giggled. "I would love to go to the redwoods and camp for a night," she said, "but where would we sleep? In the car?"

"I have a tent in the trunk," Javan replied.

"You're carrying a tent around?"

"I never took it out after we got home from Lassen."

"How many people can that thing fit?

Javan raised an eyebrow. "…Three," he answered.

Alyx glanced at him, looking completely unconvinced.

Javan turned toward Maxim again. "How 'bout it, Maxim?"

He shrugged. "A-All right."

"Don't worry," Javan assured. "We'll have a great time."

Maxim swallowed and continued to stare out the window. If something terrible happened to him, he would see to it personally that Jeff never saw the light of day again. He was an intellectual, not a freaking woodsman.

"I figure we'll spend one night up in the redwoods and drive down to Fort Bragg tomorrow," Javan continued. "We can stay there for the night maybe."

Alyx nodded. "And the morning after that we could head to Frisco."

"How many days do you want to spend there?" he asked.

"I don't care. A few. I love it there, and I haven't been in awhile."

Javan nodded. "You have any particular place you want to go, Maxim?"

Maxim looked at the back of his head. "No, not really," he replied. "I don't even know what I'm going to see."

"Do you like metal music?" Alyx asked.

"Some." He shrugged. "It's more of Jeff's thing, though."

"Speaking of which, let's listen to the radio or something," Javan suggested. "A road trip isn't a road trip until there's music." He flicked on the radio and pressed the seek button.

It landed on an oldies station, and the sounds of Simon and Garfunkle found their way back to Maxim. He frowned. "Sound of Silence"? He'd heard that song more in the last week than he had in his entire life. He sighed and wished Javan would change the station. The song was beautiful, but it saddened him. Even though he knew the song meant something else, he had always associated it with loneliness. It spoke of darkness being an old friend... How many nights had he stayed awake with the dark as his only companion?

Then it spoke of people talking without speaking and people hearing but not listening... All day people talked to him, interacted with him, but they never really had anything they wanted to share. They heard his voice, but missed what he was trying to scream... If people could only listen, they would see that he had his arms opened wide, begging for someone, anyone... Anyone at all. He just didn't know how to make the first step, to breach that barrier...and no one else ever cared to try. He didn't even know how to begin to trust someone. The rules of human relationships may as well have been a foreign language.

He blinked back sudden tears and cleared his throat. "Javan," he all but whispered.

The music was loud, but something in the tone of Maxim's voice made Javan turn in his seat, and Alyx glanced at him in the rearview mirror. "Yeah?" Javan asked.

"Can you please change the station?"

Alyx was quick to do so. Led Zeppelin came on.

Javan frowned at Maxim in concern. "You all right, man?"

Maxim swallowed again and met Javan's eyes. He stared at him for a second. No one had ever looked at him like that before. Like he had...*heard*. He blinked, then licked his lips and nodded. "Yeah, I'm fine. I just wanted to listen to something else."

Javan nodded, but didn't look like he believed him at all. He exchanged a glance with Alyx, and the way she looked back at Javan let Maxim know that she had heard the desperate note in his voice as well. He tried not to dwell on it, and let out a great sigh of relief as his ears fill with "The Immigrant Song." He leaned his head against the window and closed his eyes. He hoped he survived this trip without having a nervous breakdown or something. That would really be embarrassing.

Chapter Six

San Lorenzo, California

Taegen heaved a sigh as she rested her elbow against her car window and put her head in her hand. Traffic in the Bay Area sucked at six o'clock. She had never had this problem in Lone Pine. She rolled her eyes. Maybe that was because there was nothing in Lone Pine. "Get over it, Taegen," she grumbled. "You've been living in San Lorenzo for five years now. The traffic is like this every day." She tried to just ignore it and concentrate on the song that was playing on the radio. It was *Don't Stop Believin'* by Journey. She tapped her fingers on the wheel and sang along under her breath. She loved Journey. This was one of her favorite songs of theirs. A small town girl and a city boy both taking the midnight train and finding one another when they least expected it... She sighed, wondering why romance never existed in real life like it did in songs.

Someone behind her laid on their horn and she jumped, her teeth gnashing in irritation. She scowled and fought the impulse to stick her arm out the window and give the driver a not so polite gesture. Like she could go anywhere! She gripped the wheel tighter, and her head pounded. She noticed that the traffic Southbound was actually moving a lot faster and she toyed with the idea of just going back that direction. She worked in Hayward and didn't really want to return there, but she hadn't been to San Francisco in quite some time. Ironic, considering that the city had been her entire reason for moving to the Bay Area.

Making up her mind, she inched up to the next exit and turned off, getting on the highway Southbound. It would be the long way into Frisco, but anything was better than sitting in rush hour. The traffic was sluggish, but not at a standstill, and Taegen felt her shoulders relax a little. She leaned back in her seat and sighed. It felt good to be moving again. She did not enjoy sitting on the freeway for hours on end just trying to get from Chabot College in Hayward to her pitifully lonely house in San Lorenzo.

Soon she started to see the beginnings of South San Francisco. She usually never got around to seeing the southern part of the city. The last time she had seen it had been when she was visiting her brother. Her other reason for moving to the Bay Area... Paul...

She sighed again as she let her eyes fall on all the familiar sights. There was the Clarion...the hotel she had stayed in during one of her visits. There was the Cow Palace. She had seen a concert with him there once. She chewed on her bottom lip as memories came flooding back. Laughter...so much laughter. Perhaps there had been a good reason for her avoiding this part of the city for so long.

Suddenly, Taegen heard something that sounded like a great explosion and her car jerked to one side. The grinding of metal on asphalt made the hair on the back of her neck stand up, and she quickly maneuvered her car to the side of the road. She flicked on her emergency flashers and sat there for a second, stunned. "Unbelievable," she muttered. She turned off the ignition and got out to survey the damage.

The rear tire was completely blown out on the left side. She groaned. She didn't even have a spare! This was ridiculous! She glanced at her beaten car again and scowled at it. "Piece of junk," she grumbled, kicking it. She yanked her purse out of the front seat and grabbed her keys. "Screw this," she hissed. She slung her purse over her shoulder and stuffed the important paperwork from her glove compartment into it. "I'll deal with you later." She locked the door, slammed it, and strode along the side of the highway, praying that she didn't get flattened at any moment.

She followed the next exit into Daly City and walked until she reached the train station. She had no idea where she was going and really didn't care at this point. She was tired and frustrated and wanted nothing more than to run away from the life she had fallen captive to.

Once she had purchased the ticket, she got on the next

train and seated herself on one of the lower level seats. She didn't really want to be up near the roof. She'd always sat on the upper level when she'd come to visit Paul. "You have problems, Taegen," she grumbled to herself as she flopped into her seat. "You need a therapist." Why couldn't she just let it go? He'd been gone for two years, but it still felt like yesterday.

She was still plagued by memories of him, and it killed her. She knew that it was normal to grieve for a long time, and she knew that everyone grieved in different ways, but her sister Mary seemed to be doing all right. Sure, she still cried every year around the anniversary of his death and at family get-togethers when memories started going around, but Taegen cried almost every day. His absence had left a gaping hole in her heart. He'd been her best friend...and some irresponsible ass had taken him from her.

She sighed and closed her eyes, attempting to relax yet again. Sooner or later, she would have to take care of her car. Later, much later. She leaned her head back against the seat as the train lurched to a start. She could still remember how cold it had been the night she'd gotten the call. It had been one of those foggy, San Francisco winter nights that chilled a person to the bone. She'd been sleeping soundly in the house she rented, knowing that she had a huge final exam the next day. She was supposed to meet Paul in the city afterward for a "congratulations-on-making-it-through-the-semester-you-only-have-one-left-to-go-before-you-graduate" dinner. She'd been looking forward to it all week.

The phone had sounded muffled, like it was coming from really far away. At three in the morning, she had been very surprised to hear her mother's tear-laden voice. Of course, they had been contacted before she had. When a twenty-five-year-old man's car was found flipped and obliterated on a San Francisco street, the first thing the police did was look to see if there was any spouse. When there wasn't, they called the parents.

Taegen's heart had stopped beating that night, and two weeks later, when her boyfriend had broken up with her for being "too emotional," her heart had stopped letting people in also.

What haunted her was the fact that Paul had offered to stay at her house that night and help her study. She had told him no, thinking that helping his little sister study was prob-ably on the bottom of a successful journalist's to-do list. But if she had taken him up on his offer, he would still be alive. He wouldn't have been in the city when that drunk driver had been on the road. He would have been safe. Her parents and everyone else had assured her that there was nothing she could have done, but she couldn't help but wonder what if. Her life was full of what ifs.

She heaved a sigh and opened her eyes, banishing the troublesome memories. She'd only re-hashed the awful event seven million times since it had happened, and she never got any other results besides tremendous guilt and sorrow.

She gazed around for a moment, letting her gaze fall on the man in the seat across from her on the other side. He was sketching something and she turned her head slightly to see what it was. It was a man sitting atop a cliff overlooking the sea. The artist was putting some finishing touches on the waves and Taegen smiled. It was fabulous. She watched the artist work awhile longer, noticing how long his skilled fingers were and how he tackled the paper as a mathematician might approach an almost unsolvable equation. She let her gaze wander up his arm and then she returned to staring at the seat in front of her.

Out of the corner of her eye, Taegen noticed someone watching her. She glanced toward the person and her eyes widened in mild surprise. It was the artist she had been studying only moments ago. He regarded her with gentle eyes and a small, almost playful smile, and she swallowed. He had long, jet black hair pulled back into a ponytail that rested just past his shoulders. She felt a little embarrassed by the attention, but she smiled politely and turned to look out the window. She touched her own dark blonde locks self-consciously. She must look terrible.

Moments later, Taegen's gaze returned to the sketch the man was working on perfecting. It was beautiful. She had rarely seen such skilled black and white. She glanced up at his profile and noticed that he was frowning with a look of concentration. She also noticed that he had very attractive features. He suddenly ceased in his drawing and glanced up at her again. She quickly averted her eyes, hoping he hadn't caught her gawking again. Out of the corner of her eye, she saw him grin. She smirked to herself, barely noticing that her stop had been announced over the loud speaker. She placed her purse back on her shoulder and left the train a bit reluctantly. She wished she could see how that handsome artist's picture would turn out.

Once outside the train station, Taegen began to unwind. She looked around the busy city sparkling with a pre-dusk glitter and wandered to a bus stop. She waited for a bus that was going to Golden Gate Park and got on. She needed some time to be some place peaceful. She watched the city go by out her window and sighed. She'd moved to San Lorenzo so she could go to school in Berkeley and be close to her brother, who was going to school at the University of San Francisco. She'd had great dreams about how they were both going to take the Bay Area by storm and be a force to be reckoned with. A naïve girl's ambitions.

Even before Paul had died, she'd had horrible problems finding a job and paying her rent. She'd lived in a dorm for her first year of school until her roommate had started sneaking drunken guys in the room and making it impossible to sleep or study. After that, she'd moved to San Lorenzo because she couldn't find anything open in Berkeley that she could afford. She'd found her little house, but then lost her job. Paul had offered to let her live with him, but she had wanted to make it on her own and not have to rely on her family, so she'd spent six months flipping burgers at McDonald's and living off of pudding cups. She had been deluded about many things and she had made some irrational choices.

She sighed again as she sat down on an empty seat and closed her eyes, leaning her head against the window. She was so tired. So tired of everything…

"Hey, lady!"

Taegen jumped and blinked, her heart beating wildly. She shook her head to clear her thoughts and looked up at a scraggly older man.

"You're here," he stated.

She looked around and blinked again. "Huh?" she mumbled.

"This is the last stop, so it's yours no matter what. You slept through the others."

She ran her hand through her hair and looked out the window. Thank goodness it actually was her stop. She didn't feel like wandering around San Francisco when she barely knew where anything was. She muttered a thank you to the man and got off the bus, trying to rub the remaining sleep from her eyes. She crossed her arms and chose a path, beginning her trek through the park. It was seven o'clock and chilly from the evening fog, but she found it refreshing. The knots in her shoulders began to slowly unwind as she strolled, letting the beauty around her permeate her battered psyche.

She crossed through a field of purple flowers and came to a stop on a path surrounded by wild palms and beautiful flowers of orange and yellow. She let out a cleansing sigh and closed her eyes, grateful for the tranquility and the silence. She dealt with stress horribly. Maybe she should take some herbs, or take up yoga or something.

"Fancy meeting you here."

Taegen jumped and her shoulder knots instantly reformed. She whipped her head around to the unfamiliar voice and her eyes widened. In the hazy surreal of dusk, she saw a tall, lithe man strolling toward her. His posture was casual and his hands were resting in the pockets of tan slacks. A long, black coat was draped on his shoulders and stopped at his knees. Beneath the jacket, she could see a white dress shirt unbuttoned halfway down. His shining black hair was now free of the ponytail and fell around his shoulders and narrow face.

She was shocked, overwhelmed, and her first thought was to grab her pepper spray. "Did you follow me?" she breathed, taking a step back.

"No," he chuckled, shaking his head. "I always come here after a hard day at work. Seeing you is purely a coincidence." He came to stand in front of her and grinned.

Taegen's heart nearly stopped at that grin. She swallowed and tried to brush her hair out of her face. She knew it must be everywhere.

"I'm not an artist," he continued, "if that's what you were thinking. I'm actually an architect. I draw and paint in my spare time."

She dared glance at him again, but his handsomeness unnerved her and she averted her eyes. "You draw well," she replied lamely.

He grinned again. "So, what brings you here tonight?"

She sighed and stuffed her hands in her pockets. "A flat tire," she replied. He raised one ebony eyebrow and she shrugged. "Left my car on the side of the road and just walked away." She rocked back and forth on the balls of her feet, a nervous gesture that she couldn't help.

"Where?"

"Just outside Daly City." She looked up at him again. There was that gentle expression he had regarded her with on the train. She eased just a bit.

"Cars are evil," he stated.

She smirked.

His laid back posturing didn't change, but he bit his bottom lip as if to stop a sly smile, and looked to the right like he was debating on something. It seemed as if he came to some sort of conclusion and he straightened, offering her his left arm and a beguiling smile. "Would you consider walking with me?"

Taegen stared at him and noticed that his eyes were the most intense shade of green she had ever seen. If the forest at dusk had a color, this man's eyes would be it. Her heart flipped over and she swallowed uncomfortably. Why was it that every time people got uneasy, it became incredibly hard to swallow? And why, completely out of the blue, did *Don't Stop Believin'* start playing through her mind again? She frowned.

"I know you have no reason in the world to walk with me," he continued. "You don't know me, but I assure you, my intentions are nothing to fear. I just happen to find it interesting that, out of all the people in San Francisco, I would run into the same one twice in little less than an hour."

She took a small step back, unsure. "If you're planning on trying to seduce me later, you can just stop right now," she warned. "I don't do seduction, and I don't do commitment. I also don't really do..." She waved her hand at him. "Men at the present moment."

He grinned again. "I don't plan on seducing you," he said, though his eyes traveled up her body in a brief caress, "and I don't expect you to commit to anything. I also wasn't expecting you to *do* me. I just want to walk with you." He stepped closer and offered his arm again.

Taegen blushed horribly, but found it completely fruitless to try to resist him. His eyes captivated her, and she knew that if she did deny him, she would kick herself for the rest of her life. The last thing she wanted for herself was another what if. She had a what if about moving to San Lorenzo. She had a what if about dropping out of college when she had been so close to getting her teaching license. She had a what if about her brother. And she knew there were others. Besides, it was only a walk through the park.

She stepped forward and took his arm with caution, eyeing him. "Don't try to attack me," she said. "I know kickboxing."

"I would never dream of doing such a thing," he assured as he turned up the path.

Taegen fell into step with him and kept her eyes downcast. She felt totally weird.

"What's your name?" he asked her suddenly.

She looked up at him and shook her head. "No way." He frowned in confusion, so she elaborated. "Names are the first step to commitment. If you have a name, you have something solid, something that can be traced."

He smiled softly and pulled his arm just a little closer to his body, pulling her closer as well. "No worries," he said. "I will just call you...Pretty Lady."

She looked back down, fighting a blush. Flirt. Great, just what she needed. "What were you drawing on the train?" she asked, changing the subject.

"That's my favorite place in the Bay Area. Point Bonita. Have you ever been there?"

She shook her head.

He closed his eyes as if to recall a memory. "It's the most beautiful place. Even more beautiful than here. At night, you can stand on the cliffs in the fog and almost feel like you're flying through time and space, like the whole entire universe is your playground." He sighed. "Do you like the ocean?"

Taegen grinned. "Yes. I like it very much."

"What do you like best about it?"

"It's peaceful, and peace is a rare thing these days." Actually, the ocean was the only place that ever made her feel better. She had always gone to the beach with Paul, but the memory of being there didn't bother her like some of the others did. When she was at the ocean, she almost felt like he was with her again.

"Very true... I intruded on your peace a moment ago. Would you like me to leave you to your solitude?"

She shook her head. "I have had enough solitude to last

me my entire life," she mumbled.

He let his eyes linger on her, but didn't pursue the subject. "Do you live in the city?"

"No, I live in San Lorenzo. I'm a teacher's aide at Chabot College in Hayward. I just wanted to come to the city to relax." She fell silent. She probably shouldn't have told him that. If he turned out to be a stalker, he'd know where to find her.

The path they were on led out of the dense foliage and onto a baseball field. A group of about five boys tossed a baseball around. One of them spotted the both of them. He stopped what he was doing and jumped up, waving and grinning. "Coach!" he shouted. Taegen saw her companion wince as the baseball whizzed past the boy's head just as he began to run toward them.

"You need to pay attention to what you're doing, Chris," he said good-naturedly as the boy approached. "You almost got blasted back there. Your mom would kill me if I brought you home with a concussion."

The boy turned and looked back at his friends, confused. "Huh?"

Taegen's companion shook his head and chuckled.

"Come throw with us, coach," Chris invited.

The stranger looked over to see all of the others waving and urging for him to come over. Taegen smiled.

"I can't tonight," the stranger replied, "but you guys keep practicing, okay? You'll be great by next week."

Chris beamed up at him. "'Kay! See ya, coach!"

The stranger waved as the boy bounded back to the others. He looked down at Taegen and grinned. "I coach little league," he explained.

Well, he couldn't be all bad if he was someone parents let their children be alone with. She reached for his arm again, some of her apprehension dissipating.

The stranger couldn't suppress a surprised look.

She glanced up at him. "If a bunch of little boys love you, I figure you must be okay."

He placed his free hand over hers as they continued walking.

Taegen tried not to notice how warm his fingers felt on hers. Warm in a way that was disconcerting to her. His touch felt natural, and it soothed her more than anything had in the past few years. His gentle touch and his nearness made her feel like she was basking in rays of warm light. She never had that reaction to guys. Even her last boyfriend had to practically beg her to go out with him. She was too analytical; she thought too much. She had weighed out all the possible outcomes before she'd said yes to him. She guessed she had missed the one where he would tell her, "I can't deal with your mood swings" two weeks after her brother had died.

"I have to admit," she said, "you don't look like the coaching type."

"Oh?" he asked. "And what do I look like?"

She shrugged. *Beautiful*, she thought, frowning. What was her problem? Was she that desperate for some kind of companionship?

He smiled at her as if reading her thoughts and squeezed her hand in reassurance. "So, what kind of music do you like?" he asked. "R&B? Classical?"

She shook her head. "Oh no, I'm a hard rocker. Rob Zombie, Ozzy, System of a Down. You know, bite the heads off of chickens music. The harder the better." There. If that didn't scare him away...

"Well, Ozzy didn't actually bite the head off of a chicken. It was a bat, but a lot of people seem to think it was a bird of some sort." He gave a thoughtful look. "I think there was one incident involving a dove, but I really don't remember."

Taegen looked up at him with a frown that she knew reflected fascination as well. "You know trivia about Ozzy Osbourne?"

He laughed. "I love metal music. Nothing expresses the human emotion quite so much as head-banging, ear-splitting rock."

She giggled. "I agree totally."

"I really wanted to go see the Bleeding Passion concert at the Warfield, but they're—"

"Totally sold out," she interrupted. "I wanted to go also. They're touring with Fat Stinky."

He nodded. "It should be a great show." He stole a sidelong glance at her and sighed. "Too bad. Maybe we would have run into each other."

Taegen stopped suddenly and pulled away from him with a frown.

He turned. "Is something wrong?"

"What is this?" she asked. "What's your game?"

He cocked his head to one side and replied simply, "No game."

She let out a great sigh. She felt really confused all of a sudden. "Then what are you doing here? If you're not here to attack me, seduce me, or try to pick me up, what are you here for?" She was not about to let anyone play with her emotions. Especially not some dark, mysterious man who made her heart pound when he smiled. Those were the worst kind.

The stranger approached her and gazed down at her, all seriousness. "Why am I here?" he asked.

She nodded and folded her arms, expecting, maybe even hoping for, a lame response.

He smiled and reached down to gently unfold her arms. "There is no need to be defensive with me," he said softly. "I am very aware that the folded arms signifies a 'back off' position, but I am not going to invade your personal space." He let his hands travel down her arms as he released them and met her eyes again. "I'm here because I believe in making the most of every moment of my life. Life is a fleeting thing. You never know when you could lose everything. If you died tomorrow, wouldn't you want to know that your last moment had not been spent sitting all alone, feeling sorry for yourself, or that you had passed up a great opportunity out of fear?"

Taegen drew in a shuddering breath. All right, first off, it hadn't been nice of him to touch her when she was trying so desperately not to be attracted to him. Second, his words hit home. She *had* been feeling sorry for herself before he came. And she swore her brother had said something similar to her right before he'd gone away to college.

She'd begged him not to go because she didn't want to be left alone with Mary, who she'd thought was a shrew at the time. She asked him why he wanted to go so far away. He'd told her that he wanted to make every second of his life count. He wanted to make the most of everything. And he had. Right down to the end.

"I saw a lovely girl on a train," he continued, his eyes all dark green intensity. "By some freak chance, I saw her again. I had two choices. I could have walked on by without so much as a glance, and spent the rest of my life wondering what she was like, or I could have talked to her. I decided to take the risk." He shrugged. "Whether she feels the same way or not, I think it was worth it."

Taegen stared up at him, captivated. What he said was very true. If she died right there, her last thoughts would be that she hated men as a general rule because she didn't want to get hurt, and that she was lonely. That was depressing. People all around the world were much lonelier and much worse off than she was. She had lost her brother, yes, but she had pushed everyone else away on her own. She had no one to blame but herself for the fact that she no longer wanted to go out with her friends, and spent all her time working and brooding. She did nothing to get herself out of her depression. Paul would hate that if he could see her. She wondered why the stranger's words had made her realize that when nothing else had. "That sucks," she muttered.

The stranger arched an eyebrow. "Hm?"

She looked up at him. "Oh," she said flippantly, "I'm neurotic, I think."

His smile was warm. "Aren't we all?"

She met his eyes and took a deep breath. "You say Point Bonita is beautiful?" He nodded and she raised her chin in defiance, although she didn't know who she was defying. Herself maybe. "I'd like to see it."

The stranger's eyes took on that gentle quality that she already loved and his soft smile remained. "Would you like to go?" he offered.

She grinned wickedly, feeling very liberated all of a sudden. "Yes," she said. "Yes, I would."

Chapter Seven

Camp Redwoody
The Redwoods, California

Alyx stumbled out of the car, grateful that they had finally reached their destination. She swore she could still feel the ground turning beneath her. She found the small picnic table at their designated campsite and sat down on the bench, putting her head in her hands. She glanced up as she heard another car door slam. Maxim staggered toward her, paler than he had been all day. "That is the last time I *ever* let Javan drive," she muttered. "That was the worst, most nauseatingly twisty road I've ever been on."

Maxim nodded blankly. "I'm sure the whole pizza we ate didn't help either." He let out a long, slow breath.

They had taken a visit to the Oregon Coast before heading to the Redwoods, and Javan had decided to drive after they ate an entire meat lover's pizza with extra cheese. The road he'd taken closely resembled a carnival ride of vomitous proportions. Maxim had barely arrived with his stomach still intact.

"Where is Javan anyway?" Alyx asked. "Is he all right?"

Maxim glanced back at the car and saw Javan slumped in the driver's seat, his head resting on the steering wheel. He went over and peered in through the open window.

"You ok, Jave?" Alyx called from her place on the bench.

Javan groaned and lifted his head. He glanced up at Maxim and gave him a pained expression.

"Come on, Javan," Maxim urged. "You don't want to decorate your car with chunkage." Javan smiled and Maxim returned the expression. He opened the car door for Javan, who stumbled out and promptly sat down on the ground.

"Never again," Alyx moaned. "*Never again*."

Javan grunted something and lay down.

Maxim looked from Alyx to Javan and back again. He sighed. He was glad he'd only eaten one piece of pizza. Being nervous did have its advantages. He'd been nauseous all morning so this really wasn't that big of a deal. Although, he wasn't thrilled that because Javan and Alyx had gorged themselves, they had made him check in at the front desk in the camp office. He had not enjoyed that.

"Just out of curiosity," Maxim interjected quietly, "how are we going to camp with no supplies?"

"We have a tent," Alyx said.

"Don't worry," Javan muttered, still lying on his back. "I was a boy scout."

Alyx snorted. "There's a comfort." She met Maxim's eyes. "He dropped out of boy scouts after one year of being the worst one there."

Javan lifted his head and frowned at Alyx. "Thanks for the vote of confidence," he grumbled.

Alyx shrugged. "No sense in trying to delude yourself." She stood and went to Javan. "Gimme your keys. I'll get the tent out of your trunk."

"In the ignition," he groaned.

She retrieved the keys and opened up the trunk. She pulled out the suitcases and set them aside, then went to rummaging through Javan's scattered belongings to locate the tent. "Alyx." It came as almost a whisper. She smiled. Maxim had the most comforting voice. It gave off the same feeling as a soft caress. She looked over at him and raised an eyebrow in question.

Maxim met her eyes and drew in a breath. "Um...let me have the tent," he said. "I'll set it up, since Javan seems to be taking up permanent residency on the dirt."

"That's all right. I can do it."

"I'm sure you can," he said, "but you shouldn't have to."

She straightened and frowned at him. "Why?" she almost snarled. "Do you think I'm incompetent?"

Maxim visibly recoiled at the venom in her voice. "No," he murmured. "I don't think you're incompetent. You just don't feel well."

Alyx eased, and her demeanor softened. There was

something so sincere about how he spoke. She got the feeling that there was nothing fake about Maxim, and that was a beautiful change from the norm. Rick had been all fakeness, and it had put her on the defensive. She felt bad about snapping at Maxim, but she was so used to being undermined. It was strange for her to have someone other than Javan, or her brother, genuinely care about her well-being. "You don't feel well either," she remarked.

He shrugged with one shoulder. "Yeah, but I feel nauseous every time I have to speak with someone strange. It's normal for me." A warm smile spread across his lips, softening every feature of his face and lighting up his eyes. For a moment, Alyx could only stare at him.

"Holy crap!" Javan exclaimed.

Maxim jumped and turned to stare at Javan in bewilderment.

Alyx rolled her eyes. "What is your problem, Javan?"

Javan smiled and pointed at Maxim. "Now *that* was a real smile."

Maxim looked away, hiding a blush.

Alyx smiled and handed him the tent. "Knock yourself out."

He met her eyes and smiled again, then took the tent over to the flattest spot he could find.

"Hey, Maxim," Javan said, finally deciding to sit up, "how do you know how to set up a tent? I thought you hid out in your place like a mole or something."

Alyx scowled at him, but Maxim chuckled. "Jeff made me go backpacking with him when he was a freshman in college and I was a junior in high school. It was just me and him." He smiled at the memory. "One of my more enjoyable outings with Jeff." He pulled the tent out of the bag and began to assemble it, remembering how he and Jeff had hiked up to a lake and spent the day swimming. They had set up camp on shore and the whole weekend had been full of laughter and adventure.

Maxim sighed. When he stopped and thought about all the laughter Jeff had brought into his life, he realized that he could have been a lot lonelier than he was.

"Hey, check it out!" Javan exclaimed suddenly while rummaging through his trunk. "I found a volleyball!"

Alyx frowned. "Javan, you have the weirdest stuff hanging out in your car."

"What's wrong with having a volleyball? Jeff carries one too."

Maxim glanced up at Alyx, standing with her hands on her hips. She was wearing a pair of khaki cargo pants and a white tank top. He could see the muscles in her arms and thought they were beautiful, like a sculpture. He sighed and allowed himself to take in her slender frame and lovely curves while she watched Javan. He suddenly let out a yell as the hammer he was using to drive in a tent peg missed its target and hit his thumb. He dropped the hammer and cradled his injured thumb, fighting tears. That's what he got for watching Alyx instead of paying attention to what he was doing.

"Are you okay, Maxim?" Alyx asked.

He glanced up at her and tried to put on his best "manly" face. "I'm fine," he lied. He shook out his hand and picked up another peg, deciding that watching Alyx could wait until later. "Here," he heard Javan say. "Set me up, Alyx."

There was some general shuffling and a few smacks of the volleyball as Alyx and Javan played around. Maxim kept his head down, quietly trying not to vomit from the pain of his throbbing thumb.

"Maxim! Heads up!" Alyx suddenly shouted.

He looked up from his work. All he saw was white, and all he felt was stinging pain. He fell over onto his back and blinked a few times. The volleyball, which had rebounded off his head and into the air, bounced off his chest and rolled away.

"Javan!" Alyx cried. "What is the matter with you? That is the second time today you've decked Maxim with some kind of ball! And they're getting progressively bigger! What's next? A bowling ball? He's gonna end up with a concussion!"

Javan bit his bottom lip to keep from laughing. "Sorry, dude," he chuckled.

Maxim sighed and sat up, his glasses dangling from one ear. Try to do something nice and you get hit in the head with a volleyball... He righted his glasses and stood. "Alyx," he said calmly, "do you actually know how to play volleyball?"

She nodded. "Yeah. Bump, set, spike."

He bent and picked up the volleyball. He dusted it off and tossed it to her. "Set me up," he commanded. Alyx smiled and obeyed. Once the ball was over Maxim's head, he leapt and spiked it right toward Javan.

Javan screamed and ran as the volleyball came right at him with the force of bullet. It hit the bumper of the car and shot off into a nearby bamboo plant.

Alyx started to laugh hysterically, and Maxim smiled, feeling his cheeks redden.

"Geez, Max!" Javan exclaimed. "What are you, bookworm by day, uber volleyball player by night?"

Maxim's face flamed. "My brother is my closest companion," he replied. "He was varsity everything in school and he played volleyball at lunch intramurals all four years." He knelt and continued to assemble the tent.

Javan shook his head then frowned at Alyx. "What are you laughing at?"

Alyx wiped at the tears that were coursing down her cheeks. "Javan, you scream like a little girl!"

He frowned. "What?"

"You do, kinda," Maxim said softly.

Javan put his hands on his hips and stared at Maxim, who smiled as he worked. He glanced back at Alyx, who had started to laugh all over again. He sighed and shook his head. "Man, you guys suck."

* * * *

By dusk, the three had a nice camp set up. Maxim had assembled the tent quickly, and they decided to use three blankets from Javan's car to sleep on. Dinner wasn't really dinner considering they had not planned ahead for camping. It had basically consisted of tortilla chips, salsa, soda pop, and tuna on crackers. Javan had started a fire and he and Alyx were reminiscing about old times when Maxim slipped away to the campsite next to them.

He found the setup of the campground rather clever. A wall of bamboo separated each space so they seemed private and secluded. The camp was set up on a small cliff that overlooked a stream. Beyond that lay the dense redwood forest. It was beautiful to Maxim, so peaceful and quiet. He could hear Alyx and Javan laughing, but that was the only sound save the regular noises of the evening.

He sat down on the picnic table and gazed out into the serene forest. He took a deep breath and closed his eyes, letting the tranquility around him soak into his soul. He opened his eyes, relaxed, and sighed deeply. He frowned in thought. The ache in his heart was there, but not as acute. His thumb, on the other hand, was a different story.

Javan's laughter echoed through the camp and Maxim smiled. The ache lessened and he cocked his head to one side. The forest was the perfect setting for a story. There were so many possibilities within the leafy confines. He concentrated on the stream below and began to see a figure take shape. A character! He hadn't thought of a character in a very long time!

He brought the vision into focus. It was a woman, a beautiful woman with black hair and... He shook his head. No! That wasn't right! He had just envisioned Alyx. He sighed and ran a hand through his hair. He should have known it was too good to be true. It was too much to hope that his inspiration would come flooding back to him just because he'd been knocked in the head twice.

He thought about Javan and the volleyball and grinned. He wondered what it would be like to write a story about someone like him. Alyx's smile flashed through his mind again and he sighed. Maybe a story about someone lovely like her...

"Maxim?"

He turned quickly and saw Alyx standing a little way off. It had grown a bit chilly so she had pulled a black zip up on over her white tank top. Gnats buzzed placidly in the dusky light and he swallowed. He was unable to look at her for long and continue to function. She always managed to look so goddesslike. She had looked like a GAP model earlier that day, and now she looked like the siren of the forest. It was just wrong that someone could be so stunning all the time.

"What are you doing over here all alone?" she asked, taking a few steps toward him.

"Thinking."

She smiled. She loved the whispery voice he seemed to talk in whenever he felt uncomfortable. "Thinking?"

He nodded.

She sat down next to him. "Anything in particular?"

He shrugged. "Story stuff," he muttered.

She frowned and studied his profile. Jeffrey deBoer had always been very handsome to her, but he lacked the aura of softness that surrounded Maxim. She felt only gentleness from him, which was was something she had not felt in a long time. She looked away and touched her once bruised eye absently.

Maxim shifted and fiddled with his fingers, no doubt uncomfortable at her sudden lapse into silence. "I write novels," he blurted.

She blinked, her mind snapping back to the present. "Excuse me?" she questioned. "Did you say novels?"

He frowned and scratched at his head. "Well...at least I *attempt* to write novels. They never really get anywhere."

She smiled. "So you're out here gathering information?"

"Yeah, sorta." He gave a breathy, shy laugh and met her eyes. For a moment, he was unable to look away. There was something deep within them, a curiosity and almost awe. There was also a deep sorrow that she must try very hard to hide. He could see it just past the surface, a cloud beneath the vibrant green of her eyes.

"Tell me what you see out here," she urged.

"What do you mean?"

She shrugged. "I've never really seen the world through the eyes of a writer before."

He knew that telling her no wasn't an option. He lacked the ability. Jeff had told him that. In this instance, he was right. He folded his hands as he felt them begin to tremble. "W-Well," he stammered, "it's kind of hard to explain. It's like finding a story everywhere you look." He shrugged. "I guess it's sometimes like finding a deeper meaning in ordinary things. Take that tree, for example," he said, pointing to the tree at the far end of the site. "To most people, it's just a tree. Maybe pretty, but still just a tree. However, to a little boy, it could be where he had his first man-to-man talk with his father, or to a young couple, it could be where they first fell in love." He met her eyes again and found her smiling at him. He flushed a bit and looked away.

Alyx nudged him with her shoulder. "Same can be said for people, huh?" she asked. "Someone might look at you and never know that you could spike a volleyball like a pro."

He looked up at her and grinned.

She giggled. "That's a cool way to look at life, Maxim. To see the possibilities instead of what everyone else sees." She punctuated her statement with a nod.

He found himself staring at her hands. They were so delicate. He wondered what it would feel like to be caressed by such hands... He had never even kissed anyone before. How sad was that for a twenty-five-year-old man? He felt like one of the guys on those *Average Joe* or *Beauty and the Geek* reality shows. Put him in a room with a bunch of beautiful women and he ran straight for the nearest bathroom to hide in. He was sitting closer to Alyx right now than he had ever been to a woman, save the one he had thrown up on at that party. But that didn't make him any less of a man.

Jeff had once asked him if he had homosexual tendencies, which had made Maxim blush in angry humiliation for about two straight days. He had wants and desires just like the next guy. The strongest of which was to just be touched. Caressed. Have a pair of soft hands gliding over his skin with adoration. If he could have that, he could live the rest of his life with no kissing, no sex even. While he wanted those things too, just being touched was at the top of his list. To be touched like he mattered, like he was sexy, special... He shook his head. What was he thinking?

"Writers are also really weird," he muttered.

Alyx gave a soft laugh. "It's going to be dark soon. Why don't you come back to the fire with Javan and me? We have marshmallows we can toast."

"Javan packed marshmallows?"

She rolled her eyes. "He also packed bananas and measuring spoons. It's best if we just don't ask." She stood and offered her hand. "Care to join us, good sir?"

Maxim stared at her hand as if it was a foreign object then looked up at her. She just smiled at him. He swallowed hard and looked back at her outstretched hand. Was she really trying to kill him? He thought she might be. Didn't she see that he was a loser? Why didn't she treat him like the rest of the world did? When women came into the bookstore he worked at, they usually took one look at him and went straight for Barrett. Even though he was far from friendly, he was better looking. Pretty girls never glanced Maxim's way. They never had.

In high school, he had been avoided like the plague, called a nerd, a geek, a freak. You name it, he had been called it. All the girls had pointed and laughed behind his back. Even now, they either snickered as he walked past, or gave him those pity glances as if to say, "look at that poor guy" right before they lumped him in with computer programmers and guys who still lived in their mom's basements playing turn-based RPG's.

Yet, here was Alyx, holding her hand out to him as if she'd always been his friend... Slowly, he reached up and placed his trembling fingers in hers.

Alyx grinned and covered his hand with her other one, obviously noticing how it shook. She pulled him into a standing position, but he kept his eyes downcast.

"Maxim?"

He forced himself to look up at her.

She smiled softly. "Javan and I are both really glad you're here."

He was stunned. Had she just said that they were *glad* he was there? He swore he had fallen into a *Twilight Zone* episode. This had to be a parallel universe. Alyx's eyes held such warmth. His chest felt tight, but not from its usual ache. He whispered, "Thank you."

She grinned and squeezed his hand. "Come on," she said, releasing him. "We should get back before Javan blows himself up or something."

He nodded in agreement and followed her back to their campsite.

Chapter Eight

Point Bonita, California

Taegen had never seen such a beautiful view of San Francisco. Point Bonita was the most breathtaking place she had ever been to. It was a place filled with old overgrown WWII forts and an army barracks turned YMCA headquarters. High cliffs jutted out into the water and towered above the crashing waves below. Ice plant blanketed the sandy cliff tops and harmony permeated the whole area. On one side, a beach offered a view of the sunset and an endless expanse of diamond-studded water. On the other side, the city lay open, like a picturesque postcard. Every angle had its own unique beauty and presence. It was exquisite.

The stranger had taken her down a winding path to where an old lighthouse had once guided many a ship to safety. Taegen now stood atop an old bomb shelter, watching the fog encompass the Golden Gate Bridge and the city beyond it so that only the very tops of the bridge and the tallest buildings could be seen. She let out a long sigh and wrapped her arms around herself, closing her eyes as the cold wind blew off the ocean and tugged at her flaxen hair.

"Feeling better?"

She shivered at the sound of his voice. If his beauty didn't already undo her, his voice surely would. It was like the boldest touch with a velvet hand, and it sent chills all through her.

They had ridden in his convertible with more of the usual small talk while Taegen had tried desperately not to stare at his profile, or how the wind blew his silky black hair, or how the setting sun played upon his dramatic features. Because of her nervousness, she had nearly talked his head off, and she was surprised that he was still with her.

"Pretty Lady?" he urged.

She felt herself flush. It was rather strange to have someone calling her that. She turned to look at him over her shoulder and the wind whipped the stranger's hair around his face. Her breath caught and she met his questioning eyes, forcing a smile. "Yes, I'm feeling better."

He grinned and stuffed his hands in his pockets. "Not completely."

She frowned.

"Who are you thinking about? Someone, or something, is on your mind."

Taegen turned back around to face the bay and shook her head. "No one," she murmured. "Just my brother." She grimaced. Now why had she told him that?

"Ahh," he said. "Does he enjoy the ocean too?"

She sighed and fought sudden tears. "He did..." She swallowed. "He died two years ago."

The stranger was silent for a long moment before his gentle voice caressed over her again. "I'm so sorry. Were you close?"

"Very," she whispered. She drew in a shaky breath as years of memories invaded her thoughts. That always happened when she thought about Paul. All of her memories of him swamped her at once, making her feel like she would drown in her grief. "I miss him."

"Of course you do. I can't imagine losing a member of my family. It must be very difficult. I would probably be in a mental ward."

She liked that he made her feel validated. Most of the time, she felt like she should just get a grip. This man was the first person in a long time to not make her feel that way. He made her feel like her grieving process was a normal thing. "He died in a car accident," she continued. "My family all live in Lone Pine so I had no one but my current boyfriend." She gave a derisive snort. "He broke up with me two weeks later because he said I was too emotional and he couldn't handle my mood swings." She didn't know why she was telling him any of this. Maybe it was because he *was* a stranger. He didn't know her. He was safe. She could confide all of her problems in him and not worry about feeling stupid or insane because she would never see him after tonight.

"That's nice," he grumbled sarcastically. "What a jerk."

"Yeah, that was my conclusion also..." She shrugged. "So, I decided not forming relationships of any kind was the best course of action. That's why I don't want you to know my name and I don't want to know yours. If I don't know you, I can't become attached to you. If I can't become attached, I won't get hurt. You can't get hurt by someone who means nothing to you." Even as she said the words that had been her reasoning for the last two years, the logic sounded twisted.

Paul wouldn't have liked that philosophy either. He would have told her that she was missing out on meeting beautiful people and having awesome experiences. It hurt to realize that, in an effort to cope with his death, she had turned her back on everything he had stood for. She felt tears sting her eyes.

"I can understand where you're coming from," he said, his voice all silk and satin. "But it's horribly lonely shutting out the world. After awhile, you would really miss sharing things with someone...well, at least I would."

Taegen focused on the ground. He didn't know how completely right he was. She really missed having someone she could share absolutely everything with. She missed having close friends, and she missed having relationships. She missed laughter and adventure and playing. She had just gotten so used to living inside herself she had gotten stuck there and didn't know how to get back out. She was afraid. She was afraid of feeling her heart splinter and shatter all over again. She couldn't deal with that kind of pain. She wasn't that strong.

The stranger's voice was soft. "You look so sad," he observed.

She shuddered and wrapped her arms around herself. She shook her head. "It just sucks to remember sometimes." She knew that it was impossible for him not to notice the tears behind her voice.

"Our past always haunts us," he said, "but we can't live in it. We can't make the rest of our lives miserable because we can't let go of old grudges or past mistakes, and we can't hold onto our good memories so tightly that we leave no room for anything new. No matter how good our memories are, they are just that. Memories. You can never relive them, no matter how badly you may want to."

Taegen let out a shaky breath. She knew he was right, but it was hard to accept. "I miss those things, though," she whispered. "Those good memories." She just wanted one more night of watching Jay Leno on her couch with Paul, sharing a carton of double fudge chocolate chunk ice cream. She wanted one more phone call, one more prank, one more piece of bad brotherly advice. And that wasn't all. Not everything she wanted revolved around Paul.

She wanted to trust again. She wanted to let someone in again. She wanted to share herself and laugh with someone and not feel cold at night. She wanted to be cherished and adored and held... She closed her eyes. More than anything, she wanted to be held. She just wanted to lose herself in someone's arms and believe that everything would be okay. That the past several years had sucked really bad, but that it would be okay. That she wasn't jaded forever.

"But just because you can't relive old memories doesn't mean you have to forego new ones," he said.

She suddenly became very aware of his presence. His voice was hushed and he was standing so close to her. Had he been standing that close the whole time? She swallowed hard. He smelled good, like some kind of musky cologne mixed with incense. And he was so easy to talk to. She was spilling her guts to this man, telling him things she hadn't even told her family.

"You haven't given me a name yet," he said softly.

"Huh?" she breathed.

"You told me you wouldn't give me your name, so I call you Pretty Lady. What will you call me?"

She smiled and spoke without thinking. "Beautiful Stranger." A frown replaced her smile. Oh, man. Had she just said that out loud? She stifled a groan. How lame!

"I like that," he said with a chuckle.

She blushed.

"Hey, close your eyes."

She obeyed without hesitation.

"I want you to think only of what you feel," he instructed. "Just concentrate on that."

She took a deep breath and tried to banish all of her saddening thoughts.

"Just let your senses fill with this place."

She let her ears fill with the rhythmic sound of the waves, let her nose fill with the briny scent of the sea, let her skin feel the cold air. She let out a deep sigh and felt herself relax.

"Now, tell me what you feel," he whispered.

"Peace," she murmured, "tranquility, relaxation." She smiled. So that's what that felt like. She drew her breath in sharply as she felt his arms encircle her from behind and pull her close up against his chest.

"Keep your eyes closed," he said, his breath touching her face. "What do you feel now?"

She squeezed her eyes shut and trembled. She drew in a shuddering breath and tears cascaded down her cheeks as if someone had just turned on a faucet. "Warm," she cried. "Hurt." She trembled harder.

"Shhh," he soothed, his cheek placed against the side of her head, "it's okay." She let out a stifled sob and he held her closer. "It's okay to cry; it's okay to miss your brother. You're not broken."

Taegen turned and threw her arms around him, wanting to stay there for all eternity. He was so warm and felt so good. His body felt strong, like she could just collapse against him and he would hold her up. How did he know? How did he know that what he had just done was the deepest desire of her heart? All she had wanted was for someone to tell her that it was okay, that she wasn't out of her mind. She buried her face against his chest and cried.

"I'll hold you as long as you like," he whispered, stroking her hair.

"Why?" she murmured, fisting her hands in his shirt.

"Because I want to." He tightened his hold around her and swayed her gently from side to side.

She felt his hands on her back and she shivered. "Why do I feel like I know you?"

"Maybe you do."

She frowned and pulled away to look up at him. "What?" she asked, rubbing her eyes.

He cupped her cheek with his hand and caressed the tears away. He cocked his head to the side, making the wind catch his hair. It glistened like liquid obsidian. "Maybe your heart knows me even though you don't."

Taegen stared at him. He could tell her that he was an

alien sent from the planet of Flarb to steal her unborn children. She wouldn't care so long as he kept touching her like he was. His touch was different...better somehow.

He winked at her. "You hungry?"

She nodded. "I haven't eaten since lunch."

"Would you give me the pleasure of your company at dinner?"

She made a face. "I look awful. I can't go anywhere looking this way." She glanced down at his white shirt and her eyes widened in horror. There were black smudges all over his chest. "And I got mascara all over your shirt!" she cried.

He chuckled. "Don't worry about my shirt." He reached behind her head to the scrunchie that held her hair captive and gently tugged it loose. Her waves spilled around her shoulders. He smiled as he ran his fingers through them. "And you look beautiful," he insisted.

She smiled and went back into his arms, resting her head against his shoulder. She needed his embrace. She needed to feel his gentle strength. For some reason, his touch made everything all right. It didn't make sense, and that went strictly against the way she lived her life. She didn't find comfort in people she didn't know. She wasn't spontaneous. She planned out everything. She wrote everything in her day planner and thought everything out thoroughly before she did it... Well, except when it came to randomly leaving her car alongside the road and disappearing with strange, gorgeous men. She rolled her eyes. Man, she really was a lunatic. She didn't even make sense to herself. If this man was smart, he would hightail it far away from her as quickly as possible.

"Ever been to The Stinking Rose?" he asked. She shook her head and he made a startled noise. "That's a travesty! I have to take you. That's all there is to it." He pulled away and took her hand. "Come on, Pretty Lady. Prepare yourself for the best Italian food ever!"

She giggled as he led her back to the car, glad she was with him. She felt as if she had known him always, and he made her feel free for the first time since her brother had died. He made her feel like it was okay to laugh, okay to do something impulsive. It was a foreign but welcome feeling.

Chapter Nine

San Francisco, California

Taegen studied the stranger's hands from across the table in the same way she had studied them on the train. The graceful way they moved, the slenderness of his fingers... They were beautiful hands. She had always been one of those weird girls who looked at guys' hands. Most women looked at eyes or butts or something, but she had always been a hand person. To her, hands were important because touch was important. She remembered all too well how gentle this man's hands were.

"Did you get enough to eat?" he asked.

She met his almost iridescent green eyes and smiled. "Yes. That was a fantastic meal."

She was quite sure that she had made a glutton out of herself feasting on the best ravioli in porcini mushroom sauce this side of the equator. The beautiful stranger and she had shared laughter and pleasant conversation over dinner, and if she had embarrassed him with her barbaric eating habits, he hadn't shown it. He was a wonderful companion whom she was enjoying very much. He was easy-going and laid back, yet charisma and sex appeal radiated off of him. He had this bizarre way of making her feel comfortable while making her heart beat erratically at the same time. It was almost enough to get her to tell him her name. Almost.

"Ready then?" he asked.

She nodded and followed him out of the restaurant and back onto the street.

She took his arm automatically as they strolled down the sidewalk to where he had parked his car a few blocks away.

She felt considerably more at ease with him now that she knew he visited his grandma in Oakland once a week, had a cat named Mr. Whiskers, and loved the movie *Titanic*. Somehow, most of her suspicion had died when he told her how he had cried his eyes out the first time he'd watched it.

"That was a good idea," she said, unconsciously feeling the fabric of his sleeve. "Thank you."

"That was nothing. Are you up for more?"

"Food?" she asked, her stomach roiling in protest.

"Let's hope not." He shook his head and chuckled. "No. More fun."

She blinked. "O-Okay," she stammered. "What did you have in mind?"

He squeezed her arm and opened the car door for her. "Just a little after dinner relaxation." She halted abruptly and stared at him in a way that made him chuckle. "Away from hotel rooms and make out locations, of course."

Taegen grinned and felt her face redden. She nodded and got in. She didn't know which was worse. The shock that she thought he had been implying hotel rooms and make out locations, or the shock that her brain had actually considered it for a millisecond.

In a matter of minutes, they were on Market Street, where the beautiful stranger took her arm protectively as he helped her out of the car. "I told you I know kickboxing," she said with a teasing smile. "You don't need to hold onto me like someone's going to attack me."

He snorted. "You sure do have a high opinion of yourself, lady," he teased. "I know you know kickboxing. I'm afraid someone will attack *me*. I'm using you as protection."

She giggled. He guided her to a door a few blocks down and she looked up at the sign out front. She frowned. "The Amazing Psychotic?" He sure did know where all the bizarre places were. The Stinking Rose, The Amazing Psychotic. Who named these things?

"It's a coffeehouse with live music," he explained. "It started out as a privately owned business in New York, but they recently opened this one. The owners made enough money that they were able to have one on each coast. My friends Nasarra and Caleb run it. They are both actors. Apparently, they called up the owners in New York when they first found out this place was opening. They wanted to run it right away. They have good memories of the original."

Taegen smiled and entered the dimly lit room. Jazz played in the background and there were tables and chairs set up with candles in amber holders on them. The lamps in the room were also amber and made the whole room seem smoky, mysterious, and surreal.

"Hey! T-Man!"

The stranger turned toward the kitchen area and broke into a wide grin. He waved. "Hey, Caleb," he greeted. He touched Taegen's arm and smiled. "Come and meet Caleb."

She followed him over to the tall man with the coppery-golden hair.

"This is Caleb," the stranger introduced. "Caleb, this is a pretty lady I ran into. She refuses to tell me her name."

Caleb smiled and shook her hand. "Well, it's a pleasure to meet you, Pretty Lady."

Taegen blushed. Okay, that nickname had to go. Not only was it embarrassing, but it reminded her of a homeless man who had followed her down the street once trying to get change from her. He had kept calling her "Pretty Lady." It was unnerving.

"Where's your wife?" the stranger asked.

Caleb sighed. "She just got done with a production to-night, so she's resting at home."

"She's well, though?"

Caleb nodded. "She loves it even though it wears her out. That lady was born for the stage."

Taegen noticed how Caleb's eyes sparkled when he spoke about his wife. She sighed and looked around the place, not wanting to stare, and not wanting to focus too much on the fact that she really had no companion. She had no one to go home to. No one to call and tell about her day. For the moment, she had the seriously hot guy at her side, but he would take her home and then she'd be alone again. He would be gone. Just like everyone else was... And she had no one to blame but herself.

"Tell her hello for me, okay?" the stranger asked.

Caleb grinned. "I will. She'll be happy to hear from you. We should all go out sometime like we used to. Bring your lady."

Taegen looked up at Caleb and blushed again. If she blushed any more, she'd start to look like a Roman Candle.

Had she been reclused so long in her house that she had lost the ability to be social? Now, when anyone showed her any kind of attention, she blushed her head off?

"Yeah, if she ever tells me her name," the stranger teased.

Caleb didn't ask; he merely smiled. "You hungry?"

The stranger shook his head. "We just came from The Stinking Rose. We just wanted to relax."

"Any coffee?"

The stranger thought for a moment. "Sure. Gimme a latte."

"I'll take a mocha," Taegen replied.

"Okay, I'll bring it out to you in a sec," Caleb said with a grin.

The stranger nodded and turned to Taegen. "Take a seat," he offered.

She pulled up a chair and listened quietly to the jazz music that came from the tall, African American man on the stage at the back of the room. He finished up his song and bowed. Scattered applause followed, and a man with purple-tipped, black spiky hair and a few piercings stepped up onto the stage. He pulled a guitar over his head and began to tune it.

The stranger grinned and stood suddenly. "Someone get this loser off the stage!" he shouted.

The musician looked up and grinned. "T-Man!" he exclaimed. "Gonna play with me tonight?"

The stranger made his way up to the stage. "Just one. I have a lady I need to take home." He hopped up onto the stage and the musician handed him another guitar.

"Same as always?" he asked.

The stranger smiled as he tuned his instrument. "Always." He strummed his fingers across the strings and glanced to his friend. "Ready?"

The other man nodded and they launched into a haunting acoustic song that filled the room and made Taegen shiver. She studied the stranger, who was now free of the long, black coat and stood in just his tan slacks and un-tucked, white dress shirt. He had unbuttoned and rolled up the sleeves at the restaurant, and his muscular forearms were visible. His hair fell around his shoulders softly, and he had his eyes closed, as if the music was coming right from his soul. She sighed and didn't even notice when Caleb brought their coffee. She also barely registered the fact that his smile was sly and knowing.

When the song ended, she clapped wildly. The stranger turned to his friend and the two embraced before he set the guitar down and returned to Taegen

She shook her head, intrigued. "Is there anything you can't do?"

He frowned thoughtfully as he took a sip of his coffee. "I can't spell," he replied. She giggled and he grinned in return. "That's Charlie," he explained as the musician started another song. "We went to college together. We wrote that song and play it every time we're together. He comes here to play. Once in awhile I'll jam with him."

"Did you used to be in a band?"

His smile was almost shy. "Yes. A long time ago... Some of the best times of my life."

"So, did you always want to be an architect or did you originally want to be a musician?"

"I originally wanted to be a beekeeper," he said with a chuckle. "But that was a long time ago before I knew I was allergic to bees."

She laughed.

He took another sip of his coffee and shook his head. "No, there is barely enough life for me to do all I want to, but I do as much as I can. Drawing is my first passion, but there is no money in being a starving artist. Being an architect, I can have my creations displayed for the whole world."

She nodded, resting her chin in her hand.

"I love my job, but I always loved music. In high school and through college, I played cello and percussion. I taught myself guitar. Charlie, a few other guys, and I had a hard rock band, but we went our separate ways. Charlie went solo, but I still play with him sometimes. Acoustic, electric, I love them both." He shrugged. "It's a hobby. It's fun."

"And the little league?"

He grinned. "What can I say? I'm a renaissance man."

"Anyone else in your family as talented?" she asked.

"One sister dances on Broadway; the other one is a concert pianist. My brother, Merrill, is an actor. He lives up in Ashland, Oregon. He's part of the Oregon Shakespeare Company."

She swirled her coffee, listening.

"He's a musician also," he continued, "but he went completely classical where I went hard rock."

She smiled and looked up at him. He was so interesting and the tenderness in his eyes amazed her. She sighed. "You've changed my life tonight," she whispered suddenly.

He frowned. "How so?"

She glanced back down into her cup of coffee. "You've shown me what I've been missing. You're right, I can't live in the past." She shook her head. "My brother was a Carpe Diem kind of guy, too. I guess, in the midst of all my own issues, I forgot that... The future may be difficult and frightening to face, but it comes whether you want it to or not. I may as well enjoy it instead of trying to hide. Paul wouldn't have wanted me to hide."

He leaned forward, placing his hands over hers. "If I'd done nothing else tonight, the fact that I made you smile would be enough," he said in a hushed voice.

Taegen stared at him and her hands began to tremble. Had she ever had anyone be happy just to make her smile? She looked away. Was this guy for real? Her boyfriend broke up with her because she didn't act the way he wanted her to, but a complete stranger was content just to bring a smile to her lips? She wondered if she'd imagined him. Maybe there'd been a train wreck and she was actually in a coma. That had to be it. That was the only way she could rationalize the fact that such a breathtaking man would be so frighteningly perfect. This was her fantasy world. It had to be.

The stranger gave a soft smile and touched her cheek. "Tell me your name," he coaxed.

She felt her chest constrict and fear washed over her. She knew it was stupid, but she was so terrified of being hurt. She never wanted to go through the pain of losing someone she cared about again. In any way, shape, or form. She shook her head and met his eyes. "I can't," she whispered. He was a fantasy. A beautiful distraction. He was someone who had come charging into her life to make her get a clue. Nothing could go past that. If it did, she would just come to find out that he was the same as every other guy. He probably had some horrible bad habit that she didn't know about. He could be an alcoholic, or manic-depressive. She didn't know. She didn't want to shatter the perfection of him. She wanted to keep the memory pristine.

He nodded at her words and sighed.

"I'm sorry."

He shook his head and cupped her cheek in his palm. "It's all right," he said. "You aren't ready yet. You've been hurt. I understand... I do."

She let out a shaky breath and nodded.

"I like you," he continued, "and when you're ready, if you're ready, I think you know enough to be able to find me."

There was a little voice inside of Taegen's head screaming at her to let him in. He was different. She couldn't live in her past. She had to move forward. He was worth the risk. *Take it. Take it. Tell him. Carpe Diem...* She looked up at him and swallowed.

"Come on," he said. "I'll take you home."

The words she would have said died on the tip of her tongue and she gave a meager nod. She stood, waited for him to put on his coat, then turned toward the door.

He touched her shoulder. "Pretty Lady?" She met his eyes. He gave her a gentle smile and put his arm around her. "It's okay to be afraid," he soothed. "Don't feel bad."

She heaved a sigh and leaned against his chest. "I'm so neurotic," she groaned.

He chuckled. "At least you admit it. Admission is the first step in overcoming."

She scowled.

He laughed and held the door open for her.

San Lorenzo

Taegen was silent for the entire drive to San Lorenzo. Her mind was at war with a barricaded heart that was rather insistent on breaking free. This beautiful, beautiful man made her feel things she had not felt in a long time, and he made her look at life in a way she much preferred to how she had been looking at it. She hadn't realized how much she'd missed and needed that positive influence in her life. She was a natural pessimist. Paul had been her balance. Since he'd been gone, she'd had no one to counteract her fatalistic outlook on life. Not until now...

"Right here," she said as she spotted her house. The

stranger pulled up and turned the car off. Taegen sat in the seat for a moment, staring at her home. Dark windows, empty... She sighed and got out.

What are you doing, you idiotic girl? This man is perfect! Invite him in! Give him the guided tour and then stop in the bedroom! She shook her head. What the? She never thought like that. Ever. Either she had been working way too hard and had finally lost her last shred of sanity, or she needed some serious therapy.

Come on, how many times in your life do you run across a real-life fantasy guy? He rivals all the ones in those pathetic romance novels you read! He's a hottie! *Take advantage of it! Just imagine the way he would look naked in candle light...*

She squeezed her eyes shut as she walked up the driveway. Okay, this assault on her from her evil self was not nice. Not to mention the fact that everything that came out of his mouth was perfect. *Take a chance! What good are the lacy, black panties you're wearing if no one ever gets to see them?*

Holy cow! Shut up! She forced her brazen and out of character thoughts to stop just as she approached the door.

The stranger waited while she unlocked it. "Pretty Lady," he whispered when she opened it.

Taegen turned and met his eyes. They captured hers and her heart fluttered.

He moved closer to her. "I had a wonderful time tonight," he murmured. "Thank you for making the most of my night."

She smiled and looked down sadly. He pressed a kiss to her forehead and she shivered in response. She met his eyes again and he leaned in toward her lips. She placed her hand against his chest. "I don't think I should let you kiss me," she breathed.

His smile was ravenously beautiful. "Why not?" he asked, his voice caressing her.

"Because," she whimpered, tears returning. "If I let you kiss me, I might not let you leave."

He pulled away a bit and gazed into her eyes. He searched them for a moment, then tilted her face upward and lowered his lips to hers. Taegen's heart stopped. His lips were like the night itself, seductive, mysterious, and cloaked in a softness that shook her all the way to her soul.

She wrapped her arms around his torso, holding him close to her. His gentle hands held her face and she stifled a groan. The man was made of pure velvet, she could swear to it. When he pulled back, she felt as if her blood had stopped flowing. She felt like the very thing keeping her alive had been taken away. She trembled, hating how bereft she felt just from the absence of his kiss. *Carpe Diem! CARPE DIEM!* She closed her eyes and let out a shaky breath. If only things were that easy...

The stranger watched her, smoothed her hair, and reached behind his neck to unclasp a silver chain. He took Taegen's hand and placed it in her palm, then closed her fingers over it. "Goodnight, lovely one," he whispered. "Remember, every moment counts." He kissed her forehead again, then turned and got back in his car. He waved goodbye and drove out of Taegen's life.

Still shaking and feeling horribly empty, she opened up her hand and looked at the chain. It had a silver ring with a Celtic pattern on it. She lifted the ring and studied it. On the inside, three letters were engraved. *TLR*... His initials. She clutched the jewelry to her chest and disappeared into her house. She shut the door and leaned against it, staring at nothing. "My name is Taegen," she whispered. One tear streaked down her cheek.

Chapter Ten

Camp Redwoody

"Do you hear something?" Alyx whispered with a frown.

"Dude, I thought I was going crazy," Javan replied, rolling over.

Maxim rolled back over also. He'd heard it too. It was a faint rustling, like something snooping. "Did you pick up the trash?" he asked. He remembered when he had been backpacking with Jeff. They'd had to string their trash and food up in a tree so that bears wouldn't get into it easily. Maxim had no idea if there were bears in the redwoods, but he was pretty sure there were other animals that liked food just as much.

Javan groaned.

Alyx sighed. "Of course he didn't. He was too busy peeing on the fire."

Maxim chuckled.

"Do you think it's a bear?" Alyx asked, voicing Maxim's thoughts.

"If it is, I'll take him barehanded," Javan said dramatically, sitting up. He frowned and blinked at his own words, then chuckled. "No pun intended."

Maxim rolled his eyes.

Javan crawled across Maxim and Alyx and unzipped the tent. He poked his head out and looked around, scanning the area. "Oh, it's just a skunk," he said, climbing out. "I'll get rid of it."

"Javan," Alyx warned, "do you remember Lassen? It took me weeks to get my sleeping bag stench free. If you get sprayed, there is no way you're getting near me. Maxim and

I will just go see Bleeding Passion without you."

"Chill out," Javan said. "I'll be fine." He looked at the skunk, who didn't seem the slightest bit perturbed that Javan was even there. He unlocked the trunk of the car, opened the ice chest, and searched through it until he found something he obviously thought would make a good weapon. "This'll do," he stated. He tore the package open and hurled a hot dog at the skunk. "Get outta here!" he shouted.

Alyx's eyes bulged and she jumped out. "Javan, you idiot!" she cried. "Don't throw food at it!"

Javan stopped and blinked at her.

She shook her head and decided to take matters into her own hands. She started clapping and stamping her feet, but the skunk only gave her a bemused expression and continued about its business. Javan grabbed a wayward stick of bamboo and brandished it like a sword, thrusting it in the skunk's direction.

Maxim couldn't help but chuckle. Watching a six-foot-something man and a grown woman try to chase away something that was the size of Javan's foot was rather amusing. "Javan," he laughed, "poking at it may not be a great idea."

Javan glanced back at Maxim. "Oh, look who's talking now!" he exclaimed.

Maxim raised an eyebrow.

"You're just sitting there keeping the tent warm!"

"Well, yeah. I have no intention of joining ranks and becoming the third stooge, thank you very much."

Alyx looked at him and put her hands on her hips. "Hey! What's that supposed to mean?"

Maxim chuckled.

"Here skunky skunky skunky," Javan began calling. "Be a good skunk and go away."

Maxim laughed again. "Javan! You just called it to you one second then told it to go away in the next! You're going to confuse it to death!" Suddenly, he was blasted by a story idea and his eyes widened. It was as if a lightning bolt had hit him right between the eyes. All thoughts fled other than, *write it down; write it down*. His notebook was in the back seat of the car. He needed to write it down before he forgot. He threw the covers back and jumped up, barreling out of the tent.

He suddenly found himself face down in the dirt. Stunned, he rolled over and saw what had halted his progress. The tent door hadn't been unzipped all the way and his foot had gotten caught on it. He looked up at Alyx and Javan, who were both staring at him, and he started to chuckle.

"What was that about not being the third stooge?" Alyx asked.

He laughed harder.

The skunk made some sort of groaning noise and began to mosey away, disappearing into the nearby bamboo.

"Hey, Maxim!" Javan shouted. "You made the skunk leave!"

Maxim was laughing so hard that his stomach hurt, and he found it to be a genuinely good feeling.

Alyx giggled. "What were you doing anyway?"

"I had an idea for a book," he stated. "It's gone now." He started to laugh again and the others joined him. Javan put up the garbage, and everyone piled back into the tent. Maxim was more relaxed than he had been before and he lay down, and he thought about Javan, Alyx, and the skunk. That had seriously been one of the most comical things he had ever seen. That would be great writing material. He yawned and closed his eyes, falling asleep quickly. It had been a long day.

* * * *

Maxim's eyes opened slowly and he frowned. He had a funny feeling. A curious sensation around his heart... Like something wasn't quite right. He glanced at his watch. Four fifteen A.M... Everything was dead silent in an eerie kind of way... Yeah, he definitely wasn't a woodsman. Creeped out by the silence of the forest...

He felt a twitch next to him and he rolled over on his back. He heard a gasp and felt Alyx's body tense. With a frown, he searched for his glasses, which he had discarded near the top of the tent after the skunk incident, and sat up. He looked down at Alyx and saw that her brow was furrowed. She looked pained, and a fine sheen of sweat decorated her creamy skin.

He reached over and touched her hand lightly. She eased at his touch, then jumped as her eyes flew open. He quickly removed his hand and met her eyes. "Alyx?" he whispered.

She blinked and looked around wildly, as if trying to locate where she was. She stared up at Maxim in bewilderment. She sat up and put her head in her hands. That dream had been so real...the worst yet. She touched her cheeks and found them moist.

"Alyx, are you okay?"

She nodded, trying to block out the memory of Rick's angry face and angry fist. How many times did she have to relive it? Wasn't it bad enough that she'd had to live through it the first time? Why did she have to keep remembering the way he had beat her with such vivid clarity?

"Bad dream?" Maxim asked.

She nodded again.

He watched her for a long moment. "Do you want to talk about it?" he asked. She shook her head violently and he swallowed, looking uncomfortable and awkward. "Maybe some fresh air," he suggested.

She took a deep breath and met his kind eyes. "Yeah," she murmured. "Maybe you're right." She unzipped the tent and stepped out, sticking her feet into Javan's shoes instead of her own. She left them on and crossed the campsite, folding her arms and shivering a bit. It was so dark...and so cold. It made her feel like she was still in her dream. Her nightmares were always dark and cold. She jumped when she felt something draped over her shoulders, and she watched as Maxim pulled the blanket tight around her. "But Javan—" she protested.

"He has a sweatshirt on," he said. "He'll live for awhile."

Alyx smiled and looked up at the sky. So many beautiful stars. She closed her eyes and eased.

Maxim watched Alyx for a moment then headed back toward the tent. He probably felt like he would bother her if he hovered over her. Little did he know that his quiet company was just what she needed. "Do you like the stars, Maxim?" she asked.

He turned. "Yes. They are one of the most breathtaking sights I've ever laid eyes on."

Alyx smiled. She liked how he talked. He sounded like he cherished every word he spoke. "Do you have a favorite constellation?"

Maxim grinned. "Yeah, I love Draco and Perseus the best,

I think."

She looked at him over her shoulder and frowned. "I don't even think I've ever heard of those."

"You can see Draco the best in July and Perseus the best in December. This month is easiest to see constellations like Libra and Lupus." Okay, now he really did sound like a nerd. He looked around for a hole to crawl into, but couldn't find one. He stuffed his hands into his pockets instead.

She shook her head and gave a little nervous laugh. "And I always thought I was doing good with the Big Dipper and Orion. I think I found Cancer once, but that was one of those rare fluke things. And I never found it again."

He smiled. "Most people only ever find the Big Dipper and Orion. I was just fascinated by astronomy when I was younger. Had the telescope and everything." He scratched at the back of his head self-consciously.

"Really? I think I was too busy memorizing lines for plays when I was in science class." She shook her head with a giggle. "So, why do you like those two constellations the best?"

"Well, Draco means dragon and Perseus means hero. Two things that are commonly equated with power and strength."

"And those are things you liken to yourself?" she asked. "You're a dragon hero?" She turned and gave him a teasing smile.

He rolled his eyes. "Oh yeah. That's me. I'm really not shy at all. I'm just lulling you into a false sense of security so I can unleash my fiery heroics on you later."

She scrunched her nose playfully at his dry sense of humor. "He never liked the stars," she said, sobering. "In fact, he never really liked anything I liked. I wish he would have sat outside and pointed out constellations to me. I wouldn't mind someone showing me where something like Draco or Perseus is."

Maxim suddenly felt very uncomfortable. He had only known Alyx for a little while. He didn't know how to react. What he really wanted to do was take her in his arms and show her every constellation in the sky until all her painful memories left her, but that was probably more of a second date thing...

He rolled his eyes. He was such an idiot. Were he and Jeff even related? Maybe his mother had found him under a toadstool or something. He glanced over at Alyx again. What if he offended her or hurt her with misplaced words? He clamped his mouth shut. Silence was his ally, and it was coming to his rescue once again. He couldn't say the wrong thing if he didn't speak, so he decided to just stand there like a giant geeky statue.

Alyx glanced over her shoulder at Maxim, who was carefully maintaining his distance. "I'm sure Jeff told you about Rick."

He swallowed. Great. Now what was he supposed to do? "Uh...I-mmhmm," he stammered. "A little."

She nodded. "Jeff was there the night I left Rick. He got to see the swollen lip and lovely black eye I received as a parting gift."

He cringed. He couldn't understand how one human could do that to someone they were supposed to care about.

She gave a forced laugh. "Yeah, I'm sure you love me unloading on you." She pushed her hair back behind her ears and shook her head. "So, what do you think about domestic violence?" she asked in an attempt to sound like she was making fun of herself.

Maxim froze. "Um—I—uh—" She turned to look at him, and his eyes met her lovely green ones turned dark in the moonlight. His words came out of their own volition. "I think it's terrible," he replied calmly. "Abhorrent, abominable. The man who hurt you should be shot." Sense returned to him. Did he just say what he thought he'd said? He cleared his throat and averted his eyes. Yeah, that was a real peace-loving response. Answer violence with violence. Way to go, Maxim.

Alyx stared at him for a moment then smiled. She went over to the picnic table and sat down. "I don't know why I kept letting him hurt me," she murmured. "I knew he'd do it again even though he swore he wouldn't." She shook her head sadly. "He was always so sorry the next day."

Maxim kept his hands in his pockets and walked over to her. He was doing no good standing in the shadows. "If you don't mind me asking, why were you with him in the first place?"

She sighed. "Javan and I are actors in the Oregon Shakespeare Company," she explained. "Every Friday night before our show, Javan and I, along with our friends Merrill, Alicia and Vinnie, have dinner somewhere. Our usual place is Geppetto's Restaurant. Rick was working there last year, and he waited on our table. He flirted with me all night and just seemed so charming..." She swallowed and shut her eyes as if the memory caused her pain. "The first time he hit me was when I'd gone out with Javan and had been gone too long to suit him. He was so jealous and so possessive. He didn't even like me to spend too much time with my brother."

Maxim frowned. He'd never heard of anything so ridiculous.

"He wanted to control everything I did," she continued, "but I wasn't controllable. I love my brother more than anyone else in this world, and Javan has been my best friend practically since birth. I refused to let my boyfriend control my life." She snorted with self-disgust. "I just let him beat me instead."

The venom in her voice made Maxim's heart ache for her. He sighed and sat down next to her, shivering a bit, but saying nothing. "Why did you wait so long to leave him?"

"Because the good times were so sweet. I just kept hoping... I was stupid."

He shook his head, unable to see her look so defeated. "You weren't stupid, Alyx. You did leave him. You're safe now. It's not stupid to hope someone can change." He hated his words. He sounded like a moron.

"I was having nightmares before I left," Alyx said. "They still come. I can't get rid of them. Every night it's the same. I relive it all *every night*..."

Maxim studied her face. He hated that she felt guilty for staying with her ex, and he hated the way she was slumped and sad. Her slender shoulders were not meant to be burdened. He mostly hated that he had absolutely no idea what to do...

Literature. Literature was his forte. He couldn't think of words to say, but he could quote someone else's. Someone much more adept than him. He smiled, closed his eyes, and said softly, "Look up at the sky, Alyx. You see the Milky Way?"

"Yes," her voice came. "It's gorgeous."

He scooted a little closer to her on the bench and tried to keep his heart beating at a regular pace. He let the calm of the night surround him, and let the words come.

"She walks in beauty, like the night
Of cloudless climes and starry skies,
And all that's best of dark and bright
Meet in her aspect and her eyes.
Thus mellowed to that tender light
Which heaven to gaudy day denies.

One shade the more, one ray the less,
Had half impaired the nameless grace
Which waves in every raven tress
Or softly lightens o'er her face,
Where thoughts serenely sweet express
How pure, how dear their dwelling place.

And on that cheek and o'er that brow
So soft, so calm, yet eloquent,
The smiles that win, the tints that glow
But tell of days in goodness spent,
A mind at peace with all below,
A heart whose love is innocent."

Alyx closed her eyes and a tear trailed down her cheek. That was so beautiful. And his voice... Oh, she loved his whispering voice. His poetry against the backdrop of the canopy of stars was exquisite, so tender and peaceful "Maxim," she breathed in awe.

He opened his eyes and let his breath out slowly. "George Gordon, Lord Byron," he replied. "The truth is, you are a beautiful person, Alyx. I don't care for people as a general rule, but I like you, so that's saying an awful lot."

She smiled and turned to study his soft blue eyes, liking the gentleness that radiated from their depths.

"You were innocent in loving Rick," he continued. "You didn't know he was a raging jerk. It's not your fault. You didn't deserve to be hurt. You didn't deserve any of that."

Another tear escaped and she quickly wiped at it. "That was incredibly sweet of you, Maxim. I don't deserve those words."

"Yes, you do," he insisted.

She met his eyes again and felt as if she was being wrapped in a warm embrace. It was enough to make her want to cry forever. "Thank you."

He looked away, feeling silly all of a sudden.

"You know, you deBoers are never what you seem," she said with a little laugh.

"How so?"

"Your brother seems like such a flake when you first meet him, but he is such a caring person with so much heart. I met your sister once. She looked like she should be a model, but she's a physics major!"

He laughed softly.

"And you..." She touched his shoulder, letting her fingers trail slowly down his arm. "There is much more to you than a shy person who doesn't care for people."

He looked up at her and swallowed hard. She was touching him.... Holy cow, she was touching him. "Barrett isn't like that," he said. "Barrett seems brooding and stoic when you meet him. He pretty much is. And a turd. Barrett is a total turd. With him, what you see is what you get."

She smiled. "Well, there's one in every family."

He chuckled and shivered again.

"Oh, here," Alyx said, draping half of the blanket around his shoulders. "You're being so nice and I'm letting you freeze to death."

He would have at least attempted a nervous laugh, but in order for them to both fit under the blanket, she had to sit very close to him. Because of her close proximity, he could barely breathe or function. Laughing was completely out of the picture. She looked up at him as she tried to situate the blanket around them and their gazes locked for a moment. Time stood still for him. He wanted to drown in those eyes.

Alyx's throat suddenly went dry and her heart did a funny flip. There in the night, with the stars shining so brilliantly above him, Maxim was the most breathtaking man she had ever seen. He wasn't gawky at all. His features were very masculine. Even his glasses didn't hinder his appearance. She found something so desirable about him.

She cleared her throat and averted her eyes, her cheeks turning hot. "Do you know a lot of poems?" she asked, seeking to divert her attention.

He nodded. "I love poetry."

She neglected to tell him that she loved it also, but loved it ten times more when he recited it. Those words he had spoken would stay with her always, as would the soft caress of his voice. His kindness amazed her. Especially considering that she was a near stranger and he claimed he didn't care for people. She knew that it was the things that many people did that he didn't care for, not the people themselves. All Maxim had given since he'd met her was care.

Maxim sighed as he watched her closely. "All the world's a stage, Alyx."

She grinned. He knew Shakespeare! "'And all the men and women merely players,'" she continued. "'They have their exits and their entrances.'"

He nodded. "Rick had his moment in the spotlight, but his part is over. He took his exit. He can't hurt you anymore."

She stared at him in admiration. Not only had he recited a lovely poem for her, but he had sought to comfort her further by quoting Shakespeare and drawing a parallel to her life. She shook her head. "Maxim," she said, "I believe that you have listened to me more in the last few minutes than most people ever do."

Maxim focused on his feet. "Well, listening is what I do best." He glanced up at her again tentatively. "It's words I have a problem with."

She studied him for a moment, then reached out and took his hand in hers. "Maxim deBoer," she said, "you have no problem with words."

He offered her a small glimpse of a smile and looked away. She was touching him again. Oh geez... "Y-You should try to rest some," he stammered.

She nodded. "Javan's probably a popsicle by now." She stood and pulled the blanket gently off him. "We should do this again some time." A smile creased her lips as her eyes met his.

He chuckled nervously. "What, listen to me ramble poetry at you under the stars and look for constellations?"

She looked him directly in the eye and gave him an enigmatic smile. "Yes," she answered simply.

His heart fluttered like butterfly wings, and he had to avert his eyes again. She touched his shoulder as she walked past him, making her way back to the tent. She crawled in and flung an end of the blanket back over Javan, who had curled himself into the fetal position.

Maxim followed Alyx and zipped the tent back up. He took off his glasses and looked over at her, fighting the terrible urge to reach out and caress her face. "You going to be okay?" he asked.

She met his eyes. "I'll be fine," she assured, "but it always sucks to try and go back to sleep after a nightmare."

"Do you want to wake Javan up?" He knew Javan was her best friend. Perhaps he could make her feel better.

"No, let him sleep. I'll be fine. I'll just think of Draco and Perseus and remember your poetry." She yawned.

He smiled. "Just tell Rick that his part is over. Kick him off the stage."

She giggled. "I'll do that. Thanks, Maxim. You really helped."

"My pleasure," he replied, feeling his face grown warm.

Alyx lay there for a moment, trying to will herself back to sleep. Knowing that she was not all alone helped. She had crazy Javan sawing logs on one side of her and gentle Maxim on the other. Gentle Maxim who actually listened to her, and gentle Maxim who she knew was still awake when she finally drifted to sleep.

Chapter Eleven

Highway 1, California

Torrey relished the feeling of freedom. It was everywhere around him. In the wind blowing through his hair, in the winding coastal highway, in the California sun.

This vacation was long overdue. He'd been working way too hard lately. It would be nice to be able to relax and not have to worry about designing the layout for the new shops on The Embarcadero. He needed a nice, restful week where he could just enjoy the beauty of nature instead of 12-hour days with his boss screaming at him and his inept secretary forgetting to do *everything*. Not to mention she had spilled coffee on his shirt two days ago. *Hot* coffee. Right before he'd had a very important meeting with a client. He was, by nature, a pretty easy-going guy, but he really had to stifle the urge to strangle that woman.

He sighed and let his mind wander back to the night before. He smiled as he remembered the lovely woman with no name. He seriously could have started a relationship with her. He would have been happy to show her that not everyone she let into her heart would hurt her. He leaned his head against his hand and recalled the feeling of her soft lips. She had trembled so much when he had kissed her. It had made him want to take her in his arms and kiss all of her fear and worry away. He would have loved to show her how a lady should be treated and how a relationship could be. He wished he could have been the one to hold her close and earn her trust, and rejoice when she no longer trembled at his touch.

He had given her the ring he wore around his neck. He'd had it since high school. He'd gotten it at a street vendor and

engraved his initials on the inside. There was nothing particularly special about the ring itself, but it represented a
very happy time in his life and he wanted to pass that on to
her. It was something to remember him by, and a clue if she
ever wanted to try and find him. He doubted that she would,
but if she decided to take the risk, he would be ready and
willing. He knew it would take a long time to get her out of
his head. She had been so beautiful, and the vulnerability
he'd seen in her eyes had tugged at his heart.

He turned on the stereo in his rental car and stuck a Metallica CD in, turning it to *Wherever I May Roam*. It was a fitting song for a long awaited road trip.

He pushed thoughts of the lovely woman out of his mind
and focused on the things he planned on doing during his
trip. It wouldn't do him any good to dwell on a goddess who
didn't want him. That would only bring him pain. He sang
along softly to the lyrics of the song and smiled, feeling relaxed already.

San Lorenzo

Taegen didn't know how long she had been staring at her
ceiling. She hadn't slept very well and had been awake to
see the sun come up. She'd dozed after that, but not for
long. Her hand went to the ring around her neck. She
clutched it close and was blasted by the memory of the
beautiful stranger. His eyes, such a soul-probing green. His
touch, like the softest ray of sunlight at dawn. His voice,
which sent tremors running through her like shockwaves. His
lips... She rolled her eyes heavenward. She would kill herself
if she kept thinking this way. This had been the reason she
had stayed up practically all night. The man was going to
drive her insane. She would probably never see him again...
For some reason, she felt empty without him. How insane
was that? *It's because you liked him, stupid! And you let him
go! Stupid, stupid, stupid!*

Are you back again? Taegen shook her head. These conversations with herself had to stop. She had always been
sensible and levelheaded. This sudden emergence of the
devil on her shoulder was completely out of character.

She let her mind re-hash the evening before, even
though she'd done it a hundred times already. What had it

been about him? Why had she felt such a strong pull toward him? Why did she feel hollow inside now that he was gone? Tears came, but she quickly brushed them away. He would hate that she pitied her situation. She had chosen to let him leave. It was her own doing. Now, she had a beautiful new day to welcome...and a car to have towed. She decided she would take a jog first, get in the shower, and then call a tow truck. She would see if her neighbor would fix her tire and her poor, obliterated rim. Her neighbor could fix pretty much anything.

She rolled out of bed and slipped into some sweats and tennis shoes. She tied her hair back and burst out into the foggy morning, taking a deep breath of the cold air. It was invigorating. It was good to be alive. She thought of the stranger's kiss and how invigorating that had been. A pain shot through her heart and she winced. Man, this sucked. She blinked. Wait, no. It was good to be alive! She rolled her eyes. Okay, she was working on it. Miracles didn't happen overnight.

Camp Redwoody

Alyx awoke before everyone else, but was much too comfortable to move. Javan had rolled over sometime in the middle of the night and was pressed close up against her back. She was warm underneath the blankets and she was facing Maxim. His eyes were closed, giving her a chance to notice how thick and dark his eyelashes were. She frowned thoughtfully and took the liberty of studying him further.

His facial structure was very manly. Because of his glasses and his introverted nature, she hadn't noticed how strong and defined his features actually were. She knew he was better looking than Jeff. Jeff had the same severe features, but he looked too much like many other handsome, charming men in the world. Maxim's whole being exuded a soft tenderness that appealed to Alyx. Even the lines around his mouth that seemed to be the trademark of the deBoer men were more subtle than Jeff's. But she supposed that if Maxim smiled half as much as Jeff did, they would look just about the same.

She smiled to herself as she remembered the night before, and suddenly felt a sharp jab in her back. "Ow," she muttered with a frown. She rolled over and looked at Javan, who was propped up on his elbow and giving her a Cheshire cat grin. "What was that for?"

"I see you eyeing Maxim," he teased.

She scowled. "So what?" she asked, crawling out from beneath the covers. "I can eye anyone I please. Anything was better than staring down your gaping, cavernous mouth and breathing your toxic breath." She quietly unzipped the tent and stepped out, doing her best not to trample Maxim on her way.

Javan frowned and followed her. "You're the first girl to ever complain about my 'toxic breath,' as you so delicately put it," he said, zipping the tent back up.

She stretched and yawned. "Yeah, but how many girls actually stick around to smell you in the morning?"

He put his hand to his chest. "Ouch," he said. "Would you like your knife back after I pull it from my heart?"

She grinned. "We heading to Fort Bragg today?" she asked, turning to face the stream across the way from them.

"Sounds like a plan. You gonna let Maxim drive?'

She shrugged. "I don't care. It's your car."

"We should let him. That way he can control the radio."

Alyx turned and faced him. "What do you think that was about yesterday?"

"I don't know. You should have seen him, Alyx. He was so pale, looked like he was about to cry." He sighed and ran a hand through his hair, trying to straighten it. "There's something very lonely about that guy."

She nodded and turned her attention back to the stream. "But something very gentle also. Being around him soothes me like you wouldn't believe. Do you know what he did last night? I had this awful dream and needed to get some air. He followed me outside and proceeded to talk about the stars with me and recite poetry."

He studied her for a moment. "Seriously?"

"Yeah. Can you believe that? I didn't think people like that actually existed on the planet. He was so caring and attentive." She felt Javan's eyes on her, and she slid her gaze over to him. "What?" she asked with a frown.

"Nothing. I just think that's really cool." He raised his eyebrows at her playfully.

She rolled her eyes and tried to back out of the subject.

"Whatever, Javan," she muttered.

He chuckled. "Let's get out of here soon and hit a McDonald's or something. Tuna for breakfast doesn't really sound all that appetizing."

She nodded in agreement. "Want to wake up Maxim?"

Javan gave a devilish grin. "I thought you might want to do that."

She gave a little huff. "Whatever. Just wake him up, would you?"

He laughed and folded his arms. "I always know I've hit close to the mark when you whatever me."

"Just wake him up, Javan!"

He laughed again and went back into the tent. "Yo, Maxim!" he shouted, smacking him on the chest. "Get up, man!"

Maxim sat bolt upright.

"We're leaving soon," Javan said.

Maxim let his breath out slowly and tried to blink the remnants of sleep out of his eyes. He focused on Javan and frowned. "If that's the way you wake up everyone, I pity the woman who marries you," he grumbled.

Javan stared at him. "You know," he said, "that is the second time this morning that someone has dissed on my would-be love life." He shook his head. "I am shocked and hurt." He turned and left the tent in feigned dismay.

Maxim smiled and searched for his glasses. He had just started out of the tent when his bag began to blare. He jumped then sighed. He was never going to get used to that. He grabbed his bag and dumped the contents out in order to locate the cell phone. "Hello, Jeff," he answered.

"Hey, you're still alive!" Jeff exclaimed.

"Yes, I'm alive," he said with a sigh.

"How are you?"

He leaned back against his elbow. "Well, considering I slept all night in a two-man tent with two other people, I'm just fine."

"You slept in a tent with Javan and Alyx?"

"Yeah..." He grinned to himself as he remembered a time in the night when Alyx had rolled over and rested her head against his shoulder for just awhile. "We went camping."

Jeff chuckled. "And you didn't run out screaming?"

Maxim lowered his voice. "No... In fact, I found it rather

enjoyable." Silence. He stifled a chuckle.

"Okay, Maxim," Jeff finally said, "either you've got the hots for Alyx, or you decided to"—he cleared his throat—"swing the other way, which I wouldn't be opposed to, but—"

Maxim made a face. "Gross, Jeff," he interrupted. "That's disgusting. And I really could have done without the mental image of Javan naked."

Jeff laughed. "Too early in the morning for that?"

"Try too early in my life."

"So, you got a thing for Alyx?"

He suddenly felt a bit embarrassed. "No, I didn't say that. I just—she's—"

Jeff's laughter interrupted. "You like her!"

Maxim let out a long sigh. "Yeah," he admitted in defeat.

"Well, y'know," Jeff said after a moment, "you'd be really good for her."

Maxim blinked in surprise at his brother's statement.

"You're a very loving person," he continued. "If you like Alyx, go for it. I think your gentleness could be just what she needs right now."

Maxim swallowed, unsure how to respond.

"In fact, I think you'd be great for one another," Jeff went on. "You have everything to give and everything to gain. You are the best person I know. If anyone can make Alyx happy, you can."

"Come on, Jeff," Maxim muttered. "I'm not proposing or anything." Although, hearing such words of praise from his brother made him smile.

"No, but you both really deserve happiness. The nice guy doesn't always finish last, you know. Are you having fun?"

"Yeah, Jeff. I actually am having a reasonably good time. I don't hate you nearly as much as I did yesterday." Jeff's carefree laughter made him smile, as it always did. "I'm going to go," he said. "I think the others want to get out of here soon."

"All right, brother. You have a good time, 'kay?"

"Yeah," Maxim said. "I'll give you a call a little later. Oh, and tell Alexi that his sister says hello and she loves him."

"I will. See ya, Maxim."

Maxim hung up the phone and climbed out of the tent.

"Who were you talking to?" Javan asked, putting an obnoxiously red baseball hat on backwards.

"Jeff," Maxim replied. "He was checking up on me."

"Oh," Alyx said in disappointment. "I should have told him to tell Alex hello for me. I couldn't get a signal when I tried to call him yesterday."

"I did," Maxim said. "I told him to say hello and that you loved him."

Alyx met his eyes in mild surprise. "You did?" Maxim nodded and she grinned. "Thanks, Maxim."

He smiled and continued trying to get his things together. He had managed to drag the blanket out of the tent with him and it was still clinging to his ankle like a tentacle. He had a feeling that there was another long day ahead of him and he needed to prepare himself.

Fort Bragg, California

Torrey had never felt so relaxed in all his life. This was bliss. After turning his rental car in, he had hit the beach right away. A car was not needed during a vacation like this one. He was now enjoying the beauty and splendor of Glass Beach, loving the way the sand felt on his bare feet and the way the salty air off the sea blew through his hair. He watched the surf lap gently against the shore and sighed in contentment. He leaned back on his elbows and let the sun warm him. Small bits of polished glass glinted in the sun, making the beach seem to sparkle. The only thing that would make this better would be having that lovely girl next to him, laughing and sharing ideas and dreams. He rolled his eyes.

"She's not here, Torrey," he told himself. "She's not coming back. You'll probably never see her again. Chill." He heard a distinct feminine laugh and it caught his attention. He directed his gaze down the beach and spotted a group of three making their way toward him. There was a man with a red baseball hat carrying a woman with red-streaked black hair on his back. Walking next to them was a man with glasses who had his hands shoved in his pockets. For some reason, the girl and the man with the hat seemed somewhat familiar to him.

The girl screamed and grabbed at the man's head as he attempted to pitch her into the ocean. Torrey chuckled and continued to watch them. He found that one of the most interesting things to do was watch people. He turned to the backpack he had with him and pulled out his ever-faithful sketchpad. He turned to a clean page and began to draw the trio as they continued up the beach. It would be a wonderful picture of laughter and friendship.

* * * *

Maxim smiled to himself as Alyx squealed again. He hoped Javan realized that his life would be ending if he actually did throw her in the ocean. He let his gaze go off across the rolling waves and sighed. Alyx loved the ocean. They had already been to the Oregon coast, but she had insisted on walking this beach also. She said it made her feel at peace. After what she had been through, Maxim figured she deserved as much peace as she could get. He would gladly walk any beach in the world with her whenever she wanted to.

"Javan!" Alyx shouted. "If you don't stop it, I'm gonna kill you!"

Maxim smiled as he stopped and bent to unlace his shoes. He suddenly had the urge to walk in the surf. He had lived in Oregon his whole life, so close to the ocean, and he had never walked in the surf. Somehow, he felt as if his life would be incomplete if he didn't stick his feet in the icy waves. He rolled up his khaki pants and picked his shoes up, carrying them casually in one hand.

"What are you doing, Max?" Javan asked.

"Nothing," he murmured. He made his way to the water and let the incoming wave cover his feet. It was frigid, but strangely invigorating. It made him feel like the blood coursing through his veins was real, like he was alive instead of dormant and hibernating. He grinned and began to walk up the beach, studying the patterns in the sand and the way the waves washed up ever so gently on the shore. He had never really stopped to appreciate the great beauty of the majestic ocean. As a writer, that was wrong on the highest level.

"Excuse me."

Maxim jumped at the unexpected intrusion and looked up to see a man with long black hair and a rather flamboyant red shirt with black flames leaping up it standing in front of him. He blinked in confusion, half because he was startled and half because the slightly gothic look of the stranger's wardrobe contsracted greatly with both the beachy backdrop and the professional, put-together air the man carried.

The man grinned. "Sorry if I surprised you. I was just sitting over there watching you and your friends. I sketched this for you." He handed Maxim the paper, who took it numbly.

"What's up?" Javan asked, coming up next to Maxim.

The flaming man explained to Alyx and Javan while Maxim studied the drawing. It showed Javan toting Alyx on his back while Maxim walked up the beach ahead of them. He noted the way Alyx was laughing and it made him smile.

"Hey, lemme see that," Javan said, taking the paper from Maxim. He studied it and showed it to Alyx. "Check it out."

Alyx grinned at the artist. "It's wonderful!"

Javan nudged her with his elbow. "Look at Maxim," he whispered.

She looked closer at the rendition of Maxim and couldn't miss the expression of joy on his face as he looked down at the sand. She smiled and met Javan's eyes, who was grinning also. "Thank you so much," she said to the stranger.

"No problem. You all just looked so happy."

"Sweet shirt," Javan commented.

The stranger smiled and glanced down at his unbuttoned shirt. "Thanks."

"TLR?" Alyx asked, pointing to the initials at the bottom of the drawing.

"My name," the stranger replied. "Torrey Lucas Reed."

Alyx and Javan exchanged surprised glances.

"D-Did you say Torrey Reed?" Alyx questioned. He nodded and she glanced at Javan again. She frowned thoughtfully. "Any relation to Merrill Reed?"

He blinked in surprise. "Merrill? He's my brother."

Javan's eyes widened. "No way!" he exclaimed. "We work with Merrill!"

Torrey grinned and shook his finger at them. "That's where I recognize you from. Merrill sent me some pictures awhile back. I believe there was one with the two of you in it. I thought you looked familiar. What are your names again?"

"Javan Cox," Javan jumped in, extending his hand.

"And I'm Alyx Oncidezzerro," Alyx offered. "This is Maxim. He's a friend of ours."

Maxim offered a small smile and nodded his greeting.

"It's great to meet friends of Merrill's, but I wasn't expecting to meet you here! What are the odds?"

"We're on vacation," Javan bragged, "and on our way to

a Bleeding Passion concert."

Torrey groaned. "Man, you guys suck," he said. "I'd love to see that concert. I tried to get tickets, but they were sold out."

"Javan won ours on the radio," Alyx explained.

Javan's eyes suddenly widened in a way that Maxim swore he could see the light bulb appear over his head.

"Dude!" Javan exclaimed. "We have five tickets and only three people!"

Maxim chuckled. "Brilliant math, Javan."

Alyx laughed. Javan stuck his tongue out and continued. "Why don't you come with us? We were just going to scalp the other tickets anyway."

Torrey stared at them in shock. "Seriously?"

Javan glanced at Alyx in question.

Alyx smiled. "Yeah, come with us," she urged. "Merrill always talks about you. It would be great to get to know you. I mean, come on. Running into the brother of someone we know down here? We're *supposed* to take you."

A smile grew across Torrey's lips. "Merrill will kill me," he chuckled.

"No kidding," Javan said. "He almost killed *us*. That guy may be a classical musician, but he sure does love his rock."

Alyx nodded in agreement. "He wanted to come, but he's Javan's understudy in *Twelfth Night*. They wouldn't give him the same time off as Javan."

"I understand," Torrey said.

"So, will you come?" Javan prodded.

Torrey grinned. "You know, I live in San Francisco. This was supposed to be my week of relaxing vacation away from the city... However, I would be absolutely insane to turn down a free ticket to see Bleeding Passion."

"So you'll come?" Alyx coaxed.

He laughed. "Yeah! I just turned in my rental car, though."

"Perfect," Javan said. "You can sit in the back of my car with Maxim. We were going to stay in Fort Bragg tonight and then head out tomorrow. Is that cool?"

Torrey shrugged. "No problem here. You can stay at my place when we get to Frisco."

Javan grinned. "Thanks, that's really cool. We were going to stay for a few days. Alyx and I haven't been there in forever, and Maxim's never been. We were going to check out the sights."

Torrey shrugged. "Fine by me. Any friend of my brother's is a friend of mine."

"Cool," Javan said. "Hey, can you show us where a good place to get food is around here? I'm starved."

"Yeah, I know lots of places. Follow me."

Javan practically ran after Torrey. Alyx shook her head and laughed. "All Javan ever thinks about is his gut." She held back and waited for Maxim, who was tagging along behind. "You don't mind, do you?"

Maxim looked up at her. It impressed him that she even cared to ask. He shook his head. "No, it's fine. There is no possible way I could be more terrified than I was yesterday and I still managed to survive somehow. Adding one more person isn't going to make that much of a difference."

She stuck her lip out in a playful pout. "Aww, we weren't that bad, were we?"

He chuckled. "If you disregard the fact that I got decked in the head twice, walloped my thumb with a hammer, biffed it in the dirt trying to get out of the tent, and was forced to endure a horrendous, twisting car ride all on top of the fact that I was amid a bunch of strangers when I have the social skills of a slug..." He shrugged. "Nah, it wasn't that bad."

Alyx laughed and linked her arm with his. "It's so easy to laugh around you," she said. "It's nice."

Maxim couldn't breathe. Having her touch him at all was difficult for him to handle. Sleeping next to her had almost killed him. Now, she expected him to walk *while* she was touching him? He rolled his eyes and stifled a groan as they followed Javan and Torrey back up toward town.

Chapter Twelve

San Francisco

Taegen's attempt at a cheerful outlook had failed miserably when the tow truck transporting her car hit a semi and her car had been practically sliced in half. Luckily, the company was paying for a rental until she could buy another car, which their insurance was also paying for. As it was, they had only agreed to do that after Taegen had threatened them with a lawsuit. Two hours of arguing with an excitable Spanish guy, and one *huge* hot fudge sundae later, she found herself driving back to San Francisco. She didn't know why. Maybe just to torture herself. All she knew was that she didn't want to be in San Lorenzo. Anywhere was better than her lonely home.

She'd gone to the stretch of beach near the Hyde Street pier and read a book for a good portion of the day. It was relaxing, and had eased her frayed nerves some. She now found herself facing the end of another day and she sighed, wondering what her beautiful stranger was doing right now. Where was he? Was he thinking of her and missing her like she missed him, or had he forgotten about her as soon as he'd hit the freeway? What would he do if she saw him again?

With a heavy heart, Taegen got in her car and began to drive in no particular direction. The last thing she wanted to do was go home again. She was beginning to hate home. It was so lifeless. When had she become so boring? She hadn't always been that way. There had been a time, when Paul was alive, that she had been fun. She'd laughed and liked to do social things. They had gone out, danced, seen movies, gone to concerts. Now, the most excitement she ever got was when *Xena* re-ran on TV. It was depressing. Sure, she'd always been somewhat conservative and reserved, but she'd never been boring. She wished she could be more like the beautiful stranger. He was full of life. Life and passion and drive...

She suddenly slammed on her brakes as she drove past Golden Gate Park. She hadn't even meant to go past it. But there it was. She turned into it and found a place to park. She had been here with him yesterday.

Taegen all but leapt out of the car and started to stride toward the baseball field. He would be coaching. She could see him again and tell him her name! She had to take the chance! Carpe Diem!

She grinned and started to jog to get there faster. She would tell him how she had thought about him all night, and how she knew she had to take the chance or else regret it for the rest of her life. She stopped short upon reaching the field. She blinked. It was...completely empty. Not a child in sight. Her heart fell and she turned away, disappointed. She touched the ring around her neck and felt tears spring to her eyes. She missed him... Holy cow, she missed him more than she'd ever missed her old boyfriend. She was so stupid! How could she have let him go?

She wiped at her eyes, which continued to pour tears, and ran to her car. In the back of her mind, she knew she must look like a lunatic, fleeing to her car in tears like a soap opera actress, but she didn't care. She was coming to realize that she had a lot of pent up emotions that she wasn't sure how to deal with. She'd had a sucky day, and a really sucky past few years, so she figured she was entitled to a good waaa session.

She got in her car, slammed the door, and tore off down the street. She reached over and switched on the radio. *Thoughtless* by Korn started to blare. She let her tears flow rivers down her cheeks as the heavy music vibrated her car and soothed her aching heart. It was amazing how metal music could be so therapeutic.

She wiped at her eyes as she came to a stoplight. Instead of returning to the wheel, her fingers played with his ring. She brought it to her lips and kissed it. "I made a mistake," she whispered, "but I won't next time. You taught me that." She ignored the horn from the driver behind her, signaling that the light had turned green. "I won't forget you," she promised. "Ever." The horn honked again, less of a polite reminder and more like the beginnings of road rage. She moved ahead and began her journey back home.

Fort Bragg

Maxim had never smiled so much in his entire life. He had never met anyone like Torrey before. He was charismatic like Jeff, but there was something else about him that made Maxim feel comfortable. For as lively as Torrey was, Maxim didn't feel exasperated or uneasy in his presence. There was a laid back quality to him that made it seem like Maxim could do or say anything around him and Torrey wouldn't think less of him or look down on him.

The day had been spent exploring the town of Fort Bragg. Torrey had been there many times before and he showed them all of the good places to shop. They were now in a cove on the beach that he said was his favorite spot. They had a bonfire going and had eaten barbequed chicken. Maxim had actually succeeded in writing a bit earlier while they were at a café. The beginnings of a poem... It probably wouldn't amount to anything, but it was more than he usually wrote.

"Okay, Torrey, tell us about yourself," Javan said suddenly.

Torrey raised his eyebrows and chuckled. "Well, what do you want to know?"

"Merrill says you're an architect," Alyx said.

He nodded. "I'm also a little league coach and a musician."

Alyx grinned. "Merrill said you kicked butt in high school. He said you were on the varsity baseball team. He also said you won homecoming king *and* prom king."

Torrey looked down in an attempt to hide a blush. "I had my moments."

Maxim smiled. "I think my brother won everything in high school," he said. "At the end of every year, certain seniors were given awards. I think Jeff cleaned them out when he graduated."

"Did you ever win any awards, Maxim?" Javan asked.

Maxim snorted. "Yeah, let's see... Most likely to be a geek his whole life. Most likely to always be socially inept. Most likely to never have a girlfriend." He frowned. "I'm sure there were more."

Javan grinned and Alyx chuckled.

"Being in the arts runs in your family, doesn't it, Torrey?" Alyx questioned.

He nodded as he took a drink of a beer. "Both Merrill and I love music. My older sister is a concert pianist. My other sister is a ballet dancer on Broadway, and my baby sister is studying psychology, which is just weird, but what can you do?" He shrugged. "You can't have a complete arts family."

"So, are you going to play us anything on that guitar of yours?" Javan asked, pointing to the case sitting next to him. "Or is it just for show?"

Torrey chuckled. "I would love to play something. Do you guys have a preference?"

Maxim situated himself so that he was sitting comfortably on the sand while Torrey tuned his guitar. He glanced up at the sky and smiled then closed his eyes. He would never look at the stars again without thinking about Alyx. He sighed. This was peace. He was surrounded by weird strangers, and yet, the ache in his heart had only pained him a little bit during the course of the day.

Javan was a constant source of amusement, and Torrey had talked with him for upwards of an hour about classic novels and epic poetry. That had enabled him to climb to the top of Maxim's list pretty quick. He had gone his whole life and had never found anyone who would discuss *The Iliad* or *Beowulf* in detail. And Alyx... Just her presence was enough to take his breath away. She may not have known all of the authors Torrey and he had been spouting off, but she had definitely done her part when Shakespeare had been brought up.

After that, Torrey and she had started to talk about playwrights, which was out of Maxim's realm of reading knowledge, but he had enjoyed watching Alyx speak about them with such intense passion. Her eyes lit up when she spoke about something that was close to her heart, and he loved the way her cheeks dimpled. She was spellbinding...

Torrey strummed his fingers across the strings and finally satisfied with the pitch, began to play *Disarm* by The Smashing Pumpkins.

Alyx and Javan had both seen Merril play his cello before. As she watched Torrey play his song, she noticed how he and his brother had the same look when they concentrated. She

smiled and glanced at Maxim, who sat next to her. The flames
from the fire highlighted his face in an intriguing way, and she
remembered his kindness from the night before. It was
strange that she was attracted to him. She usually didn't go
for Maxim's type. Maybe she should start. Dating charismatic
men surely wasn't getting her anywhere.

Maxim turned his attention to the ocean, watching the
dark waves roll onto the shore. It provided a nice backdrop
for the scene that was unfolding. He let Torrey's soft, melodic
voice fill his ears and sighed. This was wonderful. He had
never thought that being in a group of people would be anything other than nerve-wracking, but he was genuinely enjoying himself.

Torrey finished the song, and it was followed by applause
from everyone.

"That was wonderful, Torrey!" Alyx exclaimed. "You have
a fantastic voice!"

He smiled. "Thanks. Want to hear another one?"

Everyone nodded in agreement.

He thought for a moment then began to play another song.

Maxim, who had turned his attention back to the darkened, rolling waves, suddenly felt his heart lurch as the song
began. He knew that song…. *Sound of Silence*… He swallowed uncomfortably and looked back at Torrey.

Alyx and Javan exchanged worried glances and Alyx
looked over at Maxim.

Maxim tried not to listen to the words, but they stabbed
at him, making him remember the awful loneliness he would
return to once this trip was over. He looked down. He could
feel his hands shaking harder, and he was having trouble
breathing. It was stupid that a song should affect him so, but
the words… Silence… All he had ever known was silence…

When his father had left, he'd shut himself inside his
closet to drown out his mother's sobbing. When his mother
had died, everyone at the funeral had been silent. They had
shot sympathetic glances at Jeff, knowing how hard it would
be for such a young person to suddenly become solely responsible for his family. Jeff had been silent. Jeff was never
silent, but after the funeral, he hadn't spoken to anyone for a
week. Not even to Maxim.

Every night, Maxim sat in silence. He hated silence, yet
he couldn't escape it.

Alyx reached over and gently placed her hand on top of his. He jumped, surprised at the touch. She smiled at him and he let out a shuddering breath. Alyx... She didn't know what it was about the song that bothered him so much, but she knew that it troubled him. And she cared. He didn't know what to do with that. He couldn't believe the concern he saw reflected in her eyes. She *saw*. He closed his eyes as her fingers ran along the back of his hand. She was caressing him. It was the only thing in the world he wanted... She was giving that to him. It was ecstasy.

When he opened his eyes again, all he saw was her. Javan was gone, and even Torrey's singing was dulled. It was just Alyx. All he wanted to see was her.

Alyx almost shied away from the intensity that washed over her when Maxim opened his eyes. His light blue orbs had turned stormy, and he looked at her as if she was the only thing in his world, the only thing in his universe. That was not something she had seen from *anyone*. Even her friends who had doting boyfriends never looked at their girls that way. It was something you read about in books, but never actually experienced. It was surprising, but definitely not unwelcome. She felt his hand turn slowly to twine his fingers with hers, and she leaned closer to him, wanting to lose herself in those powerful eyes.

Maxim took his cue from her and moved closer as well. His eyes were full of need and intensity. "Alyx," he whispered. "Alyx, I—"

She gave a soft smile. She had no idea what he was going to say, but something passed between them and she knew that he needed her. She didn't know why, and she didn't know how she knew, but she had never been more certain of anything. He needed her, and she had a stirring deep within her that let her know she might need him as well. "I know, Maxim," she murmured.

He smiled.

Torrey finished singing and strummed the last note, shooting a confused look at Javan.

Javan glanced back at Torrey and sighed. "Man, weird stuff happens when that song is played."

Maxim heard Javan's voice and suddenly noticed that Torrey wasn't playing anymore. He blinked and cleared his throat, feeling awkward and shy. What had *that* been? He averted his eyes to the ground.

Alyx came back to the present and glanced at Torrey, who was tuning his guitar again. She knew he was just trying not to look nosy. She looked away, biting her bottom lip. Maxim tried to pull his hand away, but she squeezed it, not willing to sever the connection yet. She hated to admit it, but she really liked the connection they had just made. She knew she shouldn't even be thinking about connecting with anyone after such a recent and dramatic breakup, but she couldn't deny how Maxim made her feel.

It was different than the way Rick had made her feel. When she'd first gotten together with him, he had made her feel like a giddy teenager. She'd thought he was really cute and a lot of fun. It had started out as an infatuation that she thought had turned into love. Now that she thought about it, she didn't know if she had ever really loved him, or just what he represented.

She'd wanted a serious, intense relationship her whole life. She wanted the fairy tale love story with the dashing hero on the white horse. Rick had been the stereotypical dashing man. Maybe she had just gotten so caught up in the fantasy ideal she'd created that she hadn't been able to see his flaws. If that was the case, she never wanted to be attracted to someone in that way ever again.

But Maxim made her feel different. It was an attraction, but it wasn't so superficial. She wasn't just attracted to Maxim because he had good looks or an ability to command a room when he walked into it. She smirked at that thought. He would probably choose death or dismemberment before he'd command a room in any kind of setting. No, her attraction to him was much deeper. She was attracted to the light she saw and felt resonating from his soul. He felt so pure, so genuine and good. He made her feel safe and comforted. He made her feel the way she had always wanted a man to make her feel.

"Soooo," Torrey said, breaking the uncomfortable silence, "when do I get to see a Shakespearean scene from you guys?"

Javan raised his eyebrows. "Scene?" he questioned.

Torrey grinned and placed his guitar back in its case. "Yeah. I played for you. Now I want to see some of your art."

Javan glanced at Alyx and she smiled. "Come on, Jave," she said, all too happy to have her mind on something else.

"We can do one of our scenes from *Twelfth Night*." She stood, reluctantly taking her hand away from Maxim's.

Javan groaned. "Man, Alyx. You suck. I thought I wasn't supposed to be working, y'know, on *vacation*. " He stood also and they faced one another.

Alyx rolled her eyes. "An actor never stops working, especially you. The world is your stage, remember?" She shot a wink at Maxim.

"Who do you two play?" Torrey asked.

"I am Viola and Javan is Sebastian," Alyx replied. "Brother and sister."

Torrey grinned and leaned back on his elbows, watching as they began their scene. When they finished, both he and Maxim applauded.

"Marvelous!" Torrey exclaimed. "Bravo!"

Javan and Alyx smiled and sat back down.

"Okay," Torrey continued, "Maxim's turn."

Maxim looked up, giving him a bewildered expression. "Um...I beg your pardon?"

"You must have an art you can show us," he insisted. "Otherwise you wouldn't be hanging out with us freaks."

Maxim chuckled. "Actually, I didn't really have a choice in that one."

"Come on, Maxim," Alyx urged. "Recite a poem."

He glanced at her and sighed. He would never be able to say no to her. Not in a million lifetimes. He thought hard for a moment then looked up at everyone.

> "Two roads diverged in a yellow wood,
> And sorry I could not travel both.
> And be one traveler, long I stood
> And looked down one as far as I could
> To where it bent in the undergrowth;
>
> Then took the other, as just as fair,
> And having perhaps the better claim,
> Because it was grassy and wanted wear;
> Though as for that the passing there
> Had worn them really about the same,
>
> And both that morning equally lay
> In leaves no step had trodden black.

Oh, I kept the first for another day!
Yet knowing how way leads onto way,
I doubted if I should ever come back.

I shall be telling this with a sigh
Somewhere ages and ages hence.
Two roads diverged in a wood, and I—"

He chuckled and grinned.

"I took the one less traveled by,
And that has made all the difference."

"Robert Frost," Torrey said.
Maxim nodded. "A fitting poem, I think."
Alyx grinned, knowing how hard it must have been for Maxim to even agree to come on this trip.
"Sing us another song, Torrey," Javan urged.
"Yeah," Alyx encouraged. "Sing for us again. There's something about guitar music on the beach that just fits."
Torrey grinned and pulled his guitar out again.
Alyx stole a sidelong glance at Maxim and saw that he looked deep in thought. She sighed and scooted closer to him, wanting that strange connection again. Torrey began to play Queensryche's *Silent Lucidity* and she rested her head on Maxim's shoulder.
Maxim nearly jumped out of his skin. He looked down at her in bewilderment and shot Javan a befuddled look. Javan grinned and winked, giving him a thumb's up.
Maxim sighed and felt his cheeks turn hot.
"You don't mind, do you?" Alyx asked.
He swallowed and managed to shake his head.
"Good. Otherwise, I would have to lean on Javan, and he has bony shoulders."
He gave a small smile and relaxed. Somehow, she always knew the right words to say to ease his tension. He positioned himself so he could support her better, and they continued to listen to Torrey sing. He couldn't remember the last time he'd felt so content. Probably never. It was a lot nicer than his usual feeling of isolation. This was something he could get used to.

Chapter Thirteen

Fort Bragg

After more songs from Torrey and a long night of laughter and stories, it was decided that it would be in everyone's best interest to return to the hotel. This was after Javan had suddenly fallen asleep like a narcoleptic during a lull in the conversation and fell over in the sand. Torrey revived him and suggested maybe it was about time for bed.

Alyx had fallen asleep on Maxim's shoulder shortly before Javan's episode. He didn't have the heart to wake her. She was resting so peacefully and he got the feeling that she didn't get much peaceful sleep.

"Why don't you go ahead and wake Alyx up?" Javan suggested as they put out the fire.

Maxim looked up at him and frowned. "No," he said. "She's resting."

"Yeah, but we need to go back to the hotel," he insisted.

Maxim glanced at Alyx, who was nestled close to him. He smiled and swept a piece of hair off her face, his fingers delicately brushing her soft skin. "That's fine," he said. "I'll carry her."

Javan raised his eyebrows in surprise. "All the way?"

Maxim nodded.

"Dude," Javan said, "you'll slip a disk or something."

"I'll be fine. The hotel is close by. She's tired, Javan. Just let her sleep."

Javan stared at Maxim like he wondered what planet he had migrated from. He continued to watch as Maxim stood and hoisted Alyx into his arms as if she weighed nothing at all. He glanced over at Torrey, who was grinning. "All right,"

Javan said with a shrug. "Let's go. I'm exhausted."

Maxim held Alyx close to him as they made their way back to town. He was supposed to share a room with Javan, but at least he got his own bed tonight. Even though sleeping next to Alyx had been nice, he'd gotten a Charlie horse from being so cramped.

"What time are we heading out in the morning?" Torrey asked as they reached the hotel.

Javan yawned. "Whenever I get up."

Torrey chuckled. "Gotcha."

"Hey, Max," Javan called, "here's Alyx's room key. She's two doors down from us. I'll see you soon."

Maxim nodded and took the key, although he wished Javan had just opened the door for him. Trying to situate Alyx so he could get the door while not waking her up was a very complicated task.

When he finally succeeded in kicking the door open, he carried Alyx inside and tensed when her whole body suddenly jerked. He looked down at her and she clutched at his sweatshirt, almost curling herself right around him. Maxim glanced around helplessly, not knowing what to do. He held her close and carried her to the bed, setting her down gently. "It's okay," he soothed. "You're safe." She jerked again and he stroked her hair. "Shhh, it's all right. No one's going to hurt you anymore."

Alyx's eyes fluttered open and focused on Maxim. She frowned and murmured his name in confusion.

He smiled at her. "You're in your hotel room," he explained. "We all decided to come back after Javan had a psychotic episode and fell over on his head."

She brought her hand to her forehead and blinked the remnants of sleep from her eyes. "I was dreaming," she said.

"I know."

"How did I get here?"

Maxim averted his eyes. "I carried you," he replied shyly.

Her eyes widened. "All the way?"

He nodded.

"Did you give yourself a hernia?"

He shook his head, meeting her eyes again.

Alyx gazed at him and her eyes reflected great warmth. "Where did you come from?"

He blushed and looked away. "Under a rock, I think," he

muttered. She giggled and he smiled. "Oh well," he said, "you should get your rest." He started to walk away, but Alyx grasped his wrist. He froze.

"Maxim," she whispered.

He met her eyes and his heart twisted. How could anyone have ever harmed her? She was so beautiful. He barely knew her and all he wanted to do was take care of her for the rest of his life. He still couldn't understand how someone who supposedly loved her would intentionally hurt her.

Alyx glanced away, feeling silly. How could she tell Maxim that she didn't want to be alone without sounding completely ridiculous? And he would wonder why she didn't call Javan to come be with her. How could she tell him that she felt like she could let him see the vulnerability she felt while she hid it from everyone else? The poor man would probably think she was trying to seduce him, then pass out and go into a coma.

"Do you want me to stay?" he asked.

She blinked up at him in amazement. How? How had he known? It was like he could see the battle she waged with herself. She nodded slowly.

Maxim smiled. "All right."

She frowned. "It's just that—"

"You just don't want to be alone," he answered.

She sighed and nodded, relieved that she didn't have to explain herself. Somehow, he just seemed to know.

Maxim sat down on the foot of her bed. "I understand," he said. "Sometimes, a room feels like an entire empty continent when you're alone."

She sat up, wanting to cry all of a sudden. Maxim's gentleness was overwhelming to her. She'd known gentleness from Javan and her brother, her parents even, but she had known and loved them all her life. She had only known Maxim for two days. He had no reason to show her gentleness, but he did. He gave it so freely. He exuded softness and compassion the way Torrey seemed to exude charisma and confidence... The same way Rick had exuded danger and violence once you got past his exterior charm.

"Thank you, Maxim."

"I know what it's like to feel all alone," he said softly. "Believe me, I know it so acutely that it hurts. You aren't alone, Alyx. You have Javan and your brother, and even Jeff." He cleared his throat and lowered his voice, becoming shy. "And you have me."

Alyx looked up at him and gave a soft smile. "I know," she murmured. She reached over and took his hand. "You're different, Maxim."

He chuckled. "Don't I know it."

She smiled. "Javan's my best friend. He always has been, but he lives in whatever moment he's having at the time. When Javan's eating, that's about all he can think about, but once he leaves the restaurant, he's thinking about something else. He dwells on nothing. While this makes Javan's emotions completely real and pure, it's hard for him to relate to something he's never experienced. I mean, he understands, but he's always trying to offer me some kind of advice like a shrink. How am I supposed to listen to advice coming from a man who once snorted soy sauce up his nose on a dare?"

He laughed softly.

She shrugged. "I mean, I know my own problems. I don't need a therapist to tell me what they are, and I definitely don't need Javan *trying* to be a therapist. With you, I don't feel like I'm going to have to sit through countless Confucius quotes or self-help advice. You just let me talk. And I don't feel like you just listen. I feel like you actually—"

"Hear," he finished, meeting her eyes.

She almost shivered. For a brief moment, that intensity flared in his eyes. She nodded. "It's like you read my thoughts."

"I feel the same way about you," he said with a gentle smile.

She did shiver then. She remembered the connection they had experienced on the beach. The more she thought about it, the more she knew that the connection she thought she'd had with Rick had been infatuation. Pheromones or something. The connection she had felt with Maxim had been surreal.

"Are you cold?" Maxim asked.

"Maybe a little. I'm going to change into my pajamas. I'll be right back." She stood and went into the bathroom after rummaging through her suitcase for a moment. She hoped that Maxim didn't notice how her hands shook.

He heard the door click shut and he pulled the curtains on the window closed. He turned the heater on and pulled the covers back so that everything was ready for Alyx when she returned. He wanted her to be as comfortable as possible.

When she emerged in her plaid pajama pants and black Pantera t-shirt, she seemed amazed to see that he had already prepared her room for her. She smiled and shook her head. "You amaze me, Maxim," she said as she set her clothes aside and made her way back to the bed.

He couldn't mask his confusion. He just did what he felt was right. It came natural to him. He couldn't quite understand what was so amazing about getting a room ready.

Alyx climbed back into bed and pulled the covers over her legs. She patted the end of the mattress, indicating that she wanted Maxim to sit down again. "What kind of things do you write?" she asked.

He tugged his shoes off and sat cross-legged on the end of her bed. He didn't want to invade her space, but he wanted to be able to see her while he spoke. "Oh, I don't know," he said. "Just whatever I think of at the time." He shrugged. "I actually haven't written anything with substance in awhile."

She smiled. "Tell me a story."

He paled. "N-Now?" he stammered.

She grinned and nodded.

He swallowed and thought for a moment. He hadn't written anything worth much in years. Now he was supposed to just up and produce a story from the top of his head? "I-I don't know, Alyx," he said. "I haven't written anything in such a long time."

Alyx's smile was encouraging. "Just do the best you can," she urged.

Maxim let out a heavy sigh and closed his eyes as visions and words swirled through his mind, connecting, forming thoughts. He licked his lips. "Some nights are so beautiful, so breathtakingly perfect that you can feel it in your very essence," he began. "All your senses seem heightened, and you become so acutely aware of everything around you. The stars seem to waltz across the velvet canopy of night, and everything seems so...perfect. This was one of those nights for him."

He stole a peek at her and smiled. She sat with her arms around her knees, like a little kid listening to a bedtime story. It eased his apprehension and he continued. "He had experienced something this night that could never be repeated, never duplicated. He had looked into a pair of green eyes and had

had seen his future, and his very soul." He cleared his throat suddenly, realizing where this story seemed to be headed. He opened his eyes and frowned, not knowing where to go next.

"You're doing wonderfully, Maxim," she assured. "Don't stop yet."

He sighed and shot her a pained expression, but her eyes were all warmth. "Those eyes had given him freedom while robbing him of speech." He scowled at himself. *Stop it*, he commanded his own brain. *If she figures this out and makes the connection, you're gonna sound like an idiot.* He took a deep breath. "He would remember those eyes forever and, as he began his life anew, he would find the eyes that had changed him, find the smile that haunted his dreams. If he spent the whole remainder of his life searching, it would be worth it. The eyes had a face, and the face was real. He just had to find where she was... And find her he would..." He cleared his throat again as the idea dissolved.

Alyx grasped his wrist and gave it a little squeeze. "That was good, Maxim! It sounded so mysterious."

He wrinkled his nose. "Sounded dumb to me."

She shook her head. "No, it was good. Write it down. Maybe you'll figure the rest out one day."

"He finds her," he murmured without thinking.

"What?" she asked with a thoughtful frown.

He met her eyes. "The woman. He finds her... When he least expects it." She smiled and he shook his head. He needed to go to sleep before he started confessing things he wasn't ready to confess yet. Her hand brushed over his in a friendly, gentle caress. He closed his eyes. If she knew what her touch did to him...

"I'm sorry to keep you up," she apologized, "but you..." She sighed. "Your presence gives me peace, Maxim."

He smiled. That was one of the best things he'd ever heard. No one usually even noticed his presence. "Would you like me to stay until you fall asleep?"

She met his eyes. "You would do that?"

He placed his other hand over hers. "Of course."

A shiver ran through her at his soft touch and she smiled. "Thank you." After she'd spoken with Maxim the night before, she hadn't had any more nightmares...until now. She remembered how warm his body had felt next to hers. That warmth had made her feel so safe.

"Like I said, I know what it's like to feel alone." He eased himself off the bed and sat on the floor, leaning against the bedside. "Goodnight, Alyx," he murmured.

Alyx switched off her light. "Goodnight, Maxim, and thank you again." She closed her eyes and sighed, reaching out her hand so that she could touch his hair. She needed to feel that he was there, that he wasn't leaving her. His presence was gentle, not an invasion, and she felt so much better knowing that he was beside her. It was strange, but when she was with Maxim, she felt like it was where she was supposed to be, where she had always wanted to be. He felt like home.

Chapter Fourteen

Maxim had never had the pleasure of experiencing a numb butt before, and it was definitely not an enjoyable sensation. He opened his eyes with a frown and tried to shift his weight. He was disoriented, and it took him a moment to realize that he was sitting up.

"Here, Max," a soft, tender voice came.

He looked up and saw Alyx grinning down at him with her dimpled smile. She handed a mug out to him and he grasped it blindly.

"You must be feeling sore today."

He shifted and tried to stand, but groaned when his back screamed at him. His neck felt like it was permanently bent into a right angle. "I can't feel my butt," he muttered.

She giggled.

He ran a hand through his hair and took a sip of the coffee, blinking the sleep out of his eyes. "I must have fallen asleep," he stated stupidly. *Score for Captain Obvious.* He glanced at the clock and blinked again, still feeling sluggish.

"I'm going down to the lobby to get some breakfast," she announced. She smiled at him over her shoulder. "Do you want anything?"

He swallowed another gulp of coffee and let his gaze settle on her for a moment. She was already dressed in a pair of hip-hugger jeans and a red shirt with black Chinese writing down one side. It exposed her toned stomach just slightly, and he smiled. When he met her eyes, a tender light shone from them.

Possessed by some evil demon no doubt sent to him by Jeff, he set his mug down and approached her slowly. "There is something I want."

Alyx's eyes widened as Maxim placed his arms around her and pulled her close. She rested her head against his chest and returned the hug, sighing. He smelled like wood smoke, his sweatshirt still holding the scent of the night before. Her breath caught in her throat at the feel of his strong arms tightening around her. He was tall and sturdy, and his embrace felt like protection.

He pulled away and took her face softly in his hands, pressing a kiss to her forehead. She closed her eyes as warmth rushed over her in comforting waves. She fought the urge to clutch him close to her, afraid his temporary boldness might dissolve and he would push her away.

"Good morning," he whispered, running a hand down the length of her hair.

She looked up at him. "Good morning." She placed her hand on his chest and let her fingers caress over where his heart was beating. Or racing, rather.

Maxim shuddered at her innocent touch, his eyes fixed on hers.

She smiled. "That was really smooth, Maxim," she murmured. "Does coffee always affect you like that? If that's the case, I'll give it to you more often."

He blushed furiously and looked away with a nervous chuckle.

She raised herself on her toes to press a kiss to his cheek. "You can go ahead and use the shower," she said, letting her hand travel down his arm. "Do you like bagels?"

He smiled and gave a small nod.

"I'll get you something." She touched his cheek and broke away from him, continuing out the door.

Maxim touched where Alyx had kissed him and closed his eyes. He could still feel her warm breath. He sighed and turned toward the bathroom, deciding to go ahead and use her suggestion. He could definitely use a shower... Maybe a cold one. He stepped in and let the hot water soothe the aches out of his muscles. He sighed and wondered if perhaps he had a bit of his brother in him after all. Grinning, he thought of what Jeff might say if he'd been there to witness Maxim's subtle moves on Alyx.

After washing his hair and letting his muscles relax, he turned off the water and dried himself. He picked up the shirt he had worn the day before and smelled it. He made a face.

All his clean clothes were back in his room. He sighed and wrapped the white hotel towel around his waist. His room was only two doors down, so he picked up his clothing and headed down the hallway. He found his card key in the pocket of his cargo pants and opened up the door.

Javan was awake and lounging on the bed, watching television. He glanced up at Maxim and his eyes bulged. He sat up abruptly, knocking himself off balance and landing on the floor with a crash.

Maxim raised an eyebrow and continued across the room.

"Holy crap, Maxim!" Javan shouted, scrambling to his feet.

Maxim frowned and opened up his suitcase. "What?"

His eyebrows shot upward. "What?" he asked. "Is that all you can say? You spend all night in Alyx's room, waltz in here naked, and that's all you can say?"

Maxim felt his cheeks turn hot. "I'm not naked," he stated. "I'm wearing a towel. I just got out of the shower."

Javan stared at him. "You just got out of the shower? Was Alyx in it with you?"

Maxim shot Javan an appalled look. "No!" he exclaimed. "Geez, Javan, you should have more faith in your friend than that!" He tried not to let his mind rush with the wanton images of Alyx wet and soapy in the shower. He wasn't very successful. He may be a nice guy, but he was still a guy.

Javan held his arms out. "Hey man, I never know with you. Maybe you seduced her."

Maxim heaved an exasperated sigh. "Give me a break, Javan. Do I look like the seducing type to you?"

Javan shrugged. "I don't put anything past you. You've got all sorts of secrets; I just know it. You always have to watch out for the quiet ones."

Maxim couldn't help the smile that stretched his lips. "Alyx was lonely," he explained. "I was there so she asked me if I'd stay and keep her company. She wanted me to stay until she fell asleep. I just happened to fall asleep too...on the floor." He shot Javan a pointed look.

Javan frowned in concern. "Is she okay?"

Maxim nodded. "She just felt alone, that's all."

"But she's never alone," Javan said. "Why didn't she call me?"

"I think she was afraid of seeming weak around you. She

didn't want to burden anyone."

Javan sighed. "Well, thanks, Maxim. Maybe you can get her through this rough spot in her life."

"We all can," Maxim said with a smile. "She loves you very much."

He smiled in return. "I love her too. Everyone loves Alyx. She lights up the world."

Maxim pulled some clothing out of his suitcase and gave a thoughtful frown. "How come you never went for her?"

Javan raised an eyebrow. "For Alyx? She's my best friend. We crawled around in diapers together. She's like my sister."

He nodded and headed toward the door.

"Where are you going?"

"Back to Alyx's room," he replied. "She's bringing me breakfast so I may as well just get dressed back there."

Javan's eyes widened. "She got you breakfast? She never gets *me* breakfast!"

Maxim grinned and continued on his way. He knocked on Alyx's door, hoping she was back from the lobby. He didn't feel real comfortable hanging out in the hallway wearing only a towel.

Alyx opened the door and gasped when she found herself staring at Maxim's bare chest. She blinked and tried to keep herself from drooling. How did he happen to be so beautifully sculpted? He was an introvert. Introverts were not supposed to look like Adonis. She let her eyes travel down to his stomach and she fought the urge to reach out and touch him. The towel he wore rode low on his hips, and try as she might, she could not keep herself from ogling. He was freakin' gorgeous! "Do you work out, Maxim?" she found herself asking.

He blushed horribly and pushed his way into the room. "Yeah," he muttered shyly. "I go to the gym with Jeff. I like to swim."

She smiled and closed the door. "Your food is on the table."

"Thanks, but I think I'll put my clothes on first." He threw a grin at her and made his way back into the bathroom.

The phone rang, making Alyx jump. She frowned. That was a sign that she was paying way too much attention to Maxim's rippling back muscles. She shook her head and went to answer it.

"Alyx," Javan's voice came in a cheap Ricky Ricardo imitation, "you gotta lot a 'splaining to do."

She smiled. "I don't have to 'splain anything to you. If I want Maxim to spend the night with me, that's my business."

Javan chuckled. "It *was* weird to see him saunter in here wearing nothing but a towel."

She giggled.

"Max told me you were kind of down last night," he continued. "Are you okay?"

Her heart warmed at Javan's concern. "Yeah, I'm all right, Jave. Maxim just really makes me feel safe somehow."

"That's good. You deserve to feel safe. You wanna head out in an hour or so?"

"Sure," she replied, happy he didn't push the subject. "Just call when you're ready. Let Torrey know."

Javan agreed and Alyx hung up just as Maxim re-emerged from the bathroom. She was surprised yet again. He was wearing a pair of khaki Dockers and a black muscle shirt, tucked in. A black, semi-punk style belt adorned his narrow waist. She bet he had absolutely no idea how good-looking he was. She would wager money that he worked out because it was something he could do with his brother, and he enjoyed it. Maxim was not the type to be preoccupied with his looks. She smiled, but turned away, not wanting him to feel even more self-conscious than he already did.

"So, we're off to San Francisco today, right?" he asked.

She nodded.

A knock on the door sounded and he opened it up. It was Javan with his arm extended, holding out a blaring cell phone. Maxim sighed and took it, flipping it open and turning away from the door.

"Hey Jave!" Alyx exclaimed. "Come on in!"

Javan glanced at Maxim, then back to Alyx. "I'm not interrupting anything, am I?" he purred, waggling his eyebrows at her.

She shook her head and laughed. "No, come on in. We love your company."

Javan grinned and obeyed. At least Maxim had his clothes back on. That was a plus.

Amoeba Music

Berkeley, California

Taegen stared at the back of the CD blindly. She didn't even remember which one she was looking at. She frowned and flipped it over. Creed. That's right. She shook her head and sighed, putting the CD back on the shelf. What was the matter with her? She felt like a complete zombie. She'd gone to the college earlier to take care of some stuff that wouldn't get done over summer break, but the rest of her day had been spent in a fog. She felt like she had fallen into some kind of weird abyss, and she had no idea how she was going to get out again. The stranger had given her pizzazz, but he was gone now. She had no idea how she was supposed to proceed.

It wasn't as much of an unhealthy obsession as it seemed. If Taegen was truthful with herself, she knew she had been wandering through life in a fog since Paul had died and she'd liked it that way, liked it because it was easier than facing anything that would hurt. The stranger had snapped her out of that for a little while, had been a bolt of lightning illuminating her mundane world. He'd made her remember how it felt to live her life instead of just exist. Now that she had felt that, going back to her self-made, pity-party prison felt wrong and stupid.

She moved down the row of music and picked up a Bleeding Passion CD. She studied the cover art and sighed.

"Hey, is that the last one?" a voice questioned.

Taegen glanced over her shoulder at a blond man next to her. He pointed at the CD she was looking at. "This?" she asked, holding it up. "Yeah, it's the last one, but I was only looking." She handed it to him and began to study Disturbed.

He looked at the CD for a second then moved his eyes back up to her. He smiled. "Do you like Bleeding Passion?"

Taegen glanced back at the blond man and smiled politely. "Very much."

He gave her a teasing smile. "You don't seem the type to be into metal music."

She frowned. "Oh yeah?"

He shrugged. "I mean, you just look so...I dunno. Classy?" He fixed her with an impish grin.

Taegen stared at him for a minute, wondering if he was insane. She was wearing a sweatshirt and jeans, for crying out loud. She rolled her eyes. "Yeah, look who's talking, frat boy."

He glanced down at his attire. He was wearing relaxed fit jeans and a gray t-shirt with some surf company name on it. "Hey, at least I have clothes on. My friend wandered into my hotel room this morning wearing only a towel."

She arched an eyebrow. "Is he still only wearing a towel?"

He chuckled and shook his head. "No, thank goodness."

She shrugged one shoulder and smirked at him, feeling devilish. Something about this man reminded her of her brother. "Well, at least your friend put something else on. You got up and dressed like a prep. You still look like a prep."

He raised both eyebrows and laughed. "Man, you're brutal."

She giggled. He flashed her a smile and let his eyes scan over her body briefly. She smoothed her blonde hair on instinct.

"So, are you going to the concert?" he asked.

Taegen shook her head. "I wish I could, but the tickets sold out almost as soon as they went on sale."

"I won five on the radio," he bragged.

She gave him a pointed look. "You suck."

He chuckled. "Yeah, my two friends and I decided to make a road trip out of it. We picked up another friend yesterday in Fort Bragg."

"Where are you from?" she asked, putting back the CD she had been fiddling with.

"Ashland, Oregon," he replied.

"Actors?" she asked with a smile.

He grinned and nodded. He pointed to her sweatshirt. "You go to Chabot College?"

"No, I work there. I'm a teacher's aide." She bit her bottom lip for a second before a giggle burst forth from her mouth. "I guess I shouldn't be making fun of you for looking like a frat boy, huh? I'm wearing a college sweatshirt."

He held up his hands. "I wasn't going to mention it, but since you brought it up..." He laughed then gave her a charming smile and winked.

* * * *

Alyx sighed and set her head back against the seat.

"What is Javan doing in there?"

Maxim shook his head. "I don't know, but I'm going to leave him here if he doesn't hurry up." He tapped his fingers on the steering wheel in irritation.

"How long does it take to buy a CD anyway?" she grumbled.

* * * *

He leaned against the CD stand in what she imagined was his best sexy pose. "What's your name?" he asked.

Taegen stared at him. He was flirting with her! She had gone a whole year with no one so much as glancing her direction, and now she was being hit on for the second time in three days. She grinned. He was kind of cute. "I don't tell people my name," she said, half-teasing.

"Oh come on. Tell me," he urged.

She remembered the stranger. She had made such a mistake in not letting him close enough. This man didn't have the same kind of charisma or draw that the stranger had, but he might have potential. He was easy-going and fun. She could do with some fun. Lord knew it had been awhile... She absolutely could not continue living the way she had been. She needed to make a change. "I'm Taegen," she replied.

He grinned. "I'm Javan. It's very nice to meet you."

* * * *

Torrey leaned his head back and pretended to snore.

"This is ridiculous," Alyx muttered. "What is he doing in there?"

Maxim blasted on the horn.

* * * *

Javan shot a frown toward the window. "My friends are getting annoyed."

Taegen smiled.

"We're on our way to San Francisco now," he explained, "but we decided to stop here first. I came in to buy a Bleeding Passion CD so we can listen to it. None of us had their latest."

"And you want to familiarize yourself with the new songs before the concert," Taegen assumed.

He nodded. "Hey," he said, scratching the back of his head, "do you want my fifth ticket?"

Her eyes widened. "How much?"

"Oh, you can have it. It was free anyway." He raised an eyebrow and grinned. "You just have to come with us. Hey, you could even come hang out with us for the rest of the day. My car has one seat left."

Taegen eyed him. What was it with all of these spontaneous things all of a sudden? Was it some kind of test? *Yeah right, Taegen. Who would be testing you? The spirits from the Great Beyond? Wouldn't they have something better to do than play around with your love life?* She rolled her eyes. The inner monologue *had* to go.

She studied him. Well, he didn't look like a sociopath, and she did know kickboxing. He was handing her a Bleeding Passion ticket and she was not going to let another opportunity get by her. It was about time Taegen Lane started to enjoy her life again. She needed to live up to the legacy Paul had left. She'd blown it so badly with the beautiful stranger. She would not make another stupid mistake because of her fear. She met Javan's eyes and smiled.

* * * *

"Finally!" a black-haired girl breathed when Javan got back to the car.

"Hey guys, so...I found someone who wants to take our fifth ticket, so long as it's cool with all of you," Javan announced.

"I don't care," she mumbled. "Not like we have anything planned out. The more the merrier."

"Cool. Ready to go, Max?" Javan called.

"I've been ready for twenty minutes," the driver grumbled.

"I'm Alyx and this is Maxim," the woman introduced.

Taegen smiled, glad to see there was another girl in the car instead of a bunch of drunken college guys. She got in and scooted herself over to the middle seat, trying not to listen to the voice of protest screaming in her mind. *This is so*

irrational! This is so unlike you! These people could be luna-
tics! You could end up dead in a ditch! They listen to metal
music. They could be Satan worshippers!
      Hey! I listen to metal music! I'm not a Satan worshipper!
Besides, just the other night you were telling me to show a
complete stranger my lacy, black panties.

She frowned and wondered if the first sign of insanity
was having arguments with yourself inside your own brain.
She guessed it was all right so long as she didn't start an-
swering herself out loud.

"Holy crap," she heard the man next to her murmur as
she tried to find her seatbelt. "Pretty Lady?"

Taegen's head shot up and she turned pale. All debates
within her chaotic mind ceased abruptly. Her eyes met and
held the stranger's and she wanted to cry. Her hands began
to tremble. "Beautiful Stranger?" she squeaked. How? Of all
the places and all the times... How? It wasn't possible. San
Francisco was an enormous city and they weren't even in
San Francisco. What was he doing in Berkeley?

Javan frowned as he shut the door. "You two know each
other?"

Taegen swallowed. She was unable to speak. He was so
very close. She remembered his touch, his lips. She fought
an almost uncontrollable urge to launch herself at him and
kiss him until they were both breathless and dizzy.

He grinned as he let his eyes roam over her face. "We
do," he replied.

"Aw man," Javan groaned. "Figures."

Maxim pulled out onto the road and Taegen sat back
against the seat, feeling dumbstruck. She stole a sidelong
look at the stranger and smiled. This was, by far, the best
and most bizarre thing that had ever happened to her. She
glanced at his hands, which were resting in his lap, and remembered his touch. A shiver went along her spine. She
leaned in closer. "What's your name?" she whispered.

He stared at her for a moment, obviously remembering
her fear of commitment and, well...everything.

She glanced up at him and smiled. "I'm Taegen."

His grin threatened to swallow the world. "I'm Torrey," he
returned. "Torrey Reed." He pointed to the chain at her neck
and winked. "I like that."

She looked down at the ring and felt her cheeks flush. She

closed her eyes when Torrey's fingers brushed her cheek. There was nothing she had experienced quite like his touch.

"It's a pleasure to meet you, Taegen."

She grinned and met his eyes. "I tried to find you yesterday. I went to the baseball field."

Torrey smoothed her soft, golden blonde hair, loving the feeling of it on his fingers. It was like silk and he wanted it brushing all over his body. "I wasn't there," he stated.

"I know that," she said with a giggle. "I went to The Amazing Psychotic also to ask Caleb where you were, but it was his day off."

He studied the delicate lines of her face and smiled. "You tried to find me." He couldn't pretend that wasn't a surprise. He had figured she would just write him off as a nice evening and go about her life. He'd never figured she would actually try and track him down. Maybe he had impacted her the same way she had him. He hadn't been able to get her off of his mind since he'd left her house. She had haunted his every thought, and that was odd for him. Even though he got a lot of attention from women, he'd never been a casual dater. He'd always felt like he was looking, waiting for someone special to come along. He'd been out with several women and had maintained a few relationships, but none of those girls had affected him the way Taegen had. In just one night, she had sabotaged his entire thought process.

Taegen looked up at him, instantly captivated. She gave a shy nod. Torrey cocked his head to one side and his smile tugged at her heart. He didn't need to use words when he had a smile like that.

"Well," he said softly, "you don't have to look anymore."

She smiled, wanting to cry all over again. She knew it was stupid, but she felt such a draw to this man.

"You'd better be sure that you want to do this," Torrey continued, "because I can assure you that I won't be leaving again." She would be lucky if he didn't attach himself to her permanently. What was it about her? Something was so alluring about her presence. She was a mystery. She was complicated, and he wanted to solve the puzzle. He had a feeling that when he did, the result would be the most rewarding experience of his life.

She looked up at him and wanted nothing more than to be in his arms. "You think that after this I'd actually let you leave?" His eyes softened and he held his hand out to her. She smiled and twined her fingers with his, resting her head on his shoulder.

"So, why did you decide to go with Javan?" he asked.

She smiled. "Because I wanted to make the most of my day."

Torrey grinned. "That's my girl," he whispered.

She almost shivered. *His* girl.

He wanted to pull her close, but he knew he had to go slowly. He was still so stunned that she had tried to find him. He absolutely would not let her get away this time. She had told him her name and had tried to find him. She wanted him enough to do that. He would be a fool to let her go again. He had given her the ball the last time he had been with her, content in letting her make whatever move she was comfortable with. She had chosen not to forfeit the game. Now, he was playing for keeps. He glanced over at Javan, who was scowling at the back of the driver's seat. He frowned. "What's wrong, Javan?" he asked in amusement. "You're pouting like a wet cat."

Alyx laughed and Maxim chuckled.

Javan threw his hands up in the air in frustration. "Of all the people I could choose to pick up, I chose Torrey's girlfriend!" he exclaimed.

Taegen's heart somersaulted.

"She's not my girlfriend," Torrey said, casting a glance down at Taegen. He squeezed her hand. "Unless she wants to be."

Taegen felt her face turn hot. Actually, her entire body suddenly felt like it was on fire. How did he do that? How could he elicit such a reaction from her with a mere touch or a few words? She knew he was staring at her, and she could feel Javan's eyes as well. Alyx had turned around in her seat to await her response, and she could wager that Maxim was watching in the rearview mirror.

She shrank back, trying to dissolve into the seat cushion. "Why is everyone staring at me?"

Torrey laughed.

"Crap!" Javan shouted, knowing he had lost. "You're cute too!" He pointed a finger at her as if it was a crime to be good-looking.

Torrey laughed again. "If Taegen gets any redder, she's

going to burst into flames!"

"Looks like your love life is as bleak as ever, Jave!" Alyx teased.

"Shut up!" he cried.

Taegen sniffed. "Laugh all you want," she said, "but I never even gave you my name." She scowled playfully at Torrey and raised her chin in defiance. "I decided to go to a concert with Javan."

Torrey winced. "Ouch," he said, placing a hand over his heart. "Touché."

Taegen smirked and glanced back at Javan. He was grinning like a hyena. She shook her head and laughed. "What?"

Javan chuckled. "You're going to get along with all of us just fine, Taegen."

Chapter Fifteen

Torrey's Home
San Francisco

Alyx set her suitcase down and stretched her back. It felt good to be standing after the long trip from Fort Bragg to San Francisco. Berkeley had been a nice reprieve, but she still felt like she had spent the last several hours in a sardine can. She glanced around Torrey's two-story, Victorian style home and admired how clean and modern it was. The only guy's house she ever saw was the one her brother and Javan lived in, and it always looked like a tornado had blown through. Torrey's looked like a picture out of a magazine.

What she liked the best were the many paintings that adorned his walls. Most she recognized as reproductions of famous works. Monet, Picasso, Van Gogh, but there was one that she didn't recognize. It was of a woman in a powder blue dress standing on a large, jagged rock on the shore. A wave crashed behind her, and sea spray misted around her like a cloak. Her eyes were closed and her arms were out. Her hair and dress blew with either the force of the waves, or the wind, and she had a look of complete rapture on her face, as if she could embrace the stars in the night sky above her.

"That's beautiful," Alyx remarked, going to study the painting better. "Who's the artist?"

Torrey smiled. "I am."

Alyx's eyes bulged and she stared at him. "Are you serious?"

"Wow," Javan said. "That's awesome."

"Who is she?" Alyx queried.

Torrey shrugged. "Just a girl. I came up with that image

in the middle of the night. I like to call that painting my dream woman."

Javan frowned thoughtfully as he took a closer look at the painting. "It looks kinda like Taegen," he remarked.

Torrey smirked and glanced at Taegen. "You noticed that too, huh?"

Taegen blushed. "It does a little," she murmured.

Torrey reached out and ran his hand down her arm. "Why do you think I stared on the train?" he whispered. "There are too many coincidences with us to ignore."

She met his beautiful green eyes and nodded. What were the odds? She'd seen him on the train, and then let him go. She'd met him in the park, and then let him go. Because she'd decided to go with Javan, she was with Torrey again. And he had painted a picture of his "dream woman" that looked like her... She swallowed. How was any of that even possible? The whole situation was just bizarre. It went against everything she was. She was rational. She was calm. She was analytical. She couldn't analyze her way through this even if she tried.

"So, what's the plan?" Javan questioned.

Alyx spun and her eyes riveted on Maxim. He froze and one of his eyebrows arched up slowly. He didn't like the way she was looking at him. He felt like a mouse about to be attacked by a hungry cat.

"We're going shopping," Alyx declared. "The concert is tomorrow and we need to get Maxim the proper attire."

His eyes widened and he held his hands up. "No way." Alyx gave a devilish grin.

"Torrey, you have to keep him busy," Javan added. "Alyx and I will find him clothes. It needs to be a surprise."

Maxim groaned. "You guys are gonna kill me."

"Oh come on, Maxim," Alyx said. "You already have the hair-do." She ruffled his gelled-into-a-stylish-disarray hair and grinned again. "And you have the belt." She looped her finger under his belt buckle and tugged.

Maxim let out a small squeak and his face turned three shades of red, he was sure.

"You just need the rest of the outfit and you'll look like a regular rocker." She patted him on the chest and giggled. "Just leave it to me."

He swallowed uncomfortably.

Torrey chuckled and shook his head. "Why don't you guys take your things upstairs? I have two extra bedrooms, so just figure out which ones you want."

Alyx nodded and picked up her bags. "Thanks, Torrey." She started up the staircase.

Javan picked up his bags also and grinned at Maxim. "She was totally flirting with you," he said.

Maxim averted his eyes. "She was trying to kill me," he muttered.

Javan laughed. "You want to share a room?"

Maxim nodded and picked up his bags, following after Javan.

Torrey waited until the other three were out of sight before he turned to Taegen. He placed his hands on her shoulders and let them caress down her arms. She shivered and wanted to press close to him, wanted to feel his arms around her, but she felt silly. She barely knew this man. Why was she feeling this way? Love at first sight didn't exist... Did it?

"I'm very happy we found one another again," Torrey said softly.

She swallowed and nodded her agreement.

He smiled and lifted her chin so that he could see her eyes. "Why so shy? Are you embarrassed that you're happy to see me?"

She shook her head adamantly. "Oh no, it's just, I—"

"It's very new and very sudden," he answered, caressing her cheek with the back of his forefinger.

She nodded.

He cupped her cheek in his palm. "Above all things, I don't want you to feel pressured," he said in encouragement. "Let's go shopping with Alyx and Javan. We can occupy Maxim."

She nodded again, starting to feel like a dashboard bobble head. She had no idea what she was doing. Was she completely out of her mind? She chewed on her bottom lip nervously. Torrey was so close. She could feel his warmth, could smell his fantastic cologne. How come she ached for him so? Why did she feel like he filled the missing void in her heart?

"What's wrong?" he asked with a frown.

She sighed and shook her head. "This is weird, Torrey. You make me feel really weird."

He raised an eyebrow. "Weird?"

She bit her bottom lip. "I went to find you. I wanted to tell you my name. I wanted to tell you how you consumed my thoughts and robbed me of sleep. How I woke up feeling...empty." She sighed. "Torrey, you are not like anyone I've ever known." She sighed again and let her shoulders slump. "I don't even know what I'm trying to say. I feel all flabbergasted and confused... That's so unlike me."

He studied her for a moment and smiled. "Moments, Taegen," he said. "Life is made up of moments, remember? Make the most of them and see where they lead you. Don't try to map them out before they happen. I see your fears lurking, waiting to swarm you, but give us a chance before you condemn us. I know you're confused, that you never expected this. Neither did I, but we have something. Something that shouldn't be pushed aside."

"I know. I don't want to push it aside. I-I can't let you go again, Torrey. It really messed me up. I'm all confused and arguing with myself inside my own head."

He snaked his arms around her shoulders and pulled her closer. "Then just let it happen." He gave her a soft smile. "You have a beautiful name, by the way." He touched her hair with gentle fingers. "Taegen... It's a fitting name for you. Do you know it means 'beautiful?'"

She closed her eyes and shook her head. His caressing voice... It made her melt inside. She gave a small, nervous laugh. "How in the world do you know that?"

"My sister had a baby last spring and she had me look up all these names for her. One of the ones she liked was Tegan. Spelled differently, but it means the same thing."

"And you just have that information sitting on the back-burner in your mind?"

He shrugged. "Never knew when I might meet a girl named Taegen. Thought it would make one heck of a pick-up line." He gave her a mischievous grin. "Did it work?"

She rolled her eyes, but his teasing made her feel relaxed and comfortable. Some of the confusion slipped from her, and she felt like bantering with him was the most natural thing in the world.

"Live in your moments, beautiful Taegen," he said. "See what they form."

She sighed in mock exasperation. "Well, while I was living in my moment in Berkeley, I left my rental car there."

Was she a complete imbecile? Had she taken leave of every single one of her senses?

Torrey frowned. "Rental?"

"Long story," she grumbled.

"We can go back and get it later."

She closed her eyes when she felt his fingers brush her face again. She felt like her stomach was doing a trapeze act.

"Do you mind that I touch you so much?" he asked with sincerity.

Taegen shook her head. Mind? Did she mind? She loved his touch, ached for it. She never wanted him to stop touching her.

"I'm an affectionate person by nature," he explained.

"It's fine, Torrey. I—" She smiled up at him. "I like it."

He grinned and pulled her closer.

* * * *

Maxim set his bags down on the left side of the room and frowned in thought. He turned to Javan. "Do you really think she was flirting with me?" he blurted.

Javan stared at him in disbelief. "Are you kidding me? Max, she was so flirting with you. Haven't you ever had a girl flirt with you before?"

"Once," Maxim replied dismally. "I threw up on her."

Javan made a face. "Chunkage," he muttered. "That would tend to kill the mood."

Maxim shrugged helplessly. "I was drunk."

"*You* were drunk?"

"It's not like it takes much."

Javan grinned and shook his head. "You're something else, Maxim. No wonder Alyx likes you."

Maxim frowned.

"You're different," Javan continued, sitting down on the end of the bed. "Different from Rick and all the other evil guys in the world." He sighed and lowered his voice to a serious note. "Maxim, I haven't seen Alyx smile as much as she has in the past few days in a very long time. Genuinely smile." He sighed. "She thinks she fools me, but she doesn't. I know Alyx. She's the type of person who's always trying to be positive. It's like I said, she lights up the world. She smiles even when she hurts inside. I've known her my whole life. I can see when her smiles are empty. She doesn't smile empty smiles with you."

Maxim looked away, feeling awkward. "I really like her," he admitted quietly.

Javan laughed and stood, slapping him on the back. "You don't have to ask my permission!" he teased. "Go for it, man!"

Maxim blushed. Go for it. That was a Jeff motto, not a Maxim one. He wouldn't know how to "go for it" if he tried. He heaved a sigh. "Don't get too scary of clothes for me, okay?"

Javan grinned wickedly, but didn't answer. "Come on, dude!" he exclaimed, bounding out of the room. "We're burning daylight!"

Maxim followed him with a shake of his head. He was going to come out looking like Marilyn Manson. He just knew it.

Union Square
San Francisco

Maxim was starving. He knew his stomach had to be digesting itself. He hadn't eaten since breakfast, and he had been wandering around the city with Taegen and Torrey for the last hour. They had lost Javan and Alyx. No one knew where they were, and Maxim was thoroughly convinced that he was never going to get to eat again. His original plan had been to wait until the others decided to get food, but he was quite certain that he would resort to cannibalism if he had to go any longer.

"Hey, are you all right?" Torrey asked, obviously noticing Maxim's glazed-eyed, slack-jawed expression.

Maxim glanced over at him and his stomach roared in response.

Torrey grinned. "Hungry?"

Maxim nodded. "I'm going to eat *you* pretty soon."

"I'm hungry too," Taegen said. "Where are Javan and Alyx?"

Maxim groaned. "I'm afraid to even think about it."

"Tonight is karaoke night at The Amazing Psychotic," Torrey said. "We could go there for dinner." He chuckled. "It's always fun to watch."

Taegen stopped suddenly in front of a department store window and smiled.

"What is it?" Torrey asked.

"I like that dress." She pointed to a mannequin wearing a long, powder blue evening gown. It had a silvery shimmer and the back scooped low.

Torrey stared at it and tried to imagine Taegen in it. He blinked. She would look...just like his painting. He glanced at Maxim, who raised an eyebrow. He winked and Maxim nodded.

"I think I'm going to go look around in here," Torrey said, opening the store door. "My sister wanted something from here." It wasn't a lie. His sister *had* wanted something. Taegen didn't need to know it had been a month ago.

Taegen nodded and started to follow, but Maxim took her arm. "Do you want to come into"—he looked around frantically—"that café with me?" He stabbed his finger at a tiny café across the street. "I know you said that you were hungry too. We could get something small to take the edge off while we wait for Javan and Alyx."

"All right." She looked back to Torrey. "We'll be over there."

He nodded and flashed a conspiratorial grin at Maxim.

Maxim guided Taegen across the street. It was apparent that Torrey was going to buy her that dress. How could he not? It looked like the one in his painting. If Taegen wore it, she would look even more like the woman he had created.

"So, how long have you known Torrey?" Taegen asked.

"Only two days," he replied, nabbing a bagel from the café. "Actually, none of us knew him before yesterday, but Javan and Alyx work with his brother. It was a coincidence meeting him in Fort Bragg."

"Coincidences seem to be a specialty of Torrey's."

"How long have you known him?" he questioned as he paid for his food.

She grinned and looked up at him. "Three days."

Maxim was surprised. Torrey and Taegen acted as if they had been comfortable with each other for quite a long time. He sat down at a table outside and relaxed against the chair. Sustenance...finally.

"How do you like San Francisco?" Taegen asked. "Javan said you'd never been here."

He nodded as he spread cream cheese across his bagel. "I've rarely ventured out of Ashland. I do like this city, though. It's beautiful." He flashed a friendly smile at her and noticed that it was becoming an easier practice.

Taegen returned the smile then chewed on her lip as if in thought. "What do you think of Torrey?" she asked suddenly.

He blinked, a little surprised that she was asking him. It wasn't as if he knew the man any better than she did. "He's really nice," he replied, "and a lot of fun to be around." He looked up and met her eyes. "What do *you* think of Torrey?"

Taegen's cheeks turned pink and she looked away. "I-I—" She heaved a sigh. "Do you believe in love at first sight?" she blurted, looking him straight in the eye.

Maxim pondered her question for a minute and thought of Alyx. He had adored her the moment he'd set eyes on her. Even if she never liked him that way in return, he would do pretty much anything for her. She'd made him feel for the first time in so long. Made him feel alive, accepted, like a man and not an empty chasm. She didn't look at him like a loser or a freak. She just looked at him like Maxim. If she never gave him anything else, that would be enough to merit his undying devotion for all time. "Yes," he replied softly.

She frowned. "Really? But why? I mean, it doesn't make sense!" She was so frustrated with herself and the entire situation. She hated that she kept questioning it. Torrey was the first good thing that had happened to her in years. If she had any brain left in her head, she wouldn't wonder about why a gorgeous man had been delivered into her lap. She should just accept it graciously and enjoy it. But still... It didn't make sense! She shook her head. "Okay, I know you don't really know me from Adam, but just go with me on this, okay? Last few years for me—yeah, they haven't been so great. I've been really depressed for awhile now, and nobody was able to bring me out of it. I met Torrey by complete blind chance not once, not twice, but three times! And he's the only thing to come along that makes me... " She sighed in defeat. "Smile." She was lost. She knew it. There was no sense in denying the obvious, even if the obvious made no sense. She was in serious danger of falling very hard for this man.

Maxim could relate to what she meant in a small way. He had been so lonely, but then Javan and Alyx had come along... He frowned and placed his hand over his heart. The ache. It was...gone. He blinked and thought of Javan poking at the skunk with bamboo, of Torrey singing on the beach in his crazy flaming shirt, of Taegen making everyone laugh in Berkeley, of Alyx. Alyx with her kind heart and soft touch. A smile touched his lips as the place the ache had inhabited filled with a strange warmth. He felt tears sting his eyes. Friendship. He hadn't really known the meaning of it until now. These were his friends...

Taegen frowned slightly. "Maxim?" she questioned. "Are you okay?"

He looked back at her and grinned. "I'm fine," he assured. "Taegen, I understand your skepticism, but you need to let it go. Don't push Torrey away if you think he may be worth something. My brother forced me to come on this trip. I didn't even know Javan and Alyx before three days ago. I was appalled. I felt so lost and out of my element... I still do, a little, but it's not as bad. I'm really glad I took the chance and came now. My life is better because of these people." He shook his head. "Sometimes, life throws a few wild cards at you, but just because they don't feel safe to you at the time doesn't mean they're not worth investigating."

She smiled. "Live in my moments," she murmured.

"Maxim!"

He jumped and almost knocked himself out of his chair. He frowned as Javan slung his arm around his neck, laughing. "You're so obnoxious."

Javan grinned. "Where's Torrey?"

Maxim pointed to where Torrey was crossing the street. He glanced up at Alyx who carried a black bag that he didn't have a good feeling about. She smiled down at him and he swore he felt something inside of him melt right before he felt that bolt of lightning sensation through his brain again. Words suddenly flooded through his mind. Words accompanied by pictures. Ideas. A slow smile spread across his lips. He was being barraged by ideas.

"Maxim?"

He looked up as he felt a soft touch on his shoulder. Alyx was gazing at him with curiosity. He grinned and placed his hand over hers. He stood and brought it to his lips slowly. "Muse," he murmured.

She raised an eyebrow. "Muse?"

He nodded and threaded his fingers through hers as ideas began to take form. "You are my muse."

Alyx didn't quite understand, but she loved it when he

looked at her like that. It made her feel like she was dying and coming to life all at the same time. She sighed. She wanted to fall into his bottomless eyes and never come out. She wanted to see the world through them.

"Maxim, what are you talking about?" Javan asked, looking confused.

He chuckled. "Nothing."

Torrey grinned upon his return. "Come on," he urged. "Let's go to The Amazing Psychotic and have some fun." He winked at Maxim over his shoulder.

Maxim smiled and let go of Alyx's hand. He took a deep breath and a blissful feeling washed over him. His smile turned into a grin. Maybe one of these days he would actually let Jeff know how right he had been about this trip... Maybe.

The Amazing Psychotic

"That is the coolest name for a restaurant I have ever seen," Alyx remarked as they entered the dimly lit room. Loud applause followed their entrance and she stepped back in surprise.

Torrey laughed. "Didn't know they were expecting us," he teased. He glanced over at the front counter and waved at Caleb.

Caleb grinned and made his way over to them. "Hey Torrey," he greeted. "Back so soon?"

Torrey nodded. "What was the applause for?"

Caleb chuckled. "There was this guy who just sang *Heartbreak Hotel*. He couldn't carry a tune, but he gave it a valiant effort."

"Torrey!"

Taegen glanced up to see a tall woman with curling, fiery hair wave at them. She was gorgeous. Taegen swallowed, hoping it was Caleb's wife or Torrey's sister or something. If she was some old flame of Torrey's, she was feeling mighty inadequate.

The woman ran over to them and flung her arms around Torrey. "I haven't seen you in forever!"

Torrey grinned. "That's because you're always so busy with plays."

She laughed. "If it isn't me, it's Caleb. How are you?"

"Wonderful," he replied. "Meet my friends, Alyx, Javan,

Maxim, and Taegen. Guys, this is Nasarra and Caleb. They run this place."

Caleb smiled at Torrey. "She told you her name?"

Torrey put his arm around Taegen and pulled her close. "Finally."

"Oh, is this your girlfriend?" Nasarra asked.

Taegen sighed and Torrey chuckled. "One thing at a time."

"You want something to eat?" Caleb asked. "Or are you just here to watch the general populous make fools of themselves?"

"We're starving," Javan answered. "I think Maxim's dying."

Maxim nodded in desperation. He had eaten the bagel, which had helped, but they had wandered around for another hour before reaching the restaurant, and he was back to being famished again. He was in serious need of some protein.

Caleb smiled. "All right. Have a seat. One of us will come get your orders in a sec."

Torrey led them to a table toward the front of the stage. Nasarra was there in minutes taking their orders.

"How do you know Torrey?" Alyx asked Nasarra.

"Last year I performed in a play at the Lazy Little Theatre. Torrey was trying his hand at acting and he was in it with me."

Javan grinned. "Seeing if you had what your brother does, eh?" he teased.

Torrey smiled. "I just had to see what it was like."

"Which play?" Taegen questioned.

"*Bram Stoker's Dracula*," Nasarra replied, stuffing her order pad into her apron.

Alyx's eyes widened. "Seriously? I've always wanted to be in that play. Who were you cast as, Torrey?"

Javan snorted. "Some one-liner no doubt," he scoffed.

Nasarra laughed. "No, actually, he was Dracula."

Alyx stared at him. "Your first time acting and you got the lead?"

Torrey gave a bashful smile.

"Lazy Little Theatre always takes chances on newbies," Nasarra explained. "They gave me my first break." She nudged Torrey playfully. "It wasn't like it was much of a stretch for him. Tall, black-haired, sexy vampire." She shrugged. "I think they typecast."

Everyone laughed, but Taegen leaned over to Torrey. "I agree," she whispered.

Torrey met her eyes and touched her cheek with a smile. "Careful," he breathed against her neck. "I never said I wouldn't bite." He drew his breath in slowly, creating a low hissing sound, and his fingers trailed down her neck to trace her collarbone.

Taegen's heart leapt and she closed her eyes. How had she managed to go her whole life without this man's touch? Maybe he really was a vampire, or at least enchanted in some way. How else could she explain how he affected her?

Nasarra thwapped Torrey in the back of the head with the flat of her hand. "No seducing people in my restaurant," she teased.

"Yeah," Alyx laughed. "You'd better watch out, Taegen. The animal in him is coming out."

Torrey frowned and rubbed at the back of his head, but Taegen giggled. She wouldn't really mind seeing his animalistic side. That realization both shocked and exhilarated her.

Nasarra grimaced as the current singer hit an incredibly flat note. "This is painful," she muttered. "Why don't you get up there, Torrey? Show them how it's done." She turned back toward the counter, waving as she did so.

"Dracula," Alyx muttered.

Torrey smiled.

"Who did Nasarra play?" Javan asked.

"Mina," Torrey replied. "Caleb was in it also. He played Jonathan Harker. That was before the restaurant opened and they could both be in the same play. Acting was one of the funnest things I've ever done."

Alyx glanced at Maxim, who was scrawling something on a napkin. "What are you doing?" she asked.

"Idea," he stated.

She smiled. "Will you share it?"

He glanced up at her and his eyes held hers. "Later," he said. "I promise."

Her smile grew.

Applause suddenly sounded throughout the room and Torrey sighed as the last singer made his way off the stage. He stood. "All right," he said, cracking his neck, "let's liven up this party."

Taegen grinned as she watched Torrey swagger up to the stage and select a song. Caleb and Nasarra cheered upon seeing him, and Alyx, Javan, and Maxim joined them.

Torrey shot a glance at Taegen and winked at her. Music began to play and he launched into "You Can Leave Your Hat On" by Tom Jones. His performance had the entire audience out of their seats, mostly the women.

"Please tell me he's not going to do the *Full Monty*," Javan groaned.

Laughter went around the table, but Taegen could only stare. He was the most fascinating, talented man she had ever met. He attracted people the way oxygen attracted fire. At the front of the stage, a table full of girls were shouting things at him, trying to get him to notice them. He gave them a show, but kept glancing back at Taegen. He had chosen her. He was there with her. She smiled. Her Torrey. She wanted him to be hers. She thought of Maxim's words. She needed to take this chance. She could not and would not let him go again. *Carpe Diem! Carpe Diem!*

She grinned. *Yes, yes, I hear you.*

Torrey finished his song to thunderous applause and returned to his seat laughing.

"That was marvelous!" Alyx cried. "You're such a natural performer!"

"I love showing off," he laughed.

Taegen stood abruptly. She took a deep breath and squared her shoulders. She was aware of the concerned looks her newfound companions were giving her, but she ignored them. "Moments," she whispered, closing her eyes as she firmed her resolve. "Make the most of my moments. Carpe Diem."

Slowly, she made her way onto the stage. After selecting a song, she turned toward the audience and grasped the microphone with a shaky hand. She closed her eyes and let the music of Bleeding Passion's "Consuming" fill her mind. She took a deep breath and began to sing.

"I'm black to the molten core,
Your fire consumes my soul,
Depth consuming everything,
It struck me to me heart.

        Eyes burning inferno beauty,

Passion billowing in my mind."

She opened her eyes as she relaxed a bit. She had always loved the song, but the lyrics held so much meaning to her now that she had found Torrey. She had felt so blackened and dead inside, but his fire, his passion, had brought her back to life.

"Darkness consumes the night,
I can barely breathe.
Immobile, can't move,
Look what you've done to me."

Torrey felt his heart lurch as Taegen met his eyes. Her voice was clear and soft, and she was singing straight to him. He stared at her in awe. She was choosing him. He sent her a gentle smile.

"Rose petals fall at the loss of you,
Your passion still sings to me,
Fire still consumes an empty shell,
I'm cold shaking on the floor.
I still see you everywhere I go,
I'm still bleeding for you."

"Check it out," Javan whispered to Alyx. "I think she's singing to Torrey."
Maxim grinned, knowing how hard it was for Taegen to take such a leap into the unknown. He admired her for it. Jeff had pushed him off the metaphoric cliff. Taegen had jumped all on her own.

"Darkness consumes the night,
I can barely breathe.
Immobile, can't move,
Look what you've done to me."

Taegen let it all out on the powerful ending of the song, giving it everything she had in her. At the end of the song, she met Torrey's eyes and extended her arm to him. Yes, she chose him She wanted him. Only him. He had thrown her entire world into turmoil. He had turned it upside down.

He had brought color and life back into her cold, stale existence. He reminded her what passion was.

Torrey had never, in all his dealings with women, felt what he felt for Taegen in that moment. He wanted to weep at her genuineness and the fact that she was so willing to open herself up like that. The woman he had met several days ago would never have done what she just had. He was impressed that she was trying so hard to get out of her routine and let herself feel again. He stood and threw some money on the table. "Maxim," he said.

Maxim looked up from where he was eating voraciously.

"I'm going to take Taegen and catch a cab to Berkeley. I'm going to pick her car up there. Then"—he held up the bag from the store and grinned—"I have something I have to do." He handed Maxim the keys to his car. "You drive back to my house. You seem responsible, and I don't know if I trust Javan yet."

Javan looked up from his plate and frowned. "Whats'at supposed to mean?" he asked, food falling out of his mouth.

Alyx made a face. "It means you're a barbarian," she said. "Geez, go back to decimating your dinner and call us when you come out of the cave."

Javan shrugged and continued to stuff his face.

"Hey Torrey," Maxim said, standing also, "where are you going to take her?"

"Out by Point Bonita is Rodeo Beach. I'm going to take her there. The moon is supposed to be full tonight."

Maxim smiled.

Torrey turned and met Taegen halfway across the room. She said nothing as he took her into his arms, but she trembled slightly. He stroked her hair and pressed a kiss to her forehead. "Come on," he whispered, "let's go get your car."

She stiffened. He wanted to take her home? She fought the tears that sprung to her eyes and she pushed away from him.

Torrey frowned. "What is it?"

"I can take myself home," she snarled. After she had opened up to him, chosen him...

He smiled and touched her cheek. "I never said I was taking you home. All I said was that we were going to get your car. It has to be done sometime." His smile morphed into a very desirable grin. "You think that after that performance and declaration I'll ever let you go again?"

She let her breath out slowly, relief washing over her.

He took her hand in his. "Come on," he urged. "I'm tired of the crowd in here. I just want to be with you right now."

She nodded and they started out of the restaurant.

Alyx grinned. "I think they're so cute together," she said to Maxim.

"Do you know where Rodeo Beach is?" he questioned.

"No, but it would be easy enough to find. Why?"

He grinned. "No reason."

Chapter Sixteen

San Lorenzo

Taegen frowned as Torrey turned off on the exit to her home. She felt a twinge in her heart, and she looked over at him. He sat so calmly. Her heart twisted. He'd said he didn't want to take her home, but here she was. She wanted to cry. He really didn't want her. She had decided to take the chance and risk getting hurt, and now he was going to just discard her. Had he been playing with her the whole time? She curled herself against the seat. She was a gullible idiot.

Torrey noticed her retreat and he sighed. He reached his hand over and covered hers. "Stop it, Taegen," he said softly.

She blinked and frowned at him.

"Please trust me a little," he urged. "I told you I wasn't going to leave you."

She did cry then. His tenderness undid her. How had he known? How did he always know? She put her face in her hands and just let 'er rip. He was too good to be true. He couldn't want her. He was perfect and she was just Taegen. Plain, uninteresting, completely psychotic Taegen. She had grief issues, and she had regular conversations with herself. Her analytical mind was full of more chaos than it had ever been. If she was him, she would hit the road real fast.

Torrey pulled up in front of Taegen's house and shut the engine off. He dragged her into his arms and held her close, nuzzling her hair. "I won't hurt you, Taegen," he assured her. "I won't abandon you, and I won't crush your heart."

She pressed closer to him, shaking horribly. "Why me?" she cried. "Why in the world did you choose me? Look at me. I'm a mess."

He chuckled. "You act like I deliberately sought you out," he said, running his hand down the length of her hair. "I would be a fool to ignore a beautiful girl when she's practically handed to me." He moved back slightly and gently wiped at her tears. "And you're not a mess. You're just trying to cope with some bad things that happened to you. I understand that. I don't think you're crazy." He smiled as he continued to trace the contours of her face. "I thought you were breathtaking on that train. I would have made a move on you then if I hadn't been so preoccupied with my drawing. I'm glad it worked out the way it did. It makes our story so much more interesting."

She looked up into his eyes and his smile stopped her heart. She shook her head. "Yesterday was horrible," she sniffed. "All I wanted was you. Why?" She rubbed at her eyes, feeling self-conscious and confused. "I was so used to living the way I was living. I was used to being alone, and used to not caring about anyone. You changed all of that in one night, Torrey, and I don't understand how." Was it because he had reminded her of what Paul's life had been all about? Because he had made her realize that she was living a life he would have hated her to live? Because he had made her remember for a minute what it felt like to laugh and tease and share herself with another person?

He studied her eyes for a moment. "We don't always have to understand why our hearts cry out for what they do. I just know that I think I could love you, if you let me."

Taegen coughed. "L-Love?" she stammered. Love. That word didn't exist in her world, and hadn't for some time. Love brought pain. Love brought suffering. *Don't be stupid, Taegen. You've waited your whole life for this man and you know it so stop acting so shocked.*

It was true... He was everything she had ever dreamed about. She didn't really know how she knew that, but she did. Her heart did know him. It welcomed him as if it had been waiting for him for all time. He was slowly consuming her just the way that Bleeding Passion song had described.

He grinned. "You should be pleased. Winning my heart is no easy task. I'm picky when it comes to women."

She wiped at her runny nose, trying to be discreet. The last thing she wanted was to look like a snot queen. "All women love you," she said. "You're like a male siren."

He laughed softly. "Women can gawk and lust all they want. Unless I see something special, I don't bother looking."

She fixed him with a withered expression. "Well, I see you like to go for the ones with mental problems. I don't exactly know if that should concern me."

"You don't have mental problems, Taegen. You're just recovering from a terrible loss. Now,"—he held up the bag—"go put this on."

She frowned. "Excuse me?"

"Promise you'll go in your house and put this on. Don't look until you're in there. You have to promise to wear it."

She raised an eyebrow. "I'm not putting on anything until I know what it is. It could be a see-through thong for all I know, or one of those peek-a-boo bras!"

Torrey blinked and held up his hands. "Generally, I wait until the third date to buy my lady something like that."

She giggled and felt her cheeks turn pink.

He dropped the bag into her lap. "Trust me," he whispered.

She suppressed a shiver. It was impossible to disagree when he spoke that way. "Fine," she said with a mock-exasperated sigh, "but I refuse to come back out here if it's something scary."

He nodded, his eyes sparkling like the stars in the sky. "Fair enough."

Taegen took the bag and got out of the car. "You can come in, you know," she called through the window. She knew her home was a mess, but she didn't care. If Torrey wanted to be with her, he would have to tolerate the dusty cabinets, dirty dishes, and strewn clothing as well. She liked to be comfortable, and that's what her house was. Plus, she had been suffering from severe depression for the past two years. Housecleaning kind of went on the backburner when that happened. She was just glad that she had started jogging again the month before. Otherwise, he would have had to love her messy house as well as the tubs of ice cream that had gone straight to her thighs. "Make yourself at home," she said as she made her way into the bedroom.

Torrey remained standing. He was pleased she had invited him in and was letting him catch a glimpse of her world. He wanted to learn all he could about her, but he didn't want her to think he was pushing in any way. The only way he would step into Taegen's life would be if he was invited.

He hoped he'd gotten the dress in the right size. He would wind up being very embarrassed if she was either popping out or it was falling off. He blinked. Then again...

San Francisco

Alyx and Maxim glanced at Javan, who had promptly fallen asleep on Torrey's sofa. Alyx shook her head and laughed. "What is his problem?" she asked. "He sleeps more than all of us combined. It's only nine o'clock!"

Maxim chuckled. "Selective narcolepsy."

"He's probably just power napping."

Maxim wasn't paying attention to the movie they were watching. His mind was on the poem he had hastily scrawled on that napkin, and he was also thinking about Torrey and Taegen. He frowned in thought. "Hey Alyx, you say you can find Rodeo Beach?"

She looked away from the television and shrugged. "Yeah, probably. Why?"

"Torrey was taking Taegen there," he explained. "He bought her this beautiful dress, and he was going to take her to the beach for a romantic evening." He shrugged. "I kind of wanted to..." He let the sentence remain unformed. He probably sounded like a complete dork. What kind of self respecting man wanted to help one of his friends seduce a girl by providing romantic ambiance?

"What?" Alyx prodded, obviously intrigued. "Come on, Max, what are you thinking?" She jerked her thumb in the direction of the television. "Anything's better than looking at Antonio Banderas's naked butt."

Maxim looked up at her and a slow grin spread across his lips. Oh, what the heck? "I need a battery operated CD player," he declared.

San Lorenzo

Taegen shook so badly that she thought her legs would give out. She had put the dress on, amazed that he had gotten it, but she hadn't realized how perfect it looked on her until she gazed at her reflection in the mirror. Tears hovered on her lashes. She couldn't believe he had done such a generous and loving thing. It was gorgeous, and it fit like it was made for her. How had he guessed her size so correctly? She wiped the tears from her eyes hastily and decided to make herself look presentable. She didn't know what Torrey had planned, but she wasn't going to go along with it red-nosed and puffy-eyed. She washed her face and began to apply some makeup. Torrey had seen her looking frazzled and Plain Jane both days he had been with her. It was time he saw her looking her best.

And it was about time she felt beautiful again too.

* * * *

Torrey was still in the living room, studying Taegen's pictures of family and friends. There were several framed pictures on her entertainment center. Three of them were of her with a blond man who looked a little like her. He could only assume it was her brother. In one picture, they were standing in front of The Grand Canyon, and in another, they were sitting in the teacups at Disneyland. Taegen looked a lot younger in that one, maybe in her teens. The other one was of the two of them laughing and squeezing the life out of one another. Torrey sighed. It was apparent how happy her brother had made Taegen. In every picture she was with him, she was grinning. He couldn't imagine losing not only your brother, but your best friend as well.

He stuffed his hands in his pockets and turned right as she stepped from the hallway. His breath caught in his throat at the sight of her. The icy dress looked like it had been tailored to fit only her, and she had put her flaxen hair up into a French twist. She'd done her makeup simple, but it made her beauty so much more prominent. He let his breath out slowly and stepped toward her. He ran his hands up her arms and let his eyes wander over her. "You look like a piece of art," he whispered in awe. "I've never seen anything as beautiful as you."

Taegen looked down in an attempt to hide a blush. "I can't believe you got me this."

"It was purely for selfish reasons," he teased. "I wanted to see if you really were my dream woman."

She smiled shyly. "And what is your conclusion?"

He touched a piece of hair that was too short for the twist and hung to frame her face. "You are so much better."

Taegen drew in a soft breath and looked away.

"I was looking at your pictures," he said. "I hope you don't mind."

She shook her head and glanced over at her entertainment center with a pained smile. She went to the one of the Grand Canyon and picked it up. "You know, it kills me to look at these," she said, her voice catching, "but I can't take them down." She felt like, if she did, he really would be gone.

Torrey stood next to her and ran his hand consolingly across her shoulders. "Of course you can't," he said. "You want to keep him with you."

She nodded sadly, then stared at the picture and smiled. "We went to Arizona on a spur of the moment road trip once. Paul was always forcing me into these spontaneous things that usually almost gave me a heart attack." She laughed, then sobered. "We had so much fun. We had almost no money between the two of us and spent the whole time sleeping in the car and eating the cheapest and greasiest fast food we could find." She laughed again. "And his car was this awful, beat up piece of crap that only played one station and that was the Mexican one." She shook her head as the memory came rushing back. "We blew a tire and, after we fixed it, the car started to overheat a half hour later. We had to turn the heater on to keep it cool. Imagine driving through *Arizona* in the middle of the summer with the heater on."

He chuckled and picked up the other one of them in Disneyland. "What about this one?"

She giggled. "Oh my gosh, that was right after my high school graduation. He took me to Disneyland. Mary was so jealous."

"Mary?"

"My sister. She never understood our relationship. She had nothing in common with either of us."

"When was that one taken?" He pointed to the one of them hugging and laughing.

Her smile faded. "Right before he died," she whispered. "It's my favorite... I can still feel his arms around me." A tear slipped down her cheek and she wiped it away, looking down.

Torrey pulled her against him and held her gently. "I'm

so sorry, Taegen."

"It was my fault," she whimpered.

"What?"

"It was my fault. He wanted to stay at my house that night and help me study for my exam. I told him no. If he'd stayed...he would still be alive."

Torrey sighed. "Taegen, that was not your fault. You had no way of knowing."

"But I could have prevented it." She shook her head and squeezed her eyes shut as waves of pain washed over her. "He should be here, Torrey. I want him to meet you. He would have liked you. And I know you would have liked him too."

"I'm sure I would have." He pulled back and lifted her face in his hands. "But I can still know him through your memories...if you're willing to share them with me."

She sniffled and forced a small laugh. "You'll have to stock up on tissues."

He grinned and wiped away her remaining tears. "I'll find a Costco and buy them in bulk."

She smiled in spite of herself. She shook her head as if to dispel her saddening thoughts. "Okay, enough of that. I don't want to get mascara all over you again, and I don't think this dress was made with the intention of having its wearer blubber all night in it."

He grinned. "Very well, my dear. Would you like to make the most of your night?"

She gazed up into his eyes and felt dizzy. He was so, so very *kind*. She didn't know what to do with his kindness. It was foreign to her. Her family tended to be a little on the cold side. Paul was the only one who'd felt things like she did. The rest of her family was of the mindset that you should just bulldoze your way through your problems and continue on with life like everything was fine. It was why she didn't really talk to her family about Paul. They would just tell her to get a therapist.

What she had needed was someone to show her genuine care and compassion. The way Torrey did. "Torrey," she breathed, "I will follow you anywhere."

A small smile touched his lips and his soft hands continued to caress her shoulders. "Don't do that, Taegen," he said. "Don't ever lose yourself in someone else. I see that you feel very deeply, but never feel that you have to follow a man anywhere. I want you to trust me, yes, but do not let your attraction to me drive your decisions."

She continued to stare up into his beautiful eyes. "Attraction?" she questioned. "You think my attraction to you drives my decisions?" She reached up and let her fingers trace the beautiful, sculpted lines of his cheeks, jaw, and mouth. She realized that it was the first time she had actually touched him first. "My heart drives my decisions, nothing else. For once in my life."

Torrey stared at her for a moment and pulled her just close enough so that their bodies were touching in a way that sent erotic electrical currents between the two of them. "And what does your heart decide?" he whispered against her lips.

She let her eyes close and touched her lips to his. She couldn't have stopped herself if she'd tried. She needed to kiss him. His kiss made her feel warm when she had been cold for so long.

His lips moved over hers softly as he took the time to explore the feeling of her. He was surprised when he felt her tongue tentatively touch his bottom lip, and he opened his mouth for her. Her taste assaulted him and his knees nearly buckled with the feeling of her tongue caressing his. He hadn't expected such a bold move from her, but he certainly wasn't going to complain. Every time Taegen revealed another facet of her personality, the more he realized that he didn't want to ever be without her.

He forced himself to pull away. "Come with me?" he rasped.

She nodded, her heart pounding. His eyes were dark and smoldering, and it was suddenly difficult to breathe. Holy cow, the man could kiss.

She let him take her hand and lead her back out into the night. She felt kind of silly walking out onto the street wearing an evening gown while Torrey was dressed only in black slacks and a black button down shirt, un-tucked as always, but he had an elegance about him that made him seem dressier than he was. The man could wear a paper bag and still look sexy.

They got into the car and Taegen leaned back against the seat, feeling more complete than she had in her whole life. Torrey made her feel so special. She had been so terrified that she'd blown it and would never see him again. The fact that he was with her now was incredible. She glanced at him and reached out to touch his face. She needed to sample his beauty just once more.

Torrey smiled and caught her hand in his, pressing a kiss to her palm.

She sighed in contentment and turned on the radio.

"...Fat Stinky opening for Bleeding Passion tomorrow at the Warfield," the DJ was saying. "That should be an awesome show."

Torrey grinned. "Yeah, and thanks to Javan, we'll be going," he said.

She smiled. "I really did think he was cute," she teased.

He scowled. "Yeah, I won't bring up that you told *him* your name."

"I was afraid I'd find someone else like you and blow it again."

He snorted. "Yeah, well, little did you know that I just sent Javan in as a spy for me."

"Whatever," Taegen laughed. "Javan picked me up all on his own."

"Shown up by Javan," he muttered. "What's the world coming to?"

She laughed again.

"...Apparently Fat Stinky's bassist quit right before the show in Sacramento," the DJ continued. "Walked out or something. Guess they had to hire some local guy real quick. Supposed to be real good, though. Named Darren Hayes..."

Torrey's eyes widened. "Darren Hayes?" He laughed. "I know him! I went to college with him! He was in my music theory class and in my band!"

Taegen looked over at Torrey in disbelief. "Are you serious?" she squeaked. "You know the bassist of Fat Stinky?"

"I guess I do now. That's cool!"

She shook her head. People like Torrey should be cloned and mass produced. It would definitely make the world a much more interesting place.

Chapter Seventeen

Rodeo Beach

Maxim had managed to locate a portable CD player and a burned CD labeled "Torrey's art music." It had slow, instrumental songs along with some rock on it that would suit his purposes just as well. They had left Javan snoring on the couch and had been able to find Rodeo Beach with a little bit of difficulty.

The turn off to get to Point Bonita was only accessible from the inbound side of the Golden Gate Bridge, and it was in such a weird place that they'd had to drive back and forth over the bridge three times before they'd finally found it. Then they'd had to navigate up a mountain on a winding dirt road in the fog. And, of course, there'd been no guard rails of any sort. Maxim's hands had been sweating the entire time. He was just relieved they had arrived in one piece.

"Now, all we need to do is find Torrey and Taegen," he said as they parked in the Point Bonita YMCA parking lot.

"Yeah, and we need to figure out how we're going to get down to that beach without killing ourselves," Alyx muttered.

There was a small cliff they had to climb down in order to get to the beach and, while it wasn't that steep, the path was rather treacherous. The foggy night air blasted them as they got out of the car. Alyx shivered into her sweatshirt, stuffing her hands in her pockets.

Maxim pulled out the CD player and a backpack from the trunk. He turned and went to Alyx. The moon was high in the sky, making the fog seem like milky tendrils.

"This place is beautiful," she murmured, taking a good look around.

"Yeah, Torrey has good taste." The wisping fog made everything seem unreal, like a fantasy from a dream. Maxim glanced at Alyx, whose face was highlighted by moonlight. It caused her to look pale and delicate and it made him want to touch her so badly that he had to glance away. He hefted the backpack onto his shoulder and started toward the cliff.

* * * *

Taegen tugged her coat closer around her, shivering with the dampness of the fog. Torrey put his arm around her and pulled her against him as they walked down the beach. The ocean was thunderous, its waves crashing against the shore violently.

"My intent was not to have you freeze to death," Torrey said as he rubbed his hand up her arm. "I just wanted to share this with you….and I wanted to take your picture."

She frowned. "What?"

He grinned down at her. "Look." He pointed to a large boulder just out of the way of the pounding waves. "Stand on it, Taegen," he urged. "Let me see if you're my dream woman."

Taegen felt a flush creep into her cheeks and she smiled. "You just happen to have a camera handy?"

"It was actually in my glove compartment, if you can believe it. Sometimes when I'm out, I see things that are particularly beautiful. I like to capture them and use the images for my drawings."

She stepped away from Torrey and pulled her coat off. She discarded it, as well as her shoes. She held her arms out, ignoring the cold fog licking across her bare arms. "Do I look all right?"

His smile was soft, and he reached out to remove the pin holding her hair. Her golden tresses fell in thick waves around her shoulders and turned platinum in the moonlight. He ran his fingers through the silken strands and sighed. "You look like a goddess," he breathed.

Her face went crimson and she looked away. With a bashful smile, she turned and headed toward the rock. She stepped up onto it carefully and held her arms out. "Like this?"

His heart melted at the sight of her. He pulled his camera

from his pocket. "Just like that," he said. "Now, look happy."

Taegen laughed. "I *am* happy!"

He was quick to snap while she was laughing. It was perfect. She looked as if she'd stepped directly from his painting, thus stepping right out of his subconscious fantasies. He took a few more for good measure then put his camera back into his pocket. "You are radiant, Taegen," he murmured.

She smiled, loving the feeling of the damp tendrils of fog curling around her. She was cold, but it was invigorating. It made her feel alive after feeling stagnant for so long. She closed her eyes and sighed, letting the sounds of the ocean surround her. For the first time since her brother had died, she actually was happy. Torrey made her forget all her pain. All she felt was joy when she was with him.

"Watch out for the wave behind you, Taegen," he called. "It's kind of enormous."

She turned to look at the incoming wave and hurried to step down from the rock. She stubbed her toe on a jagged edge and started to plummet forward, her dress making it difficult to catch herself. Torrey instantly covered the distance between them and caught her in his arms, falling backwards onto the sand. She landed on top of him and he looked up at her, gazing deeply into her eyes. The wave crashed behind them with a deafening roar, sending tiny droplets of salty spray over them.

She froze, unable to take her eyes from his. He looked so sexy lying there in the sand, his eyes dark with their burning intensity. She wanted to stare into those eyes forever, to know that he only looked at her with that heated expression.

He reached up to brush her cheek with his fingers and he closed his eyes as if savoring the texture of her skin. His arm tightened around her waist and he rolled her beneath him. She found it impossible to breathe. Torrey's body blanketed hers with gentle strength, and the wind tossed his hair carelessly. His eyes held her in their power, and she could do nothing other than lose herself in them.

"I see you have a few dominant qualities," she teased, making a stab at humor.

His easy smile gleamed white against the black of night, and he shrugged one shoulder. "Just a few." He whispered it over her lips and he took her hand in his, raising her arm above her head so that he could press closer to her. "Do you trust me?"

She giggled. "Not at all."

He grinned broadly and lowered his lips to hers in a teasing caress. Her fingers tightened around his and he pressed his mouth fully to hers. She began to tremble and he deepened the kiss, coaxing her to follow him down an erotic path that she was powerless to resist. The velvet touch of his mouth and tongue made her shaking increase. He pulled away, looking concerned.

"Taegen, you don't need to shake like that," he assured. "I won't hurt you."

She blinked and tried to comprehend what he was saying. Her mind reeled from the touch of his lips, and all she wanted was to feel them again. Now was not the time for talking. Even her meddlesome inner voice had silenced its opinion for the moment, thank goodness.

He sighed. "I don't want to push you, Taegen," he said. "Would you like me to stop?"

"No!" she protested. Was he insane? She shook her head. "Don't you understand, Torrey?" She reached her free hand up to run it down his jaw. "It's your touch that makes me tremble. I'm not afraid. *You* make me tremble...for all kinds of reasons, but not from fear."

Torrey stared at her in wonderment, obviously surprised by her admission. He smiled and lowered his lips to hers again, deliberately teasing her mouth with his. He tasted each of her lips, playing with them until her free hand came up to tangle in his hair. He let out something between a groan and a growl and pressed lingering kisses along her jaw. "I know I will never get enough of you," he whispered.

She closed her eyes, wanting to die of bliss. His kisses were like sampling heaven. It was wrong that someone should kiss the way Torrey did. Everything about him was just sinful. A small noise of pleasure escaped her throat and she ran her hand down his shoulders, relishing the feel of him. She had thought she'd messed up so badly, letting him go the way she had. She would have to remember to thank Javan later. If it hadn't been for him, she wouldn't be here right now. She probably never would have found Torrey again.

She sighed contentedly into Torrey's kiss as his lips claimed hers once more, holding him as close to her as she could. She wouldn't give him up again without a fight. He was worth fighting for. She felt his hand come up to cradle her face as he explored her mouth with gentle passion. Her world began to spin. There was no one like Torrey. She didn't want anyone but him.

* * * *

Maxim was having trouble making his way down the cliff. They had spotted Taegen and Torrey, who were now in the midst of a rather...private moment, and they were trying desperately to be quiet. This was difficult to do while climbing down a badly marked trail with a backpack and a portable CD player. It briefly occurred to him that there had to be an easier way down considering Taegen was in an evening gown. Leave it to him to pick the difficult way.

"Maxim," Alyx whispered, turning to face him. "Be careful. There's a root sticking out down here."

He stepped closer to Alyx. "Huh?" His foot caught on the very root she had warned him about and he went plowing right into her. Her eyes widened and she held her hands out to try and catch him, but it was all downhill...literally. She fell backwards and Maxim went rolling over her. He tried to balance his weight so that he could stop, but it was useless. He did something of a somersault and landed at the bottom of the cliff, followed by Alyx who had managed to half-run down it. The CD player went flying and landed itself behind a dune. *Moonlight Sonata* started to play instantly.

"Maxim!" Alyx whispered frantically. "Are you okay?"

He grabbed her arm and pulled her down next to him. He started crawling commando style toward the dune.

Alyx followed him, stifling laughter. "What are we doing?"

* * * *

Torrey blinked and pulled away from Taegen with a frown. Was that...*Moonlight Sonata*?

Taegen frowned also. "What is that?"

"It's...music," he replied, perplexed. He stood and offered his hand to her, helping her up.

* * * *

"We can't let them see us," Maxim said. "That would ruin the entire plan." He examined the CD player, which was now sitting placidly, amazingly unharmed.

"That's a terrible plan," Alyx laughed. "They'll come searching for us if we don't let them know somehow. Phantom music isn't a normal occurrence."

Maxim peered over the hill. He wanted to laugh aloud at the confused expression on Torrey's face. He jumped up and waved wildly to get his attention while Taegen's back was turned.

* * * *

Torrey frowned as he suddenly saw Maxim pop up from behind a nearby hill. Sand poured out of his hair and he looked entirely too pleased with himself. He gave a dramatic thumbs up and Torrey chuckled. He caught Taegen around the waist to keep her from turning to see Maxim, and he curled his hand into a thumbs up behind her back.

"What's going on?" Taegen questioned as Torrey took her in his arms and began to sway softly to the music.

"Oh nothing," he said, "but I do believe we may have stumbled upon a couple of very cool friends."

Taegen didn't quite understand, but Torrey no longer seemed concerned with where the music was coming from, so she leaned her head against his shoulder and closed her eyes as they danced. The song switched from *Moonlight Sonata* to *Dolphin's Cry* by Live and he pulled her closer, burying his face in her neck. He sang the words against her skin, making her shiver.

* * * *

Alyx smiled. "Maxim, look," she whispered. She peered over the edge of the hill and Maxim joined her. Torrey and Taegen were completely fixed on one another. No one else existed to them.

Maxim smiled. Mission accomplished.

* * * *

Torrey sang the entire song to Taegen, murmured the words in her ear. He sang all the way through the second chorus, but then he couldn't concentrate on the music any longer. He pulled back, took her face in his hands, and gazed directly into her eyes before he crushed his lips to hers, deciding right then that he would never let this woman go if he had anything to do with it. No one had ever made him feel so intensely in such a short amount of time. Taegen was special, and she was his.

Chapter Eighteen

Maxim and Alyx sank back down below the hill and leaned against it. Alyx glanced over at Maxim and smiled. "They're very dynamic," she observed. "I can almost see the sparks fly when they're together."

He nodded, shaking more sand out of his hair. "I'm going to be hurting tomorrow," he chuckled.

"That was the funniest thing I've ever seen."

"Glad I could amuse you. My backpack nearly strangled me."

"And then with the soldier belly crawling!" She laughed.

He joined in her laughter. "I was just trying to do something nice!"

She sighed and reached over to touch his hand. "You're always nice, Maxim, and such a romantic."

He looked up at her and a shiver went through him. If she had any idea how her touch made him feel... He let his eyes roam over her moonlit face and thought of what Javan had said earlier. *"Alyx never smiles empty smiles with you..."* He swallowed and his heart beat just a little faster as he turned his hand palm up to hold hers. "Do you want to hear what I was working on?" he queried, running his thumb across the back of her hand.

Alyx frowned in question.

"At the restaurant," he explained. "My idea?"

Her eyes brightened. "Yes!"

He reached for his bag. "It's actually not an idea," he said. "It's a poem." She sat up straighter as he rummaged through his bag and pulled out the near-demolished napkin from the Amazing Psychotic. "It's not going to get any points for presentation," he laughed, trying to mask his nervousness.

She smiled.

He glanced up at her and took a deep breath. He briefly wished that the boldness demon that had possessed him earlier would return, but it refused. He was going to have to go it alone. He let his breath out slowly and tried to still the shaking in his hands.

"Maxim."

He looked up at her. She gazed at him with an understanding that broke his heart.

"It's okay," she assured. "Don't be nervous. I won't laugh at you."

"That's not what I'm worried about," he whispered. She frowned, but he waved it away and turned back to his napkin.

"I have never known true wonder,
Until now.
I have gazed upon the shimmering waters
Of a tranquil sea,
And felt completely at peace.
I have stared up at a star-filled sky,
And felt awe untold.
I have listened to the wind in the pines,
And have known
There is nothing greater
Than the world around me.
I have had my greatest inspiration staring at the sunset,
Bathing the sky in a tapestry of color,
And yet,
Those shimmering waters are nothing
Compared to the peace you give me.
They cannot quiet my restless heart
As you can.
And the stars hold no power
When matched with your intelligence.
That is truly an awe-inspiring thing.
The wind cannot compete with
The sound of your voice.
And, even when twined in the trees,
It is forced and droning
Compared to the grandeur with which you speak.
And there has never been anything to inspire me

As much as you.
You cause the words to flow from me
Like water bursting from a dam.
You evoke my best work.
You are my muse.
The sunset pales
When next to you.
And as we continue to live and breathe,
The waters will flow,
The wind will blow,
The stars will shine,
And the sun will set.
But all these things lose a little more power
Each time you step into my life.
You are the true definition of wonder.
I have found you at last."

He finished up with a shaky breath and glanced at Alyx, who stared at him in awe.

"That was absolutely beautiful. The imagery was wonderful."

He swallowed and looked down. "It was about you," he blurted.

She sucked her breath in sharply and she stared at him. "Me?"

He nodded, still not looking up. He couldn't. He was too afraid that he would see rejection in her eyes.

Alyx couldn't formulate any words. That beautiful poem… He had written it for her? "Maxim…" She sighed. She shook her head. She didn't think men wrote poetry anymore. Not like that. Not romantic poetry from the heart. It was one reason why she loved Shakespeare so much. Everyone spoke in poetry. After a day of listening to men use horrid pick-up lines, or yammer on about the Lakers and video games, there was nothing she loved more than to go to work and lose herself in a world that no longer existed. When poetry was the language of love, and men were courteous and kind.

She really hadn't thought that chivalry existed anymore. And sensitive men? Well, she'd given up on them too. Especially after Rick.

But Maxim… "Why?" she questioned.

He swallowed, still staring down at his lap. "Because…"

He took a deep breath. "Because you're exquisite, Alyx. There is no other word to describe you."

She stared at him. She thought of Rick again. The nicest thing he'd ever done for her was get her flowers. This was so much more than flowers. This was Maxim's art. He had created this for her. She felt tears sting her eyes and she bit her bottom lip. Exquisite. He thought she was exquisite. She glanced at Maxim, who looked as if he was preparing himself for the end of the world. He sat with his shoulders hunched and his head down, expecting the worst. She smiled and reached out to touch his hair.

Maxim blinked and his breath caught audibly. He looked at her and she knew he saw the pure emotion in her eyes.

"Thank you," she whispered. "Thank you so much."

He gave her a shy smile and shrugged.

She shook her head. "You don't understand," she said in a choked voice. "That meant so much to me."

He was quick to catch the tear that made its way down her cheek, wiping it away like it was second nature. Her eyes fluttered closed at his touch. He was so gentle, so kind. Her throat tightened painfully and she leaned against him, hiding her face against his chest. He felt strong at that moment, a tower of refuge for her.

Maxim's arms crept around her and he pulled her closer. *Pachelbel in D* was now weaving its haunting melody through the night and he sighed, resting his head on top of hers. "I meant all of those words," he murmured. "Everything."

She wiped her eyes and positioned herself so that she was more comfortable but still in Maxim's arms. She rested her head on his shoulder and heaved a sigh. "When I was a little girl, I was a hopeless romantic," she said suddenly. "I guess I still am, but I was like a fairytale princess back then. I would watch *Cinderella* and *Beauty and the Beast* every day." She smiled. "I would even try to get myself into trouble, convinced that my Prince Charming would come and rescue me. Unfortunately, my Prince Charming always wound up being my brother. Then I would have to endure Javan's merciless teasing."

Maxim allowed himself to play with her luxurious hair. He ran a few strands through his fingers, marveling at the silkiness of it. "You say you and Javan have always been friends?"

She nodded. "Our families knew one another. Javan lived down the street from me. He used to come over and play *Zelda* all the time with Alexi. We went to school together too. He's been my best friend for as long as I can remember."

Maxim smiled.

"Anyway," she continued, "I grew out of that phase, but the romantic dreams have always been with me. I dated two guys in high school. Both relationships lasted for two years. The first one, Greg, was in the drama department with Javan and me. I played his wife in a play once and I guess we rehearsed the kissing scenes too many times. He was very intense, a typical artist, very temperamental. He couldn't separate his life from his work. His work was his life. I fell second and that was a lonely place to be.

"The other guy was Lucas Lord." She shook her head. "Just his name was enough to make girls swoon. He was the most popular guy in school, the quarterback, very cute."

He grinned.

"I don't really know what he saw in me. We had nothing in common. After I realized that if I stayed with him, I would be spending the better part of my life with a guy who couldn't add two and two, I moved on. Lucas was my last serious relationship before Rick."

Maxim briefly wondered why she was telling him all of this, but he just pulled her closer and listened. He could listen to her forever. He wanted to know about her past. He wanted to know about her life and her thoughts and feelings. He wanted to know it all because everything about her seemed so beautiful to him.

"I was always searching for the prince," she went on. "To this day, I have some kind of sick Prince Charming obsession. I thought I'd found him in Rick. That guy was all charisma and charm." She shook her head. "Now that I think about it, he never really did make me feel special...not like you." She looked up at him, meeting his eyes. "You have made me feel special since the first time you called my apartment." She reached up to touch his cheek with her forefinger. "Perhaps the prince is not always the dashing warrior everyone is after." She let her hand rest on his chest, over his heart.

Maxim closed his eyes, feeling her touch in his very soul.

"Perhaps he is the one who remains quiet. The stoic one

with the beautiful eyes and kind heart. The one who is stronger than all the warriors in the land, but never lets anyone know it."

He felt like his heart was going to burst from pumping too hard. "Alyx," he whispered. He shook his head. "I think you're trying to kill me."

She smiled and curled her arm around his waist.

"How could anyone ever want to hurt you?" he asked.

She swallowed hard and looked away. "Just lucky, I guess." She sighed. "He beat me up so badly once that I had to take three days off of work and stay in bed. I always went back... I was *so stupid*!"

"No, Alyx. You *did* leave. A lot of people aren't that strong." He let his gaze roam over her beautiful face for a moment, and he sat up taller. "Where did he hurt you?" he asked. "Show me."

She frowned, but she knew she could never resist the look in those soft eyes. For some reason, he made her want to tell him things she usually just kept inside. She placed her hand over her stomach, remembering how he had kicked her.

Maxim placed his hand over the spot she touched and caressed his thumb over it tenderly. "Where else?"

She reached one trembling hand to her right cheek. He feathered his fingers over it and let out a shaky breath. He leaned in and placed the lightest of kisses on her skin. Alyx closed her eyes at his touch and found it difficult to breathe. When he moved away, she touched her fingers to her once injured eye and he replaced her touch with his, soothing the painful memories and replacing every once marred spot with gentleness. Her eyes drifted closed again at the touch of his lips.

Maxim didn't know what was wrong with him. All he knew was that Alyx had confided in him, told him things in her heart, and she was still hurting. He would do anything to take away that pain. When he pulled away this time, she met his eyes and raised her hand slowly to her mouth. He winced inwardly. He had hurt her perfect mouth...the man should be dragged out and shot. He touched his fingers to her lips very softly, tracing their fullness. Something like electricity started to course through his veins and he couldn't hear anything for his own heart pounding in his ears. He brought his mouth closer to Alyx's, and saw her eyes close halfway in anticipation. It was all the invitation he needed.

He touched his lips lightly to hers, only wanting to heal, not alarm. When he pulled away, he was shaking slightly, but the look in Alyx's eyes was enough to stop his heart forever.

"I could live forever on kisses like that," she whispered. So gentle... He was so very gentle. No one had ever kissed her like that. Even the boyfriends she'd had before Rick. Even when they'd been gentle, their kisses had still seemed slightly possessive. As if they were claiming her for their own and reminding her of that fact. Maxim's kiss had been nothing like that. He didn't want anything from her, didn't want to take. He only wanted to offer comfort and warmth.

She searched his eyes and found only sincerity in their light blue depths. She reached up and touched his face, cupping his cheek in her palm and loving the roughness of his stubble underneath her fingers. There was a rugged man in there. She could see him even if Maxim couldn't.

His eyes closed and he leaned into her touch.

"I'm very happy you decided to come on this trip with us," she said. "My life is better because of you."

Maxim couldn't understand how he could make anyone's life better when he couldn't even manage his own, but he didn't have time to dwell on it. Alyx's lips found his again and the firm press of them made his blood turn from electricity to fire. She pulled his bottom lip into her mouth. He groaned, deepening his kiss and wrapping his arms around her. He lost all rational thought and let his hands run up her back to twine in her dark tresses. He wanted to drown in the taste of her, the pure sweetness of her. His tongue tangled with hers, and his mind was a blur of passion and Alyx. Just Alyx. All he wanted was her.

"Maxim," Alyx gasped, pulling away and collapsing against his chest. "Where did you learn to kiss like that?"

He blinked and tried to focus. "Don't know," he stated, trying to keep his head from spinning right off.

"Your kisses are like drugs," she said with a nervous laugh. "I just want more."

He smiled and his cheeks burned as he stroked her hair. "I'm not entirely opposed to that idea."

She lifted her head and grinned up at him, pressing her lips to his once more. She kissed him tenderly, relishing in the suppleness of his beautiful lips, and in the way he moved them over hers in such an ardent, seductive way. There was nothing demanding about his kiss, nothing harsh at all, but geez Louise... She could seriously see herself being his slave forever after kisses like that. They were pure, raw sensuality.

She knew he would laugh and get embarrassed if she told him that. The last thing he saw himself as was sensual, but the sexual energy radiating off him was incredible. In that moment, he had more chemistry and draw to him than Rick, or any of the other "charming" men she'd encountered. The vibe he threw off as he held and kissed her, and looked at her in that intense way, was enough to rival Torrey. It made her head swim in a deliriously intoxicating way and all she really wanted was to have more of him.

Maxim knew he could never possibly feel the same after this. These people, his friends, they were changing him. Alyx was changing him, making him better. He let out a shuddering breath and pulled her close to him, squeezing his eyes shut at the flood of emotion he felt so intensely. He wanted to hold her forever. He fought tears as she went pliant against him and wrapped her arms around his waist. For the first time in a very long time, the ache in his heart was completely and totally gone.

Chapter Nineteen

Alyx and Maxim returned before Torrey, and they found Javan awake with an enormous bowl of popcorn. He was watching something on television and glanced up at them when they entered. He frowned. "Oh, lo and behold, the deserters return."

Maxim set Torrey's CD player down and went to sit on the couch next to him. "It's not my fault you decided to turn into Rip Van Winkle."

"Where were you?" he asked.

"We snuck out to Rodeo Beach and played mood music for Taegen and Torrey," Maxim replied.

"Yeah," she laughed, "and Maxim did acrobatics down a cliff."

Maxim smiled and put his arm around her as she sat next to him. Javan blinked at the action in slight confusion.

"What are you watching?" Alyx asked.

"Something lame," Javan replied. "But it was either this or brain surgery, so I decided I would give my gag reflexes a break and just watch this." He frowned as Maxim pressed a kiss to Alyx's forehead. "What's up with you guys?"

Maxim reddened and Alyx grinned. She winked at Javan and he raised an eyebrow. "Maxim and I just had a good time," she replied vaguely.

Javan's eyes narrowed. "I'll just bet." He gave her a look that promised he would be interrogating her later.

Alyx simply smiled and pressed herself closer to Maxim. She couldn't seem to keep herself away from him after the intimate moment they'd shared at the beach. Even driving home, she'd attempted to hold his hand, but he'd almost had a heart attack. The fog was so thick and the road so treacherous that he'd had a death grip on the steering wheel and wasn't about to let go. So she'd settled with resting her palm on his thigh, which she was sure hadn't helped his nerves any. She just couldn't help it. She needed more of that warm connection.

She smiled as she settled against his chest and felt the tremendous pounding of his heart. She draped her arm across his waist and sighed in contentment.

* * * *

Torrey glanced at Taegen as they neared the freeway. He stopped the car close to the entrance and turned toward her.

She looked over at him and frowned. "What are you doing?"

He sighed and reached out to touch her hair. "You are at a crossroads, Taegen," he murmured.

She blinked. "A crossroads?" That didn't sound very good to her. Sounded too much like something a psychiatrist would say.

"One path is the one leading into the city...and my home. At my home sit three people." He smiled. "One of which should still be dumping sand out of his hair. Three people whom I am considering my friends. I enjoy their company, but I will tell you truthfully, Taegen, I will be lonelier than I've ever been in my life tonight if you are not with me."

Taegen's breath hitched in her throat. Was he saying what she thought he was saying? She closed her eyes, trying to rid herself of the images that filled her mind. Torrey's elegant body moving above her, his velvet hands on her body, his perfect mouth... She shook her head. Like she needed to be thinking about *that* right now. Her inner voice started to sing Queen's *We Will Rock You* suddenly and she flushed. She forced herself to think rationally. She was attracted to him on more than one level, but it was still too soon for her to take that step. Besides, if she was intimate with Torrey, she was pretty sure she would spontaneously combust.

Torrey smiled at Taegen's obvious thoughts. He held his hands up in an "unarmed" gesture. "I'm not like that," he said. "I'm not out for sex. I genuinely care about you." He shook his head and frowned. "Okay, that made me sound like every college jerk on the planet who's just looking for a good time."

She laughed as the tension eased.

He sighed. "What I mean is... I feel more for you than I should at this point. More than just attraction to your body, as tempting as that is. I am attracted to you in every way possible, and that means much more to me than just a night spent between the sheets."

Taegen's smile was shy; she was embarrassed at being so easy to read.

"The other path," he continued, "is the road leading you to your home. Everything you know is there and it's familiar and safe. You can return there, and that would be fine. I will call you tomorrow and see you then. However, if you wish, you can come to my house and stay there with the rest of us. There's no pressure," he assured. "Just the invitation."

Taegen stared at him, speechless. She glanced over to the city and sighed. It was so beautiful, sparkling like a diamond beacon full of hope and promises. She'd had so much fun with everyone today. Alyx, Javan, and Maxim were easy to get along with. They made her smile, and precious little made her smile anymore.

She glanced over at Torrey. He was waiting patiently for her answer. Always patient, never pushing. She smiled at him. Her life had been so dull a few days ago. Torrey had changed that. He made her see everything differently. He made her look at life in a perspective that was exciting and new.

She reached out and touched his hand. She didn't want to go back to what she knew. She didn't want to return to what she tried to convince herself was safe. Not now. Not after he'd made her remember what her brother's life had been all about. Not after she'd had a taste of feeling daring and free. Not after she'd had a taste of him. "It's like the song said," she murmured. "You're consuming me... And I like it."

Torrey had never actually thought it possible for one to feel their heart soar, but his did. He reached over and took Taegen's face in his hands. "Taegen," he whispered, "you are going to be the end of me." He kissed her full on the mouth, loving her softness and subtle passion.

Taegen wanted to spend the rest of her life kissing this man. She never wanted to leave him again. He was so beautiful, so different. He was everything that she wasn't but wished she had the courage to be. She pulled away and reached up to touch his face.

He smiled and pressed a kiss to her forehead. He shifted

the car into gear and started off toward his house before she had a chance to change her mind.

* * * *

Javan managed to fall asleep again while all three of them were watching television, and Maxim and Alyx decided to head to bed also.

"We have a big day tomorrow," Alyx remarked as they climbed the stairs. "Maybe we can go to the wharf before the concert."

Maxim made a face. "I'm still terrified over what you're going to dress me in."

She grinned. "It's not that bad."

They reached Alyx's room and she turned to face Maxim. He watched her calmly with his serene blue eyes. "I'm going to change into my pajamas," she said. "Give me five minutes. Then do you want to come in and talk for awhile?"

He smiled softly and nodded.

"All right. Five minutes."

He leaned in to kiss her cheek then pulled away with a twinkle in his eyes. "I look forward to it."

Her smile felt like a timid little girl's. "Me too." She fought the insane urge to giggle as she closed the door. Geez, what was this? Maxim made her have that stupid giddy teenager feeling. He made her forget that she had kissed several guys before him and had been in several relationships. He made her feel like she was doing everything for the first time all over again. It made her forget all about Rick, all about being hurt. It wasn't rebound attraction. It was genuine.

* * * *

Maxim watched Alyx disappear into her room and he went to his own. He was grinning like an idiot. He couldn't help it. He wanted to let out a really loud yell, and do one of those victory dances like the NFL football players did after a touchdown. It took every bit of self-control he had not to. He pulled out his cell phone instead and dialed Jeff. It took five rings before his brother finally answered.

"This had better be good, man," Jeff said. "I am really trying to pick up this girl, and you interrupted me in the middle of my best line."

Maxim rolled his eyes. "If it was that 'if I said you had a nice body, would you hold it against me' one you should thank me."

"So what's up?" Jeff asked.

"You're the best brother in the world," he said at the risk of sounding horribly silly.

"How did I manage this?"

"I kissed Alyx," he whispered confidentially.

"You *what*?"

"I don't even know what I was doing! We were on the beach talking..." He shrugged as if his brother could see it.

Jeff laughed. "Way to go, Maxim!" he exclaimed. "I'm totally proud of you!"

Maxim chuckled. "I'm writing again too." He shook his head. "It's like I'm awake after being asleep for a really long time."

He laughed again. "A good woman will do that to you!"

Maxim grinned. "Well, I'll let you go so you can get back to your woman."

"I'll talk to you tomorrow, Max," he said. "You can tell me all about it."

"Right, Old Lady Gossip. Talk to you later." He hung up the phone and shook his head. There was only one Jeff. He glanced at his watch and sniffed the armpits of his shirt for good measure. He checked himself over in a mirror that was hanging on the wall then made his way back down to Alyx's room. He took a deep breath and knocked lightly on the door. She opened it with a grin.

He smiled. "Hello."

She took his hand and pulled him into the room. "Hello," she said, kicking the door shut. She turned to him and wrapped her arms around his waist, resting her head against his chest. "I missed you." She squeezed her eyes shut, cleared her throat, and looked up at him. "Sorry, that sounded lame."

He raised an eyebrow. Lame? That had been music to his ears. He reached out to wrap a strand of hair around his fingers. "You think I'm going to think you're stupid for missing me?"

She blushed. "Well...it just sounded kind of sudden, I guess. I mean...I just saw you. Made me sound like a kid with a crush." She cleared her throat again and shrugged.

He chuckled. "You think you're going to scare me away?" He brought her raven waves to his lips. "It's not going to happen."

A funny tremor went through her heart as she watched him do that very simple gesture. She smiled and led him over to the bed. "Tell me something about yourself," she said.

He blinked in bewilderment as he took a seat next to her. "What do you mean?"

"Well, I told you all about myself earlier. I want to know more about you. I know you're shy, and I know about your family from Jeff, but other than that, all I really know is that you're a writer, know a lot about stars and literature, and are a magnificent kisser."

Maxim's face turned hot and he looked down at his hand, which was being caressed absently. He sighed, loving that feeling more than anything else in the world. "I've been alone my whole life," he murmured. "Jeff's been my only friend until now. Even Barrett and Meg don't really understand me. Barrett is very businesslike, very focused. He can't understand my passion for writing and he can't understand why I haven't accomplished anything yet. I imagine he thinks I'm worthless. Meg is more like Jeff. She's in college. She has so many friends that she doesn't even remember she has siblings... This is the first time in my life that I can remember ever having friends, Alyx. I know that sounds pathetic, but I never really cared for people. I mean, in high school there was this one guy who I used to pull out of the garbage can after the football team got through with him, but he wasn't really what I'd call a friend. My life has been very lonely. These past three days have been like a liberation for me."

Her smile was soft. "You aren't alone anymore."

He sighed and met her eyes.

She reached up and touched his jaw. "You will never be alone again. We are all your friends."

He leaned into her touch. "I thought my brother had lost it when he told me he'd volunteered me for this trip. I was so angry at him." He chuckled. "I'm really glad he made me come."

She leaned in close to him. "So am I," she whispered. She touched her lips to his and felt him shiver. It made her feel very desirable to know that her touch made him do that. It was empowering in the best way. She pulled back with a grin. "Tell me something else," she prodded.

He leaned back on the bed and began to tell her stories of his life, about Jeff and what he had put Maxim through over the years. He talked until they ran out of things and it was very late. They'd heard Torrey come home, and it sounded like Taegen might be with him, but they said nothing.

"I've never talked so much in my life," Maxim chuckled when he had finally exhausted his vocal cords.

Alyx gave a sleepy grin. "I like to listen to you talk."

He smiled and reached out to touch her cheek. "You look tired," he observed. "We should go to sleep. Tomorrow is going to be a very long day." He sat up.

She laughed and sat up as well. "Don't sound so enthused," she teased.

He stood, hating that he had to leave her. He was nowhere near being finished with gazing at her, or touching her, or listening to her talk. "Thank you for a beautiful night, Alyx," he said. "Sleep well." He turned to go, but stopped when she grabbed his hand.

"Maxim," she murmured.

He turned and gave her a gentle smile as his heart surged with hope. "Would you like me to stay?"

She swallowed and looked away, as if she felt ashamed. She nodded and glanced up at him. "Maybe you could…" She chewed on her bottom lip. "Sleep on the bed tonight?"

He blinked, and his heart flipped dramatically.

She averted her eyes. "I mean, if you want to. It has to be better than sleeping on the floor."

He watched her for a moment then tightened his fingers around hers. "That would be great," he said. "I never want to experience dead-butt again."

Alyx giggled and her expression reflected what almost looked like relief. Could she be happy that he wanted to stay with her? Could he actually offer her something worthwhile? Something that mattered?

He kicked his shoes off while she pulled the covers back on the bed. He tugged off his shirt and crawled beneath the comforter, trying to still the jackhammer that had replaced his heart. He took a chance when Alyx had settled herself, and he slipped his arm around her waist. "Is this okay?" he murmured, his body smoldering at the feel of her against him.

Alyx let out a contented sigh. "This is wonderful."

He grinned and gave her a little squeeze.

She relaxed into his hold and giggled. "Maxim."

He tried with all his might not to notice that magma had apparently replaced his usual blood flow. "Hm?"

"You're trembling."

He let out a nervous chuckle. "Yeah, I know."

She smiled and turned in his arms so she faced him. She placed one hand on his chest and traced the line of a muscle. In the pale light from the moon, she could see the rough outlines of his sculpted frame, and it made her blush. He was so strong, so cut. She never would have guessed that he was hiding a godlike physique underneath that shy exterior. "Are you sure you're not a super hero?"

He frowned. "Not the last time I checked. Why?" He forced the words out when all he really wanted to do was die. Die a fantastic, blissful death as her delicate hands trailed across his chest and abdomen, tracing every line and curve.

"Well, I'm just trying to figure out how you can claim to be such a recluse, but have such a delicious body."

Delicious. His entire body flamed at that word being used to describe him. He was embarrassed; he was elated. He was...really aroused. And that just made him blush even worse.

"I really like you," she admitted softly.

Maxim felt like he'd swallowed a basketball. "I really like you too."

She smiled. "Maybe we could stay like this. Y'know..." She shrugged. "Like a relationship."

Getting kicked in the chest didn't have as much power as those words. He drew in a breath that almost resembled a wheeze. "Relationship?"

She smiled. "If you want. I mean, I know I just got out of one and you probably think I'm just rebounding, but I really do like you, Maxim. You're different." She heaved a sigh and shook her head. "I was hoping maybe you might turn out to be my prince."

Maxim wanted to hold this woman forever. She was everything beautiful to him. Everything beautiful and pure and inspiring. He pulled her up close to him and pressed his forehead to hers. "I make no promises, Alyx," he said quietly. "I can only be what I am. I may never be your prince, but I can always be Maxim."

She closed her eyes and rested her head in the space be-tween his neck and his shoulder. "Maxim may be all I want," she whispered. She pressed a kiss to his neck and his body spasmed.

"I would be a fool not to try," he murmured, "but I am new at this."

"That's okay. It's nice to be with someone who doesn't think he knows it all."

He sighed. "Rest, Alyx. The first test of our relationship will come when I find out what you bought me tomorrow."

She giggled. "Goodnight, Maxim," she whispered.

"Goodnight." He lay awake for a long while after she fell asleep, marveling at the fact that he had such a soft, beauti-ful woman in his arms. His girlfriend... Alyx was his girlfriend now. He blinked at that realization. How had this happened? How had he managed this? It was insane... It was wonderful. He closed his eyes and let her warmth surround him. He had received the best of his life in only three days.

* * * *

Taegen swallowed uncomfortably upon reaching Torrey's bedroom. She didn't know what she was doing and she felt terribly awkward. As if sensing her unease, Torrey turned and offered her a warm smile as he removed her coat. "I forgot that you would need some clothes," he said, pressing a kiss to one shoulder. "You can wear some of mine until to-morrow. We can buzz you home before the concert." He hung both of their coats up and pulled a pair of sweatpants and a sweatshirt from one of his drawers. "Now, where would you like to sleep?" he asked. She met his eyes and he smiled softly. "My bed is open to you, as are my arms, but I don't know if you're that comfortable with me yet. You can sleep on the sofa if it would make you feel better."

She smiled. "Javan was sleeping on the sofa."

"Well, kicking him off would be easy enough."

She giggled and glanced around Torrey's room. It felt warm and welcoming, like him. The walls were light blue, the bedspread was a rich cream color, and beautiful works of art adorned the walls. She swallowed as her eyes fell on him. Yeah, like she was going to sleep on the sofa when she had a man like *that* standing in front of her. As rational as she was, even she wasn't that stupid. "I'll stay," she whispered.

He stared at her in surprise. "You will?"

She grinned. "Yeah." She reached out and took Torrey's hand in hers, liking that she had caught him off guard. She squeezed his hand and kissed his lips tenderly. Shockwaves went through her. "I'll be right back," she whispered with a smile.

Torrey nodded and watched her go to change. He let out a long breath and shook his head. That woman... He sat on the foot end of his bed and removed his shoes. He unbuttoned his shirt and donned a pair of loose-fitting, black drawstring pants. He heard Taegen re-enter and his heart leapt. He smiled. That was something he wasn't used to, but he liked it. He liked the way his heart and body reacted to her presence. He glanced at her over his shoulder and sighed.

She had been absolutely gorgeous in that dress, but there was something very attractive about seeing her in his couch potato attire. Even though he loved going out, a very large part of him was a homebody. He could see her staying in bed with him all day, watching movies and talking and...doing other things. Desire flared to life inside of him and he had to look away to collect himself.

Taegen grinned as she pulled the covers on the bed back and crawled beneath them. Torrey slid into bed beside her. She shivered as he pulled her close. "You smell really good, Torrey," she murmured. He felt really good too. He felt right. He felt like beauty and sanity and salvation. She didn't even want to think of what she would be doing if she wasn't with him. Sitting at home, crying probably. She never wanted to go back there again.

He sought her lips and gave her a long, drugging kiss. "Thank you for making the most of my night."

She snuggled closer to him. "Thank you for making the most of my life."

He gazed down at her and touched her cheek with tender fingers. "Sleep well, dear one."

She smiled and closed her eyes. "Will you be here when I wake up?"

"I hope so. This is my house."

She giggled. "No, I mean *here*."

"Next to you?" he asked, smoothing her hair. "Always."

Chapter Twenty

When Torrey awoke, his first thought was that he had to be one of the luckiest men in the world to have such a beautiful woman sleeping next to him. Taegen's back was up against his chest and her golden hair fanned all around her. He smiled and slipped an arm around her, pulling her close. He touched his lips to her neck and ran his hand lightly up her arm. She felt so soft and right, like she was meant to be there. It was the oddest thing. He'd felt like she was supposed to be his from the moment he'd seen her.

"What are the lyrics of that Madonna song?" Taegen's voice murmured suddenly. She started to hum the melody of *Beautiful Stranger*.

He grinned.

"Blah blah something 'bout a beautiful stranger..." She turned to look up at him and giggled.

He smoothed her hair back and kissed her smiling mouth. "Good morning."

She snuggled closer to him, saying nothing, but grinning. Oh yes. Waking up to Torrey every morning was definitely something she could get used to.

"You hungry?" he asked. "I'll make you breakfast."

She looked up at him and reached out to touch his now disheveled hair. "Maybe we can make it together," she suggested.

His eyes softened and he sighed. "I think you're perfect," he said, taking her hand and kissing the palm. He then broke into a wide grin and kissed her on the forehead. "Come on," he urged. "Let's see how much noise we can make before Javan wakes up."

She giggled and rolled out of bed, following him out of

the room.

* * * *

Alyx awoke to find herself lying across Maxim's chest. Her head was on his shoulder and her arm was draped around his waist. She let herself listen to the rhythm of his breathing and she smiled. She caressed his side, feeling the texture of his skin. She fought sudden tears and raised her head so she could look at him. She touched his face with gentle fingers, tracing the intriguing lines around his mouth. She lowered her lips to his with tenderness and he stirred slightly. His breathing pattern changed, letting her know he was awake.

"You're trying to kill me in my sleep now," he said softly.

She smiled and met his eyes. She laid her head back on his chest and listened to his heart. It sounded so strong, so steady, like he was. "Maxim," she whispered.

He tangled his fingers in her hair. "Yes, assassin," he teased.

"I had no dreams last night," she confessed. She looked up at him. "No nightmares."

He frowned thoughtfully.

"For a year I have had them every night," she continued. "I didn't have any last night." She sat up and ran her fingers through his hair. "You chased my demons away."

He blushed and they heard laughter downstairs.

Alyx frowned. "Sounds like Torrey's up. Taegen must have stayed the night. Want to go down?"

Someone knocked on the door, and Maxim propped himself up on his elbows, searching for his glasses on the night-stand.

"Alyx?" Javan's voice called. "You awake?"

She grinned and winked at Maxim. "Yeah, come on in."

Javan opened the door, a disheveled mess, rubbing his eyes. "Hey, have you seen Maxim?" he asked. "His stupid cell keeps—" He stopped suddenly and his eyes widened. His mouth dropped open. "Aw," he groaned. "Aw man. Don't tell me you—" He waved his hands as if to erase all thoughts from his mind.

"Maxim just slept in here last night," Alyx explained. "I didn't want him to have to sleep on the floor again."

Javan continued to stare. "Unbelievable," he muttered.

She threw the covers back and went over to her friend. She hugged him and smiled. "Maxim's my boyfriend now, by the way," she said with a grin. "Be nice, hmm?" She looked back at Maxim and winked again. "Why don't you come down to the kitchen? We can join Torrey and Taegen."

Javan looked genuinely distressed now. "Taegen's here also?" He threw his hands up in the air. "What is this? I wake up one morning and everyone on the planet has gotten some action but me?"

Maxim smiled and stood. "Well, if you'd come to the beach with us last night you might have had better luck," he said. "I think there was something in the air."

"Yeah, instead you fell asleep on the sofa," Alyx teased.

Maxim pushed his way past Javan, and Alyx turned to follow, but Javan grabbed a hold of her arm.

"Not so fast, turbo," he said.

Alyx wailed helplessly and reached for Maxim, but he shook his head with a laugh and all but fled down the stairs.

"You don't waste any time, do you?" Javan asked.

She sighed. "You weren't there, Javan. He wrote this beautiful poem for me. We were sitting on the beach just talking. Talking, Javan. Like he actually enjoyed my company and valued what I had to say. We'd gone down there to surprise Torrey and Taegen and..." She shrugged. "It was like magic. Like real magic. Do you remember when I was a little girl and I was always imagining that some prince would come and rescue me?"

"How could I forget? Alexi was always saving your butt."

She laughed then met his eyes. "Alex was always my knight in shining armor," she said, "but last night, when Maxim was sleeping next to me, I had no nightmares, Javan." His brow furrowed and she shook her head. "Even sleeping next to my brother after I left Rick didn't make them stop, and you know how safe I feel with Alex. They stopped with Maxim. I felt so protected, Jave. Like nothing could ever hurt me. It's different with him... Everything's different with him."

Javan studied her for a moment and smiled. "What was it like?" he asked, crossing his arms over his chest.

She frowned. "What?"

"When he kissed you?"

She raised an eyebrow in alarm. "Why are you asking me

what it was like to kiss Maxim?"

Javan let his breath out in an exasperated growl. "That is not what I meant!" he cried. "Come on!" He shook his head and tried to regain his thought process as Alyx dissolved into giggles. "What I meant *was*... What did it feel like to know that the person you were kissing wanted nothing from you but that kiss? Not sex, not submission. He just wanted you."

"How do you know that? You weren't there."

Javan tapped his finger against his temple and gave her a smug smirk. "That man is not capable of hurting anyone," he said. "And he really likes you."

Tears stung Alyx's eyes and she looked down. "He's so nice," she whispered. "I almost don't know what to do with him."

He sighed and wrapped his arms around her, pulling her close. "He's good for you, Alyx."

"I hope so. I've dated such losers, and it would be nice to have someone other than Alex saving me all the time."

He grinned and pushed back some of her hair. "Save you? I think Max may already have."

Alyx looked down, feeling embarrassed. "Come on, Jave," she said. "Let's go down to breakfast. You make me nervous when you get serious."

He laughed and put his arm around her as they descended the staircase.

* * * *

Alyx hummed softly to herself while she played with her hair in front of the mirror. She was trying to figure out what she wanted to do with it for the concert. She liked it down best, but she knew how hot it got at a show, and she didn't want it to be hanging all stringy later. If she'd just been with Javan, she wouldn't have cared, but she was going to be with Maxim too. And even though she knew that Maxim could probably care less about her hair being stringy after a rock concert, she wanted to look her best. He made her feel sexy and alluring, and she liked that. She wanted to keep feeling that way, and the image was just kind of tainted for her when she thought of herself with B.O. and straw-head.

She sighed and glanced down at her cell phone, which was sitting face up on the dresser in the bedroom so she could keep track of the time. She frowned when she noticed that she'd apparently missed a call. The number was unlisted. That was weird. She quickly picked up her phone and dialed her voicemail, hoping everything was all right at home. Chills ran down her body as she recognized the voice in the message.

"Alyx, it's me. I know I should have called you sooner, but I wanted to give you time to cool off. I figured if I waited awhile, you would be more inclined to listen to me. Look, I really need to talk to you. I miss you, baby. It's been torture without you. I'm so sorry for what happened. You know I didn't mean it. I love you so much. I would never hurt you on purpose. Please call me. I don't want to lose you. I need you."

She stared ahead blankly for a minute before scowling and stabbing the button on the phone to erase the message. What a...oh man, there were no words in the English language that would properly describe what that man was. He had more audacity than any person she had ever known. She flung her phone back down on the dresser and glowered at nothing in particular. How dare he try to play the remorse card with her again! Like she would ever actually consider taking him back? Not unless she was a masochist and liked the pain, emotional as well as physical. She had been stupid in the past, but she wasn't *that* stupid.

She turned back to the mirror and angrily started to twist pieces of her hair up into little buns and secure them with bobby pins so that some of the hair stuck out. A knock sounded on her door, and she had just turned in her seat when a frowning Taegen burst into the room holding a duffel bag.

Alyx arched an eyebrow, but was grateful for the distraction. She didn't want to think about Rick anymore than she absolutely had to, which in her book, was never. "What's up?"

Taegen dropped her bag down onto the bed and faced Alyx with a huff. "Okay, here's the deal. Quick version, I've been kind of a dud the past few years. A really moody, pissy, depressed dud. Donuts for breakfast, lots of chocolate and ice cream. I ditched makeup awhile ago and usually wear jeans and t-shirts."

Alyx blinked. "Okay..."

She sighed and her shoulders sagged. "I'm tired of feeling like a hag, Alyx. Torrey blazed into my life a few days ago and changed everything in my world. He lit it up like an explosion. I want to dress like he makes me feel, but I think any feminine charm I had went out the window with that last tub of mint chocolate chip."

Alyx laughed and stood up. "What is it with these guys anyway?" She went over to the duffel bag and pointed to it. "This your stuff?"

Taegen nodded.

"Do you mind if I look?"

She shook her head. "No, by all means. You always look good. If you can help me in any way, shape, or form, I'll be eternally grateful."

Alyx rolled her eyes. "Come on, Taegen. It's not like you dress in track suits and haven't shaved your legs in a century." She opened up the duffel and began to rifle through it. "What kind of look were you going for?"

"Something fit for a goth metal concert that I'm going to with a guy who once played Dracula."

Alyx grinned and found a few things that had potential, but she decided against them. "You know, I think you're about the same size as me. I'm going to give you The Dress."

Taegen almost retreated from the way Alyx stared at her when she said that. It would have been fitting if her voice had echoed. "The Dress?" she queried.

Alyx nodded with a devilish gleam in her eye. She went over to her garment bag and pulled out a short black dress with spaghetti straps. "Sure it looks simple," she said, "but trust me. When Torrey sees you in this, he'll drop dead."

Taegen eyeballed it. "You think?"

"I don't think. I know. Go put it on."

* * * *

Maxim paced for a few ridiculous minutes outside of Torrey's room before he ran his fingers through his hair and rapped on the door.

Torrey opened it within seconds and raised an eyebrow when he saw Maxim standing there in distress. "What's up?"

"Torrey, I need your help."

He sobered. "Who died?"

Maxim frowned. "No one died."

"Did Javan blow something up?"

Maxim chuckled. "No, nothing like that."

"Well good lord, what then? You look like you have ulcers."

"I might be getting them. Look, I need help with Alyx."

"In what way?"

"Can I just come in? This standing in the hall thing is driving me crazy."

He stepped aside. "What's wrong, Maxim? Girl problems?" He gave him a teasing smile.

Maxim sighed and sat down on Torrey's bed. "I want to do something special for her. She's special. So she deserves something special."

"Special. Got it. Did you have anything in mind?"

"No." He looked up helplessly.

Torrey chuckled at Maxim's undoubtedly distraught expression and sat down next to him. "Max, you need to give me something to work with here."

He sighed. "Okay. Alyx has been through a really tough time, and she suddenly decided that she thinks I'm boyfriend material. I'm not complaining, mind you, but I am freaking out a little. I've never been in a relationship before, and I've never even let myself fantasize about a girl on Alyx's level. She's so gorgeous and soft and perfect..." He shook his head. "I just thought that she deserved something nice, something special. I know we're all supposed to be going out as a group tonight, but I thought it would be cool to surprise her with something and then meet up with you guys before the concert. She spends so much time in 'performance mode,' you know? She's always laughing and smiling and making everyone think she's absolutely fine all the time. I just want her to be able to relax, let her guard down. I want to see her and I want her to see me."

Torrey smiled. "Without the masks."

Maxim nodded.

"Why ask me?" he queried. "Wouldn't Javan be a better choice? He's Alyx's best friend."

Maxim gave him a dry expression. "Have you seen Javan's love life lately? It's dryer than the Sahara. You want me to take advice from him?"

Torrey laughed. "Point taken."

"Besides, you're so suave. Taegen practically melts when you come in the room. I thought you could give me some pointers."

Torrey patted Maxim on the shoulder and smiled. "Just be you. That's the best advice I could offer you. Plan something for you to do that will show her a glimpse into yourself. It's…"—he glanced at his watch—"one o'clock right now. We're all heading out of here in about an hour. That gives you five hours of alone time with Alyx. Think of what you'd like to do, and I'll help you find the places that would be best to do them."

Maxim nodded and frowned, thinking…

* * * *

"Come on, Maxim!" Javan shouted from the bottom of the staircase. "Torrey and I are all ready! What are you doing up there? You're as bad as the girls!"

Torrey chuckled as he leaned nonchalantly against the banister of the staircase. He couldn't keep his mind off of Taegen. He'd taken her back to her house that morning so she could get something to wear for the show. He'd imagined she would change there. Instead, she had come out toting an entire duffle bag of her belongings. He hadn't asked, but he wondered if that meant she was planning on staying with him for awhile. It was summer break at her school, so she didn't need to worry about working.

His heart beat faster at the possibility. It made him think that maybe she was being affected by him the same way he was by her. He didn't know what it was, but good lord, he could swear the air got thinner when the woman left the room.

He heard a door shut, and glanced up to the top of the stairs to see Alyx descending with a grin. She was wearing a pair of low-rise jeans and a black corset top that laced up. Her hair was in a crazy concoction of tiny red and black buns, and the layered ends stuck out in varying directions. She looked fantastic, and he was pretty sure Maxim would have a coronary when he saw her.

"Hey, guys," Alyx greeted. "You two are lookin' stylish."

Torrey glanced down at his attire. He was dressed in a pair of black leather pants and a maroon button-down shirt that hugged his body. He had his hair down and he was wearing a long, black coat. He glanced to Javan, who wore a pair of wide leg, black denim pants and a loose-fitting, button-down black shirt with leopard print panels down the sides.

Alyx cocked an eyebrow. "Where did you get the pimp shirt, Jave?"

Javan glanced down at his shirt and frowned. "What's wrong with it? I got it at Hot Topic!"

She giggled. "I didn't say anything was wrong with it. I was just teasing you." She cleared her throat. "Now, gentlemen, turn your attention, if you will, to the top of the staircase." She gave an elegant gesture to the stairs with her hand. "May I present to you, Miss Taegen Lane."

Torrey stood up straight and turned just in time to see her step into his line of vision. Time slowed to a stop. She wore a black dress that came to just above her knees. It was form fitting and hugged her luscious curves. Her legs seemed to go on for days. He hadn't noticed she had such gorgeous, long legs while she was wearing jeans. Her flaxen hair was pulled up with a claw clip that left the loose ends spilling over the top of it. A black choker adorned her slender neck, and her makeup... He swallowed because his throat suddenly seemed very dry. Her eyes were smoky and sultry, and her lips looked like she had just taken a bite out of somebody. So red...so perfect... She could have been a model for the cover of a *Gothic Beauty* magazine.

His hand went to where his heart was pounding. "My gosh..."

Alyx grinned up at Javan and watched as Taegen descended.

Taegen couldn't believe the look of complete awe on Torrey's face. Alyx had been right. The Dress had done its job well. She hadn't expected such a powerful reaction. She thought maybe he would give her a large grin or something, but the look he was giving her... He looked like he wanted to devour her. Shivers ran up her spine. For the first time in her reserved life, she really wanted to be devoured.

Torrey took her hand as she reached the bottom step and, to her astonishment, he fell to one knee and pressed a lingering kiss to the back of her hand as he bowed his head over it. She felt a flush creep up her neck and into her face, and she glanced at Alyx, who covered her mouth to stop a giggle.

He stood and pulled her into his arms. "You are ravish-ing," he whispered against her ear. "You've ruined all other women for me after this. You have to know that."

She hid her face against his neck, both embrarrassed and flattered at his showy display. His strong arms pulled her closer and she sighed as she leaned into his body.

"Yo! Maxim!" Javan shouted. "Come on!"

"Shut up, Javan!" he yelled down. "My belt is stuck!"

Javan frowned. "On what?"

"It's one of those sliding buckles," Alyx explained. "They get jammed sometimes."

He raised an eyebrow at her. "Why don't you go help him with it?"

She scowled and slugged him playfully in the arm.

Maxim appeared at the top of the stairs, glaring down at Javan. Alyx grinned. He wore a regular pair of jeans and a black Avenged Sevenfold shirt. It clung to his body enough to show off his broad shoulders and lean frame. He also wore a studded belt.

Javan whistled. "Lookin' hot, Max!"

Maxim rolled his eyes and smiled timidly as he came down the stairs. Alyx met him at the bottom and pressed a kiss to the hollow of his throat. He went hot all over. "You look beautiful," he rasped. Actually, beautiful was an under-statement, but he was having trouble making his brain work properly. All he wanted to do was stare at her.

She smiled.

"Now we are concert worthy," Javan declared. "Let's go tear up the town!" He grabbed his keys and headed for the door.

Torrey wrapped his arm around Taegen's waist, not wanting to be away from her for a second. He also wanted everyone else to just get out of the house so he could wor-ship her body the way he wanted to. Unfortunately, that wasn't going to happen. As appealing as the idea sounded, he didn't want to scare her off with his boldness, and he def-initely didn't want her to miss Bleeding Passion because of him. He let his gaze sweep over her and sighed. He would just have to content himself with staring at her radiance for the time being.

Alyx smiled up at Maxim as they made their way to the door. "What do you think?" she asked. "I told you we didn't get you anything too scary."

He nodded. "I don't mind, actually. I kinda like it."

"I think you look sexy."

He gave her a bashful smile. "Well, thanks." He took her hand and twined his fingers with hers as they headed toward the door.

Torrey and Taegen lagged behind, and he turned her to face him. "You're bewitching me," he murmured, tracing his fingers along the lines of her collarbone.

She closed her eyes at his touch and tried to stay upright. He made her dizzy just by being near her. "How so?" she whispered.

He nuzzled her neck and wrapped his arms tightly around her waist. "I can't stop touching you."

She gasped when she felt his lips touch her neck, kissing and nibbling the sensitive skin. "Torrey..." She breathed his name like it was a secret, something dark and sacred that only she could utter. She tangled her fingers in his hair as his lips came up to claim hers in a passionate kiss. She would never be able to get enough of this man. Not even if she lived forever.

"Hey guys—aw man!"

Torrey and Taegen parted reluctantly to see Javan shaking his head and backing out of the doorway.

"Come on, do you have to do that in my line of sight?" he whined.

Torrey grinned and met Taegen's eyes. He kissed her again before leading her out the door and toward the next adventure on their path.

Chapter Twenty-One

Alyx watched the trees whiz past the window, wondering what in the world was going on. She'd driven with the others down to Fisherman's Wharf under the impression that she was going to spend the evening with her friends before the concert, but right as Javan had parked the car and she had been about to step out, Maxim had jumped in the driver's seat and informed her that he was kidnapping her. She didn't mind, really. She had never been kidnapped before. Still, she was curious as to what he had up his sleeve.

She slid her gaze over to him and watched him as he drove. He hadn't spoken at all, which gave her a pretty good indication that he was really nervous. She smirked to herself, finding delight in his discomfort. She knew that sounded horrible, but it was such a nice change of pace. He wasn't sitting there, sagging casually in the seat like he owned the entire universe. He wasn't looking over at her and giving her smug glances that let her know she'd better like what he had planned, or else. He was sitting ramrod stiff and gripped the wheel so tightly that his knuckles were turning white. Plus, he hadn't looked at her once the entire drive. It was so real, so genuine.

Maxim found a place to park the car outside of Golden Gate Park. He stole a quick glance at Alyx and got out of the car, trying to remember how to breathe. Oh yeah, that's right. Inhale, exhale... Inhale, exhale... He took a few deep breaths and opened up the trunk. What was the matter with him? He'd already kissed her. He'd already slept in her bed, for crying out loud... But this was different. This was something he had planned. What if she didn't like it? What if she thought he was a complete loser like everyone else did? His fingers trembled as they grasped the handle of a medium-sized lunch box Torrey had packed for him. He wished it was a picnic basket. Red and white plastic just wasn't the same.

"Maxim?"

He jumped and whacked his head on the hood of the trunk.

Alyx let out a startled yelp and put her hand over her mouth.

Maxim sucked his breath in sharply and rubbed at the top of his head.

"Oh, I'm sorry!" she cried. "Are you okay?" She put her hand on his arm in consolation.

He forced a smile and tried to blink the tears out of his watering eyes. "I'm fine." He was lying. His noggin was so *not* okay. After this trip, he would be surprised if he didn't go home with some kind of permanent damage to his skull. He pulled the lunch box out, as well as a soft fleece blanket and his backpack, and then turned back to Alyx.

"What's this all about?" she asked with a coy smile and a raised eyebrow.

He grinned and looked down to hide a blush. Aw man, he felt like such a fool. Did all guys go through this? He somehow had a hard time picturing his brother being all worried about impressing a girl. Maybe he just hid it well. Maxim didn't. He was twenty-five years old and had never been on a date with a woman. Not one. The safety zone boundary didn't even exist anymore. It was way, way back in Oregon with his dilapidated apartment and comfortable routine.

Taking a deep breath, he shut the trunk and gave Alyx a tremulous smile as he led them through the park.

Alyx couldn't help but grin at Maxim as she walked along beside him. His shy uncertainty was adorable. She let herself enjoy the stunning scenery, the lush green trees and beautiful flowers. They were every color of the rainbow, and the splendor of it, coupled with the sounds of the birds chattering happily in the treetops, filled her with peace.

They stopped suddenly and she frowned, looking up at Maxim in question. He grinned and pointed over to something. She followed his gaze to a black iron gate that read Shakespeare Garden. Her eyes widened and she turned to face him in elation.

Maxim smiled as he started through the gate and down a

path set in between overhanging trees and brilliant flower-beds of pink and white. "There is supposed to be every plant mentioned in Shakespeare's sonnets and plays in here," he supplied.

"Are you serious?" Her heart leapt in excitement as she looked around at the beautiful trees, shrubs, and flowers. She noticed an elegant brick wall on the far side of the garden and headed toward it. "What's that?"

"All of the pertinent quotes set on plaques," he explained. He found a soft, grassy spot and spread the blanket out as Alyx went to study the wall.

"Who thought of this?" she asked, glancing at him over her shoulder. "Who actually had the thought 'let's make a garden with all of Shakespeare's plants'?"

He shrugged. "I don't know. Someone who probably loved the bard as much as you do."

She turned and focused her eyes on him. He was sitting on the blanket, pulling plastic containers out of the lunch box. She wondered if he had any idea just how fantastic he was. She doubted it. He saw himself as someone who just disappeared in a crowd, someone who was insignificant and boring. She wished he could see himself through her eyes. He was a breath of fresh air to her.

Smiling, she went over to him and sat down. "So, what's this project?" she asked, trying to peek inside the lunch box.

He smiled in return and opened up one of the containers. It had two turkey sandwiches in it and he removed one of them. "I didn't have a whole lot of time, so I had Torrey help me out. He just packed what he had in his fridge, I think." He frowned as he noticed small green, fuzzy spots on the side of the sandwich. He scowled. "Oh come on!" he exclaimed.

Alyx raised her eyebrows in surprise at his outburst. "What's wrong?"

"The bread is moldy! Torrey gave me moldy bread!" He sighed in exasperation and flung the sandwich back down into the container. "You know, this never happens in books. Ever. Dashing fictional heroes never have to ask their friends for help to impress their date. They don't plan romantic dinners only to knock themselves in the head for the umpteenth time and then have moldy bread!"

She smirked in amusement at his tangent.

"Man, I should have known this was too good to be true," he went on. "You can't just take a guy who has no social skills and make him a Casanova. It just doesn't happen." He shook his head, feeling like he was going to lose his mind. What did he think he was doing? He'd been a nervous wreck the entire drive over and hadn't even spoken to her. What kind of an impression was that going to make? What did he think he could accomplish by trying to be romantic? He didn't know the first thing about being romantic. "This was so stupid. I'm just making myself look like an idiot."

"Maxim," Alyx interrupted, "calm down."

"I can't calm down! Why in the world would you even be interested in me, Alyx? I'm a complete freak of nature! I'm not suave like Torrey. I'm not even funny like Javan. I'm just...blah. I read books and I write bad poetry. Big whoop. What does that matter? I mean—"

She leaned forward to press her lips forcefully against his.

He stopped talking immediately and his head spun in a way that made him have to close his eyes to keep from passing out. His heart skipped a beat before it proceeded to pound as if it wanted to come right out of his chest cavity.

"Maxim," she said as she pulled away, "shut up."

"Okay..." he whispered.

She smiled and reached up to run her fingers along his stubbled jaw. "You are not a freak of nature. You are a beautiful, caring, and gentle person. And you write amazing poetry. I know you haven't had a lot of practice with dating. That doesn't matter to me. I don't want a Casanova. I told you, all I want is for you to be you."

He sighed in defeat. Hadn't that been the whole point of this date in the first place? For them to get to know one another without the pretenses? He looked down at the grass and played with the hem of his shirt.

"This was not a stupid idea," she went on. "I love that you brought me here. Maxim, you listen to me. You planned a date around something you knew I would like. A lot of guys wouldn't be so thoughtful." She gave him a soft smile and ran her hand down his arm. "You don't need to impress me. You did that already."

He chuckled with uncertainty. "Can't think of how I managed that."

She lifted his chin so that he was looking at her. "By being you."

He met her eyes and sighed. She was being sincere. She really meant what she said. He didn't know what he had done to get so lucky, but he decided he wasn't going to question it. The last thing he wanted to do was wreck the one good thing he had going for him by acting like a psychopath. "Sorry I kinda went ballistic on you there." He chuckled.

"Yeah. Who would have thought moldy bread would put you over the edge?"

He rolled his eyes.

She looked into the lunch box again and grinned as she pulled out a container with strawberries in it. "Who cares about the bread?" she said. "We still have these." She opened the container and showed it to him. She took a double check in the lunch box and pulled out a can of whipped cream. She shook the can and sprayed a bunch of it onto the lid of the strawberry container. When she had finished, she dipped one of the berries in it and held it up to Maxim.

He frowned in confusion. "You're going to feed me?"

"Yes." When he still looked puzzled, she gave him a wry smile. "It's romantic."

He smirked. "It is?"

She nodded.

"Oh. Okay then." Her giggle sent chills all through him as he took a bite of the strawberry she offered. Her eyes held his, and her fingers brushed against his lips. It was strangely intimate, and some of his inhibitions disappeared. This wasn't just some random woman he had met on the street and asked out. Sure, he was very attracted to her, and that was nerve-wracking enough, but he had been with her constantly for the past three days. She had seen him do and say a multitude of dumb things and she still seemed to like him anyway. He didn't need to be so uptight.

Alyx grinned when he'd finished. She licked the juice off of her fingers. "See? Romantic."

He nodded as if he was thinking very hard, and then shrugged. "Not bad."

"Not bad?" She raised her eyebrows at him.

He smiled. "I always preferred this, myself." He grabbed the can of whipped cream, shook it, and proceeded to spray so much of it in his mouth that he could barely swallow. Alyx burst into laughter, which made it worse. He fought a chuckle and only succeeded in almost making it come out of his nose. When he was finally able to down all of it, he turned to Alyx and held the can above her. She opened her mouth with a giggle and he sprayed an equal amount into hers.

Her eyes bulged and whipped cream oozed out the sides of her mouth as she laughed. She managed to swallow it, and looked up at Maxim. She shook her head. "Man, you are a bachelor!"

He grinned and watched as she wiped the cream off of her mouth with her fingers. He reached out and grabbed her hand before she could lick it off and, acting on pure instinct, placed her fingers in his mouth and gently sucked them clean.

Alyx froze and her blood turned molten in her veins. She actually burned. She'd never had that reaction to someone before. One of Rick's favorite complaints about her had been that she was too cold. That she was an ice queen when it came to intimacy. She'd started to think that maybe something was wrong with her, but those thoughts vanished as she felt Maxim swirl his tongue along her fingers, then release them and place a tender kiss to the inside of her wrist. He made her body turn into a raging inferno. It made her think that maybe she hadn't been the one with the problem.

Maxim blushed as he looked up at Alyx, realizing what he had just done. He smiled and looked around for something to divert his attention. His eyes fell on his backpack, and he dragged it over to him. "I thought maybe I could share my favorite work of literature with you," he said softly.

She scooted closer to him as he pulled out *The Princess Bride* by William Goldman. She rested her chin on his shoulder and grinned. "*The Princess Bride*?"

He nodded. "Silly, I know, but I love it."

"It's not silly. Alexi and I used to watch the movie all the time when we were little. He can still quote it."

Maxim smiled and ran his fingers over the cover. "I used to read this all the time. Especially when I was in high school. I don't know what it was about it, but it comforted me the most out of all of the books I love. I guess it made me feel like, no matter what kind of horrible things were going on in my life at the time, I could always have a happy ending. I mean, Westley died and he still got the girl in the end."

She snuggled up to him with a soft laugh and reached down to link her fingers with his. "Read me some."

"Really?" He couldn't hide the surprise in his voice. He'd thought that reading out loud to her would probably seem strange and dull, but when he looked down at her, he saw nothing but her gorgeous green eyes staring up at him. They were full of genuine interest, and he cupped her cheek with his palm, lowering his lips to hers in a brief kiss.

She smiled and brushed her fingers against his cheek in a delicate caress. "Read me your favorite part," she urged.

He turned back to the book and opened it to the fire swamp part. He started to read, losing himself easily in the adventure he so loved. Alyx sat with her head on his shoulder for about two pages, but then she shifted, and he assumed she'd lost interest so he stopped.

"What are you doing?" she asked. "Keep reading."

He frowned, but obeyed and almost jumped clear out of his skin when he suddenly felt her tongue run along the outside of his ear. All of the breath slammed out of his lungs and he dropped the book into his lap. "Oh my gosh," he almost wheezed. "How am I supposed to read with you doing that?"

She laughed an evil, sexy laugh. "Read." She whispered the command directly into his ear, making him shiver. She grinned in satisfaction.

Maxim forced himself to pick his book up again. He stammered his way through a few lines as Alyx trailed hot kisses along the line of his neck and down his jaw. His eyes rolled up into his head and he couldn't concentrate anymore. She was robbing him of all thought, all logic. All he could do was feel. Feel her touches, feel her kisses, feel the way his body responded to them. Most importantly, the way his heart responded to them.

"Why did you stop? I didn't say you could stop," she reprimanded.

"Somehow, I get the feeling you're not paying attention," he replied breathlessly.

"Why would you say that?" She ran her tongue slowly up his throat and he groaned, tilting his head back to give her better access. She smiled and inched her way closer to his lips, spreading kisses across his chin and cheeks. She gasped as his arm came around her waist and, before she had time to even register what was happening, she was lying on her back with him beside her. He cradled her in his arms and gazed down at her with that expression she loved. The one that made her feel like she was the only woman he'd ever seen. For several beats of her heart, all he did was stare down at her, as if he was memorizing every detail of her face. His fingers spanned across her neck and he threw off that raw sensuality he'd had that night on the beach.

"Meet me at the crossroads," he murmured. "Meet me at the edge of town, outskirts of the city. Just you and I and the evening sky…"

She blinked up at him. "Did you write that?"

He shook his head. "No, that was Jim Morrison, actually." He gave a soft laugh.

She couldn't help but giggle. "Jim Morrison?" She never would have pegged him as someone who would be into The Doors.

He nodded, his smile playful and sexy. "Hey, the guy may have been a little on the bizarre side, but he wrote some good poetry." He traced his fingertips across the lines of her face, over her delicate cheekbones, the bridge of her nose, her satin soft lips. "I've realized something about myself on this trip."

"What's that?"

He gave her a lopsided smile. "I discovered that I quote literature when I'm nervous."

She grinned and toyed with the neckline of his shirt. "Why are you nervous?"

He swallowed and shook his head. "Because you're the most beautiful woman I've ever seen and you rob me of all rational thought."

Alyx stared at him in quiet wonder. She reached up to remove his glasses. "I could get used to hearing words like that," she whispered.

"I could get used to saying them." He tightened his arms around her and lowered his lips to hers. He closed his eyes and forced any thought out of his mind. He didn't want to think, or question, or doubt. He just wanted to feel her. He wanted to feel her softness and her passion. He caressed his lips over hers and deepened the kiss, drawing a delightful noise from her throat. It made everything inside him come alive. Knowing that he had the power to bring her pleasure. Him. The shy one. The hopeless introvert. His kiss was what caused her to gasp and moan. He pulled her closer to him, pressing her pliant body against his. Her arms went around his shoulders and her fingers ran down his spine, making him tingle. He continued his unhurried exploration of her mouth, knowing he was completely, hopelessly lost to this woman.

She'd had him wrapped around her finger from day one, and for some absurd reason, she wanted to be with him. It almost seemed too good to be true. He had no idea how he had managed to get so amazingly lucky. He'd asked himself over and over, and it still baffled him. He had a feeling that it would continue to baffle him for a very long time.

Alyx was breathless when Maxim finally broke the kiss. Her head was foggy, and every part of her ached for him. It was like she had been waiting for him forever. Like her body recognized him and warmed only for him. She wanted his lips on hers, his whispering voice in her head, his gentle hands on her skin. She wanted *him*. All of him, completely. She suddenly hated that they were lying in a public park. A nice, private place would have been so much better.

What was it about him? His voice soothed her instantly. It had before she'd even met him, when he'd called her that day at her apartment. It was like the softest strains of music, or wind chimes in a summer breeze. It was the most relaxing sound she'd ever heard. And his eyes made her feel so at peace. Maybe because they reminded her of the ocean. The ocean had always been ultimate tranquility to her, and that was what she saw when she looked into his eyes. Calm, blue, with a kind of depth that was unreal. His eyes looked like they held a thousand secrets, and she wanted to know each and every one.

What was it about him that caused her blood to burn? It was like she had been denied passion only have it to awaken at his simplest touch. And she didn't just want a heated make-out session. She wanted the kind of lustful encounter that you only saw in the movies. She remembered all too well what his gorgeous body looked like, and she wanted to run her hands over every inch of buffness. Oh yeah.... She was having naughty thoughts.

Maxim raised a curious eyebrow as a devilish smile

crossed her lips. "What are you thinking about?"

She sighed and met his eyes. "Maxim, if you knew, you would blush your head off."

He frowned. "Tell me anyway."

She grinned and raised herself up on her elbows so she could whisper in his ear. "You do know that you're an incredibly sexy man, don't you?"

There went blush number one. He cleared his throat. "Uh... No, I actually didn't know that."

"You are. You really turn me on."

Okay, blush number two.

"I want to ravage you."

Holy cow! Somebody call the fire department because his face just burst into flames! "Aw man," he muttered. "Alyx, you're the devil. You really are trying to kill me. I can't take this."

She laughed and wrapped her arms around his neck, pulling him down close to her. She sobered. "Maxim, in all seriousness, I'm so grateful I found you. Thank you for coming on this trip. Thank you, thank you." She punctuated her words with little kisses on his face. "There's no man like you in the whole world."

He chuckled. "Is that a good thing?"

"Oh yes. That's a very good thing."

"Why?"

She grinned, feeling so happy in that moment that she didn't really know how to react to it. "Because you're all mine."

Chapter Twenty-Two

"What are you doing?" Javan exclaimed in frustration. "Read the map!"

"I'm trying to read the map!" Alyx insisted. "It's weird!" She turned it around and around, trying to find the street that the Warfield was on. "Everything looks the same."

"Turn here," Taegen suggested.

"I can't!" Javan shouted. "No left turn! What is this? You can't turn left in this stinkin' city!"

"Maybe turn here, Javan," Alyx suggested. "If you turn right here, maybe you can get over."

Javan obeyed and promptly let out a yell. "Oh, look!" he cried. "What a surprise! I'm on Market Street again!"

Torrey chuckled. They had been on Market Street three times already. He glanced at Maxim. "I'd help," he said, "but this is too amusing."

Maxim smiled.

"Turn here!" Alyx commanded.

"I can't turn there!" Javan shouted. "No friggin' left turn!" He beat his palm against the steering wheel in agitation. "What is this? You are a terrible co-pilot!"

"It's not my fault this map is freaky!"

"Gimme that effing thing," he demanded. "Let me see it."

Alyx handed him the map and huffed. "Really? You just said 'effing?' Just swear already. We're not in a car full of little kids." She sat back against the seat. "We're never going to get to the concert," she conceded.

"It's upside down, Alyx!" Javan cried. "No wonder you can't read it!"

"Well how am I supposed to know?" she grumbled. "Everything looks the same."

"Here's a clue," he griped. "The words are upside down!" He turned the map and tried to figure out which direction he was going. He grasped for the stick shift, but when the car didn't change gears, he frowned and tried again. He scowled. "What the—"

Alyx looked over at Javan and gave him a bemused expression. "Javan."

"What?" he snapped.

"Do you really think that my knee will shift your car into gear, or are you just trying to feel me up?"

He blinked and looked over at her. He rolled his eyes and took his hand off her knee.

"Turn here, Javan," Torrey finally relinquished.

Javan obeyed and listened as Torrey guided him to a parking place about a block away from the Warfield.

"See, that wasn't so hard," Torrey said.

Javan scowled at him. "Shut up, Mr. Native San Franciscan. You could have, you know, like, piped up sooner."

Torrey smirked and got out of the car after Maxim. He helped Taegen out and took her hand, bringing it to his lips. "Come on, my gorgeous goth."

Taegen grinned and wrapped her arms around his neck. "My Dracula."

He chuckled and turned back to the others. "Hey, everyone! I want a group picture." He set his camera up on the roof of the car and set the timer. He ran back to the group and put his arm around Taegen's shoulders.

Taegen nestled against Torrey, happy to be so close to him. After the picture was taken, she kept a hold of his hand as they made their way to the concert. She loved walking with him. He didn't walk, he swaggered. Like a panther. Graceful, confident, powerful. All the women stared at him, but he didn't look back. He was there with her. He could have any woman he wanted and he was there with her. It made her feel special and wanted and, against her better judgment, her heart was slowly being taken over by intense feeling for the man beside her. It was as if it was binding itself to him, making her unable to be without him for long. It was foreign, frightening, and strangely delightful all at the same time.

The Warfield was packed with people and the five of them threaded through the throng to their places, which happened to be in the very top of the nosebleed section.

"Man, this sucks," Javan complained. "Isn't it just like a radio station to give away crap tickets?"

"Oh well," Alyx said. "At least we're here. That's more than we would have been." She sat down next to Maxim and took his hand. "You okay?"

He nodded and smiled at her. "I'm perfect."

She grinned, admiring how far he had come in such a short amount of time. Maxim had completely altered his perception of life in only a few short days. It had been forced upon him, and instead of fighting it, he had taken it in stride to the best of his ability. She thought it took an amazing amount of courage.

The lights dimmed suddenly and Javan jumped into his seat. "Here we go!" he exclaimed in excitement.

There was a moment of silence, then one chord strummed on a guitar in the dark and the crowd went mad. Everyone leapt from their seats and began to scream and cheer. Someone on stage chuckled into a microphone, but still no lights. "Good evening, San Francisco!" The crowd reached a deafening roar. Another chord was strummed, and the lights came on with a bang as the song began full force.

Alyx jumped up and took Maxim's hand, pulling him out of his seat as well. He blinked, confused as to where the sudden cloud of marijuana smoke had come from. He wrinkled his nose. Just what he needed was to leave his first rock concert with a contact high. He glanced over at the girl who was sitting in front of him. She wore extremely low leather pants that she was fairly spilling out of, and her bright pink thong was showing for the whole world to see. He sighed. Somehow, in all his wildest imaginings, he never thought he'd be doing this. Apparently, his imaginings weren't really that wild.

Torrey nudged Taegen and pointed down on the stage to the blond man playing the bass. "That's Darren!" he said.

The concert continued until Fat Stinky ended their session and a short intermission ensued. Alyx sat down, out of breath from laughing and rocking out with Javan. She looked over at Maxim, who felt shell-shocked, and grinned. "You still okay?" she asked.

He nodded and let his eyes take in all the colors and smells. So many people... He locked everything away into compartments in his mind to be used later. There was some good material here. He then sat back in his chair and listened to Torrey as he told them all about Darren.

It wasn't long before the lights went down again, and the same dark silence filled the smoky room. The crowd began to cheer at nothing, and the longer the silence, the louder they cheered. Suddenly and without warning, pyrotechnics exploded on the stage, sending pillars of fire and spark up into the air. The crowd went crazy, and a spotlight was directed down into Maxim's section on the balcony. A tall man with long, dark hair stood with his head down and the people around him went berserk.

Maxim frowned. "Who's that?" he shouted at Alyx.

She was grinning. "Van Marshall! The front man!" She pointed down at the main stage where a woman with shining black hair stood in a spotlight with her head down as well. "And that's Nyah Densmoore! She's the other singer!"

Javan tugged on her arm as the man lifted his eyes to the audience and began to sing. His deep, rich voice filled the auditorium and everyone started to run toward where he stood in a crazed, psychotic stampede. "Come on!" Javan shouted. "Let's go over there!"

Alyx grabbed Maxim's hand and pulled him after them. He followed and looked up at the singer. Good lord. The man was the very picture of gothic beauty. He was tall and slender with dark brown hair that shone in the spotlight. He was wearing tight black leather pants that rode low on his hips and a black long-sleeved shirt with Fender written on it. Maxim was elated that he actually knew that Fender was a brand of guitar. Back in high school, Jeff had gone through a musician phase. That was the only reason he remembered.

He was awestruck as he watched the rock star perform. All of his movements were fluid elegance, as if he was made out of music and not just playing it. He cradled his guitar in his arms like he cherished it above all things, and the sex appeal and charisma that emanated off of him made Torrey look tame.

Maxim was not known to stare at men as a general rule, but he did study people, and he couldn't help but be captivated by the singer. He commanded the entire auditorium all on his own. His eyes were lined with thick, black eye shadow and his fingernails were painted black as well. He was the complete goth package, but Maxim found something odd in his actions that not a lot of people would have noticed. Though he was charming the crowd, he sang most of his songs with his eyes closed, and when he did look up at the audience, it was almost as if he was looking over them, scanning them instead of really connecting. It was a strange kind of look. Like he was locked inside of himself. Maxim recognized it because it was the same kind of look he had seen in his own eyes for years. The look that there was a barrier keeping him from the rest of the world, one that he hadn't known how to get past until Jeff had forced him to.

Maxim followed Javan to the hoard of girls surrounding the singer, and frowned as he realized that Alyx had disappeared. He glanced around and turned to look up the stairs they had just descended. His eyes widened as he saw Alyx fly through the air. He held his arms out just in time to catch her and fall backward into the crowd. He landed hard on his elbow and a tall, mocha-skinned woman stumbled over Alyx and landed right on top of Maxim. Dark, almost black eyes burned into his and a sly smile spread across her full, red lips.

"So sorry about that," the woman purred.

His eyes widened as she seemed to settle herself provocatively against him.

"Who are you?" she asked.

"M-M—" He blinked. "Maxim," he rasped.

"Hello, Maxim." She tilted her head to one side and grinned. "I was in that magazine once." She raised an eyebrow. "If you like, I can show *you* what I showed *them.*"

Maxim had never seen anyone raise an eyebrow in such a sensual manner. He swallowed, his mouth going dry.

The woman moved suggestively against him and toyed with his hair. "How about it? Do you want to see?"

"Hey!" Alyx shouted suddenly. "Get off my man, slick!" She pushed the woman off and helped Maxim up.

He let out a grateful sigh and grinned at Alyx. She pressed a quick kiss to his lips and turned back to the handsome singer.

"Man!" Javan laughed, slapping Maxim on the back. "You get all the luck!"

Maxim chuckled and shook his head. He glanced over at the woman, who was still standing close. She smiled at him in a way that made him think of a succubus. He shivered and looked away. That hadn't been luck. It had just been scary.

Van Marshall remained on their level for the duration of two songs before going back down to the main stage with his band. Maxim actually found himself really enjoying Bleeding Passion and he even rocked out a little bit with Alyx, loving the laughter in her eyes.

The concert was over much too quickly to suit everyone, and Javan grumbled the entire time they were leaving the building. Torrey held Taegen's hand as they stepped out into the night. He smiled down at her. "Awesome show," he remarked. "I especially loved *Consuming*."

Taegen grinned and blushed. "It was fantastic! Javan, I'm so glad you tried to pick me up in Berkeley! I wouldn't have been able to come to the show if you hadn't!"

Javan chuckled and stuffed his hands in his pockets as they meandered past the tour bus where eager fans were waiting. Torrey stopped. He glanced across the crowd, then looked over to Alyx, Maxim, and Javan, who were talking happily about the high points of the show. "Hey, guys."

They looked up at him.

"Let's wait," he suggested. "I want to see if I can snatch a hello with Darren."

Suddenly, the crowd started to scream and rushed at the band members as they emerged. Torrey was shoved one way and another and he couldn't see anything past the hysterical girls. He sighed. So much for seeing his old friend. He would get eaten alive if he tried to get through there.

Alyx frowned. She whispered something in Maxim's ear and he nodded, hoisting Alyx up onto his shoulders.

"Darren Hayes!" she bellowed. "Darren Hayes! Your old friend Torrey has come to see you! Torrey Reed!"

Torrey chuckled, but to his surprise, he heard his name being shouted through the crowd. The blond bassist came bounding through the fans, grinning like an idiot. People pressed in from all sides, begging for autographs and any kind of attention, but Darren ignored them. He gave Torrey an enormous hug, almost picking him right off the ground. "Torrey!" he exclaimed. "How have you been, man?"

Torrey laughed. "I just about had a heart attack when I heard that you were Fat Stinky's new bassist!"

Darren grinned. "I was kind of surprised when it happened. Remember our old garage days?"

"Darren!" a fat man with glasses called suddenly. "Get on the bus! If you must continue your high school reunion, get your friends in with you, but come on! These people are going to knock the bus over!"

Darren nodded and looked back to Torrey. "Our manager. He tends to exaggerate. Hey, we've booked a private dinner party at Steps of Rome before we head out tonight. Meet me there at the front door and I'll get you and your friends in."

Torrey grinned and nodded. "I'll see you there." Darren waved as he disappeared back into the crowd. Torrey turned back to see Javan's jaw almost on the ground. He laughed and patted him on the back. "Come on, driver. We'd better leave now. It'll take you all night to find the place."

Chapter Twenty-Three

Javan felt like he was in a bad recurring nightmare. This was the fifth time they had circled this particular block. He snarled. "Where is Stockton Street?" he hissed. "This is ridiculous."

"What's ridiculous is you driving in circles!" Alyx cried. "Javan, how many opportunities do you get to eat with a bunch of rock stars? I don't know about you, but this is the first time it's ever happened to me! You're going to blow it!"

Javan scowled at nothing. "Maybe if you could read the map, we wouldn't be having this problem," he retorted.

"Holy—" Torrey flung his hands up into the air in a gesture of frustration. "You both are making me nuts! Just park the car for crying out loud! We can walk to the restaurant!"

Javan obeyed and quickly pulled into the first spot he could find. The five got out in annoyed silence and Torrey took the lead. He saw Taegen shiver and he placed an arm around her shoulders, bringing her close up against his body. "Did you like the concert?" he questioned, seeking to talk about something other than Javan's abhorrent sense of direction.

Taegen grinned and looked up at him. "It was a blast. Especially when Van Marshall came up to our level to perform."

"Yeah, until I took that embarrassing header," Alyx said.

"What happened to you anyway?" Javan asked. "One minute you were behind me and the next you were flattening Maxim."

"Correction," Maxim interrupted. "That frightening woman was flattening me."

"I got pushed aside by some scary, sweaty Mexican guy,"

Alyx explained. "Then I tripped while I was going down the stairs."

"I almost died," Maxim muttered.

Alyx grinned and laced her fingers with his.

"Look!" Torrey exclaimed suddenly. "There's Darren! Come on guys!"

Alyx shook her head in wonderment. "I can't believe I'm going to a private dinner party with the members of Fat Stinky and Bleeding Passion."

Javan chuckled. "Yeah, Torrey really comes in handy."

Darren embraced Torrey at the entrance of the restaurant and grinned. "Where've you been, man?" he asked. "I've been standing out here forever." He pointed to the bulky man next to him. "Rex is going to freeze to death."

Torrey glanced at the small Titanic standing next to Darren and raised an eyebrow. "Rex?"

Darren smiled. "Bodyguard. Come on in, guys. Everyone is welcome."

Torrey entered first with Darren, and the others followed closely behind. Rex brought up the rear and stood at the door like a menacing statue. The bands, as well as a few roadies and some others, were all seated around the restaurant, laughing and talking loudly.

"Hey Darren!" the drummer of Fat Stinky called. "Who are your friends? Is this the guy you used to play with?"

Darren nodded with a grin.

"Bring 'em over!" he invited.

Darren led everyone over to the table where the members of Fat Stinky sat, and he indicated Torrey. "This is Torrey Reed," he introduced. "He was in a band with me in college. Torrey, this is Jacob Pike,"—he pointed to the drummer—"Link Fox,"—he pointed at a tattooed blond guy—"and Dane Thompson."

Dane was tall, lean, and a sex symbol. He was the front man and he exuded suaveness, like many other famous rock stars. He gripped Torrey's hand and smiled. "Good to meet you," he said, his voice naturally soft and seductive. "Darren has mentioned you before. Says you're a real good musician."

Torrey smiled. "Well, I do my best."

Dane let his eyes scan the rest of the group and they fell on Alyx. He raised an eyebrow and smiled appreciatively.

"You going to introduce us to the rest of your friends?"

Torrey pulled Taegen up beside him and smiled when he saw her baffled expression. She had been casting uneasy glances back at Rex since they had entered and hadn't quite noticed what was going on. She blinked up at the tall man in awe. "Dane Thompson," she whispered. Holy cow... she was actually standing right in front of Dane Thompson. And she dare not even look over to the other table where she knew Van Marshall sat. She would either scream or pass out if she did, and neither one of those options would make her look very glamorous.

Dane grinned and nodded a greeting.

Torrey chuckled. "This is Taegen, my girlfriend. Behind me are Javan, Maxim, and Alyx."

Dane moved gracefully around Torrey and came to stand in front of Alyx. He took her hand and brought it to his lips. "Hello, Alyx," he greeted.

Alyx turned several shades of red and grinned.

"Come and eat something," he invited, still holding onto her hand. "There's an empty seat next to me."

She giggled and allowed him to lead her to the table.

Javan nudged Maxim in the shoulder. "Careful," he warned. "He's making moves on your girl."

Maxim glanced at Alyx as she took her seat. She looked back at him and gave him a surprised and elated look. He grinned. "I'm not worried." Alyx didn't need anyone else trying to dictate how she should live her life. She'd gotten enough of that from her ex. Maxim would never tell her what to do. He wanted her to stay with him because she wanted him, not because he kept her on a leash.

Javan smiled and patted him on the back in a gesture of brotherly affection.

"Come on," Darren urged. "Come meet Bleeding Passion." He grinned. "Alyx can catch up as soon as Dane is finished charming her."

The others followed Darren over to a larger table where they were introduced to all of the band members. Erik Vandenburg was the keyboardist and he was a quiet, rather stoic fellow. Lance Lawson was the bass player and he was blond, vivacious, and looked like he should either be surfing or skateboarding. The drummer, Jack, was Nyah's brother and he seemed very friendly and down to earth. Nyah reminded

Maxim of the woman who had fallen on him at the concert, and he would have been concerned if not for the fact that she kept clinging onto Van's arm like she was permanently attached. Van himself was very polite, and as he reached out to shake hands with everyone, Maxim got that same impression that the musician was watching the world behind a barrier. It intrigued him. It fascinated him to think that someone with such charisma and stage presence could be hiding behind a mask as well.

"Let's just sit at this table," Darren suggested. "Dane just gave away my seat to your friend Alyx."

Torrey chuckled and they all took seats around the Bleeding Passion table. Maxim sat the farthest from the conversation and listened as Torrey jumped right in like he belonged there. Maxim had to shake his head. Torrey amazed him. He was never uncomfortable in any situation. He always seemed so calm and confident. Maxim admired that since it was something so foreign to his nature.

Taegen turned to face Maxim and smiled, voicing his own thoughts. "Look at him," she said. "Like he knows these people. How does he do that?"

Maxim chuckled. "I don't know. I'm crapping my pants."

She giggled and touched Maxim on the arm in a gesture of affection. He looked down at her hand. A small smile touched his lips and he thought of how Javan had patted him on the back. Affection. Friendship. His friends. He sat back in his chair and let himself soak in everything that was going on around him. He watched Dane Thompson touch Alyx's cheek at the next table, and he saw Link Fox roll his eyes. Link Fox. What kind of a name was that? He watched Link as he looked at Dane and pointed back to Maxim. "Look at that dude," Link warned. "He's watching you. You better watch out. I bet he could kick your sorry little butt into next Tuesday."

Maxim laughed out loud and turned away before Alyx could see how red he turned. Like he could kick *anyone's* butt into any day of the week... He looked over at Van Marshall as he sat casually in his chair, his arm draped around Nyah's shoulders. He seemed so composed and serene, sipping his beer and laughing with Torrey, but there was something about him. Something else. Something...sad? Detached?

Two other band members listened to Javan. Maxim had

no idea what he was talking about, but he was flailing his arms about wildly. There were a few roadies drunk in the back corner. They were loud and obnoxious and trying to pick up some girls that were there. Maxim's eyes wandered back to Fat Stinky's table. Dane Thompson had long, blond hair. What was it with women and long hair? And what was it with rock stars all having long hair? Was it a prerequisite or something? Dane had his arm around Alyx and he leaned in close to her. Maxim smiled, hoping she was enjoying herself. No doubt she was, being hit on by a famous rocker. If he'd been sitting next to Sylvia Plath and she had been putting her arm around *his* shoulders, he would have been hyperventilating. Alyx was actually handling herself very well.

"Maxim?"

Maxim blinked and pulled himself from his observations to look at Torrey.

Torrey chuckled. "What are you thinking about?"

He smiled shyly. "Just watching."

"Gathering ideas?"

Maxim felt his cheeks turn hot.

"Ideas?" Van questioned.

Torrey nodded and pointed to Maxim. "He's an aspiring novelist."

Maxim looked around for a hole he could crawl into. He was quite happy sitting there, pretending to be invisible. He didn't need a famous rock star asking him questions about his horrendous writing career.

Van grinned. "Are you? That's wonderful. I watch people to get inspiration for songs also."

Maxim scratched at the back of his head and gave a tremulous smile.

"Did any ideas find you?" Van asked.

"Ideas are everywhere," Maxim replied, braving a look up at the man. "In every shadow, every smile. If you look hard enough, everything tells a story."

Van arched an eyebrow and held up his beer. "Amen, brother."

Maxim chuckled and raised his glass to touch Van's beer bottle.

"So, where's your next show?" Torrey asked suddenly.

"Vegas," Van replied. "We meet up with our other opening band there."

"You're touring with another band?" Javan questioned.

"They're just opening for one show. They're going on their own tour soon, but the singer is a friend of mine. They're opening for us just for fun."

"Which band?" Torrey asked.

"Dead Vampire," Lance replied.

Maxim frowned. Dead Vampire? How was that possible? Weren't vampires supposed to be dead anyway? That name made no logical sense. Then again, it was a heavy metal band. He supposed the names were allowed to not make sense.

"It's a shame we aren't in town longer," Darren said to Torrey. "We could get together."

Van shrugged his broad shoulders. "Why don't you guys just come with us to Vegas?"

Maxim's eyes bulged and Javan nearly fell straight out of his seat. "You mean *with* you?" he squealed.

Van chuckled. "Sure. Just come on the bus with us. There's room. That way, you and Darren can catch up." He gestured to Torrey. "The rest of you can have some fun." He grinned. "I know about having fun with friends and making things memorable."

Taegen stared at Maxim in shock and tugged on his arm. "This is amazing!" she whispered to him.

Maxim re-entered the conversation after talking with Taegen just as Torrey was agreeing they would go. He sighed. Jeff *would* kill him now. He was certain of it.

"Alyx!" Javan shouted suddenly. She jumped and spun in her seat at the urgent tone of his voice. "We're going to go to Las Vegas with these guys! And we'll get to stay backstage when they perform!"

Alyx looked shocked. Dane's arm snaked around her shoulders again. "Stay in our bus, Alyx," he invited. "I can show you where all the comfortable places are." He ran his finger down her bare arm slowly. Alyx met Maxim's eyes and rolled hers.

Maxim smirked and glanced up at Link, who was shaking his head. "Next Tuesday, Dane," he continued to warn. Maxim chuckled and let himself fall back into his observational state. He sighed. No one would ever believe that shy, bookish Maxim deBoer would be eating dinner with a bunch of rock stars. No one would believe that he would be standing backstage at a concert of one of the most popular rock bands of the year. No one would believe that he had a beautiful girlfriend who was making her way over to him now instead of taking Dane Thompson up on his offer.

He smiled as Alyx placed her hands on his shoulders. How had he managed to get so very lucky? He looked up at her. She kissed him on the forehead and Maxim glanced around at his friends. Javan with his big mouth and laughing eyes. Torrey with his suave mannerisms and charming smile. Taegen, who was currently biting all her nails off in excitement while Torrey toyed absently with the hair at the nape of her neck. Alyx. Beautiful Alyx. These people were what true characters were made of. They were real people who had overcome real obstacles and they were his friends. They deserved to grace the pages of a great work of fiction... Maybe one day they would.

* * * *

Maxim watched the city go by as the bus made its way out of San Francisco. He, Javan, and Alyx had been placed on the Bleeding Passion bus while the others traveled with Fat Stinky. He looked around the bus, which had fallen very quiet. Erik, Lance, and Nyah had retired to their bunks, Jack was passed out on the sofa, and Van was strumming softly on an acoustic guitar. Javan sat next to Maxim with his head back. Maxim assumed he was dozing.

He looked down at Alyx, who had fallen asleep on his lap. He stroked her hair softly and smiled. He heaved a sigh and studied her quietly.

"The starlight dances on your face,
Leaving behind a subtle trace
Of heaven's splendor, nature's perfection.
Before you, my loneliness escaped detection.
You saw my heart,
In darkness and sorrow.
You soothed the ache,
Gave hope for tomorrow.
How can I express to you what you have done
When your love for me has just barely begun?"

He murmured it very softly, more or less thinking out loud, but it was enough to make Van stop playing and stare.

"Did you just make that up off the top of your head?" he asked.

Maxim met his eyes and diverted his attention, embarrassed that someone had overheard his uncensored thoughts. "Yeah," he muttered. "I think better in verse."

Van shook his head. "That was incredible," he said in awe. "Have you ever considered becoming a lyricist?"

Maxim swallowed uncomfortably, but a faint smile touched his lips. "No, not really."

"You should."

Maxim's smile grew when he gazed back down at Alyx. She snuggled closer to him, as if she could tell he was watching her. He sighed. He was aware of Van's eyes still on him, so he glanced up.

Van smiled softly. "She your girl?"

Maxim looked back down at Alyx and returned to stroking her hair in adoration. "Yeah," he murmured. "She's my girl." He shook his head. "I have no idea what she sees in me, though." He didn't know why that flew out of his mouth. He would normally never divulge such a personal thought to a stranger, but he felt some sort of weird, instant kinship with Van. It was stupid, since he was not the adoring fan type, but there was something so familiar about the look in his eyes. Made him wonder if maybe "The Sound of Silence" freaked him out too.

Van looked away for a moment. He sighed. "There are times in life that don't make sense," he said. "Times when rare beauties find something in men like us that we can't see."

Maxim frowned. "Men like us?"

"Creative, quiet, shy."

Maxim arched an eyebrow. "You don't seem quiet and shy to me."

Van smiled enigmatically as his skilled fingers continued to absently pluck the guitar strings. "I used to be... I used to be a mess, actually." He gave a dry chuckle and shook his head before a warm light came to life in his eyes. "Someone changed all that for me."

"Nyah?" Maxim assumed.

He frowned. "No, not Nyah. Someone else..." He stared

off wistfully for a minute before shaking his head sadly. "Just hold onto her, Maxim. Women like that only come along once in your life. Believe me, I know."

Maxim found it strange and interesting that Van seemed to be able to read him so well. He met the man's gaze and frowned in curiosity. "How do you know I'm the quiet, shy, creative type anyway?" he asked. "For all you know I could be the biggest jock on the planet."

Van laughed. "I find that very hard to believe. Maxim, you sat at my table all night watching people to gather ideas for your novels. You hardly spoke, and besides, I can tell. Eccentrics can sense each other."

Maxim studied him for a moment, trying to sense if he was being genuine. When Van looked up and met his gaze head-on, an involuntary shiver went up Maxim's spine. "Okay, you're a creepy man."

Van chuckled and went back to playing his guitar.

Maxim wondered what Van was hiding. What painful secret or memory did he keep locked inside? He knew that the hollow look he had seen in his own eyes for years was a product of loneliness, of pain from feeling like an outcast. He wondered what caused it in such a dynamic man like Van. "So, you really used to be shy and quiet?" He couldn't help it. His curiosity was hopelessly piqued.

Van glanced back up at him. "Yeah... I was the definition of freak in my adolescence, but that was mainly because I had so much creativity and so much anxiety all rolled into one. It came out in this angsty, dark poet thing." He chuckled. "Not too many people appreciated that in high school." He met Maxim's eyes and grinned playfully. "Now I can get away with it by slapping 'musician' on myself as a title."

Maxim smiled. "So you're still dark and full of angst then?"

"I'm dark in the sense that I like gothic things. Edgar Alan Poe, medieval architecture, Celtic design, the movie *The Crow*. You know, stuff like that. So, yeah, I guess I'm basically the same."

"Not to mention the anxiety problems," Javan said suddenly.

Maxim glanced at Javan in surprise. He thought he'd been sleeping. "Anxiety problems?" The question shot right out of Maxim's mouth, his curiosity getting the best of him before he had a chance to sensor himself.

Van nodded. "Yeah, I have panic disorder."

Maxim blinked, stunned that a man like Van had trouble with anxiety, and even more stunned that Javan had hit the nail on the head. "And you can still perform in front of thousands of screaming fans? That's impressive." Suddenly, everything made sense. How he sang with his eyes closed and seemed like he was watching the world from behind a barrier. It was a barrier erected to protect himself, to keep everyone at a certain distance so he would be safe. It was a barrier to keep his anxiety at bay. He frowned thoughtfully. "Do you think we all spend our lives hiding behind masks?"

Van looked up at him and held his gaze for a moment. He nodded slowly. "Yeah, I think we do. I mean, the world is a cruel, mean place. Who wants to go out into it vulnerable and naked to assault? We put on fronts to keep ourselves protected."

"But then we just spend our entire lives lying to people."

"Not lying," Javan spoke up. "Just acting." He raised his head. "That line 'all the world's a stage,' it's true. We all put on an act for the rest of the world and keep our true selves locked behind a front. It's protection." He looked at Maxim. "I bet you would never guess that I graduated from high school with honors, would you? Or that I was top of my class in college, and graduated with a bachelor's in psychology." He smirked as Maxim raised his eyebrows. "See, I've always been really good at making fun of myself when I make a mistake. It makes people laugh. Making people laugh causes them to like you. So, I just play the part of the clown, the jokester, when the truth is, I'm afraid to let people know the serious side of me for fear they won't like me. I act. We all act. Van hides behind his status as a sex symbol. It keeps him safe. No one would ever suspect that he's having a heart attack when he steps out on stage. Just like no one would ever suspect that I can diagnose a whole lot of psychological problems in only a few minutes. Just like no one would ever suspect that you are a creative genius and have quite a bit of hidden charisma yourself." He shrugged. "We play parts. It's human. We all do it. It's not deceitful, Maxim. It's just survival."

Maxim couldn't even formulate a thought for a long while. Javan had a bachelor's in psychology? The man who had peed on a fire to put it out and chased a skunk with bamboo had graduated with honors? That was insane. But his words made sense. He himself had spent most of his life hiding behind the fact that he thought he disliked people when, in all truth, he was just terrified of being rejected and made fun of. Alyx hid her pain behind her warmth and laughter. He guessed everyone had something to hide, but he thought it was kind of a sad way to live. If you spent your entire life keeping who you really were secret, no one would ever get to know you for real. They would know a front, a façade, and that really wasn't fair to anyone involved.

He heaved a sigh and leaned his head back against the sofa cushion. He closed his eyes as exhaustion set in. The rhythm of the bus slowly lulled him to sleep, and his last thought was that he hoped he could hold onto Alyx like Van had said. He hoped he could show her who he really was, and that she would show him all of her. He just hoped he could make her as happy as she deserved.

Chapter Twenty-Four

Las Vegas, Nevada

Taegen was pretty certain that the only way she was going to make it through the day was if someone hooked her up to an IV full of coffee. Torrey had stayed up for the entire journey playing various instruments with Darren and the other band members. Taegen had enjoyed watching and listening to them so much that she hadn't been able to go to sleep either.

Now it was nine-thirty in the morning and they had just checked into their hotel suite a half hour ago. Fat Stinky had put them up in a room at The Luxor, and they were all free to explore Vegas for the next day and a half. The show wasn't until the next evening and Javan was already planning on where he was going to lose his money the fastest.

Torrey smiled as he came up to Taegen, holding out a cup of her much coveted coffee. "Good morning, sweetheart," he said, pressing a kiss to her temple.

She reached up and took the cup from him with a small smile. "Hello," she muttered. She took a sip and closed her eyes as the warm liquid filled her with caffeinated comfort. Torrey sat down next to her and began to run teasing kisses up the side of her neck.

Taegen closed her eyes and turned her head to the side to give him better access. She sighed softly as tingles spread throughout her body at his gentle assault. "You've turned my world upside down," she whispered.

He smiled as he reached up to cradle her head in his palm and continued to lavish her neck with kisses and teasing nibbles. "How so?"

"A few days ago, I was boring old Taegen Lane," she said breathlessly. "Lonely teacher's aide unable to move past her problems and her grief. I met a beautiful man who blew every theory on life I had right out of the water."

He grinned as she melted in his arms. He reached out and took her cup of coffee from her, setting it on the table in front of the sofa. He gently pushed her back against the cushions and leaned over, moving to the other side of her neck and giving it equal attention.

She reached up to tangle her fingers in his hair. "I don't know what to do with him now." Her voice was a throaty whisper, laden with passion.

He smiled and trailed his fingers down her neck as he playfully nipped on her earlobe. "I have a few ideas." He seized her lips in a searing kiss that left her gasping for air, and he could feel her furious heartbeat. It matched his own. He caressed her hair. "What do you feel, Taegen?" he whispered.

She let out a ragged sigh and shook her head, keeping her eyes closed. "On fire."

He smiled and kissed her again, taking his time, delighting in how her fingers dug slightly into his shoulders. One of her legs came up around his waist, trapping him against her. His entire body jolted at the contact, and he growled low in his throat. He had never in his whole life wanted someone so badly. Sure, he had been sexually attracted to a number of women, but what he felt for Taegen made all of that seem silly.

He wanted to explore every single inch of her body, wanted to lose himself inside of her until reality faded away and all he knew was her. She was like an addiction that just kept growing stronger. Not just her body, but her heart and her soul. He wanted all of it. He wanted all of it for his own. He wanted to take all her grief away. He wanted to make her smile and laugh. He wanted to erase all the fear from her and replace it with love. Love... He loved her. He really did. In only a few days, he had fallen so hard for her that he feared he would be lost forever.

She was strong, and he liked that. He liked that she could stand on her own two feet and be resilient. She was also vulnerable, and that was attractive to him as well. He was someone who loved to take care of people, and he wanted nothing

more than to make Taegen feel safe and protected. He wanted to hold her in his arms and have her confide in him, tell
him every secret fear and wish in her heart. He knew it was
insane, but he could close his eyes and see his entire future
stretched out before him like a clear map...and every vision
had Taegen in it. It was surreal, but he felt like he had been
waiting his whole life for her, just biding his time until that
moment he first glimpsed her on the train. In that brief moment, everything in his life had clicked into place.

Taegen's mind spun in the way it liked to do when he
kissed her. He made everything go away. Any pain, uncertainty, or grief that she might be feeling vanished as soon as
he touched her. She didn't understand it. All she felt when
she was close to Torrey was passion. Blind, raw, all-
consuming passion. It was unusual. It wasn't her way. She
was generally conservative, but he made her fill with wild,
wanton desire. He made her feel alive.

She tucked her hands under his shirt and ran them slowly
down his spine. His skin was smooth and warm on her palms
and she could feel the lines of muscle rippling beneath her
exploring fingers. Without much thought, she deftly unbuttoned his shirt, pulled it off, and flung it to the floor. He met
her eyes briefly in mild surprise, but she only grinned. She
wanted to touch him. She wanted to see his delicious body.
She pulled him back down to her, capturing his lips in another breathtaking kiss.

Torrey trailed his lips along Taegen's throat and across
her collarbone. She was still wearing the black dress Alyx
had let her borrow, and he traced his hand along her feminine curves. His fingers found the edge of her skirt and he
spanned his hand across her thigh, nudging the material up
ever so slightly.

"Hey, we're gonna have to find somewhere to buy some
clothes 'cause—Dude!" Javan spun and averted his eyes as
he came into the living room.

Taegen jumped and all but threw Torrey off her as she
struggled to pull her skirt back down and sit up. Her hair was
a mess and she tried in vain to smooth it while her lips
burned with the after effects of Torrey's hungry kisses.

"Could you guys, like, put a sign up next time or something? I have seen you two sucking face a lot more than I
really would have liked," Javan grumbled, keeping his back

turned to them.

Torrey picked his shirt up and pulled it back on with a smirk. "We can go out whenever you want," he said. "I know we need to get some clothes. I really doubt Taegen wants to be running around for two days in a tight black dress." He let his eyes rake over her for a second, and his grin was devilish. "Not that I would mind."

Taegen felt her face flush.

"Yeah, I'll just let you know when Alyx and Maxim are ready. Are you guys going to stay fully clothed for awhile or should I shout a warning next time I come looking for you?"

"I think we're good," Torrey chuckled.

Javan rolled his eyes and muttered something under his breath as he left the room.

Taegen put her hands over her face in embarrassment. What in the world was wrong with her? She didn't act like this. She didn't wrap her legs around guys and yank off their clothes.

Torrey frowned, picking up on her anxiety. "What is it?" he asked, gently caressing her arm.

"Torrey, this is insane."

"Why? What's insane?"

"You and me. This whole thing. It's just...not normal." She shook her head. "This all has been so magical, but what happens when this trip is all over? What happens after Javan and Maxim and Alyx go home and it's just you and me?" What if what they felt for one another was just based on a fantasy? What if it was only fueled by the adventures they kept having together? What if there was nothing solid there at all?

He smiled and brought her fingers to his lips. "I'm coaching a little league game next weekend," he said. "Why don't you come?"

She smiled at his simple reply. "And after that?"

He shrugged casually. "I dunno. Pizza at the pier?"

She sighed in exasperation and met his eyes. "Is everything so easy for you?"

He took her face in his hands and feathered his thumbs across her skin. "Taegen, what is this all about? Where is this coming from? Do you think I'm going to disappear and leave you all alone after the others go back to Oregon?"

She averted her gaze. "This has all just been too magical." Magic didn't exist in real life. Especially not in her life.

Torrey kissed her on the forehead. "My dear little fatalist," he teased. "I am not going anywhere. I told you that. Besides, everyone needs a bit of magic in their lives, don't you think?"

She swallowed and leaned against him, resting her head on his shoulder. All of this was so hard for her to wrap her mind around. Everything about Torrey conflicted so heavily with everything she had trained herself to believe about life. "I've never met anyone like you before, so free and spontaneous. Do you worry about anything?"

He tangled his fingers in her hair. "Of course I do. I am human. But life is made of moments, as I said before. I genuinely believe that each one should count. I try to make every second of my day as full as it can be. There is no way to predict the future. All I really know is that I care for you very much, and that there was awesome chemistry between us before the Ashland trio ever entered into the picture." He paused and studied her for a moment, his dark eyes capturing hers. "At least, I thought we had awesome chemistry. Perhaps I was only imagining it?"

Taegen frowned and shook her head adamantly. "No, Torrey, you didn't imagine anything."

He smiled and pulled her closer to him.

She couldn't look into his eyes. They were so powerful. They made her feel like he could see every thought and feeling she possessed.

He ran his hand up her arm, and his fingers stopped to massage the nape of her neck. "And do you feel the magic now?"

Her breath caught and she nodded, her heart picking up its pace. There was no one in the world like Torrey. He was so intense, so sexy, so smooth. He was the closest thing to a romance novel hero she had ever seen...and she had read her share. She shivered as his fingers brushed her cheek.

"Taegen," he whispered, "look at me."

"I can't," she stated with a small frown. "Your eyes are just wrong. They drive me crazy. They make me melt inside."

His chuckle was soft, and he caught her chin with his forefinger. "Come on," he urged. "Let me look at you."

She relented and gazed up into his fantastic green eyes.

They were so soft, holding nothing but sincerity. She sighed.

A smile tugged at his perfect lips and he leaned in to caress her nose with his. "Tell me something," he murmured. "Why were you staring at me on the train?"

She blushed and smiled shyly. "I liked your drawing." She stole a peek up at him. "I realized a little later that the artist wasn't so bad either."

"My heart almost stopped when I saw you in that park. I had been kicking myself for not talking to you when I first saw you."

"I thought you were following me."

"I frightened you."

"A little. Beautiful men don't just pop out of nowhere that often, and if they do, they usually don't have the best of intentions."

"I had perfect intentions."

Taegen grinned, then sobered. "I'm glad I found you again."

"So am I." He gazed intently into her eyes for a moment, memorizing her lovely face and remembering the second verse of *Consuming*. Had she really felt that way when she thought she'd lost him? Like she was an empty shell? He'd never imagined he could affect someone that way. He lowered his lips to hers in a deliberate teasing stroke. He felt her shiver and he smiled. He cupped her cheek with his hand and pressed his lips to hers, losing himself in her gentle passion and silken kisses.

Chapter Twenty-Five

Van let out a soft sigh as he felt Nyah's arms circle around his neck. He watched the cover band on the stage at Carnival Court at Harrah's with little interest, which wasn't like him. Usually music of any kind held his rapt attention, but tonight his mind wandered to other things. Things from his past that continued to haunt him, regrets he couldn't get over. It was the worst when he looked at Maxim and Alyx.

The five strangers they had picked up in San Francisco had spent a good portion of the day out shopping with Darren, but when they'd returned, Darren had managed to convince Lance to go out with them for dinner and dancing. Lance hadn't even given Van a choice, and the next thing he knew, he was being dragged along as well. He didn't mind really, but watching Maxim and Alyx interact was difficult for him. He saw so much of himself in Maxim. The awkward shyness, the look of depth in his eyes that suggested his mind was always dwelling on something beyond himself. He seemed out of place when he was sitting alone. He didn't look like he belonged with a bunch of metal fans and goth rockers, but when Alyx was around him, he blossomed. It was easy to spot for a person who would understand. Van understood. He understood more than anyone there.

"Are you okay, baby?" Nyah's sultry voice purred in his ear. "You're so quiet tonight."

Van sighed and forced a small smile. He covered her hand with his. "I'm fine, honey. Just tired. Why don't you go dance? You don't need to sit here and watch over me all night. I think those guys over there recognize you." He pointed to a table in a dimly lit corner. "Why don't you go make their night and dance with them?"

"But I want to dance with you," she practically whined.

"I know, but I don't feel much like dancing. Go on, have a good time. I don't mind."

She pressed a kiss to his cheek and sauntered over to the corner table. The men sitting there looked so shocked that Van had to chuckle. Nyah did have that effect. Most every man on the planet would sell a vital organ for just one look from Nyah Densmoore. She was all curves and smoldering sensuality. He should consider himself very lucky to have such a gorgeous woman at his side, but it just felt so...empty to him.

She didn't make him laugh. Not the way Alyx made Maxim laugh. Not the way *she* had... He shook his head and went to go sit at the table with Torrey, Taegen, and Darren. Dwelling on things long past would do him no good. He was the one who had messed up. It was his own fault. No one else's.

* * * *

Taegen was staring at the drink menu when Van pulled up a chair and joined them at their table. She knew nothing about alcohol. Whenever she'd gone out with Paul, he had always ordered for her.

"Can I get you something?" the cocktail waitress asked suddenly.

Taegen looked up and then glanced back down at the menu. "Sure, gimme...one of those." She pointed to a random beer and Torrey raised his eyebrows. He chuckled and she looked up at him. "What?"

He shook his head. "Nothing." He reached over and covered her hand with his, toying with her fingers as he watched the band play. They were playing everything from classic rock to funk.

"Taegen!" Alyx shouted suddenly as Wilson Pickett's "Mustang Sally" started to play. "Come on! Dance with me! I love this song! Please?"

Taegen grinned and stood. Alyx grabbed her hand and the two of them headed out onto the dance floor with Javan in tow.

Torrey smiled and went over to Maxim's table as Darren started talking to Van. "How you doing over here?" he asked.

Maxim looked at him and smiled. "I'm good, actually." He chuckled. "Can't believe I'm sitting in a club in Vegas with a bunch of rock stars and I just said I'm good, but it's true."

Torrey laughed. "You've definitely made progress, Max."

Maxim sighed as he watched Alyx laugh with Taegen as Javan started to shake his butt in a ridiculous way during the chorus.

"Oh, now that's just wrong," Torrey remarked.

Maxim laughed and looked at Torrey, smiling at the look of adoration on his face. He wondered if he even knew that he was staring at Taegen that way. Like she was an angel just descended from heaven. "You love her, don't you?"

Torrey met Maxim's eyes and smiled shyly. "It's that obvious, huh?"

Maxim smirked. "I only noticed because you're staring at her like she's the only woman here."

"Kind of like the way you look at Alyx?"

He chuckled. "Exactly."

Torrey shook his head and let his eyes wander back to the object of his affection. "I think I loved her the moment I saw her," he said. "As crazy as that sounds."

"I've stopped trying to figure out what's crazy and what's not. When I was first forced into this, I thought coming on a trip with two strangers was the craziest thing I'd ever done. Three head injuries, a Yeti, a skunk, two random people, a girl who actually likes me, and a bunch of rock stars in Las Vegas later..." He rolled his eyes. "Crazy is a word that's no longer in my vocabulary."

Torrey laughed. "You know, my greatest fear in life is to end up in a loveless marriage and die alone and miserable," he blurted. "I guess that's why I'm so picky with women. I'm terrified I'll end up loving someone so much that it blinds me to reality. Then one day I'll wake up stuck in some life I never wanted, holding onto a dream that will never happen."

Maxim frowned, more than a little surprised at Torrey's admission. He seemed so collected, so suave and sure of himself. To know that he hid a secret fear of that magnitude was strange to Maxim. Who would marry Torrey and not love him? He was a fantastic person. He was fun and exciting and full of passion for life. He shook his head. "I don't think you need to worry about Taegen, Torrey. She looks at you like you're plated in gold."

"You think so?"

Maxim nodded. "Yeah." He turned toward Alyx as the three of them headed back over to the table. They were laughing, and Alyx leaned over to press a quick kiss to Maxim's lips. A small jolt shot through him and he wondered if he would ever get used to her showing him affection. Every time she touched him, he felt like it was the first time all over again.

"I have to call Merrill," Alyx stated as she pulled out her cell phone. "He's seriously going to crap a brick when he finds out where we are right now." She switched the mode to speaker phone.

Torrey laughed. "Don't forget to tell him who you picked up along the way." He reached over to grab his drink from Van's table as the waitress delivered them.

"How was the concert?" Merrill's voice drawled as he answered the phone.

Alyx grinned. "Awesome, of course, but do you know what's even better?"

"What?"

"The fact that your brother knows the bassist of Fat Stinky and got us on their tour bus. We are currently sitting in Vegas with Van Marshall, Lance Lawson, and Nyah Densmoore, and we get to see their show again tomorrow!"

"What?" he screeched. "No way! How did—wait a second. What did you say about my brother?"

She giggled. "We picked him up in Fort Bragg by complete bizarre coincidence. Javan gave him one of our extra tickets and we've been staying at his house."

"Man, I hate you all," he stated. "But I really hate Torrey. It's bad enough that you guys left me here to rot while you went to the show, but to have my brother go and not me is just wrong. You're my friends, not his."

"Well, no offense Merrill, but it wasn't you who knew the bassist of Fat Stinky." He grumbled something she couldn't understand and she giggled.

"Hey guess where I'm at right now?" he asked.

"Where?"

"Geppetto's, being waited on by your heinous ex boyfriend."

She frowned. "Are you serious?"

"Yeah, he just brought me bread." He sighed. "I can't believe you're in Vegas, Alyx! With Bleeding Passion no less!"

She laughed again. "I know! It's unreal! I'll take lots of pictures, I promise."

"Yeah, whatever. Hey, let me talk to Tor."

Alyx took it off speaker phone and handed it over to Torrey, then turned back to Maxim with a grin. He smiled and reached his hand up to lightly rub across her shoulders. She closed her eyes, her heart doing somersaults at the tender touch.

"Alyx?" he said as The Righteous Brothers' "Unchained Melody" started to play. "Would you like to dance?"

She looked up at him in surprise and a slow grin spread across her lips. She nodded and let him lead her out onto the dance floor. His arm slipped around her waist and she wrapped hers around his neck as her body fit perfectly against his. They swayed slowly to the music and she rested her cheek against Maxim's shoulder, getting lost in the feel of being in his arms. It was divine. It was heaven. It was where she was meant to be.

* * * *

Over the course of the night, all of them danced way too much. Javan was pretty sure that his legs were going to fall off, and Alyx was out of breath and sweaty. Taegen kept throwing back beer after beer, and any inhibitions she had went sailing out the window. What was the point? She only had one life. Paul would want her to have fun, and that was what she was going to do. She danced until she didn't think she would be able to anymore, but she kept it up purely for her own enjoyment. She loved to watch Torrey's body move. She would dance herself right into her grave if she could continue to watch him. She wanted to spend the rest of her life watching him. Watching him move, watching him laugh, watching him do a hundred little things that most people took for granted. She wanted to watch life pass by with him at her side. She realized that she hadn't even really been living until Torrey had come into her life. She'd just been existing. The day she'd seen him on the train was the day her life had really started. She would be stupid if she didn't stay with him forever... Really stupid.

She frowned and looked over at him. He laughed at

something Van said. He had the most beautiful smile she had ever seen. Why was she always such a freak anyway? He was enchanting. He brought magic to her life. Everyone needed a bit of magic. He had said so himself... Right, she wasn't going to analyze this one. She didn't care that she was drunk. She just wanted to be with him for the rest of her life. That was all that mattered to her at the moment. She loved this man.

Taegen reached out and grabbed Torrey's wrist with urgency, causing him to look over at her in alarm. "What is it?" he asked. "Are you all right?"

"Come with me," she demanded. "Now."

He raised an eyebrow, but stood slowly. "Okay..."

She grinned, laced her fingers with his, and led him out of the club.

* * * *

"Does anyone know where Taegen and Torrey went?" Javan grumbled as he flopped down in one of the hotel chairs.

"I have no idea," Alyx said with a yawn. "One minute they were there, and the next, they'd disappeared." She shrugged. "I'm not that worried. They're adults. They know where the hotel is." She sat down next to Maxim on the sofa and sighed. She rested her head against his shoulder and closed her eyes. "I don't know about you, but I'm exhausted. I've never danced so much in my life." She grinned and glanced up at Maxim. "Even you were out there busting some moves."

He chuckled. "Yeah, well..."

The door burst open suddenly and Torrey and Taegen stumbled in, laughing and kissing. Torrey pushed Taegen back against the door, pinning her there with his body as he kissed her thoroughly.

Javan raised an eyebrow and glanced at Alyx and Maxim. He cleared his throat.

Torrey spun and grinned when he saw his friends. "Hey guys," he greeted.

Javan frowned. "Dude, where have you two been? You disappear on us and all you have to say for yourselves is 'hey guys?'"

Taegen giggled and came to stand next to Torrey. His arm encircled her shoulders and she leaned into his body.

"Yeah, where did you guys go anyway?" Alyx prodded.

Torrey's grin was bright enough to light an entire town. He pulled Taegen close and kissed her on the forehead.

Taegen laughed jubilantly and held her left hand up. Her ring finger sported a thin, gold band. "We got married."

Chapter Twenty-Six

"You *what*?!" Javan screeched. He jumped to his feet like an angry father would after waiting up all night for his child. "Did I just hallucinate?"

Torrey grinned and Taegen giggled. She shook her head.

Maxim blinked rapidly, his brain refusing to take in the knowledge that was being handed to him. Alyx was apparently having the same problem because she just stared at them awhile before shaking her head violently like she was trying to get her thoughts to coalesce.

Javan opened his mouth in an attempt to say something, but for once, nothing came out.

"I-I think that would be our cue to leave the room," Maxim interjected, standing up.

"No, that's okay," Torrey said. "I don't want to kick you guys out. It's a suite. We'll just go in the bedroom."

"And we can sleep on the pullout while you guys do the horizontal polka in the next room. Gee, how thoughtful of you," Javan muttered.

"Just uh...turn up the TV," Alyx suggested, switching it on.

Taegen blushed a bright shade of crimson and buried her face against Torrey's shoulder. "This is really embarrassing," she whispered.

He grinned in obvious jubilation. He bent, swept Taegen up into his arms, and carried her to the bedroom as she squealed with laughter. He kicked the door shut, leaving Maxim, Javan, and Alyx staring in stunned silence.

Javan shook his head and ran his fingers through his hair. "Dude, I did not expect that."

"Yeah, I'm a little surprised myself," Alyx said.

Maxim smiled. "I'm not."

They both turned and stared at him with a frown.

He shrugged. "I mean, it's kind of surprising that Taegen actually did it. Especially since she's always trying to analyze things to death, but why not? He loves her, and she loves him. Why not get married?"

"Maxim, they've only known each other for, what, a week?" Alyx cried.

"So? I've only known you for a week."

She paled.

He chuckled. "No, I'm not asking you to marry me. I'm just saying, who are we to judge? Come on, let's just watch TV and try not to pay attention to the back room."

Javan shook his head and was still muttering under his breath as he sat back down.

Maxim smiled and resumed his seat on the couch. He pulled Alyx into his arms, secretly delighted for Torrey and Taegen. It was more than obvious how much Torrey loved her, and he was happy that she had actually followed her heart instead of trying to convince herself that every move she made outside of her safe zone was the wrong one. Sometimes, the safe zone needed to be obliterated. It was the most important lesson he had learned.

* * * *

Taegen's mind spun like she was back on the teacups at Disneyland. She wasn't sure if it was from all the alcohol she had consumed, or if it was from the blur of the past several hours. Her breath left her body in a rush as Torrey lay her down gently on the bed and leaned over her. She became acutely aware of how hard her heart was beating and of how silent it was in the room. It struck her as odd because she'd always heard that alcohol dulled your senses. But, seeing as how she'd never been drunk before, she wouldn't know.

She closed her eyes as Torrey traced his fingers lightly across her lips and jaw, drawing them along the column of her throat toward the V of her neckline. He dipped to press a kiss there, and her breath hitched in her throat.

Torrey smiled at her reaction to his touch and he mar-veled over the fact that she was his now. Really and truly his. His wife... He had been beyond surprised when she had brought up the idea to him. Especially since she had expressed her fear of commitment and impulsiveness on more than one occasion, but she had seemed so sincere. Her eyes when she'd told him that she wanted to be with him forever... He would remember the look in them for the rest of his life. It was the kind of look he had been waiting an eternity for. And he had no doubts in his mind that she was the one for him. The only one. The only one he would ever want. He knew that there were some who would condemn them and say that eloping in Vegas with a woman who, in all respects, he barely knew was a ridiculous and foolish gamble, but what was life worth if you didn't take chances? He wanted to make the most of every moment, and he knew beyond a shadow of a doubt that he did not want one more moment without Taegen.

He lowered his body to rest against hers as he caught her lips in a slow, languorous kiss. He inched his fingers below her shirt and slid them up her satin skin. He felt her shudder, and heard her small gasp. He moved his lips to her neck, lavishing it with attention in the way he knew she loved as he pulled her shirt up and off in an unhurried movement. Her fingers instantly grasped at his shirt, tugging the cloth upward until he moved away to yank it off. He bent back down to kiss her, but she stopped him with a palm against his chest. He froze with a frown.

Taegen pushed him back until they sat facing one another, and she raised both of her hands to his shoulders. She had wanted to see his elegant body from the moment she'd met him, and she was going to take her time with it. She trailed her palms across his chest and shoulders, down his toned stomach and up his sides, feeling every inch of his smooth skin. He closed his eyes and tangled his fingers in her hair, leaning in to claim another kiss.

Her fingers continued their exploration as he kissed her, going around the back of his shoulders and down his spine in a slow, sweeping caress. She felt him reach up to unhook the clasp on her bra, and her cheeks turned hot as the fabric fell away from her body. She wasn't very confident about the way she looked naked, and having such a perfect man stare at her made her feel so vulnerable that she almost wanted to run away. She hated feeling vulnerable. Instinctively, she pulled back to cover herself.

Torrey frowned and shook his head, gently moving her hands aside. "Don't hide yourself from me, Taegen," he whispered. "You're my wife, and you're gorgeous. Let me worship your body the way it deserves." He eased her back down on the bed and let his eyes take in all of her pale, silken skin. She was so beautiful. So beautiful that he ached when he looked at her. He knew that she was uncomfortable and felt awkward, but she had nothing to worry about. She was flawless. Even if in her eyes, she felt otherwise, she was perfect to him.

He smiled softly and spanned his fingers across her stomach and narrow waist, running them gently up her body in the way she had done to him, exploring every inch of her feminine softness.

Any awkwardness Taegen had felt at being exposed in front of him quickly fled at his tender assault. His touch set her body aflame, and after he had finished exploring, he bent to replace where his fingers had traveled with his lips and tongue. She drew her breath in sharply and arched her body up, offering more of herself to him. Before her mind had a chance to come back to reality, he had pulled her jeans off, thrown them on the floor, and was tugging at the edge of her lacy, black panties. She fought the urge to laugh as she remembered the conversation she'd had with herself the night she'd first met him. *What good are those lacy, black panties you have if no one ever gets to see them?* Well, someone was looking right at them now. Maybe her inner voice would finally shut up. It had only been wreaking havoc since she'd met Torrey. It was annoying at best, even if some small part of her felt like it was Paul's influence in the back of her mind still working on her. This entire experience would have been right up her brother's alley.

Her heart hammered as she felt him slip the thin strip of material down her legs. She closed her eyes to try and keep herself grounded. Was she really about to make love to Torrey? The most extraordinary man ever created was married to her? Was going to share his body with her? It made no sense. None of this made sense, but she didn't have time to dwell on it because Torrey stood swiftly, removed his remaining clothing, and came to lay beside her, all of his velvety skin sliding against hers in the most intoxicatingly seductive caress she had ever experienced. He was magnificent, so stunning it should be against the law. His hands continued their lazy, torturous journey, and she let out a deep groan as he sought out every secret place on her body while he continued to shower her chest and neck with searing kisses.

* * * *

Javan flipped absently through the channels on the television, searching for anything to keep his mind off what was transpiring in the next room. "How is it that there is absolutely nothing on?" he grumbled.

Alyx smirked. "You're just irritated because Torrey's getting some and you aren't," she teased.

He scowled. "Yeah, rub it in, why don't you?"

She giggled and snuggled closer to Maxim. A loud moan suddenly sounded from the bedroom and she raised her eyebrows. "Hey whatever Torrey's doing must be good," she remarked. Another moan came, this one louder than the first.

Javan bristled. "Okay, I don't know about all of you, but I'm not really in the mood to listen to this all night."

Maxim smiled and was already starting to stand up. "Anyone up for a late night snack at the coffee shop downstairs?"

"Count me in," Javan volunteered.

Alyx stood. "Yeah, me too."

* * * *

Taegen's breath came in shallow, ragged gasps after Torrey's relentless onslaught of passion. The way he touched and kissed, the things he made her feel...all of it was deliciously wicked. Her body tingled and burned, crying out for him in every way. "Now you know what it's like to be worshipped," he whispered with a smile, taking her hands in his and raising her arms above her head.

She nodded, unable to do anything else. The tumultuous chaos he had awakened in her did not allow her to speak. All she could do was stare up at him helplessly, aching for him to give her what she wanted and needed more than anything else. Tears waited just behind her eyes. She could feel them.

He had brought them forth with the way he had so selflessly explored her body. She could feel the kindness in his touch, the love in every sweep of his hand or brush of his lips. He handled her like she was a precious gift that was to be savored, and he had no idea how badly she had needed that. To feel like she mattered to someone in the world, to feel like she was lovable and know that she was able to love in return. She thought her heart had frozen, that it would never feel anything but sorrow again. Torrey had changed all of that. He had brought her back to life, had given her beauty again.

One tear succeeded in slipping down her cheek and she closed her eyes. "Torrey," she whispered.

He looked down at her in concern and cupped her cheek in his palm, catching the falling tear. "What is it?" he asked softly. "Why are you crying?"

She forced herself to look up into his green eyes, and she loved that she could see the desire smoldering in them. She gave him a wobbly smile and forced her tears away. She wasn't going to flip out on him now. Now was not the time for her overwhelming emotions. She reached up to stroke his hair, letting the strands fall through her fingers. "I love you."

Torrey let out a long, slow breath and everything in his universe fell into place as she uttered those words. He closed his eyes and let them echo through his mind and take root in his soul. His entire body coiled tight and turned molten as the soft words left her and wrapped around his heart. He gripped her hands in his and lavished her lips with ardent, fevered kisses as he gave himself over to the passion he felt and lost himself inside of her body. He caught her gasp in his mouth and he shuddered as she reached up around his shoulders and dug her fingernails gently into his back.

"Torrey," she murmured, her voice breathy and thick with the exquisite pleasure she felt.

"Yes, love?" He looked down at her, brushing his lips across her cheeks and forehead.

She met his eyes and gave him a small, warm smile. "With you, I am whole again."

He stared down into her eyes and lost himself there. He stroked her hair and kissed her again as he moved against her. A smile pulled at his lips at the small noises she made in her throat. His heart was dancing in the heavens, and before the night was over, he planned on showing her just how much he loved and appreciated her. She didn't know it, but she had completed him as well. He had been waiting for her, and his life was full now. Every day would be ten times more radiant with Taegen in it. He knew that in the very depths of him. He could never love another like he loved her. It wasn't possible. He believed in soul mates and she was his. She was the other half of his heart. She was his entire world.

* * * *

Alyx, Maxim, and Javan lay side by side on the pullout bed, staring up at the ceiling.

"This has been a really weird trip," Javan commented.

Maxim chuckled. "Got that right."

"Well, at least we were down there long enough to miss the festivities," Alyx said.

Suddenly, Taegen's laughter echoed through the suite and all three of them tensed.

"Oh come on, don't they sleep?" Javan grumbled.

As if in response, another one of those dead-giveaway moans followed the laugh, only this time it was a much lower octave and the words, "Oh good lord, woman" came after it.

Alyx raised an eyebrow. "Sounds like it's Torrey's turn to be...conquered...taken? I don't know, ewwww." Alyx made a face and squirmed uncomfortably.

Javan started to whimper like he was going to cry and he flopped the pillow over his head. "Come *on*!" he cried. "This is *so wrong*!"

Alyx and Maxim laughed and she reached down for the television remote. She flicked it on again and turned the volume up as high as it could go without blowing them out of the room. She found some old episode of *Saturday Night Live* and left it on, cuddling up next to Maxim and ignoring their friends in the next room.

Chapter Twenty-Seven

It was with blurred eyes and sleep-deprived brains that Maxim, Javan, and Alyx left the hotel room with the intent of going down to get breakfast at the same coffee shop they had eaten at the night before. They'd left the TV on all night just to be safe, and as a result, they'd really only snagged snippets of decent sleep.

Alyx let out a monstrous yawn as they left the elevator and made their way to the coffee shop. When they got there, she groaned and rolled her eyes. "I left my purse back in the room," she grumbled. "You guys go ahead and get a table. I'll be right back."

Javan and Maxim nodded and headed into the restaurant.

* * * *

Alyx sighed as she left their hotel room and started back toward the elevators. She seriously needed some coffee or something because she felt like she was walking in a fog. She smiled to herself as she thought of Taegen and Torrey. It was insane that they had just up and eloped, but she guessed Maxim was right. It wasn't really her place to judge. As long as they were happy together... And last night had definitely led her to believe that they were very happy.

She pushed the button on the elevator and hummed softly to herself as she waited. It was all right that she'd had to share the pullout with Javan and Maxim. It had forced her to sleep extra close to Maxim, and she had enjoyed every minute of it. She had awakened with one of his hands tangled in her hair and the other one resting on her exposed stomach while she was nestled safely in his arms. It was a wonderful way to wake up, one she could get used to.

The elevator chimed suddenly and she started to get in, but all of the blood drained from her face as she looked up at the man stepping out into the hall. She almost choked and she retreated several steps. He swaggered up to her, his lips twisted into that fake apologetic smile. His posture resonated with casual menace.

"Hey, baby," he greeted.

"Rick," she whispered. "How..." She swallowed hard and forced herself to remain calm. "What are you doing here?"

"You never returned my call so I thought I'd come and find you. I needed to see you, baby. I was dying without you."

"How did you find me?" She glanced around her, but realized it was stupid. There was no one around to help her if he decided to attack. The only good thing was that she was by the elevators. Maybe a random stranger would come by.

"I overheard your friend talking to you at the restaurant last night." He shrugged his shoulders and looked sheepish. "I know I shouldn't have done that, eavesdropped, but I needed to talk to you somehow, Alyx. You wouldn't return my calls. So I just hopped a red-eye and tracked you down." He chuckled. "Kind of interesting how you ended up getting to hang with a famous band. What did you have to do to get that shoe in the door?" His dark eyes flashed for a moment, but he masked it quickly.

"Look, I didn't return your calls for a reason, you jerk," she stated bravely. "I don't want anything to do with you so get out of my life." She tried to step past him, but he blocked her.

"Alyx, listen to me for a second," he begged. "Please, you don't know what it's been like without you. I know I messed up, but I promise I'll never lift a finger to you again. I was just so angry. You know how I get sometimes."

She glowered up at him. "You mean how you sometimes get the craving to beat the crap out of me for no reason? Yeah, I know that part of you real well."

His eyes narrowed. "I would never hurt you on purpose and you know it," he hissed. "I only lashed out at you because you like to do things that you know will piss me off. If you just—"

She snorted. "If I just what, Rick? If I just cut all of my friends and family out of my life, bat my eyes and do whatever you say, and tie myself naked to your bed so you can use me whenever you feel like it, you'll stop beating me? I'll pass, thanks." She didn't need this right now. The guy was more of a lunatic than she'd given him credit for. She couldn't believe he'd actually *followed* her to Las Vegas. The man had serious problems.

"Stop being so over dramatic," he spat. "Come on, Alyx. Just come home with me. What are you doing here anyway? Who are you with?" He fixed her with a black scowl. "You're with Javan, aren't you?"

She met his eyes and folded her arms. "Yeah, actually, I am, but Javan isn't who you need to worry about." She knew she should just shut up and get out of there, but he didn't seem as intimidating to her as he once had. Not now. Not after she knew what it was like to be with a real man who treated her the way she deserved.

The look in his eyes changed from slightly irritated to dark and dangerous. He raised himself taller and stepped closer so that he towered over her. "And who exactly should I be worried about then?" he snarled.

"Maxim," she stated. "My boyfriend."

* * * *

Maxim tapped his fingers on the table and frowned as he glanced at his watch. "Alyx has been gone a long time," he said.

Javan looked up from his menu and shrugged. "Maybe she needed to use the bathroom."

"She went before we left the hotel room."

"Well then, maybe she got lost."

Maxim fixed Javan with an incredulous stare. "It's a giant pyramid, Javan. How lost could she possibly get?"

"Hey, don't ask me. Alyx never was very good at geometry."

He shook his head, his chest feeling tight all of a sudden. "No, something's wrong." He stood. "I have to find her."

Javan frowned and looked up at him. "What? What do you mean something's wrong?"

"I-I don't know. Something's just—" He grabbed Javan's arm and hauled him out of his chair. "Come on, we have to go. Something's not right."

"How do you know?" he asked as he stumbled after him out of the restaurant.

"I can feel it."

* * * *

"Well, you don't waste any time, do you?" he growled. "Congratulations, Alyx. I didn't know you had it in you. You certainly never let on to me what a slut you are. So, where'd you pick him up? Did you do your famous song and dance? Flash your pretty smile and show a little skin, and then turn into the ice queen I know you to be, or did this guy actually get some out of you? Please tell me he didn't because that would definitely hurt my feelings."

He had backed her up against the wall, but she continued to meet his unrelenting gaze. "Is that all I was to you? A sex toy? Is that all that mattered?"

"Of course not. How can you say that? I loved you!"

She didn't even have time to blink before the flat of his hand smacked across her cheek, sending her head jerking sideways. Tears burned in her eyes and her ear rang in the way she was used to it doing after he hit her. What she wasn't used to was the sudden way Rick stumbled away from her as Maxim's fist connected with his jaw.

"You abhorrent creature," Maxim snarled, looking anything like the quiet, awkward man she was used to. His eyes were flashing blue fire and his fists were balled at his sides. He stood tall and unrelenting, staring Rick down like he was a bug about to be squashed. "So help me, if you ever raise a hand to her again, I will hunt you down and kill you."

Rick recovered from the blow quickly and turned to face Maxim. "So, you must be the famous new boyfriend I just heard about." He laughed and shook his head. "Well, I have to admit I was worried for a minute." He looked at Alyx like it was all just a big joke. "Honestly, Alyx, I can forgive you for this one. It's obvious that you only went out with this computer geek out of pity. Come home with me now. You need a real man after this sorry excuse."

"It wasn't a sorry excuse who just punched you in the jaw," Javan said. "What are you doing here anyway? Are you a stalker now?" He put a well-placed hand on Rick's shoulder and shoved, just enough to make him knock back into the wall.

Rick snorted. "I just came to get what's mine." He bumped into the wall and then righted himself quickly, cracking his neck as if that somehow made him seem tougher.

"She's not your property," Maxim snarled. "You're not even fit to breathe the same air as her."

He laughed. "Aw, are you going to protect her? How sweet. Too bad you hit like a girl."

"Yeah, you'd know all about how to beat up on someone, wouldn't you?" Javan interrupted.

Rick rolled his eyes. "Please, I never 'beat up' on Alyx. I did, however, have to discipline her. Otherwise, she never would have learned. You were the bad influence on her, turning her against me. It's you she needed to stay away from. You and her idiot brother—"

"Don't you *dare* insult my brother!" Alyx shouted, shoving Rick back with enough vehemence to make him stumble.

He laughed and held his arms out to the sides in a taunting fashion. "Let's face it, baby. I'm the best you're ever going to get and you know it. Stupid, fat cows like you will never get the guy trimmed in gold, the 'knight in shining armor.' Awww, so sweet." He rolled his eyes in mockery. "You're just lucky I love you enough to accept you with all your obvious flaws. I can even overlook the fact that you're the biggest cock tease on the planet, but that's going to get old real fast so you'd better rethink this whole frigid thing. One of the only reasons I've been putting up with you this long is because I just know you're gonna be an awesome piece of ass—"

Maxim didn't really know what happened. He had been infuriated when he'd stepped out of the elevator and had seen Rick slap Alyx, but that was nothing compared to the rage that boiled up inside of him as Rick assaulted her with his horrible words. *No one* would say things like that to her and get away with it. Not while he was alive.

He pulled his fist back again and let it fly with every ounce of strength in his body. It made contact with Rick's nose, and made a sick cracking noise. Rick stumbled backwards and instinctively went to grab his bleeding nose, but Maxim didn't give him the chance. He punched him again in the stomach and flung him back against the wall, making Alyx shriek and jump. "This is what *you* deserve, you bastard." He drove his fist once more into the man's eye and hit him again across the mouth. Every place Alyx had told him she'd been struck he gave back to him. "Not bad for a computer geek, huh?" he spat. "Stay away from Alyx. If I see you near her again, I'm going for your cock and balls. And, rest assured, I *won't* tease." He let the man slump to the floor and turned to Alyx.

Alyx stared at Maxim, trembling so badly that she could hardly stand. She couldn't even believe what she had just witnessed. If she remembered nothing for the rest of her life, the vision of Maxim standing over Rick like some great avenging angel would stay with her forever. He looked so strong, so capable and powerful.

"Are you all right?" he asked tenderly. He took her face in his hands and gently wiped at the tears that had fallen down her cheeks.

She met his eyes, and the blue that had moments before been blazing like the hottest part of a flame were back to the tranquil sea she was used to. She fell into his arms and sagged against him. "My prince," she breathed. "I knew you were." She held on tight, never wanting to let him go again. She had seen fear in Rick's eyes. Genuine fear. Fear of the great and terrible Maxim. Her Maxim.

"I never thought I'd live to see the day when Maxim de-Boer would beat the crap out of someone," Javan said. He seemed so awestruck he could barely speak. He just shook his head in bewilderment.

Maxim frowned. "He hurt Alyx." He stated it very matter-of-factly and tangled his fingers in Alyx's hair. "I didn't think. I just reacted."

"I think you broke his nose," he said, glancing over at Rick who was moaning on the ground. "Maybe I should... Yeah, I'm going to call an ambulance." He laughed as he pulled out his cell phone. "Man, wait 'til I tell Jeff about this. You have, like, an Incredible Hulk hiding in your body, don't you?"

Maxim felt his face flush. His entire body was charged from the adrenaline that still coursed through him. It made him feel...powerful somehow.

"You rock, Max," Javan said quietly.

Maxim continued to touch Alyx's face as if he was inspecting it to see if there was any permanent damage. "I don't even know what happened," he admitted softly. "I've never hit anyone in my whole life. All I know is that I couldn't let that raging jerk keep speaking to you that way."

Alyx smiled up at him. "My whole life I've been pretty okay to defend myself. Rick was the only person who ever made me feel worthless."

"That's because you've never been worth jack—"

Maxim's anger boiled and raged again at the sound of Rick's voice and he turned back to him, his fingers curling into a fist.

"Ok, turbo," Javan said, intercepting Maxim and pushing him back a little. "You don't need to kill him. Let's just get out of here, okay?"

Maxim let out a sinister snarl, but he grabbed Alyx's hand and started to lead her back toward the hotel room. He stopped in front of Rick on his way, glanced up at Javan, who was heading down the hall, and kicked him a good one in the ribs. "Think about that while you wait for your ride," he spat. He led Alyx down the hall after Javan, leaving Rick in a whimpering pile on the floor. He ran his fingers across Alyx's knuckles. "You are not worthless," he said. "You're beautiful and special and—"

Grinning, she stopped, turned Maxim to face her, and placed her fingers to his lips. "Rick doesn't matter anymore. What he said doesn't matter and what he thinks doesn't matter. What you think matters."

He shook his head slowly and stroked her fingers. "No, Alyx. It's what *you* think that matters."

She studied his face for a moment and sighed. "I think I should have found you a long time ago."

He gazed into her eyes for several heartbeats, then took her face in his hands and kissed her with a slow, sensual passion. He relished the feel of her soft lips under his, and in knowing that he was the one who could save her from harm and kiss all the pain away. "Alyx, you rob me of everything I thought I knew and fill me with wonder and light."

She smiled and kissed his chin. "My beautiful poet." She caressed her hands across his chest and sighed. "Come on, let's go back to the room. I'm not really hungry anymore, and I just want to be with you."

Chapter Twenty-Eight

The first thing Taegen noticed when she awoke was that she didn't have a headache. She found that strange. Given the fact that she had been so inebriated the night before, she thought for sure that she would wake up with a horrendous migraine, but there was no pain in her head at all. She didn't feel sick to her stomach either.

She rolled over with a sigh and smiled as she gazed at Torrey's beautiful face. He was still asleep and she reached out to touch his cheek with her left hand. She caught sight of the gold band around her ring finger and her heart lurched. She blinked rapidly.

Torrey's eyes fluttered open. He smiled at her as he wrapped his arm around her waist and pulled her close up against him.

Taegen's senses were assaulted as she felt his bare skin against hers and she closed her eyes, feeling dizzy.

"Good morning, my beautiful wife." He grinned and traced her lips with his forefinger.

Wife. That word was like a bucket of ice water on her head. She jumped as her mind flooded with memories of the night before. She remembered dragging Torrey out of the club and going to some chapel on The Strip. They'd been married by some scary old dude, and one of their witnesses had been an Elvis impersonator. Torrey had found the ring she was wearing at a gift shop in The Excalibur, and they had used the Celtic ring he had given her for his. She remembered it all in a clarity that startled her. They'd gotten married. They'd actually eloped. In Las Vegas!

Her breath started coming in short gasps and she scrambled out of the bed. No, no, no, she couldn't have eloped in

Vegas with a man she barely knew. That was not something she would do. *Ever.*

Torrey frowned and he swung his legs out of bed. "Taegen, what's wrong?"

"You, you—I—" She shook her head. "Please tell me we didn't really get married last night." She grabbed the sheet and hastily held it up in front of herself.

He stared at her like she had lost her mind. "Of course we did. It was your idea!"

She shook her head violently. "No, that's not possible." She would never do something so impulsive, so rash, so stupid! She didn't even know this man! He was practically a stranger! *A beautiful stranger. You can't forget that.*

Shut up! She tangled her fingers in her hair and looked around frantically for her clothing. She started to pick them up and clutch them to her chest.

Torrey went over to her. "Taegen, what's the matter?"

She averted her eyes to keep herself from staring at his naked form, but her cheeks turned red anyway. "I couldn't have eloped in Vegas with you. That's not who I am. That's not what I do! I'm not some Britney Spears wannabe!" She flung her clothes on the bed and began to pull them on in a rush.

He put his hands on her shoulders in an attempt to calm her down. "Taegen, take a deep breath. We had a wonderful night together. Why are you freaking out on me?"

She jerked away from his touch and yanked her shirt on. "Because, Torrey, I married you last night when I wasn't even in my right mInd!"

He stepped back, folding his arms. "You seemed pretty coherent to me." Cold dread moved through him like poison. This couldn't be happening. She couldn't be trying to take back everything they had shared the night before. His heart trembled in fear at her words.

"How can you say that?" she spat. "I was drunk, Torrey!"

He frowned. "What?"

"You saw how much I had to drink! When I came up to you with the insane idea to get married, why didn't you take me back to the hotel room and make me go to sleep? You took advantage of me in a drunken state!"

"Taegen, you were drinking O'Doul's!" he shouted in exasperation. Unaccustomed to shouting, he was taken aback at his own outburst, but he couldn't believe she was trying to deny everything they had shared.

"So?"

"So, that's a non-alcoholic beer!"

She froze and stared at him in confusion and horror. "W-What?"

He raised an eyebrow. "You were drinking non-alcoholic beer, Taegen. You just thought you were drunk. You were perfectly sober."

She stood there for a moment, trying to process what he had just said. She really hadn't been drunk? She had done all of that with a completely clear mind? She swallowed hard, and her hands stared to shake. "No, something had to be wrong with me. I would never have married you in my right mind." Hurt and betrayal flashed in his eyes and clouded his beautiful face. "I just can't believe this," she went on. "We have to find somewhere to get a quick divorce."

His attention snapped to her. "What?"

"Well, it's Vegas. I imagine there has to be somewhere that we can get it done." She tried to get past him, but he stopped her.

"What are you saying?" he asked, his voice laced with pain. "That you're just going to marry me and then discard me? That everything you said to me was a complete lie?"

The hurt in his eyes stabbed at her heart and she looked down. She didn't want to hurt him. Good lord, she would never wish him pain, but she couldn't do this. She didn't know him. She couldn't pledge her life to a man she barely knew. It wasn't right. It went against everything she'd ever believed. How could she have done such an insane and spontaneous thing? It made no sense. It was so unlike her. She hadn't even wanted to go on a last minute road trip with Paul. How was it that she had managed to *marry* somebody? "I'm sorry, Torrey," she whispered.

He winced. "You told me you loved me."

She snorted. "Yeah, well I told my sixth grade teacher I loved him too. Didn't mean I knew what I was talking about."

He stepped away from her, flinching at her harsh words. He found his clothes and pulled them on, then left the bedroom and started for the front door. "So much for making the most of my moments," he grumbled. "So much for finding my soul mate."

"Where are you going?" Taegen called.

"To go find somewhere we can get divorced," he snapped. "Heaven forbid I keep you shackled to me any longer than necessary."

She squeezed her eyes shut at the cold tone of his voice. She had never heard him sound cold. "Wait," she called. "Torrey, wait."

He ignored her and yanked open the door only to find Maxim, Alyx, and Javan preparing to come in.

"Hey!" Javan cried. "You're up! I thought you guys would be asleep all day considering..."

"Please get out of my way," Torrey said icily.

Alyx frowned. "What's wrong?"

"My wife is sick of me already," he spat. "I guess she got out of me what she wanted."

"Torrey!" Taegen called. She ran up to him and grasped his arm, guilt washing over her in waves. She felt so confused. She thought she'd been drunk when she'd married Torrey, but now that she knew she hadn't been, nothing made sense. She couldn't understand what she had done when it was something she would never do. And she couldn't bear Torrey's cold words. She didn't want to lose him. He was the best thing to ever happen to her. She wasn't rejecting *him*. She was just rejecting the fact that she had leapt so blindly into something so enormous. How could she make him understand that? She couldn't pledge herself to him. Not like that. Not yet. Not for a long time. It left her too open, too vulnerable. Too...out of control.

"Wait, what?" Javan asked with a puzzled frown.

"Taegen is apparently the first woman in history to get drunk off of O'Doul's," Torrey said, his voice all smooth frigidness. "And I guess that means that she wasn't thinking clearly when she married me last night. She wants a divorce now, so I'm going to go grant her wish." He shook Taegen's hand off of his arm and tried to push past the three in the doorway, but Maxim let out an angry growl and shoved him backwards.

"Enough of this!" he bellowed. "Everybody just stop it!"

Torrey blinked in bewilderment and Taegen jumped back in surprise at Maxim's forcefulness.

"Taegen, stop being a baby." Maxim stabbed his finger at her. "And Torrey, maybe you could calm down for about two seconds and realize where Taegen is coming from."

Torrey scowled. "I've tried my best to figure out where she is coming from this entire time and—"

Maxim held his hands up and shook his head. "Dude, I am so not even finished yet." He fixed everyone with a measured stare and his tone silenced any further protests. "How many people here, besides Javan, know that Van Marshall has panic disorder?"

Everyone glanced at one another in bewildered silence.

"Nobody? How many people here know *why* Javan knows that Van Marshall has panic disorder?"

Again, no one said a word.

"It's because Javan graduated top of his class with a bachelor's in psychology. I bet you wouldn't have imagined that either. You know why? You know why no one would have guessed these things? It's because all people do is lie to one another! To their friends, the people they are closest to! We all put on this fake front to cover over some bizarre fear or insecurity. Alyx smiles all the time. She's always happy. You never see her depressed or irritated. She's always warm and fun when inside, she's hurting. Not five minutes ago, she was being assaulted by her abusive ex-boyfriend and you would never know it now because she's so good at pretending."

Alyx looked down self-consciously.

"Javan is a friggin' genius, but he plays the fool because he knows that, if he makes people laugh, they'll like him. Torrey, suave, charismatic, put together Torrey, his greatest fear is that he'll end up in a loveless marriage and die alone and heartbroken. You would never know that by being around him. He seems so self-assured."

Taegen looked up at Torrey in surprise and he averted his eyes, swallowing hard.

Maxim went on. "Taegen, she spends so much time overanalyzing just so she can find something wrong with everything. That way, she never has to leave the safe little box she's put herself in..."

Her eyes snapped to Maxim in anger. "You hide too, Maxim."

"Oh yeah!" he cried. "I'm an old pro at it! I hide behind the fact that I'm an introvert so that I never have to let people close to me. I pretend that I don't let people in because

I'm afraid they'll abandon me like my father, or die like my mother, or stab me in the back like Jeff's friends have done. It's all BS! The reason I don't let people get close to me is because I am terrified that if they see the real me, they'll hate me. They'll think I'm a freak, or a loser, or a weirdo..." He shook his head. "I've lived my whole life in that safe little box, but I realized that if you shut yourself in and shut the world out just to avoid being hurt, you're going to die alone in there.

"I didn't want to come on this trip. I wanted to kill my brother for making me do it, but it is the greatest thing he could have ever done for me. I've realized something about myself on this trip. See, I've always been passive Maxim, shy Maxim, but just a little bit ago, I saw Alyx being threatened and I didn't like it. What did I do, Javan?"

Javan glanced over at him. "You beat the snot out of Rick."

Maxim snorted. "Yeah, I did. Me! You see, I realized that I'm strong, and capable, and fiercely protective of people that I care about. I wouldn't have known that about myself if I hadn't let Alyx close to me..." He heaved a sigh and ran a hand through his hair. "We can't spend our lives letting fear dictate who we are. Sometimes, you just have to be you and take the risk... You taught me that. All of you. In five days."

He gave Taegen a pointed look. "Taegen, so you tricked yourself into thinking that you were drunk to give yourself an excuse to do what you really wanted to do. Who cares? You did something real, something genuine. That moment was all you and not the person you like to pretend to be. Torrey loves you. He worships the ground you walk on. Don't jack it up because you're afraid people will see through you and judge you for it. That's no way to live your life." He sighed and his shoulders sagged. He felt like all of the life had just been sucked out of him. He shook his head. "Excuse me, I think I need to lie down." He headed for the living room and Alyx followed close behind him.

Javan glanced at Torrey and Taegen, offered a small smile, and headed after Maxim as well.

Taegen sighed and let her head hang in shame as Maxim's words swam around in her brain. He was right... So right it was eerie.

"Well..." Torrey said softly. "I do believe we just got told."

She giggled and glanced up at him. He met her gaze with a faint glimmer of the gentle warmth she loved, and her heart melted. "Torrey, I'm so sorry," she said. "I'm ridiculous... I'm a spaz. You did not deserve any of what I just put you through."

He sighed in defeat and put his hands on her arms. "Taegen, I agreed to marry you last night because I love you. It wasn't just a game to me. I've loved you since the minute I saw you."

She shook her head. "But how is that possible?"

"What does it matter? What fun is life if you know the answer and solution to every little thing? Taegen." He met her eyes forcefully. "I want to spend the rest of my life convincing you that marrying me was not a mistake. I'll give you as much time as you want to figure things out. Just, please, don't throw me aside like a used towel."

She laughed a little and moved closer to his warm body. She placed her palm on his chest and remembered the way she had done that the night before. She smiled. "I really married you on my own," she murmured. "It's insane... I can't believe it." She met his eyes. "You're really my husband."

He smiled. "If you want me to be."

She sighed and slipped her arms around his waist. "I guess I can give it a try." It was hard for her to get the words out. They stuck in her throat. Letting herself do this, no matter how badly she may want it, was the most difficult thing she had ever done. Giving herself over to a man, letting her guard down and leaving herself open for attack. It was so hard... But she had married Torrey in a lucid state, even if she hadn't believed it at the time. Her heart had dictated that move for her. She needed to start listening to it. Carpe Diem all the way... She trembled as his lips gently caressed across hers, and she bunched her fingers in the fabric of his shirt.

Torrey cradled her in his arms, aware of her apprehension and her great fear. He ran his hands across her back, coaxing her to relax, kissing her with soft tenderness. Slowly, he felt her grip loosen on him and her body went pliant against his. He smiled and his heart rose from its momentary blackness with hope like a Phoenix rising from the ashes. She was choosing him again. She was giving him a chance. She wouldn't regret it. He would spend his life making her happy and showing her that sharing herself with another person didn't always have to bring pain. He would love her in a way that put every love story to shame. She deserved that, and he would give that gift to her.

* * * *

Maxim had a raging headache and his hand felt like it had been shattered. He lay on the couch with his fist in the ice bucket and his head on Alyx's lap. This knight in shining armor thing...it wasn't for him. Just give him a book and a latte any day.

He sighed as he felt Alyx's delicate fingers caressing his forehead and he smiled. "I think maybe I have multiple personality disorder," he commented.

She giggled. "You were crazy today," she teased. "You saved me, and Torrey and Taegen's spur of the moment marriage. I knew you were a super hero in disguise."

He chuckled and shook his head.

"We'll paint an S on your chest," she said, tracing the letter on him with her fingertip. "Call you Super Max instead of Super Man."

He laughed. "Equipped with his volleyball of doom and his useless trivia, Super Max bores villains into insanity. His only weakness is moldy bread." Alyx let out a loud laugh and he shook his head. "Man, what a sad super hero I would be."

She bent down to kiss his lips. "You're the perfect super hero. You know why?"

He looked up at her. "Why?"

"Because you're real. You're just a real guy doing what he thinks is right, and that makes you the best hero of all."

He rolled his eyes and waved her statement away, but he blushed anyway. He closed his eyes, intent on catching some sleep while he could. He wanted to get rid of his headache before the concert, and there was no better place to find sanctuary than Alyx's arms. She may think that he had saved her, but all he had done was punch a well-deserving jerk. She had saved him in so many ways he couldn't name them all. She was the real hero.

Chapter Twenty-Nine

Alyx and Taegen couldn't believe what they were seeing. They had watched Fat Stinky perform from the wings of the stage, but Dead Vampire had managed to hold their complete attention. The lead singer was tall with shining black short hair and a mysterious look about his chiseled face. He matched Van in appearance. Gothic, black clothes, eye makeup, but his voice... Alyx and Taegen exchanged rapturous glances as he hit the climax of the song.

Torrey and Maxim sighed as they watched their women drool over the singer. "I can't believe this," Torrey said. "I've been shown up by a dead vampire."

Maxim smiled. "I really don't think you need to worry," he assured.

Torrey raised an eyebrow. "Yeah, thanks to you. Your speech made a world of difference."

"She decided not to ditch you then?" Javan asked.

Torrey sighed. "For the moment. I'm hoping she doesn't have another one of those out of control moments and decide to divorce me again. My heart can't take it."

Alyx leaned over to Taegen as they watched the show. "That guy is really hot," she murmured.

Taegen nodded emphatically. "Do you think we'll get to meet him?"

"I hope so."

The girls continued to stand with their eyes glued to the stage for the duration of the concert. When Dead Vampire finished playing, Taegen and Alyx tried to find a way to the dressing room, but the lead singer stayed on stage to perform a bit with Bleeding Passion. When he wasn't on stage, he was in the opposite wing, and Rex refused to let anyone move around until the show was over. Disappointed, the girls returned to their guys to enjoy the rest of the concert.

"Oh, I see how it is," Torrey teased as he pulled Taegen into his embrace. "You only come to me when you can't get to the goth."

Taegen grinned and leaned back against him. "Can't I appreciate talent when I see it?"

Torrey snorted. "Right. Talent. Just so long as you don't decide he's a better choice and try to divorce me again."

Taegen's face flamed and she smacked him playfully in the arm. "Shut up. You're not being nice."

He chuckled and squeezed her tighter. "I'm sorry if I'm protective of my wife."

She shook her head. "Torrey, you freak me out every time you say that. Can we just cool it with the husband/wife thing for a bit? I'm trying not to flip on you."

He rested his chin on her shoulder and nodded. "Of course. Whatever you want, beautiful."

Bleeding Passion was just as dynamic that night as they had been before. Van played to the crowd like a true entertainer, and coupled with the lead singer of Dead Vampire, the show was incredible.

As Bleeding Passion went out for their last encore, Alyx sighed and looked up at Maxim. "Look at us," she said. "How many people can say they've been where we are right now?"

He grinned down at her. "Not many." He chuckled. "I sure never would have thought I'd be here." He actually never would have thought up half of the stuff that had happened on this trip.

"Hey!" Darren exclaimed suddenly, popping his head through the stage door. "Do you want to come meet Dead Vampire?"

Taegen and Alyx's eyes lit up and they flew after Darren. Javan rolled his eyes and Maxim chuckled as they followed behind. They were introduced to the rest of the band first, then taken over to the lead singer who was sitting placidly in a chair. Darren grinned and pointed to him. "That's Chris Copenhagen," he said.

Chris rolled his eyes as a woman knelt down next to him. "Regina," he said, "you have got to get me some new conditioner. I had to use the hotel stuff last night and it has been wreaking havoc on my hair all day." He ran his fingers through it a few times and made a disgusted noise. "I mean, look at it. It's been screaming at me!"

The woman smiled. "No problem, Chris."

Alyx and Taegen exchanged a look.

"Oh!" he called. "And could you book an appointment with my manicurist? I broke a nail tonight and my cuticles look like they've been put through a blender." He flopped his hand in a feminine manner.

Regina smiled. "Will do."

He smiled. "Thanks, sweetie!"

Taegen blinked. "Alyx," she muttered, "does he seem a little...feminine to you?"

Alyx raised an eyebrow. "In a flaming, stereotypical *Will and Grace* kind of way, yeah." They exchanged another look and stifled laughter.

"Chris!" Darren called. "Come here! Meet my friends!"

Chris grinned and all but leapt out of his chair. He shook Alyx's and Taegen's hands, as well as Maxim's and Torrey's, but he stopped when he reached Javan. "Mmmm," he purred, "you're cute." He ran a finger down Javan's arm. "I'd like to suck *your* blood."

Javan blinked in horrified bewilderment.

Alyx couldn't help herself. She folded her arms and smirked. "Hey, look, Javan," she said. "Your love life's improving."

Javan shot Alyx a scathing look and Chris erupted into high-pitched, cackling laughter that made everyone jump.

He clapped his hands together. "I like you," Chris said, sashaying over to Alyx.

Javan snorted. "Yeah, she generally thinks she's pretty funny."

Chris laughed again. "Oh don't worry, Javan," he assured, flopping his arm around Javan's shoulders. "I don't bite..." He threw a suggestive wink at him. "Unless you want me to."

Javan raised an eyebrow and chuckled. "I'll take a rain check, but thanks."

Chris wrinkled his nose in a flirtatious manner and turned back to the girls. "So, Van says you're just staying for this concert?"

Alyx nodded. "It's amazing we even got to come. Torrey knew Darren and we just happened to get lucky."

"Where are you from?" he asked.

"Javan, Maxim, and I are from Oregon," she replied. "Taegen and Torrey are from San Francisco."

Chris nodded. "I'm returning to San Francisco tomorrow. My band is in the process of booking a tour and I have to pick up my sister. I promised she could travel with us."

Torrey frowned. "That's a thought," he said suddenly. "How are we getting home? We left Javan's car at Steps of Rome."

"Oh that sucks," Javan grumbled.

"Yeah, impulsiveness is not always a good thing," Taegen put in.

Chris eyed them for a moment as if assessing their worth, then clapped his hands together again. "Well, since you're Darren's friends, you are more than welcome to ride back to San Francisco with me. My car is practically a boat. It seats six. Unless you would rather ride a bus or something. That's an awfully long bus ride."

The five exchanged glances. "That's very nice of you to offer," Torrey said, acting as spokesperson. "Are you sure it wouldn't put you out in any way?"

Chris shook his head. "Not at all! I'm going to San Francisco anyway. I would be happy to help!"

"Thank you," Alyx said with a grin. "It's very much appreciated."

"Are you guys going to the party tonight?"

Alyx shrugged and glanced at Torrey. "I didn't know there was a party."

"Of course there's a party!" Darren exclaimed. "And you all have to go. I won't see you again in who knows how long." He turned to Torrey. "You have to go."

Torrey smiled. "I'll be there," he said, "but I can't speak for everyone." He looked down at Taegen. "Would you like to go?"

She gave him a look that said she was surprised he would even ask. "Of course."

"I'm in," Javan volunteered.

"Hey, me too," Alyx added.

Maxim sighed. "I guess that means I have to go also."

Torrey grinned and patted him on the back. "It'll be fine," he assured. "Just don't drink anyone else's water."

"Great," he muttered.

Chris smiled. "I'll see you there, then!" he said excitedly. "And I'll pick you up at your hotel tomorrow around noon."

Torrey nodded. "Thanks again."

"No problem."

Alyx turned to Maxim and gave him a reassuring smile. "The party will be fun," she assured. "Did you ever go to any raves in high school?"

Maxim blinked. "Alyx, I've been to three parties in my lifetime. My brother's graduation party, my sister's graduation party, and that embarrassing office party that I threw up at last year."

Alyx giggled and put her arms around his waist. "Well, I bet Jeff's never been to a rock party."

He sighed. "Yeah, and he's gonna kill me when I get home... Probably in several different ways."

She ran her hands up his chest and absently picked at a piece of lint. "You'll dance with me, right?"

Maxim gave her a pained expression. "I danced with you last night. Do I have to?"

She frowned. "Of course. It's your duty as my boyfriend."

He groaned. "I think I'm going to re-nig on this whole boyfriend thing."

She punched him in the shoulder. "You'd be missing out," she teased.

Maxim sobered and cupped Alyx's cheek in his hand. "Don't tell me what I already know," he whispered. He nuzzled his lips against her temple and smiled when she rested her head against his chest. He pulled her close, studying the way her soft body fit against his.

Alyx closed her eyes as Maxim's arms encompassed her. She sighed. She didn't ever want this vacation to end. So it had been a little...out of the ordinary. She didn't care. It had been wonderful. She didn't want to return to the mundane routine of everyday life. She liked seeing the world though Maxim's eyes. He made everything seem so much more beautiful, and he made her feel so special. There was nothing but soft love in Maxim's touch.

"Come on, guys!" Darren called suddenly. "Everyone's heading out!"

Maxim turned and began to follow the others. He sighed as he caught a glimpse of Chris Copenhagen messing with his hair in front of a mirror again. He had seen enough in the past four days to write an entire book.

He chuckled. Heck, maybe he would.

Vibrations Night Club

Maxim watched Alyx from his place at the table he sat at with his friends. Although, his friends were no longer there. They had left him there all alone to go and rub up against a bunch of sweaty people. He was guarding his water carefully after what Torrey had said to him. He didn't really know why he was supposed to do that, but he decided that it would be best to just listen to him and not take any chances. He enjoyed watching Alyx as she laughed and danced with the others. He smiled as Torrey spun her around. There was nothing in the world like watching her laugh.

"Hey, Maxim."

Maxim glanced over his shoulder to see Van sitting in a corner booth in the shadows. He motioned Maxim over and he obeyed, a little confused by the request.

Van smiled at him. "Gathering more ideas?" he questioned.

"Always." It amazed him how Van was so interested in his writing career. No one other than Alyx and Jeff had ever really cared before. But, then again, Van was creative too, and he'd said himself that eccentrics sensed one another. He probably understood Maxim's passion more than anyone else.

Van's smile morphed into a grin. "I overheard Torrey telling Darren something backstage." He chuckled. "It sounds like you guys all had an interesting twenty-four hours."

Maxim rolled his eyes. "Please, don't get me started."

"Did you actually pulverize somebody in the hallway?"

Maxim's face burned and he held his hand up. His knuckles had split when he'd punched Rick and they were scabbed over.

Van raised his eyebrows and laughed. "Man, Maxim, you're something else. You're one of those rare people who blaze right through life, aren't you?"

Maxim frowned in puzzlement. "I think maybe you're confusing me with Torrey."

"Nah. Torrey is a great person with a lot to offer and an amazing passion for life, but he doesn't stick out like you do.

Not in the same way. You shine, even if you don't mean to."

Maxim smiled tremulously and didn't know what to say. He hadn't spent any part of his life up till now blazing through anything. Hiding was more like it. Never wanted to shine. Always wanted to be invisible. Maybe Van had just had one too many alcoholic beverages and was hallucinating.

"It's a subtle shine," the rock star said, as if he had read Maxim's thoughts. "You think Torrey shines because he is social and outgoing, and that's true. He's the type of person that always gets attention. You may spend most of your time being relatively quiet, but when you decide to speak up, people listen. They stand up and take notice. You get what I'm saying?"

Maxim scratched at the back of his neck. "Not really," he mumbled, and turned his attention back to the dance floor where the lead singer of Fat Stinky was trying to bump and grind with Alyx. She kept evading him and positioning Javan between them so that he was getting all of the action. Javan didn't look very amused by the situation. Maxim laughed.

Van regarded Maxim for a moment then smiled. He pulled off a silver necklace he was wearing and handed it to him. "I want you to have this," he said.

Maxim looked at the necklace and his eyes widened. It was the Bleeding Passion logo, an eye crying rose petals instead of tears. He shook his head. "Uh...I..."

"Dude, what are you doing?" Lance interrupted. "You already gave your jacket away to that girl last year. Do you just pick an annual person to give your custom made stuff to?"

Van scowled half-heartedly at his friend. "Shut up, Lance. It's just a necklace. Besides, I don't know why I gave that girl my jacket."

Lance rolled his eyes and looked at Maxim. "Van here had his own bout of heroics last year. We played in some sleazy club in L.A and some girl was getting manhandled outside the bathroom. Not only did Van jump in there like Zorro or something, but he gave the girl his custom made leather jacket."

Van shrugged. "Something about her... I don't know. Anyway, I'm a grown man, Lance. Thanks. I think I have enough money to get both another necklace and jacket made." He held it out to Maxim again. "Bleeding Passion is exactly what the name implies. All of us in the band love what we do so much that it actually runs through our blood. This necklace symbolizes that. It belongs to one whose life is his passion. I know passion, and you have it. I see it burning in the depths of your eyes. You just haven't really realized it was there until now. Write your stories, Maxim. Write every-thing you can. Rarely a person with such passion is able to fail. Bleed it onto the page, and when you do, think of all the eccentrics out there you'll be standing for." He grinned and set the necklace down in front of Maxim.

Maxim stared at Van, still completely and ridiculously speechless. Who was this guy? Rock Yoda? He reached out and took the necklace. He studied the symbol. He had no idea if Van knew what he was talking about, but somewhere in the back of his heart—because his mind would never be able to process this—he felt a tiny flame where there had once been an ache. He knew this experience had changed him completely. Javan with his understanding and humor. Torrey and Taegen with their fairy tale romance. Alyx with her love and acceptance. He could never return to skulking around Barrett's bookstore and being as elusive as possible after he had fallen in love, learned to laugh and trust, and learned to stand up for and protect those people who had brought light streaming into his dreary world.

He did want to write it down. He wanted to share his journey with everyone so that other shy loners out there like him—the eccentrics, as Van had put it—would know that tak-ing that road less traveled, while sometimes frightening, and sometimes difficult, could lead to unfathomable treaures.

Maxim glanced up at Van again with a soft smile. "Thank you."

Van grinned.

Maxim slipped the necklace on, liking the way the cool metal felt against his skin. He extended his hand to Van. "I will most certainly never forget you," he said.

Van shook his hand and nodded. "Brothers in oddness always," he teased. He sat back in his chair with a grin.

Maxim played with the necklace. It made him feel power-ful for some stupid reason...as if he needed to feel any more powerful today. Now Jeff would kill him even more than be-fore. He chuckled. Maxim deBoer... In one day he'd beat up a guy, given all of his friends a very loud lecture, and had acquired Van Marshall's necklace. Who would have ever thought? Blaze through life indeed. After so many years of being stagnant, it seemed like maybe he was onto a decent start.

The Highway

Javan didn't think it was right that his friends were evil and had all called their seats as soon as they'd set foot out of the hotel, leaving him to sit next to Chris Copenhagen. It was wrong. The man was wearing a bright purple shirt and he kept winking at him and trying to touch his knee. Plus, they were in a giant boat of a classic convertible car that looked like it had come right out of *Too Wong Foo: Thanks for Everything, Julie Newmar.* It was just wrong. Everyone else, of course, thought it was hilarious.

He glanced at Torrey, who sat next to him, and sighed. "How is it that Maxim gets Van's necklace?" he asked. "Maxim's about as social as a barnacle. How in the world can he bleed passion?"

Torrey laughed. "Stop pouting, Javan," he teased. "Seemed like he was doing a pretty good job of bleeding passion all over us yesterday when he was telling us what for."

Javan rolled his eyes and chuckled. "Yeah, no kidding." He turned in his seat and looked back at Maxim. "How did you remember all that stuff about us anyway?"

Maxim met his eyes. "Because I don't listen. I *hear.*"

Javan raised an inquisitive eyebrow, but he grinned and turned back around.

Chris turned the radio station and laughed as one of his own songs started to play back at him. He sang along, his rich, baritone voice filling the car.

Alyx and Taegen exchanged glances, grinning at one another. Maybe Chris was a little...eccentric, but there was no denying that he had serious talent.

The song ended suddenly and Chris changed the station to avoid the commercials that followed. Helen Reddy's *I Am Woman* started to play and he let out a high-pitched squeal that made everyone jump. "I love this song!" he exclaimed. He sang along, dancing in the driver's seat.

Javan's eyes widened as Chris accidentally jerked the

wheel a little too far to the left, causing them to almost veer off the road. "Want to watch the road there, slick?" he cried.

Chris returned the car to the road and giggled. "Sorry, I think I got a little carried away."

Javan stared at him for a moment and tried desperately to scoot closer to Torrey.

Maxim could not contain his laughter. He let his eyes go from Chris to Javan, who was practically sitting in Torrey's lap, and he shook his head. All of this was so insane and such a perfect piece in the most outrageous adventure of his life. "'Two roads diverged in a wood and I—'" he quoted.

Everyone grinned and spoke simultaneously. "'I took the one less traveled by. And that has made all the difference!'"

Chapter Thirty

Maxim began to recognize the looks of home before he even saw the sign saying it was only twenty miles away. He sighed. Part of him was happy to see the familiar sights, the things that were ever-constant. It would be good to get back to his apartment and sleep in his own bed. On the other hand, he would miss the adventures. He would especially miss Torrey. He had bonded with the man from day one over literature, and he had continued to be a great companion to him for the duration of their odyssey together. He would miss having him around.

The rest of the trip had been a lot of fun. They had managed to get back to San Francisco in one piece...barely. After they had said goodbye to the flamboyant Chris Copenhagen, they had continued to tour the city and had gone to Six Flags Marine World one day. Javan and Torrey had convinced Maxim to go on the Medusa roller coaster with them, which he would never forgive them for.

Maxim glanced in the rearview mirror. Javan was draped across the back seat, dead to the world and probably drooling all over the upholstery. He looked down at his lap, where Alyx's head was resting, and he smiled to himself. Van had told him to write, and that was exactly what he was planning to do.

He passed another sign stating that Ashland was only ten miles away. He gripped the steering wheel tighter. Tomorrow, he would start his book...

And he planned on finishing this one.

San Francisco

Taegen stirred and her eyes fluttered open. She frowned, wondering why she had awoken. Deciding it must have been a dream, she turned and let her gaze focus on Torrey. She smiled. He was sleeping peacefully. She reached out to touch his face gently and he smiled a little, turning to pull her into his arms. She nestled against him, closing her eyes again.

The last few days of Maxim, Alyx, and Javan's stay had been kind of weird. Getting used to the idea that she was actually married to Torrey was very hard for her to handle, but he had been so patient with her. He never pushed. He was always so compassionate and encouraging. Her beautiful stranger. The man who had touched her life as no other could.

They had decided that she would move her things into his house, and he currently had boxes strewn all through his living room. It was strange because she had lived in her little house for so long, but part of her found the moving process somewhat therapeutic. It was like she was leaving all of the painful memories behind her. She could put her pictures of Paul up in Torrey's house and remember him, but she didn't have to lie in her bed reliving how she had been awakened that horrid night. There was nothing in Torrey's house that held any bad memory. Only good.

She sighed softly and traced patterns across Torrey's chest. "Darkness consumes the night, I can barely breathe," she sang quietly. "'Immobile, can't move. Look what you've done to me...'"

He pressed a kiss to the top of Taegen's head. "Sleep, Pretty Lady," he whispered. "I'll be here when you wake up."

She smiled. She knew he would be. He wouldn't leave her. A strange, surreal calm came over her as that realization sunk in. He wouldn't leave her...

She felt herself begin to drift back to sleep, and she knew that she had never felt such warm contentment. Torrey was hers. Despite her fears, insecurities, and clumsy attempts to protect herself, deep in her heart, she knew that he was hers. "Torrey," she whispered, "I-I—" she swallowed. "Torrey, I love you." The admission should have frightened her, but it didn't. She needed to say it. She needed to say it because it was true. She listened to his heartbeat and it accelerated just slightly.

Torrey tightened his arms around her. "I love you too, my beautiful Taegen," he whispered, kissing her forehead.

"My husband," she murmured, her voice so soft she could barely hear it.

Torrey heard and he held her close. "My wife... Now sleep, sweetheart."

Taegen grinned and obeyed, knowing deep in her soul that her life would hold many more happy days with the man beside her.

Ashland, Oregon

Maxim pressed a soft kiss to Alyx's lips as Javan stumbled into the driver's seat, looking like the living dead.

"Is he gonna be all right?" Maxim asked.

"Yeah, he'll wake up once he starts driving. I'll blast some music at him and turn on the AC." She hugged Maxim close. "Will I see you tomorrow?"

He smiled and touched her hair. "I thought maybe I could come over and cook you dinner," he suggested.

"I'd like that very much."

He held her face gently in his hands. He pressed a kiss to her forehead and sought her lips again.

Alyx sighed into his kiss and rested her head against his shoulder.

His arms wrapped around her and held her close. "Don't worry about your nightmares," he assured. "Nothing will dare touch you while I am with you. And you know I will be with you, holding you close and safe. All night long. Even if I'm not there in person, I'm there in your heart."

She looked up at him and smiled. "You always know what I'm thinking, and always know exactly what to say." She shook her head. "I'll see you tomorrow?" she questioned again.

He nodded, touched that she seemed so reluctant to be parted. "Definitely. Sleep well, beautiful."

She reached up to trace the lines around his mouth. "You too." She raised herself on her toes to press another kiss to his lips. He watched as she got back into the car.

"See you later, Maxim!" Javan called, waving.

Maxim smiled and waved in return. He waited until the car was out of sight to enter his apartment building. He lugged his bags up the stairs, trying to be as quiet as possible, and entered his apartment to see Jeff playing Solitaire on his computer.

"Maxim!" Jeff exclaimed, jumping out of the chair. "I was wondering when you'd finally get home!"

Maxim let his bags drop and he closed the door quietly. "What are you still doing up?"

Jeff shrugged. "Just wanted to make sure you got home okay."

Maxim smiled. "How many days have you been living in my apartment?"

Jeff made a face. "Only today. This place gives me the creeps." He frowned as he caught sight of the necklace that Maxim wore. His eyes bulged. "That's the Bleeding Passion symbol!" he shouted.

Maxim grinned.

"Where did you get that?"

"Van Marshall," Maxim replied.

Jeff blinked, uncomprehending. "You met Van Marshall?"

He nodded and staggered to his sofa. He flopped down on his stomach. "We went to Vegas with the band." He yawned. "Got to go backstage, meet everybody, and watch them perform. Torrey Reed has some good connections."

Jeff had a rare speechless moment for several seconds. "You're kidding me."

"And then we got to ride back to San Francisco with a very gay rock star who was trying to pick up Javan." He chuckled. "I'll tell you about in the morning."

Another speechless moment. "Unreal."

"You can just sleep on my bed," Maxim muttered. "I'm not moving from this couch." He closed his eyes and sighed. "I'm exhausted." He didn't hear any noise that would indicate movement and Maxim knew his brother was staring at him.

"You still going to see Alyx?" he finally asked.

Maxim smiled as he peeked up at his brother. "Yeah, I'm seeing her tomorrow... Gonna cook dinner."

A smile quirked Jeff's lips. "That's great, Max..." He sighed. "Hey, you get some rest, all right?" He headed off toward the bedroom.

"Hey, Jeff?"

He turned. "Yeah?"

Maxim grinned. "Thanks...I had the time of my life."

Jeff's grin could have dwarfed the sun. "No problem, bro. Get some rest. I'll see you tomorrow."

Maxim waited until Jeff was in his room before he chuckled to himself. Jeff never would have believed that any of this could have happened. His antisocial brother went on a trip he was forced into, met rock stars, and found a girlfriend. It was so not in Maxim deBoer's profile. He smiled as he thought once again of all the adventures he'd had, the friends he had made. Friends he was sure he would have for the rest of his life. Friends he had never had before and who had inspired him to find his passion once again.

He sighed and reached out to turn on the radio. He looked forward to seeing Alyx the next day. It was strange to not be with her and he missed holding her. He wanted to spend his whole life holding her.

His eyes opened suddenly as the familiar strains of "The Sound of Silence" filled his ears. He frowned, wondering why the song seemed to follow him. He briefly searched his heart, but found no ache there. He smiled and closed his eyes, letting the beautiful music lull him to sleep.

Epilogue

Ashland, Oregon
One Year Later
1:02 P.M.

Maxim stared at his manuscript and swallowed nervously. He glanced over at Alyx, who was sitting on the couch eating popcorn and watching a movie. He closed his eyes and tried to calm the rapid pounding of his heart. One year. One year ago, Alyx and he had begun their journey through love together. She'd had crimson streaks in her hair then. They were gone now and her hair was longer, falling past her shoulders and down her back in gleaming ebony.

He smiled as his eyes fell on the two pictures on his end table. One of him and Jeff at that humiliating party, the other of all of them before the concert. That trip had been the inspiration for the novel he now held in his hand. It was the only thing he had ever completed. He had poured his soul, his very essence into it. Now, he only needed an ending...

He took a deep breath and stood from where he had been sitting at his desk. "Alyx," he croaked.

She looked up at him and smiled. He looked like a lost little boy, clutching his manuscript to his chest. She briefly recalled when she had first seen him. He had been standing in much the same manner, only clutching his backpack. "What is it, babe?"

He took another deep breath and stepped forward. "I need your help with something."

She sat up and set her bowl of popcorn aside. She loved helping Maxim with his work. He had been nonstop at it ever since they had returned from their insane trip.

Maxim sat next to her and sighed. "I need an ending," he replied," but you have to read the whole thing first."

She met his eyes. "You mean you're finished?"

He smiled. "Almost, but I need you to help me with the ending."

She grinned. "All right." She took the manuscript and sat back, preparing to read. "I won't put it down until I'm done."

Maxim watched her for a moment, then grew restless and stood. "I'm going to go see Jeff," he stated. "I'll be back later."

She looked up at him with a frown. "You're going to go see him at work?"

He ran a hand through his hair and nodded. "Just want to say hello." He strode to the door, the Bleeding Passion necklace that Van Marshall had given him dangling from his neck.

Alyx knew something wasn't right. The only time Maxim wore that necklace was when he wanted to feel invincible. It was like his power item. The fact that he was wearing it to go see his brother in the middle of the day at his law office let her know that something was definitely up. She sighed and shook her head. Sometimes Maxim was the most mysterious man she knew. She looked back down at the manuscript and smiled as she began to read. He had been working so hard. It made her proud to see that all of his efforts had paid off.

6:40 P.M.

"Maxim," Alexi said, coming out of his office, "you have to go home. You can't hang out in our lobby anymore. We have to close."

Maxim looked up at Alexi. He was minus his suit jacket and his shirt was already un-tucked. Maxim heaved a sigh.

Alexi chuckled. "I'm sure she's finished reading it by now. Alyx is a fast reader."

Maxim felt himself turn what he was positive was a faint shade of green.

Jeff appeared suddenly, grinning like a hyena. "Go on, loiterer," he teased. "Go home to your girl."

Maxim twisted his fingers nervously. "I think I'm dying," he muttered.

Jeff laughed. "You're not dying," he assured, "but you do look like you could use a stiff drink. Wait here." He disappeared into a back room and emerged a moment later carrying a shot glass full of amber liquid.

Maxim frowned. "You have liquor in your office?"

Jeff shrugged. "In our meeting room. It's mostly for show. Here."

Maxim downed the shot and coughed. "What is that?" he rasped.

"Bourbon."

He made a face as his insides burned like fire. He thrust the glass back to Jeff. "That is vile."

Alexi chuckled. "You ready to go home now?"

Maxim looked up at him and knew that his eyes reflected the terror he felt.

Alexi put his arm around Maxim's shoulders and gave him half a hug. "Go home, brother," he said with a conspiratorial wink.

Maxim took a deep breath and nodded. It was now or never. He went to the door and looked back at Jeff and Alexi.

"Call me later," Jeff said. "I'll be dying to know."

Maxim grinned and nodded, heading back out into the warm summer evening.

* * * *

Alyx glanced up as she heard the door open. She rolled her eyes as Maxim entered. "Only going to say hello, were you? What, did you decide to take on a case while you were there?"

Maxim smiled weakly. "Are you finished yet?"

"I'm on the last page."

He tried to swallow the lump in his throat, but it remained. His timing was terrifyingly impecible. "Read it out loud." He went and sat down next to her.

She looked up at him and smiled. "I really like it. You captured everything so wonderfully."

"Thank you," he murmured. "Read the last page."

She looked back down at the text. "'Brandon knew that he loved her, would love her forever. There was no one else in the world for him but her...'"

Maxim's heart started to thump wildly. Brandon, his middle name. He had kept everyone's name but his own. He felt weird writing about himself in the third person. Somehow, it didn't seem as strange if he was using his middle name.

"'Alyx was his soul mate,'" she continued. "'She was his match, and she was the only one he wanted to be with. Taking a deep breath, he took her hand in his.'"

Maxim reached out his shaking hands and took one of Alyx's gently between them. He let out a slow breath.

Alyx smiled. "'He looked deeply into her eyes, the eyes he lost himself in at every chance. 'Alyxandra,' he whispered, 'you are my breath, my life, everything that makes me what I am. Without you, I would be nothing. You are the water that quenches the thirst of my soul. I love you.'"

Maxim felt like he was going to die. Why had he made this paragraph so incredibly long?

She glanced up at him. "You are so sweet."

He smiled, his heart melting. He gestured for her to continue reading.

"'I love you. You are my heart. Stay with me and be my muse forever. Alyx...will you...'" Her eyes widened. "'Marry me?'" she squeaked. She looked up at Maxim, tears hovering on her lashes.

Maxim averted his eyes and cleared his throat. "Yeah, you see, that's the part I need help with." He scratched his head. "I can't decide what her answer should be..." He stole a glance up at her, his heart racing like a locomotive. "What—what do you think her answer should be?"

One tear streaked down her cheek. "I think her answer should be yes," she murmured, a slow grin spreading across her lips.

Maxim let out an enormous sigh and grinned. "Yeah that's what I was thinking also."

She giggled.

"Oh, I need help with one more thing," he said, groping around in his pocket. He pulled out a small black box and held it out to her. "Do you think that Alyx would like this engagement ring?" He opened it up to reveal a white gold band with two small diamonds on the sides and a ruby in the middle.

Alyx drew in a sharp breath, looked up at Maxim, then let out a strangled half-laugh, half-sob. "I think Alyx would like that very much!" she cried.

He grinned and snapped the box shut. "Oh good. Now that I know that, I can finish my book." He stood and started toward his computer.

"Hey!" Alyx exclaimed. She stood up and launched herself at him.

He laughed and caught her in his arms, pulling her close up against him. He buried his face in her hair and closed his eyes. "Oh Alyx," he breathed, "I love you so much."

She wrapped her arms around his waist and rested her head on his chest. "I love you too, Maxim." She looked up at him and grinned. "Can I have my ring now?"

He grinned and pulled the ring out of the box. He placed it on Alyx's finger, then took her hand and pressed a gentle kiss to her palm. He smiled as she reached up and removed his glasses.

"Let me see your eyes," she murmured. "I love your blue eyes."

He caressed her face as if to memorize every delicate feature. "Alyxandra deBoer," he said. He nodded in satisfaction. "Sounds good."

Alyx reached up to trace the lines around his mouth, more prominent now that he smiled so much more. She raised herself on her toes to touch her lips to his. Maxim held her close and kissed her so slowly that he thought he might die of pure bliss and longing. Her kisses were enough to get drunk off of. He deepened the kiss, wanting to lose himself in her for all time.

The door burst open suddenly and Jeff flew in. "They're kissing!" he shouted. "That's a good sign!"

Maxim reddened. "Can't I have any privacy? Is nothing sacred?"

Jeff laughed and ran over to him, followed by Javan and Alexi. "No way, man! You're my brother! You should be proud of us. You have no idea how hard it was to listen at the door and not make any noise."

Maxim stared at him in shock.

"I can't believe it!" Jeff exclaimed. "My little brother's getting married! The shy one!"

Maxim chuckled. "Never thought I'd be first."

Jeff laughed and embraced Alyx. "My little sister-in-law!"

She laughed and turned to Javan and her brother.

Maxim managed to escape the crowd for a moment and he turned to his computer. He typed in the last few paragraphs then printed it out, adding the final page to the man-

manuscript. It was finished... His book. He felt a soft touch on his hand and he looked up to see Alyx smiling at him. He kissed her again, feeling so much joy that he thought he would burst.

"Come on!" Jeff shouted. "This calls for a celebration!"

Javan shoved a cell phone into Maxim's hand. "It's Torrey and Taegen," he said. "They want to hear the news."

Maxim took the phone. He followed the rowdy group out as he started to talk to Torrey, casting a look back at his manuscript as he closed the door. He grinned. He had finished it. Finally, after so long, he had finished something worthy of publication. He closed the door and took Alyx's hand as they descended the staircase. He kissed her fingers. It was all because of her. She was the source of his happiness. And now, she would be his wife.

About the Author

I have been telling stories since I was able to comprehend words. While most kids in the first grade were playing tag, I was the one all by myself in the corner of the soccer field pretending it was a gateway to a different world. For as long as I can remember, there have always been people in my head begging to have their stories told.

I write love stories. Contemporary and fantasy. The world we live in is greatly devoid of love and true friendship. I write stories that revolve around these themes, as well as the overall message to be true to yourself. We were created as individuals. We should strive to be just that.